EXORSISTERS

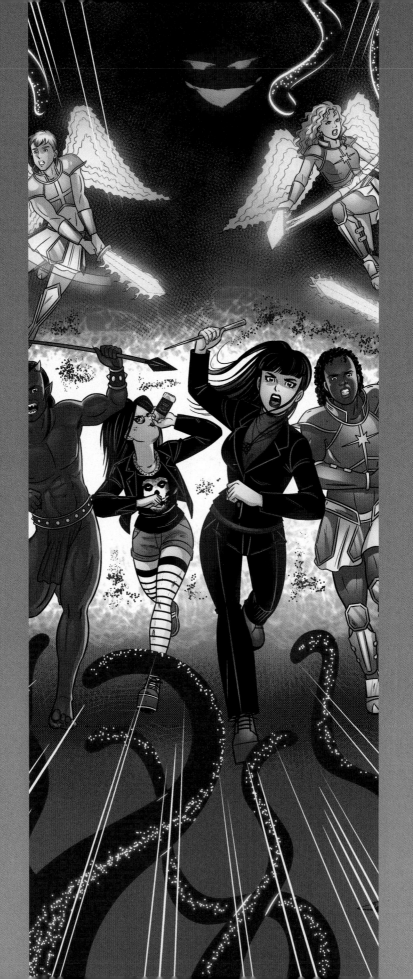

WRITER
IAN BOOTHBY

ARTIST
GISÈLE LAGACÉ

COLORIST
PETE PANTAZIS

LETTERER
TAYLOR ESPOSITO

EDITOR
BRANWYN BIGGLESTONE

PRODUCTION
DEANNA PHELPS

COVER ART
**GISÈLE LAGACÉ &
PETE PANTAZIS (COLORS)**

IMAGE COMICS, INC.
Todd McFarlane: President
Jim Valentino: Vice President
Marc Silvestri: Chief Executive Officer
Erik Larsen: Chief Financial Officer
Robert Kirkman: Chief Operating Officer

Eric Stephenson: Publisher / Chief Creative Officer
Shanna Matuszak: Editorial Coordinator
Marla Eizik: Talent Liaison

Nicole Lapalme: Controller
Leanna Caunter: Accounting Analyst
Sue Korpela: Accounting & HR Manager

Jeff Boison: Director of Sales & Publishing Planning
Dirk Wood: Director of International Sales & Licensing
Alex Cox: Director of Direct Market & Speciality Sales
Chloe Ramos-Peterson: Book Market & Library Sales Manager
Emilio Bautista: Digital Sales Coordinator

Kat Salazar: Director of PR & Marketing
Drew Fitzgerald: Marketing Content Associate

Heather Doornink: Production Director
Drew Gill: Art Director
Hilary DiLoreto: Print Manager
Tricia Ramos: Traffic Manager
Erika Schnatz: Senior Production Artist
Ryan Brewer: Production Artist
Deanna Phelps: Production Artist
IMAGECOMICS.COM

image

EXORSISTERS, VOL. 2. First printing. October 2020.
Published by Image Comics, Inc. Office of publication:
2701 NW Vaughn St., Suite 780, Portland, OR 97210.
Copyright © 2020 Ian Boothby & Gisèle Lagacé.
All rights reserved. Contains material originally
published in single magazine form as EXORSISTERS
#6–10. "EXORSISTERS," its logos, and the
likenesses of all characters herein are trademarks of
Ian Boothby & Gisèle Lagacé, unless otherwise noted.
"Image" and the Image Comics logos are registered
trademarks of Image Comics, Inc. No part of this
publication may be reproduced or transmitted, in any
form or by any means (except for short excerpts for
journalistic or review purposes), without the express
written permission of Ian Boothby & Gisèle Lagacé,
or Image Comics, Inc. All names, characters,
events, and locales in this publication are entirely
fictional. Any resemblance to actual persons (living
or dead), events, or places, without satirical intent,
is coincidental. Printed in the USA. For international
rights, contact: foreignlicensing@imagecomics.com.
ISBN: 978-1-5343-1701-7.

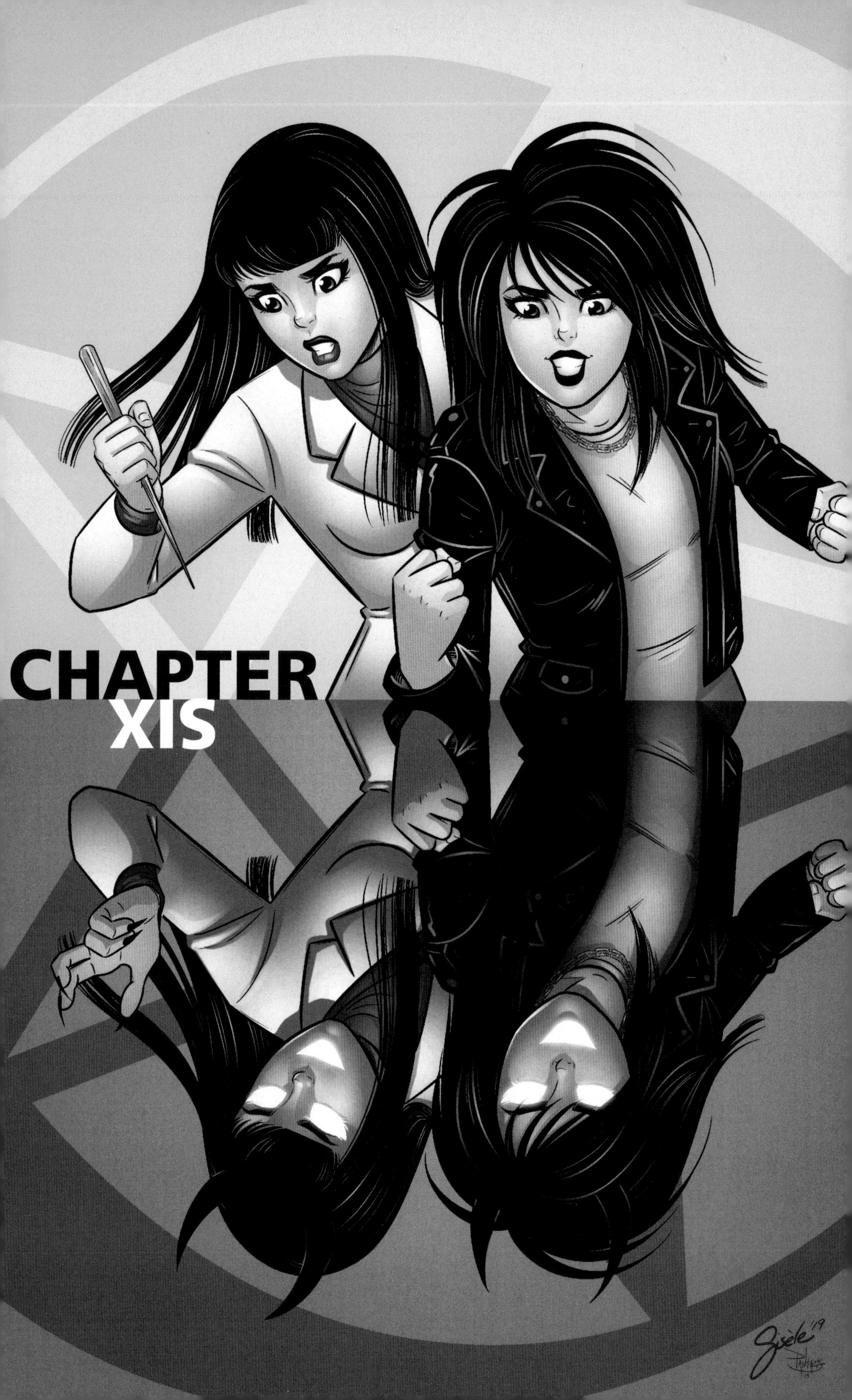
CHAPTER
XIS

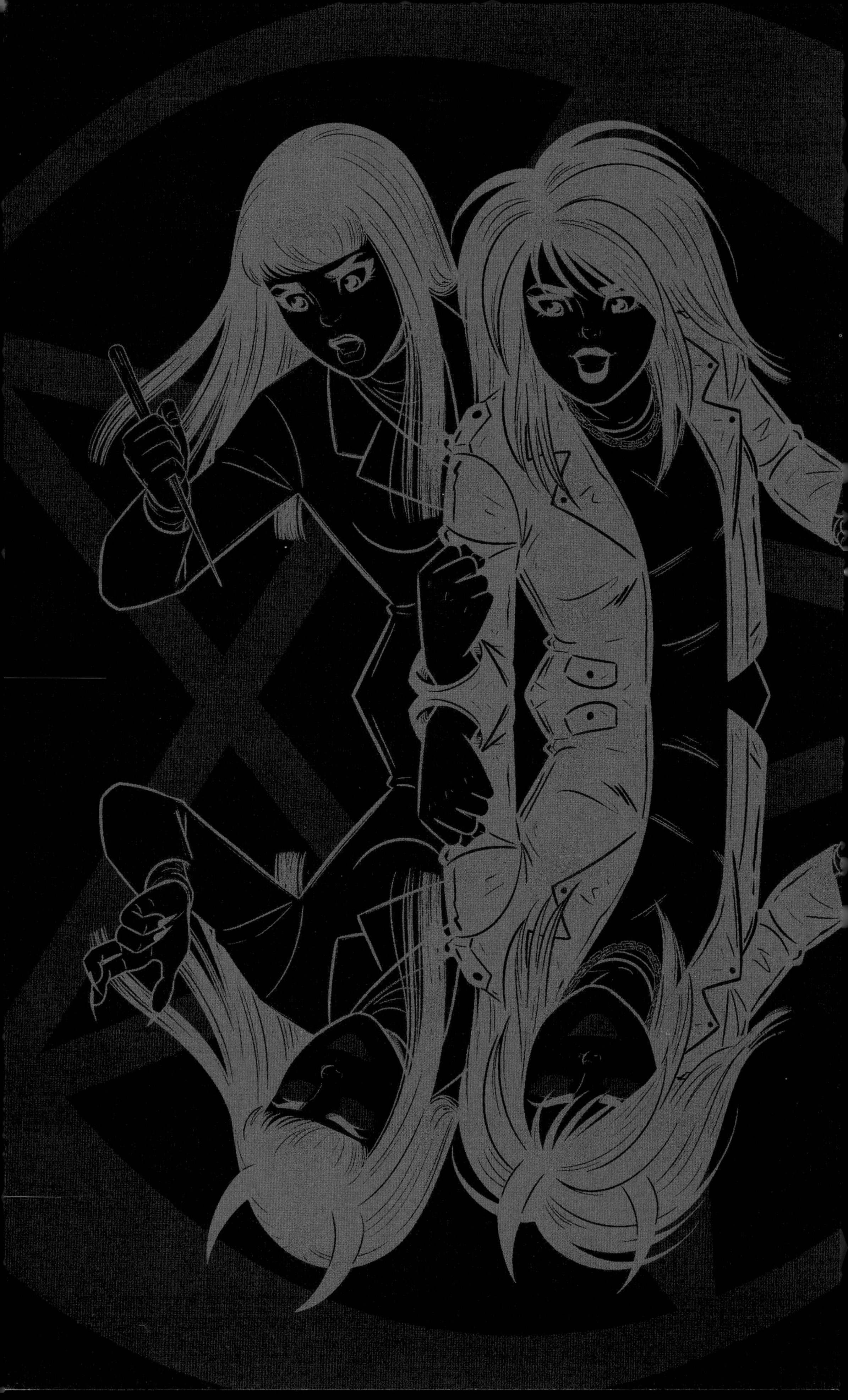

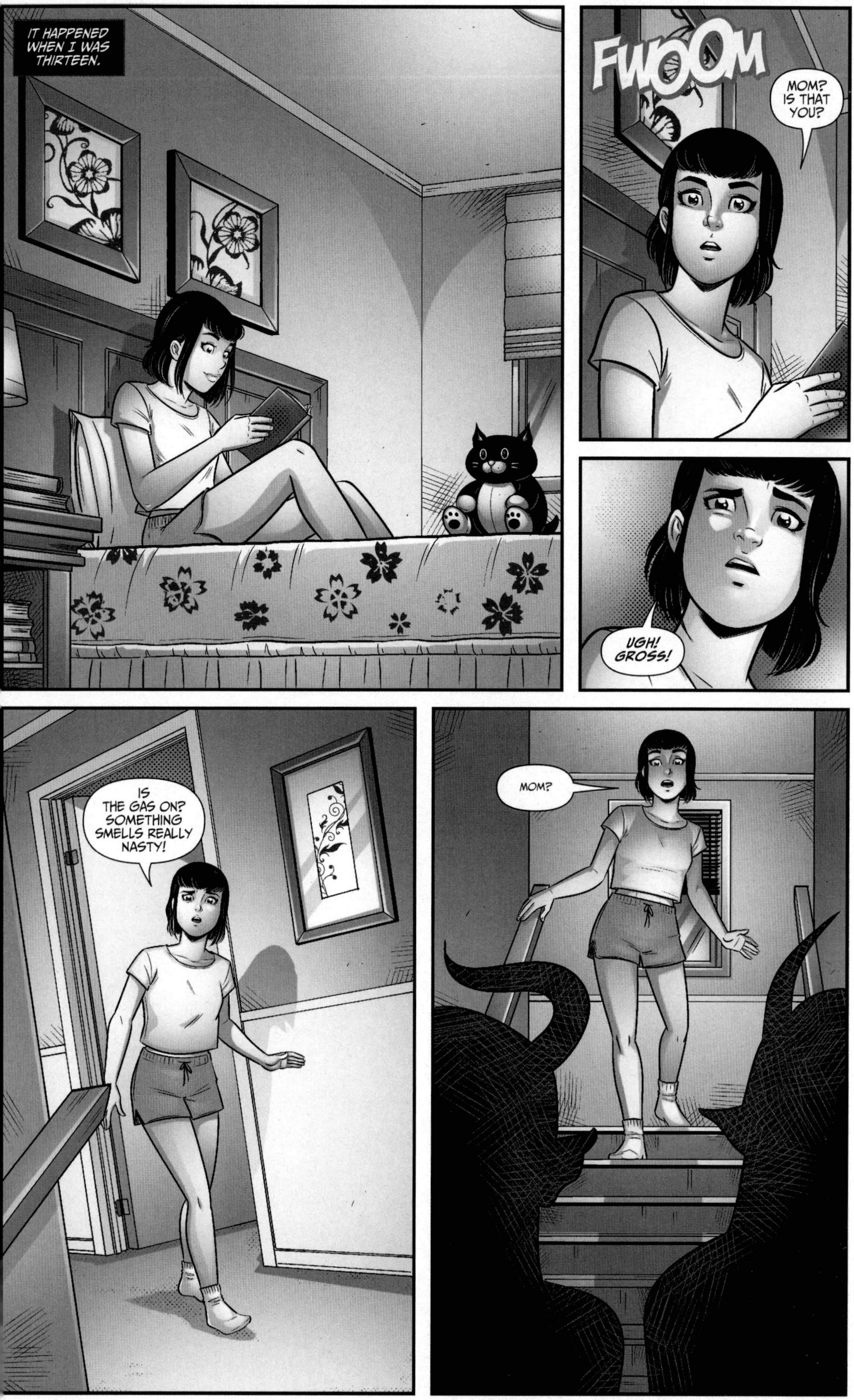
IT HAPPENED WHEN I WAS THIRTEEN.
FWOOM
MOM? IS THAT YOU?
UGH! GROSS!
IS THE GAS ON? SOMETHING SMELLS REALLY NASTY!
MOM?

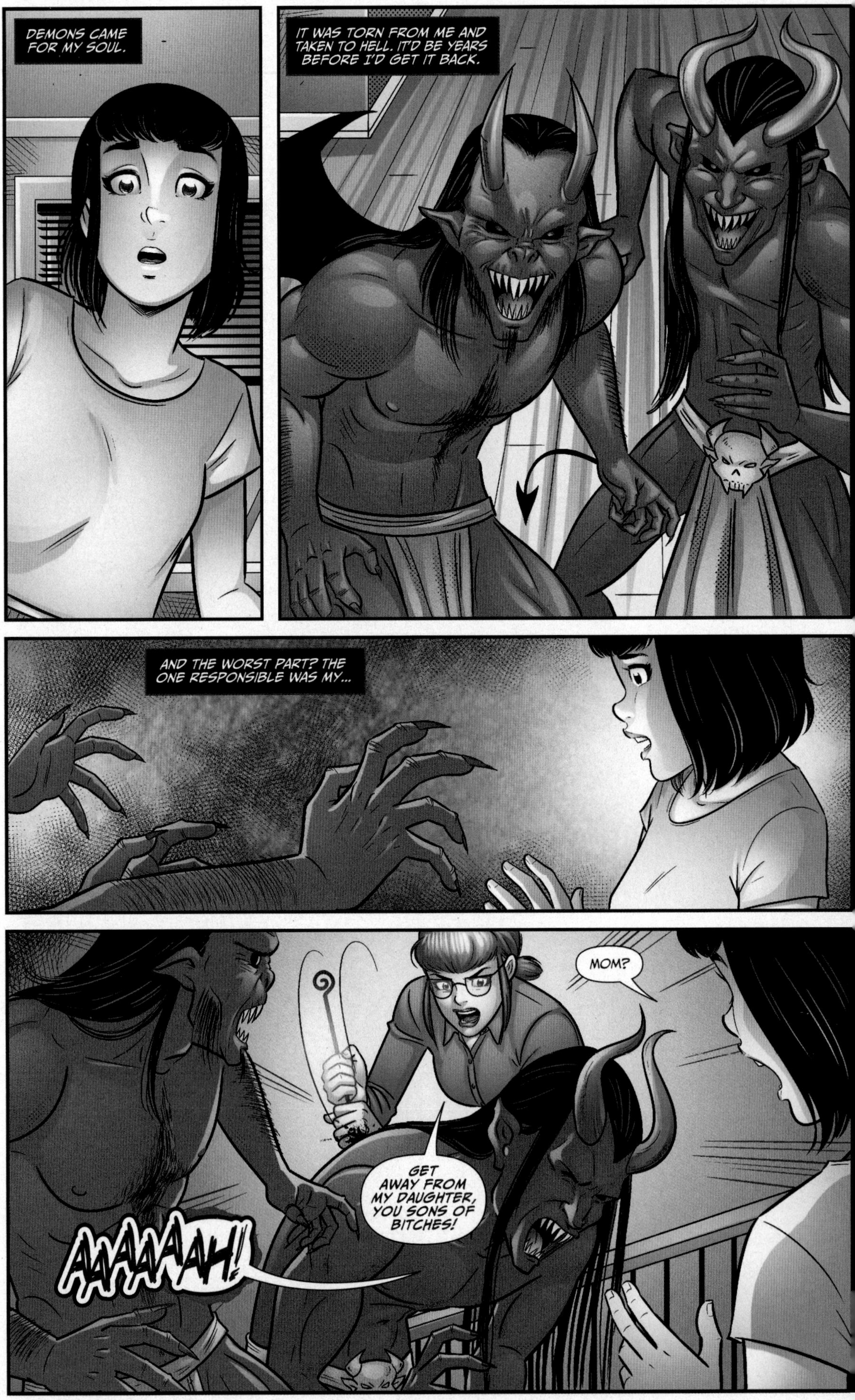
DEMONS CAME FOR MY SOUL.
IT WAS TORN FROM ME AND TAKEN TO HELL. IT'D BE YEARS BEFORE I'D GET IT BACK.
AND THE WORST PART? THE ONE RESPONSIBLE WAS MY...
MOM?
GET AWAY FROM MY DAUGHTER, YOU SONS OF BITCHES!
AAAAAAAH!

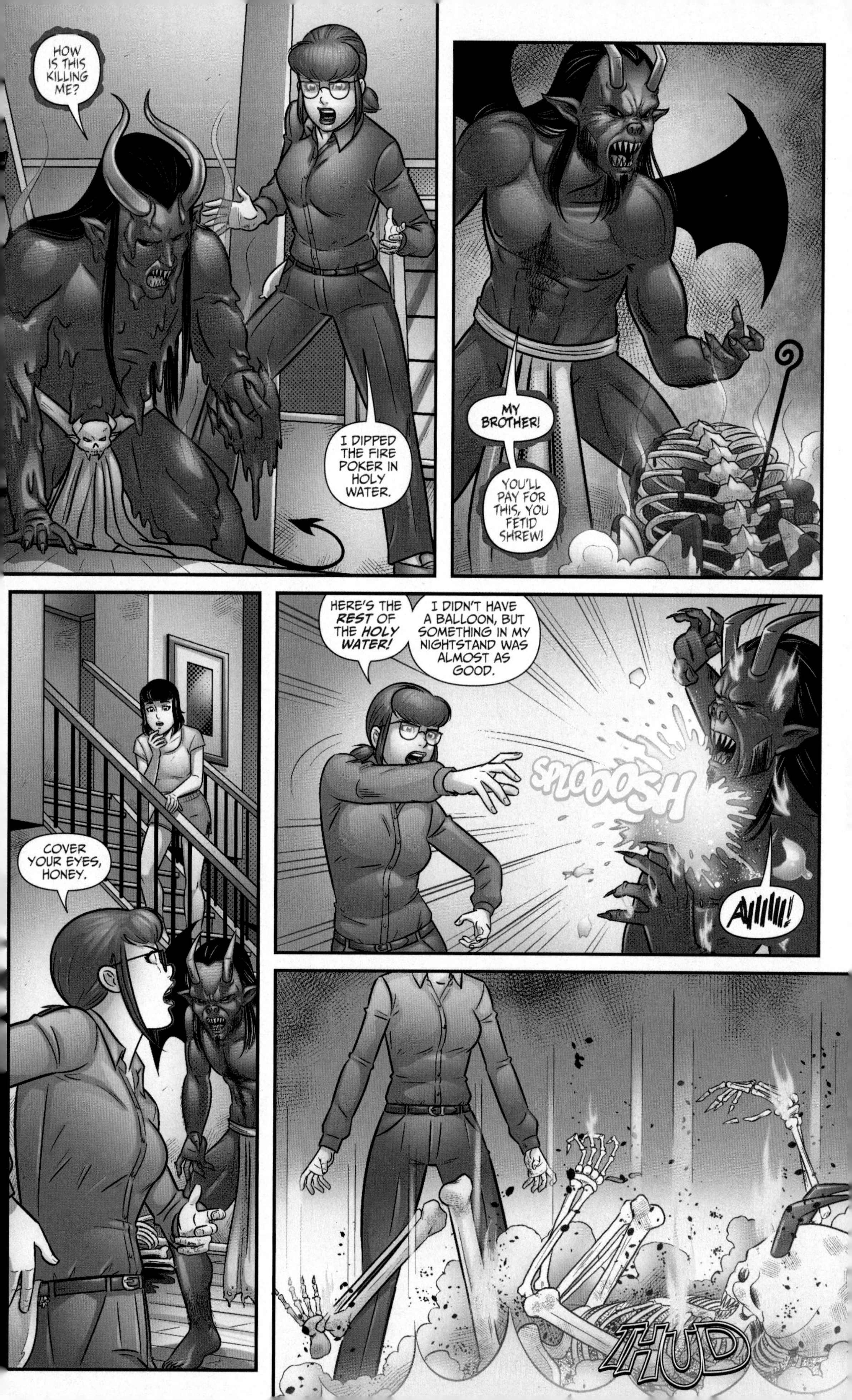
HOW IS THIS KILLING ME?
I DIPPED THE FIRE POKER IN HOLY WATER.
MY BROTHER!
YOU'LL PAY FOR THIS, YOU FETID SHREW!
COVER YOUR EYES, HONEY.
HERE'S THE REST OF THE HOLY WATER!
I DIDN'T HAVE A BALLOON, BUT SOMETHING IN MY NIGHTSTAND WAS ALMOST AS GOOD.
SPLOOOSH
AIIIIII!
THUD

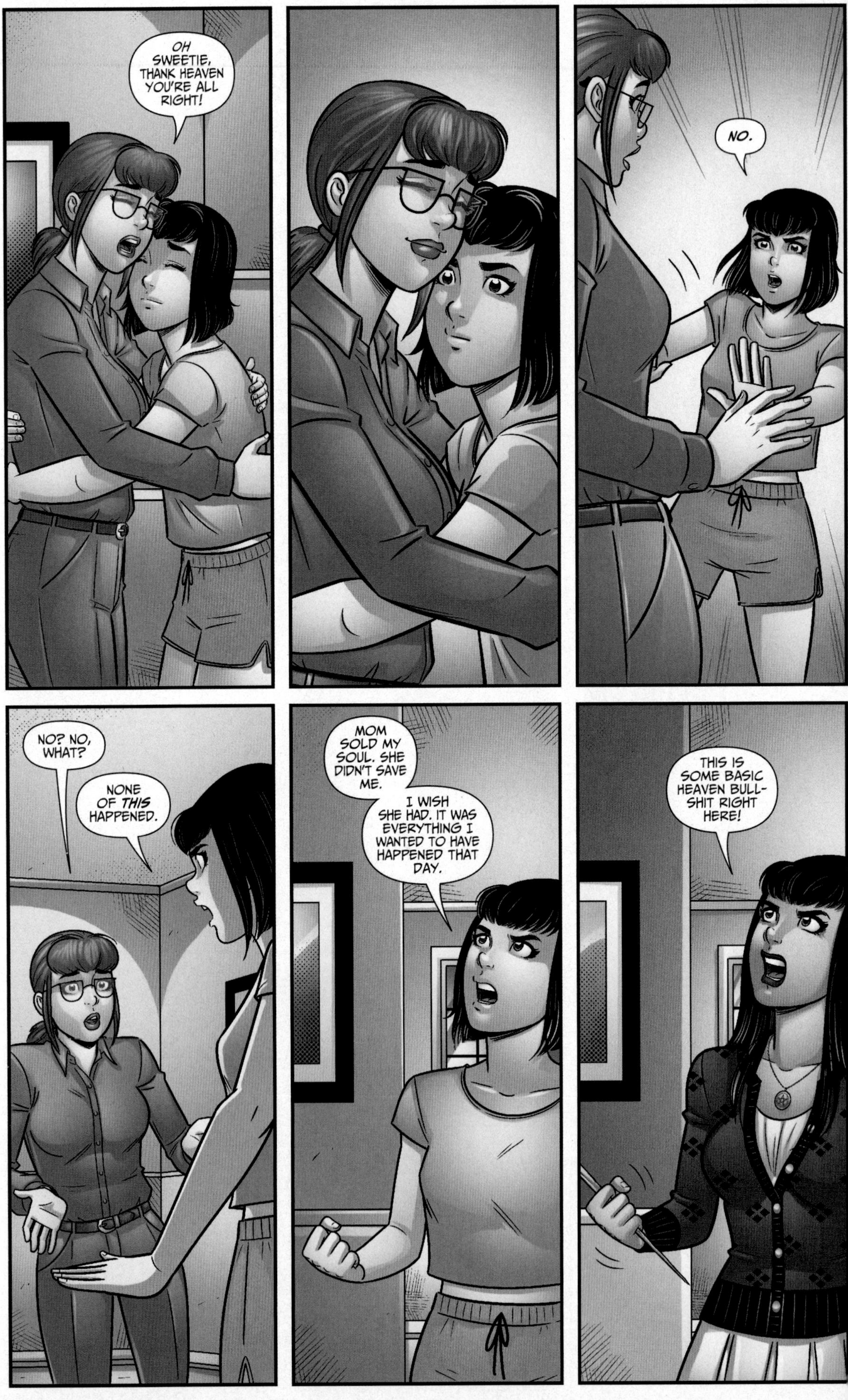
OH SWEETIE, THANK HEAVEN YOU'RE ALL RIGHT!
NO.
NO? NO, WHAT?
NONE OF THIS HAPPENED.
MOM SOLD MY SOUL. SHE DIDN'T SAVE ME.
I WISH SHE HAD. IT WAS EVERYTHING I WANTED TO HAVE HAPPENED THAT DAY.
THIS IS SOME BASIC HEAVEN BULL-SHIT RIGHT HERE!

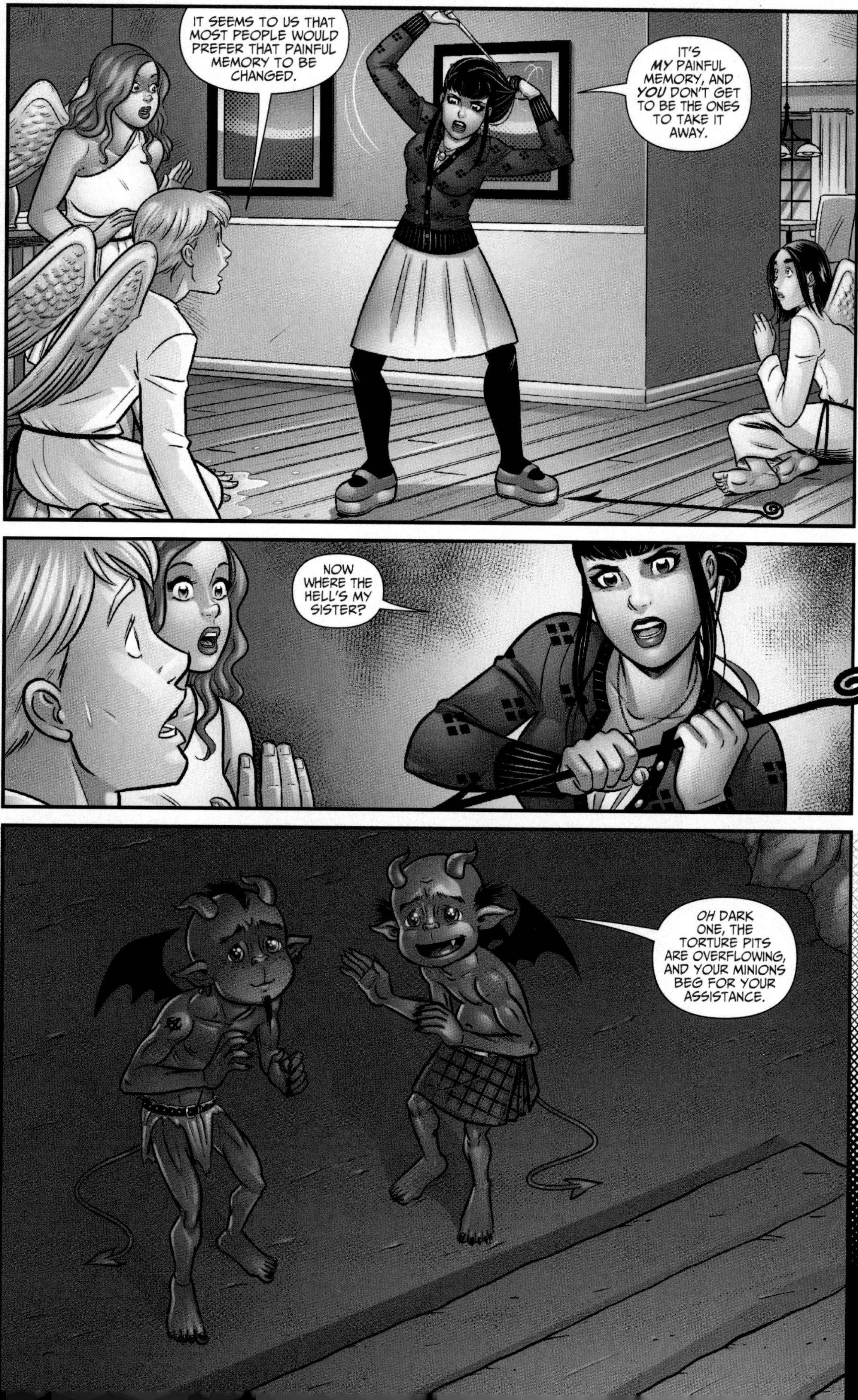
IT SEEMS TO US THAT MOST PEOPLE WOULD PREFER THAT PAINFUL MEMORY TO BE CHANGED.
IT'S MY PAINFUL MEMORY, AND YOU DON'T GET TO BE THE ONES TO TAKE IT AWAY.
NOW WHERE THE HELL'S MY SISTER?
OH DARK ONE, THE TORTURE PITS ARE OVERFLOWING, AND YOUR MINIONS BEG FOR YOUR ASSISTANCE.

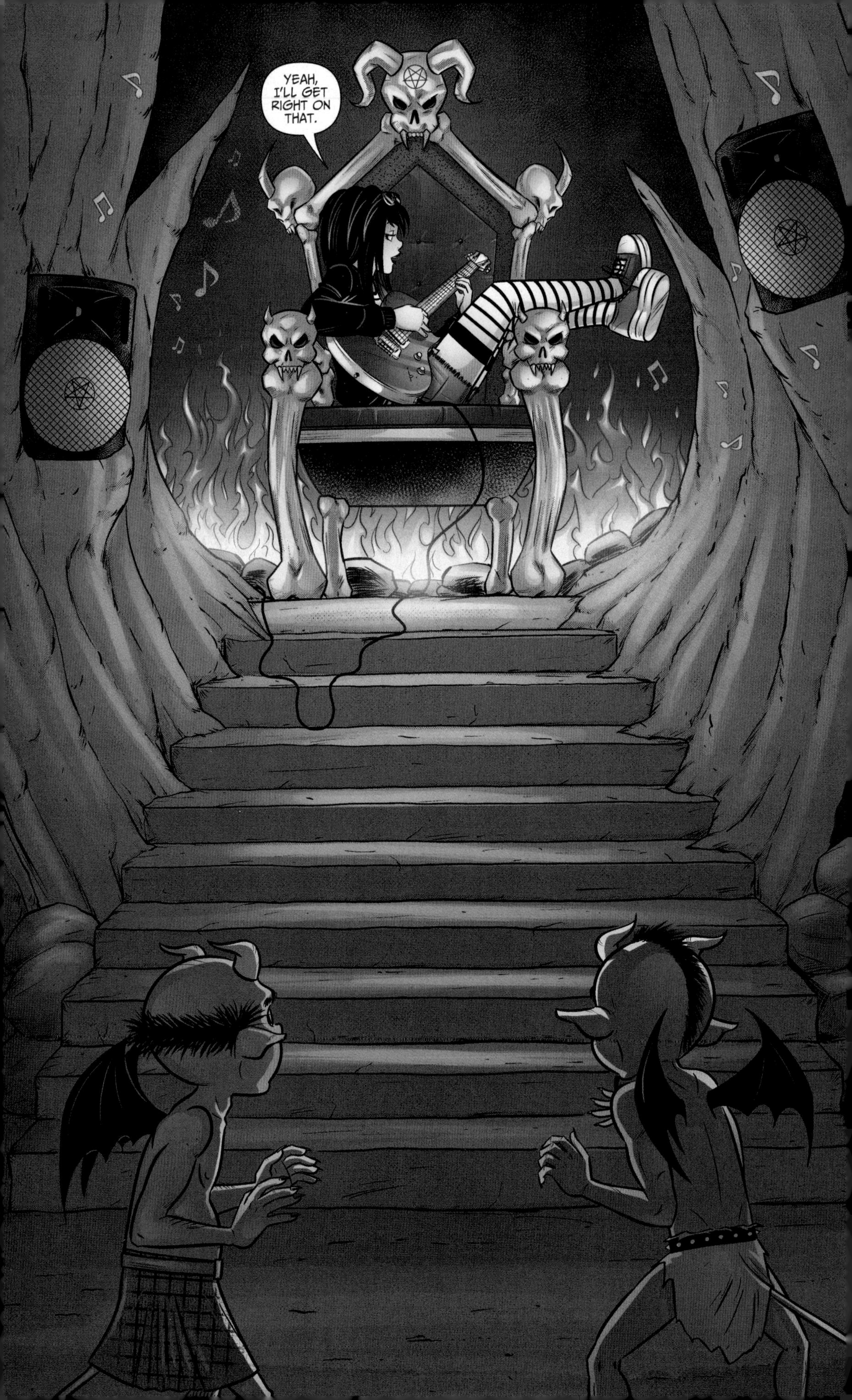
YEAH, I'LL GET RIGHT ON THAT.

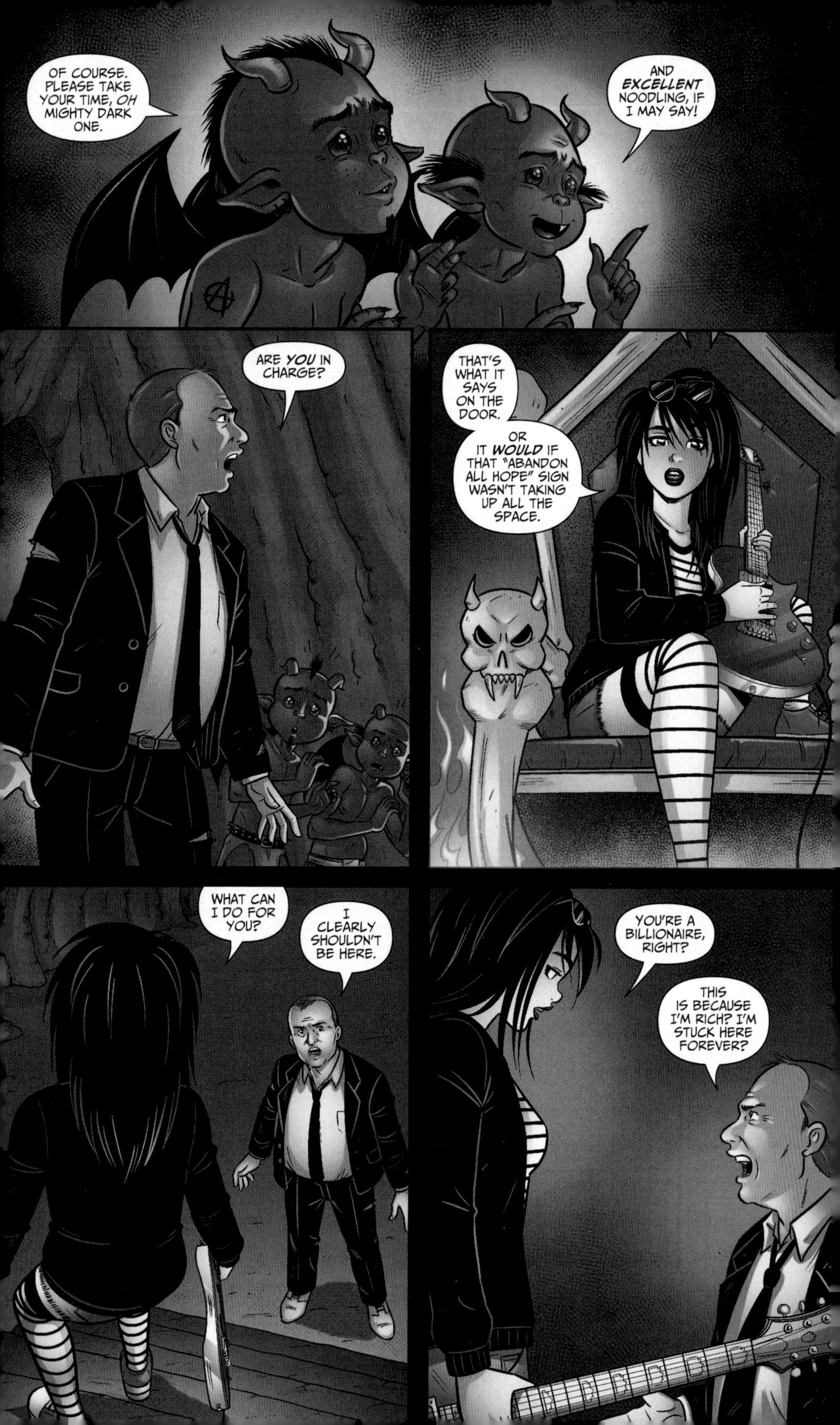
OF COURSE. PLEASE TAKE YOUR TIME, *OH* MIGHTY DARK ONE.
AND ***EXCELLENT*** NOODLING, IF I MAY SAY!
ARE *YOU* IN CHARGE?
THAT'S WHAT IT SAYS ON THE DOOR.
OR IT ***WOULD*** IF THAT "ABANDON ALL HOPE" SIGN WASN'T TAKING UP ALL THE SPACE.
WHAT CAN I DO FOR YOU?
I CLEARLY SHOULDN'T BE HERE.
YOU'RE A BILLIONAIRE, RIGHT?
THIS IS BECAUSE I'M RICH? I'M STUCK HERE FOREVER?

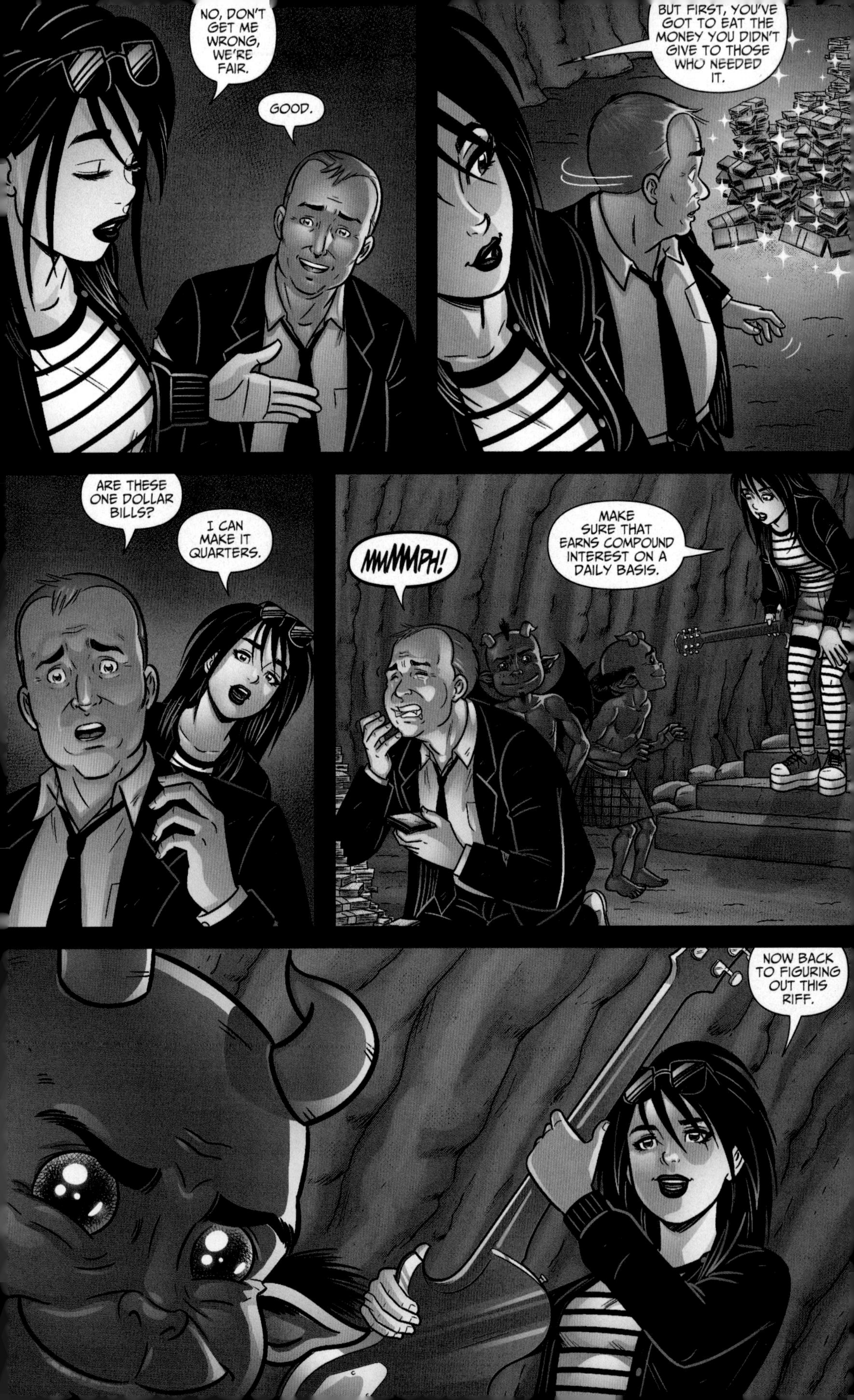

NO, DON'T GET ME WRONG, WE'RE FAIR.
GOOD.
BUT FIRST, YOU'VE GOT TO EAT THE MONEY YOU DIDN'T GIVE TO THOSE WHO NEEDED IT.
ARE THESE ONE DOLLAR BILLS?
I CAN MAKE IT QUARTERS.
MMMMPH!
MAKE SURE THAT EARNS COMPOUND INTEREST ON A DAILY BASIS.
NOW BACK TO FIGURING OUT THIS RIFF.

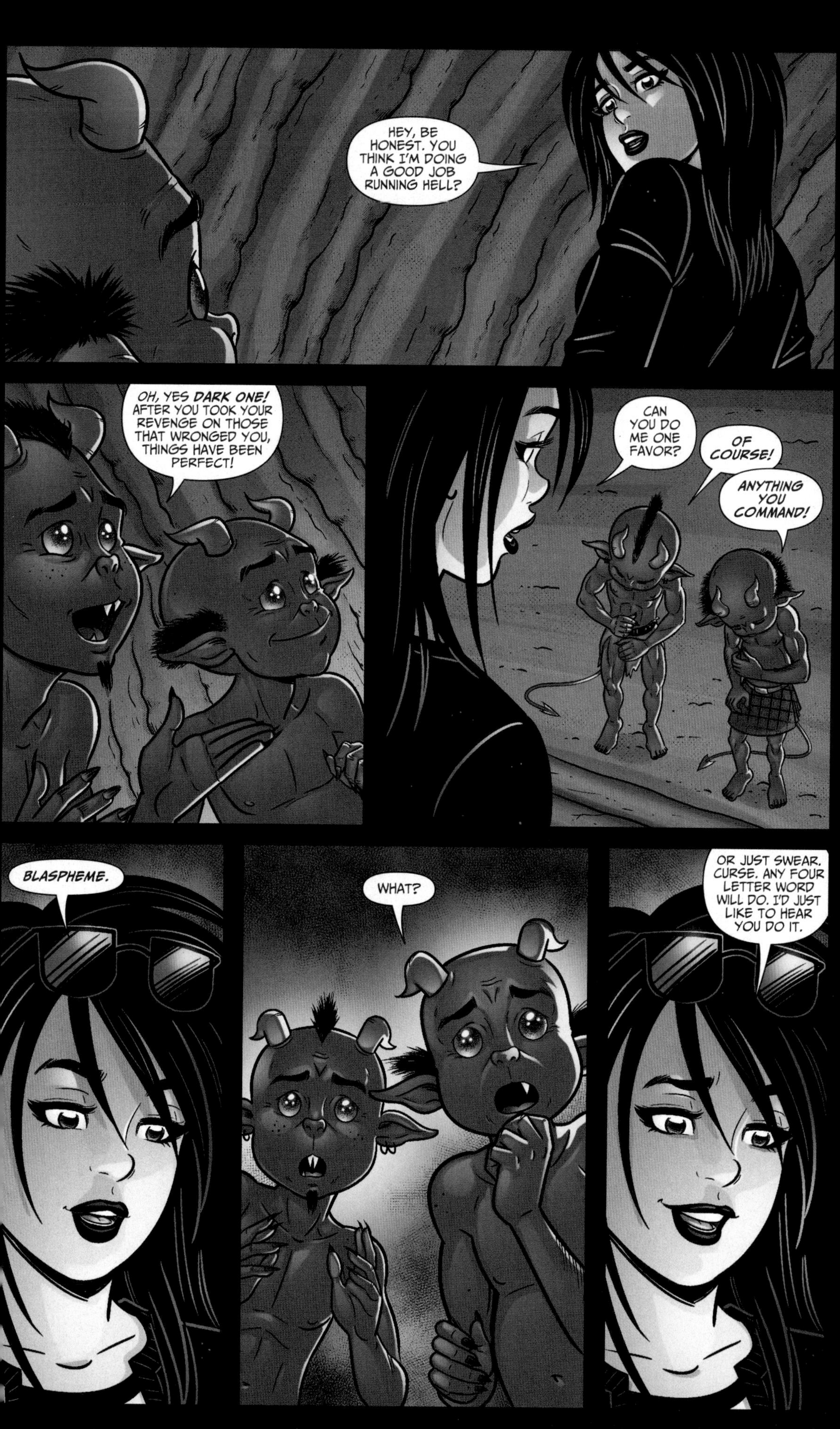
HEY, BE HONEST. YOU THINK I'M DOING A GOOD JOB RUNNING HELL?
OH, YES DARK ONE! AFTER YOU TOOK YOUR REVENGE ON THOSE THAT WRONGED YOU, THINGS HAVE BEEN PERFECT!
CAN YOU DO ME ONE FAVOR?
OF COURSE!
ANYTHING YOU COMMAND!
BLASPHEME.
WHAT?
OR JUST SWEAR. CURSE. ANY FOUR LETTER WORD WILL DO. I'D JUST LIKE TO HEAR YOU DO IT.

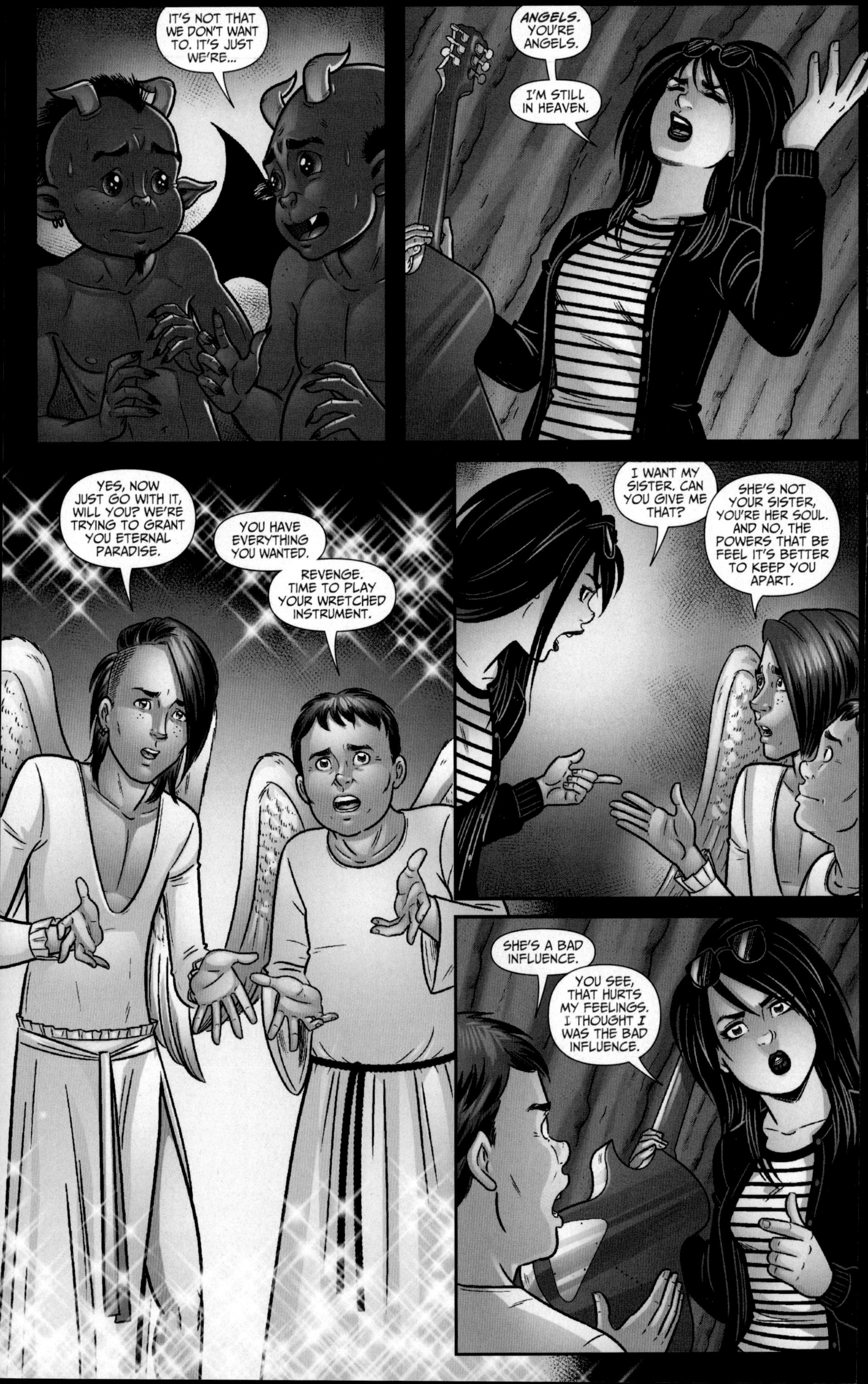
IT'S NOT THAT WE DON'T WANT TO. IT'S JUST WE'RE...
ANGELS. YOU'RE ANGELS.
I'M STILL IN HEAVEN.
YES, NOW JUST GO WITH IT, WILL YOU? WE'RE TRYING TO GRANT YOU ETERNAL PARADISE.
YOU HAVE EVERYTHING YOU WANTED.
REVENGE. TIME TO PLAY YOUR WRETCHED INSTRUMENT.
I WANT MY SISTER. CAN YOU GIVE ME THAT?
SHE'S NOT YOUR SISTER, YOU'RE HER SOUL. AND NO, THE POWERS THAT BE FEEL IT'S BETTER TO KEEP YOU APART.
SHE'S A BAD INFLUENCE.
YOU SEE, THAT HURTS MY FEELINGS. I THOUGHT I WAS THE BAD INFLUENCE.

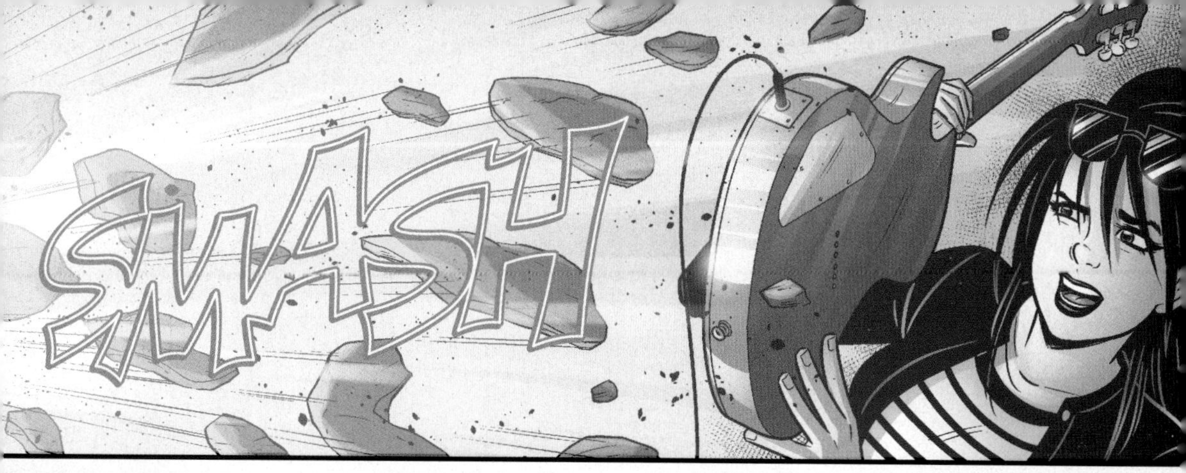
SMASH

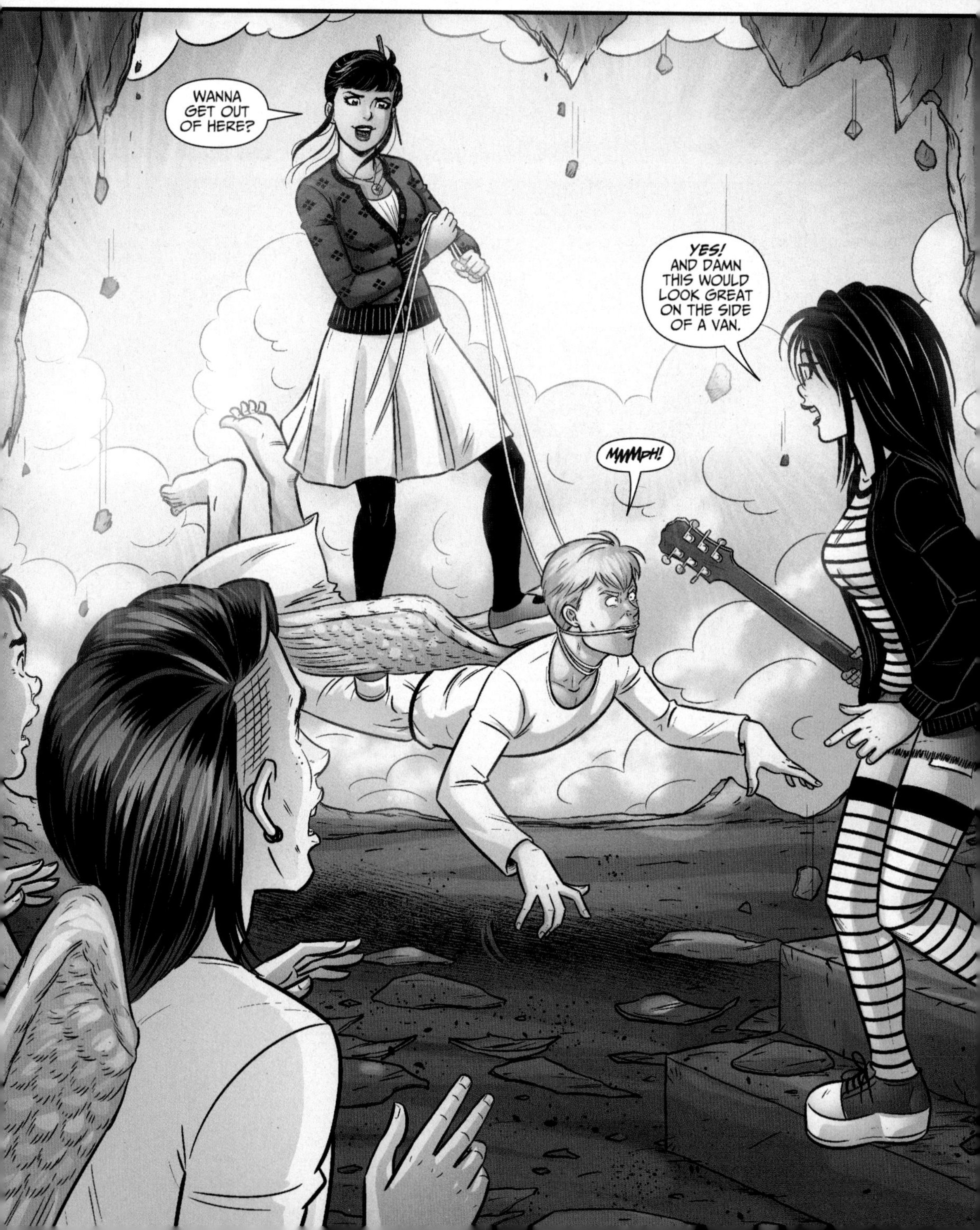
WANNA GET OUT OF HERE?
YES! AND DAMN THIS WOULD LOOK GREAT ON THE SIDE OF A VAN.
MMMPH!

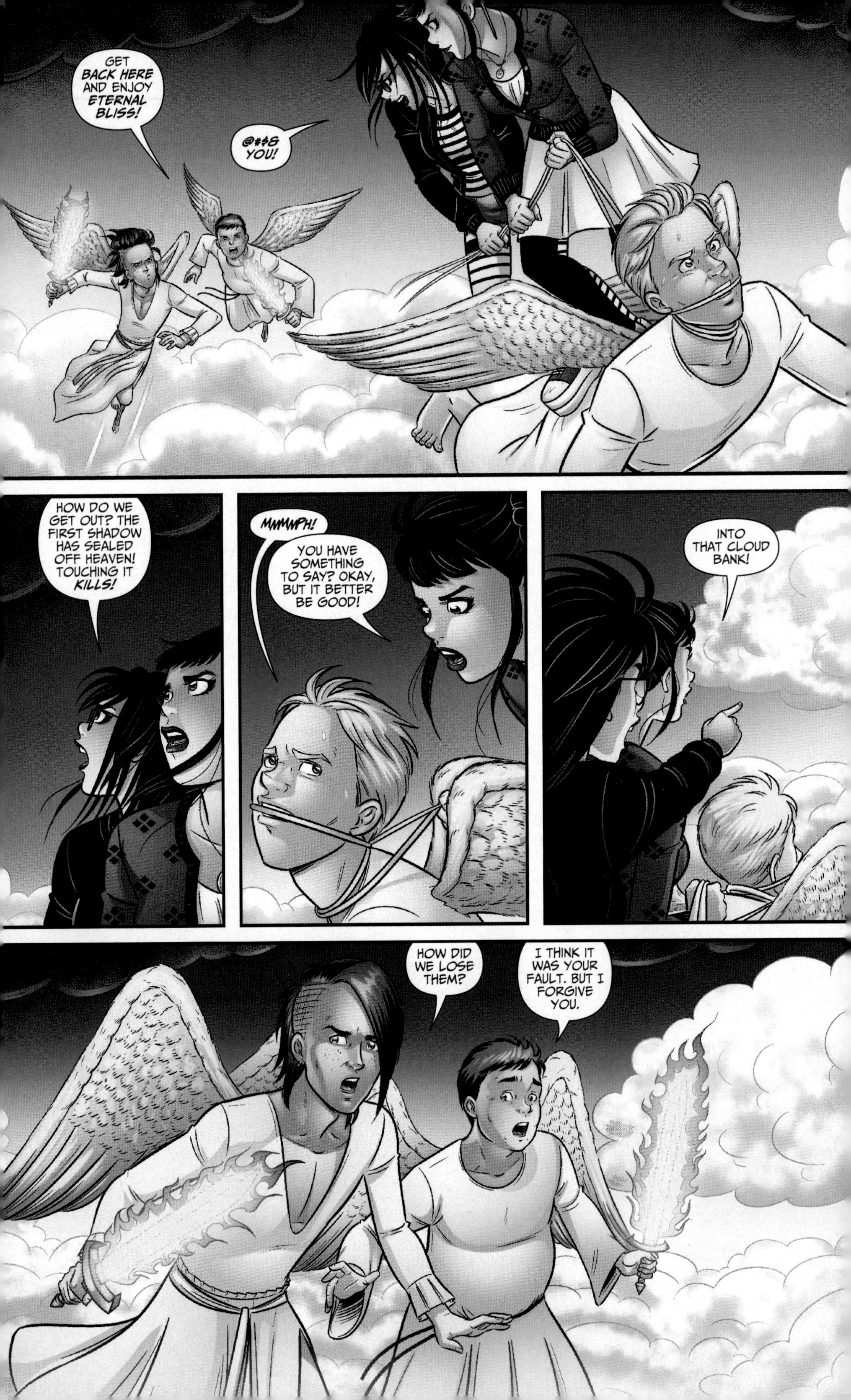

GET BACK HERE AND ENJOY ETERNAL BLISS!
@#$& YOU!
HOW DO WE GET OUT? THE FIRST SHADOW HAS SEALED OFF HEAVEN! TOUCHING IT KILLS!
MMMMPH!
YOU HAVE SOMETHING TO SAY? OKAY, BUT IT BETTER BE GOOD!
INTO THAT CLOUD BANK!
HOW DID WE LOSE THEM?
I THINK IT WAS YOUR FAULT. BUT I FORGIVE YOU.

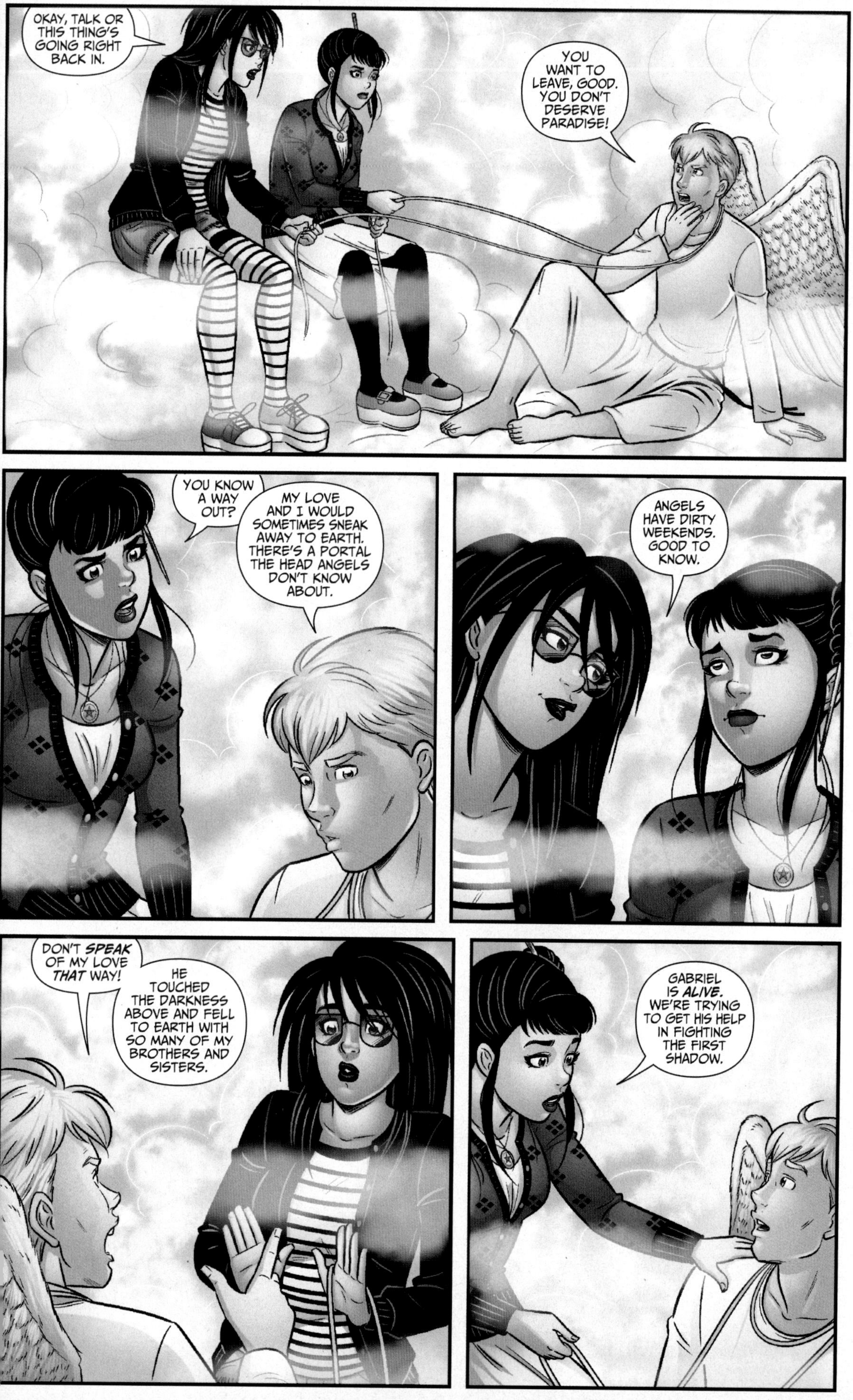
OKAY, TALK OR THIS THING'S GOING RIGHT BACK IN.
YOU WANT TO LEAVE, GOOD. YOU DON'T DESERVE PARADISE!
YOU KNOW A WAY OUT?
MY LOVE AND I WOULD SOMETIMES SNEAK AWAY TO EARTH. THERE'S A PORTAL THE HEAD ANGELS DON'T KNOW ABOUT.
ANGELS HAVE DIRTY WEEKENDS. GOOD TO KNOW.
DON'T *SPEAK* OF MY LOVE *THAT* WAY!
HE TOUCHED THE DARKNESS ABOVE AND FELL TO EARTH WITH SO MANY OF MY BROTHERS AND SISTERS.
GABRIEL IS ***ALIVE.*** WE'RE TRYING TO GET HIS HELP IN FIGHTING THE FIRST SHADOW.

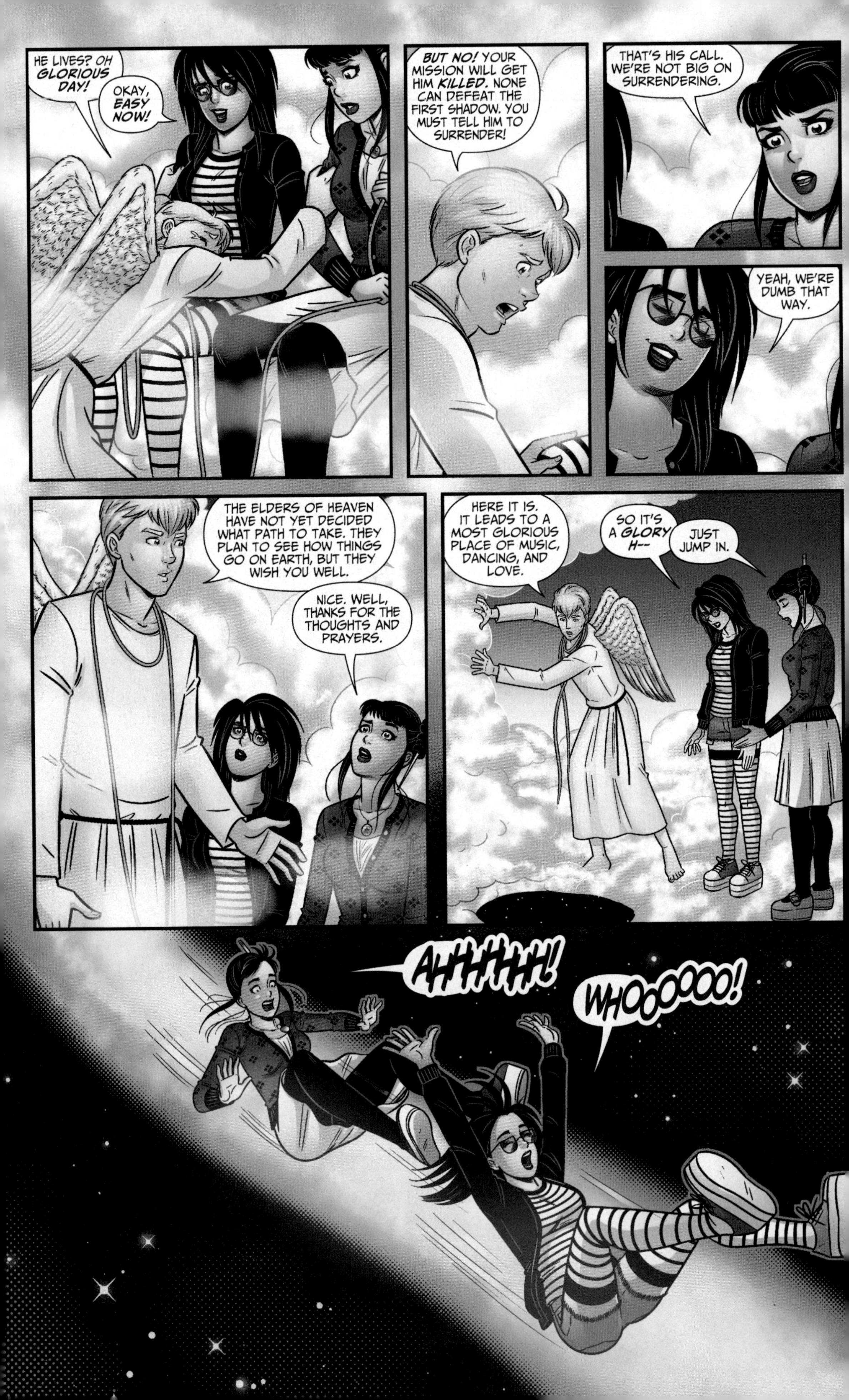
HE LIVES? OH GLORIOUS DAY!
OKAY, EASY NOW!
BUT NO! YOUR MISSION WILL GET HIM KILLED. NONE CAN DEFEAT THE FIRST SHADOW. YOU MUST TELL HIM TO SURRENDER!
THAT'S HIS CALL. WE'RE NOT BIG ON SURRENDERING.
YEAH, WE'RE DUMB THAT WAY.
THE ELDERS OF HEAVEN HAVE NOT YET DECIDED WHAT PATH TO TAKE. THEY PLAN TO SEE HOW THINGS GO ON EARTH, BUT THEY WISH YOU WELL.
NICE. WELL, THANKS FOR THE THOUGHTS AND PRAYERS.
HERE IT IS. IT LEADS TO A MOST GLORIOUS PLACE OF MUSIC, DANCING, AND LOVE.
SO IT'S A GLORY H--
JUST JUMP IN.
AHHHHHH!
WHOOOOOO!

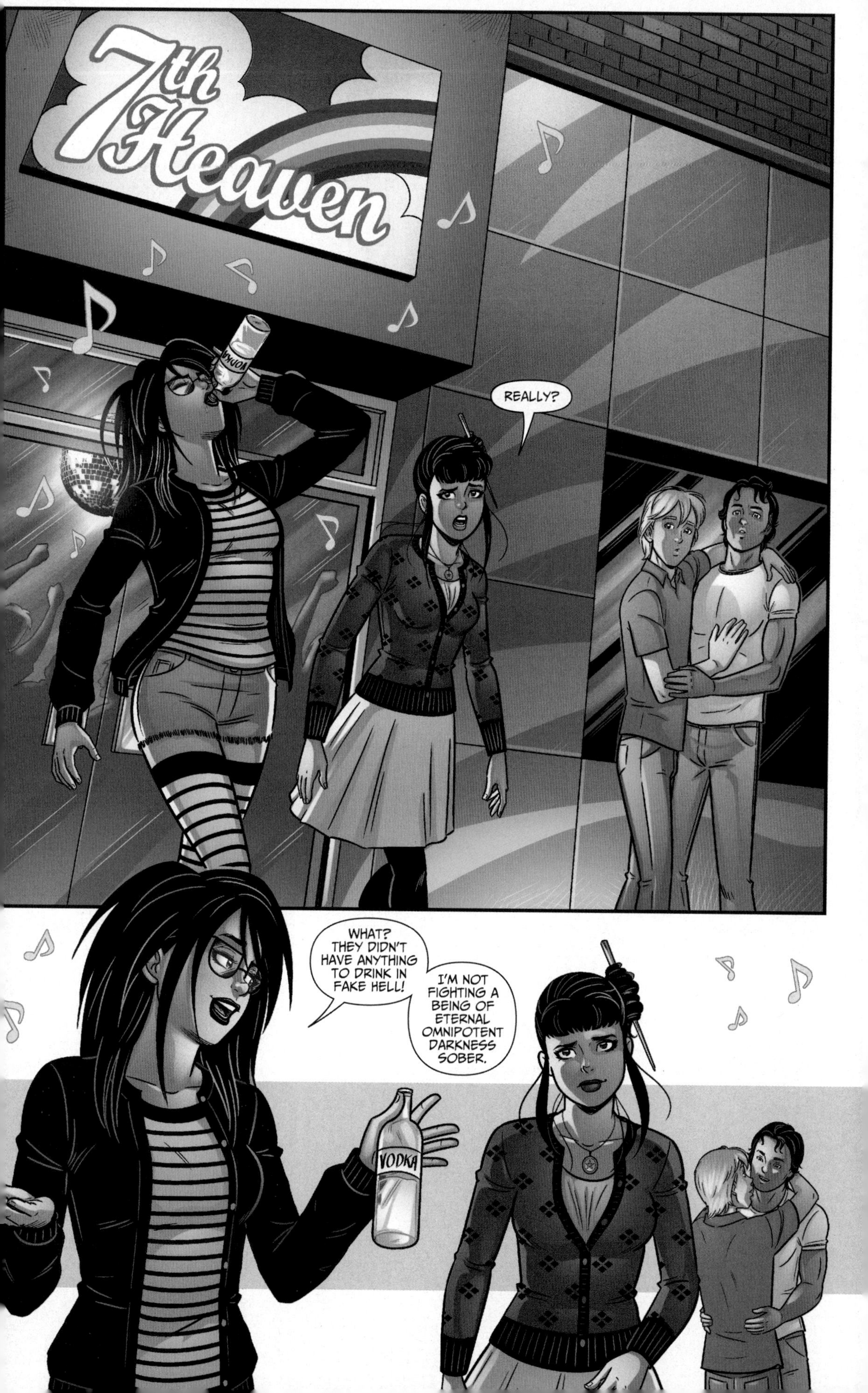
7th Heaven
VODKA
REALLY?
WHAT? THEY DIDN'T HAVE ANYTHING TO DRINK IN FAKE HELL!
I'M NOT FIGHTING A BEING OF ETERNAL OMNIPOTENT DARKNESS SOBER.
VODKA

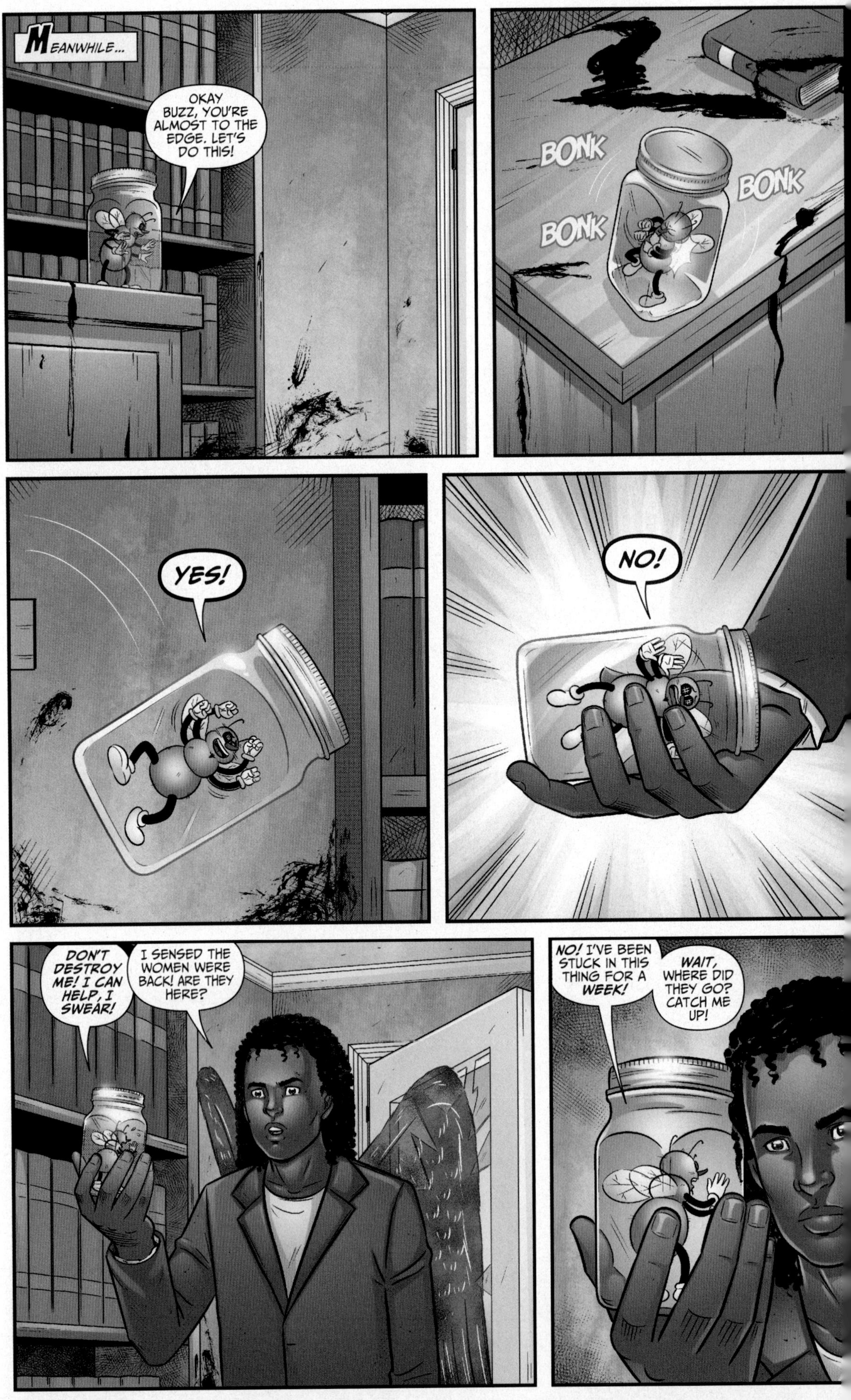
MEANWHILE...
OKAY BUZZ, YOU'RE ALMOST TO THE EDGE. LET'S DO THIS!
BONK
BONK
BONK
YES!
NO!
DON'T DESTROY ME! I CAN HELP, I SWEAR!
I SENSED THE WOMEN WERE BACK! ARE THEY HERE?
NO! I'VE BEEN STUCK IN THIS THING FOR A WEEK!
WAIT, WHERE DID THEY GO? CATCH ME UP!

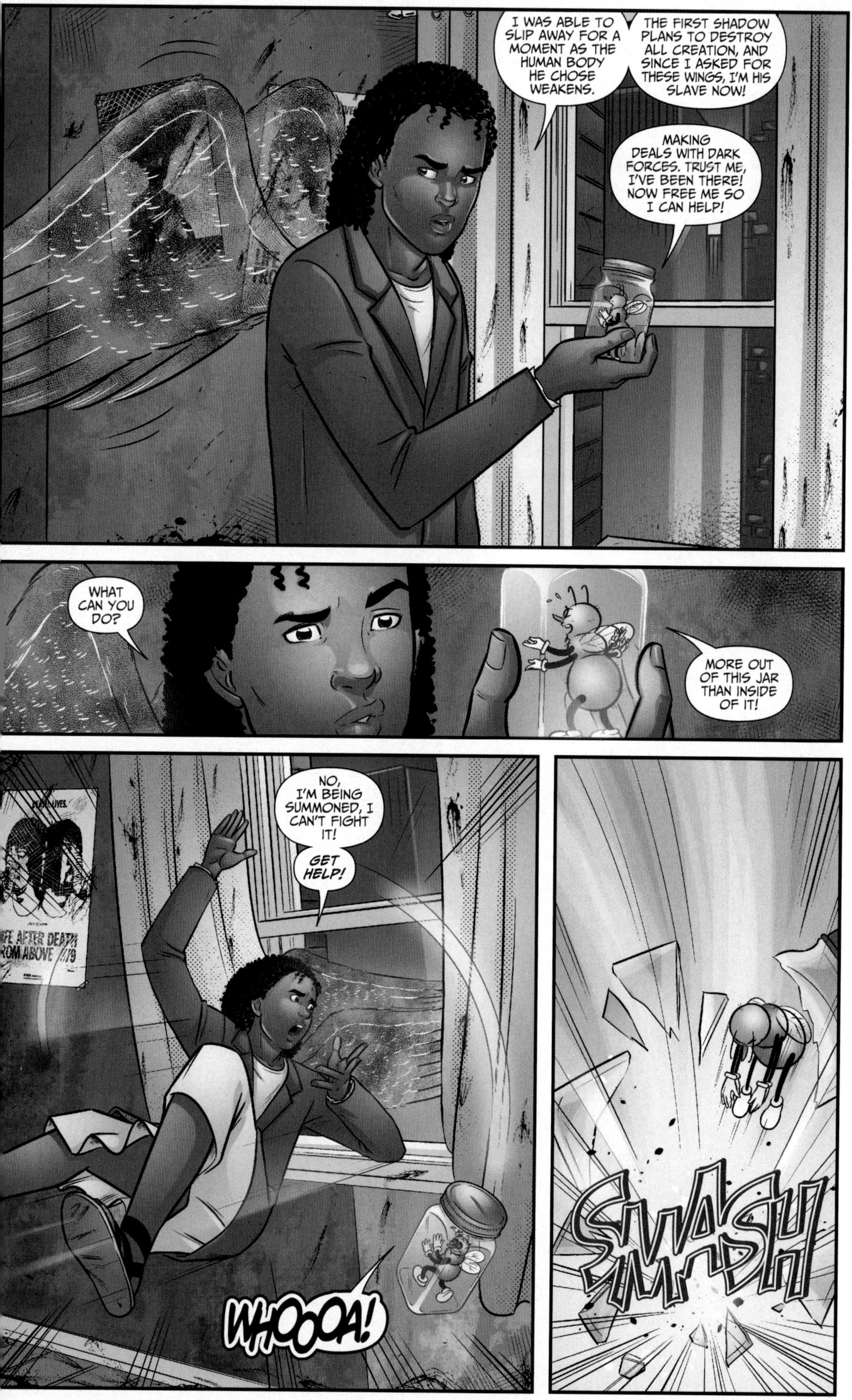

I WAS ABLE TO SLIP AWAY FOR A MOMENT AS THE HUMAN BODY HE CHOSE WEAKENS.
THE FIRST SHADOW PLANS TO DESTROY ALL CREATION, AND SINCE I ASKED FOR THESE WINGS, I'M HIS SLAVE NOW!
MAKING DEALS WITH DARK FORCES. TRUST ME, I'VE BEEN THERE! NOW FREE ME SO I CAN HELP!
WHAT CAN YOU DO?
MORE OUT OF THIS JAR THAN INSIDE OF IT!
FE AFTER DEATH
ROM ABOVE 11/9
NO, I'M BEING SUMMONED, I CAN'T FIGHT IT!
GET HELP!
WHOOOA!
SMASH

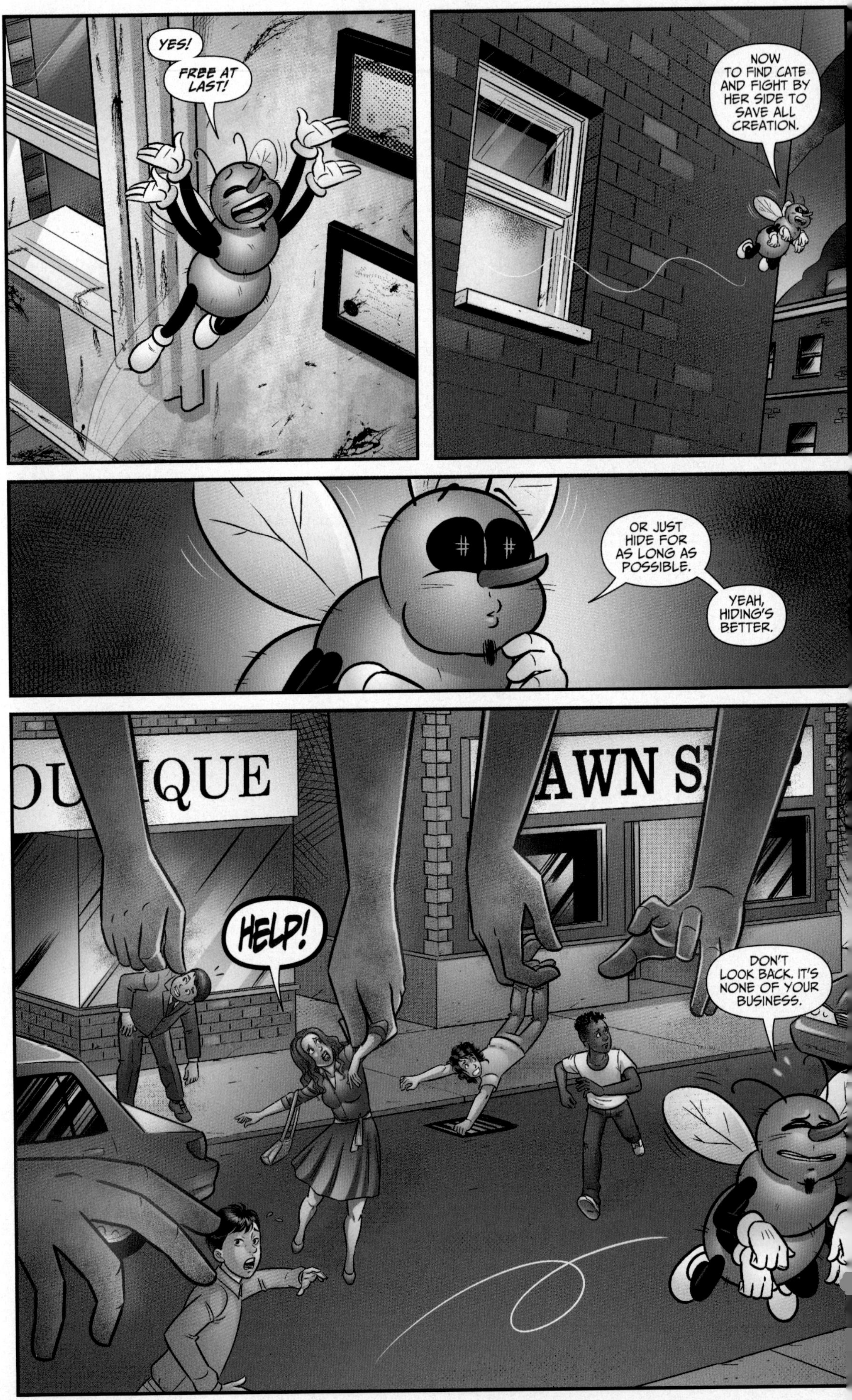
YES!
FREE AT LAST!
NOW TO FIND CATE AND FIGHT BY HER SIDE TO SAVE ALL CREATION.
OR JUST HIDE FOR AS LONG AS POSSIBLE.
YEAH, HIDING'S BETTER.
OU IQUE
AWN S
HELP!
DON'T LOOK BACK. IT'S NONE OF YOUR BUSINESS.

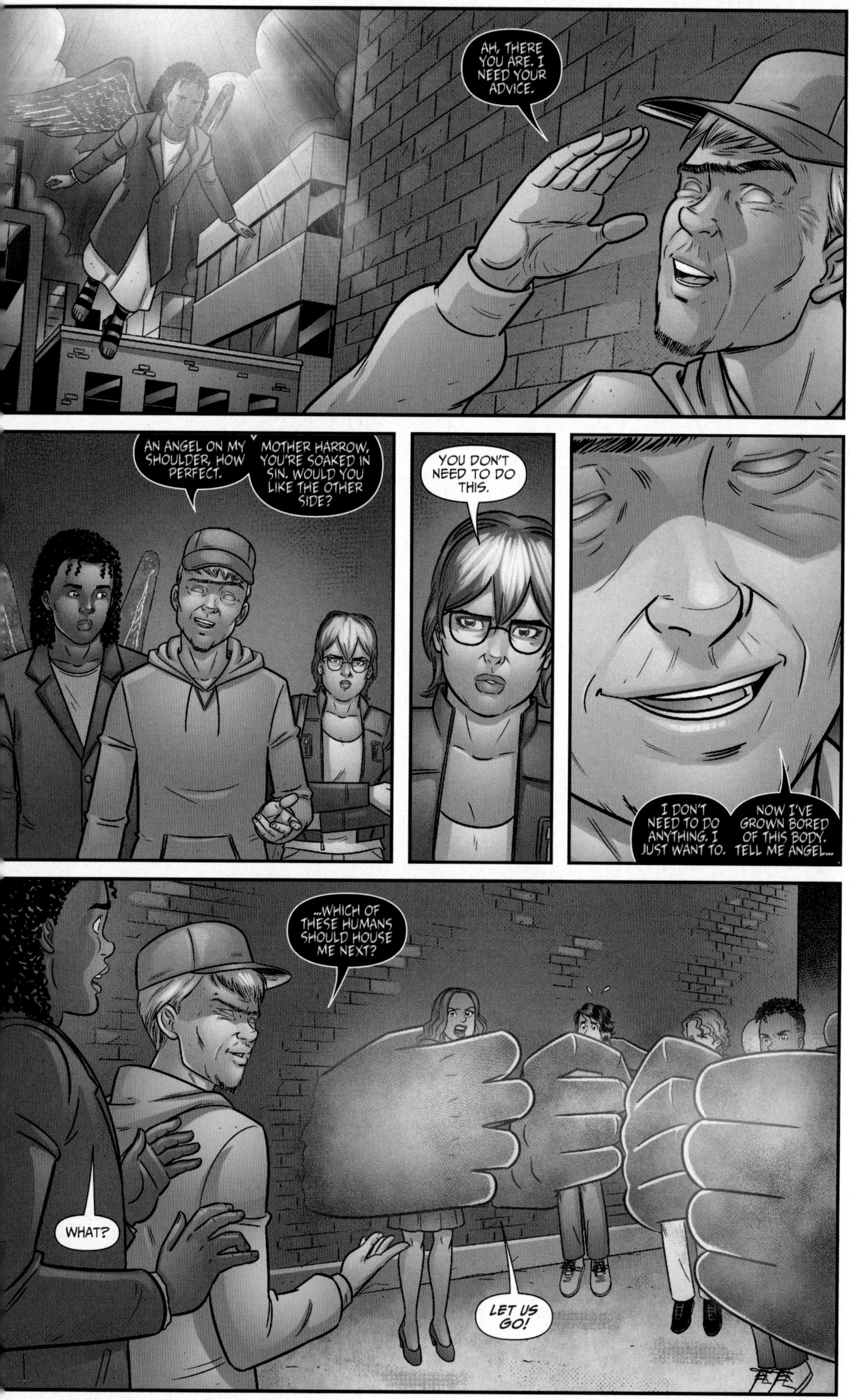
AH, THERE YOU ARE. I NEED YOUR ADVICE.
AN ANGEL ON MY SHOULDER, HOW PERFECT.
MOTHER HARROW, YOU'RE SOAKED IN SIN. WOULD YOU LIKE THE OTHER SIDE?
YOU DON'T NEED TO DO THIS.
I DON'T NEED TO DO ANYTHING. I JUST WANT TO.
NOW I'VE GROWN BORED OF THIS BODY. TELL ME ANGEL...
...WHICH OF THESE HUMANS SHOULD HOUSE ME NEXT?
WHAT?
LET US GO!

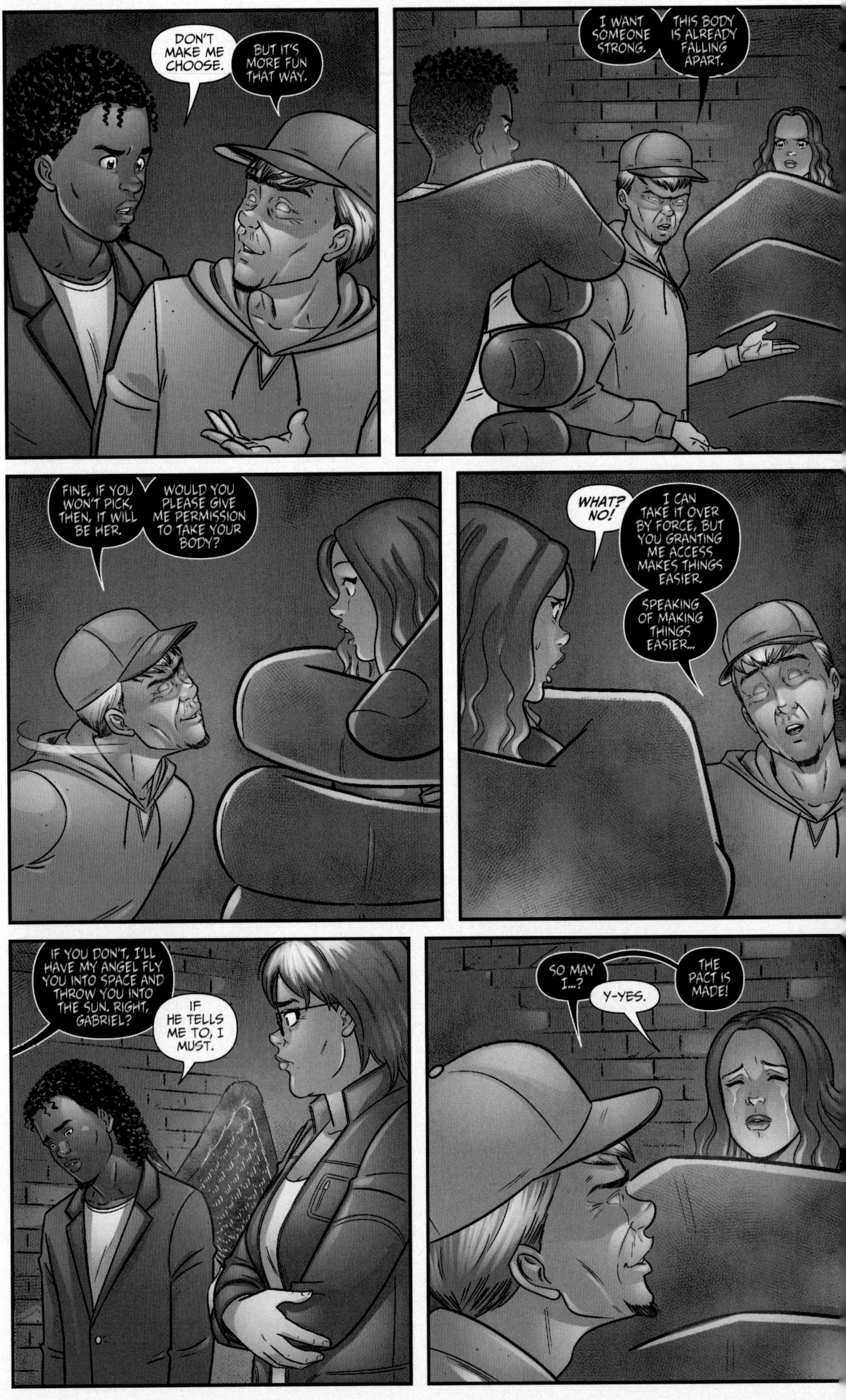
DON'T MAKE ME CHOOSE.
BUT IT'S MORE FUN THAT WAY.
I WANT SOMEONE STRONG.
THIS BODY IS ALREADY FALLING APART.
FINE, IF YOU WON'T PICK, THEN, IT WILL BE HER.
WOULD YOU PLEASE GIVE ME PERMISSION TO TAKE YOUR BODY?
WHAT? NO!
I CAN TAKE IT OVER BY FORCE, BUT YOU GRANTING ME ACCESS MAKES THINGS EASIER.
SPEAKING OF MAKING THINGS EASIER...
IF YOU DON'T, I'LL HAVE MY ANGEL FLY YOU INTO SPACE AND THROW YOU INTO THE SUN. RIGHT, GABRIEL?
IF HE TELLS ME TO, I MUST.
SO MAY I...?
Y-YES.
THE PACT IS MADE!

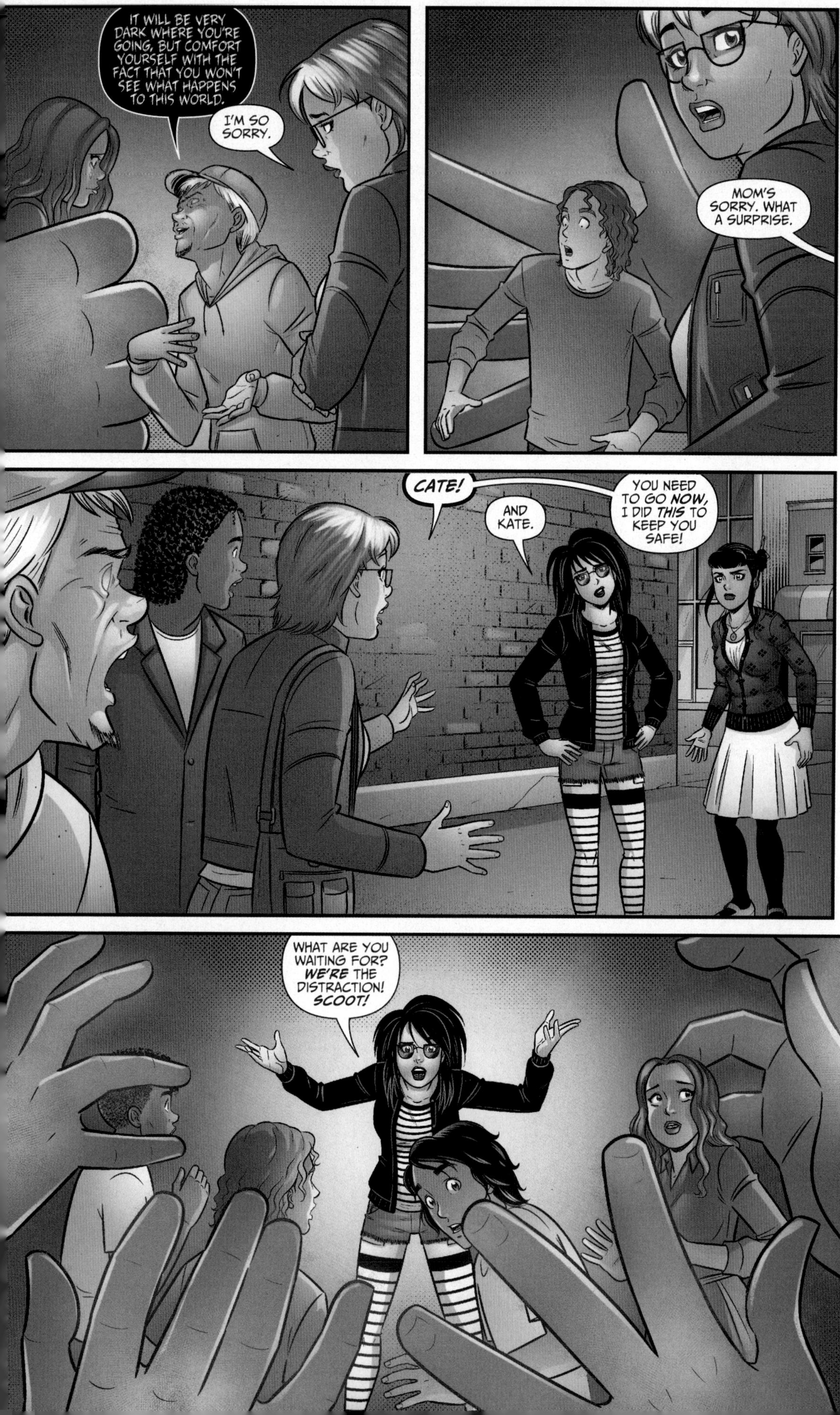
IT WILL BE VERY DARK WHERE YOU'RE GOING, BUT COMFORT YOURSELF WITH THE FACT THAT YOU WON'T SEE WHAT HAPPENS TO THIS WORLD.
I'M SO SORRY.
MOM'S SORRY. WHAT A SURPRISE.
CATE!
AND KATE.
YOU NEED TO GO NOW, I DID THIS TO KEEP YOU SAFE!
WHAT ARE YOU WAITING FOR? WE'RE THE DISTRACTION! SCOOT!

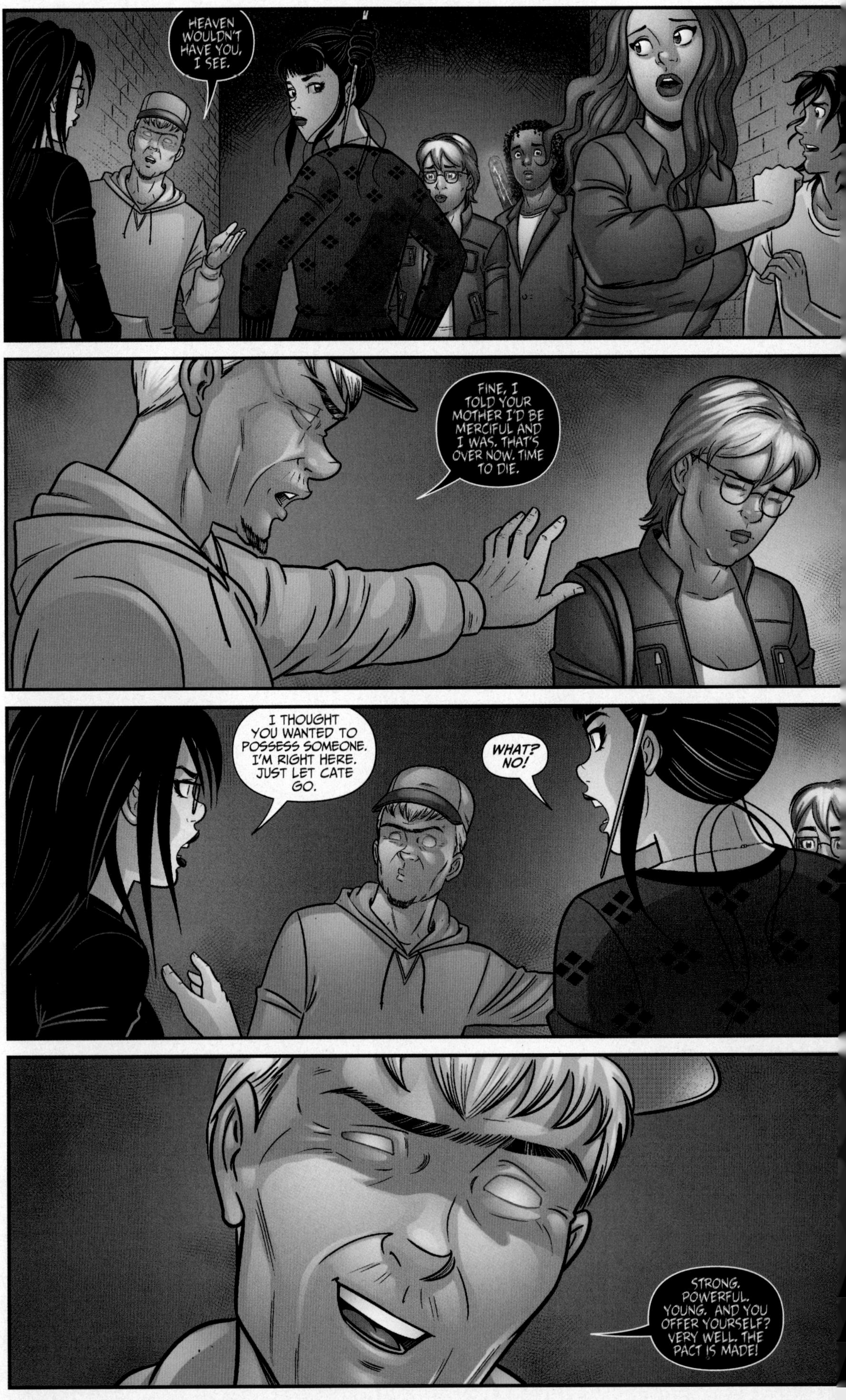
HEAVEN WOULDN'T HAVE YOU, I SEE.
FINE, I TOLD YOUR MOTHER I'D BE MERCIFUL AND I WAS. THAT'S OVER NOW. TIME TO DIE.
I THOUGHT YOU WANTED TO POSSESS SOMEONE. I'M RIGHT HERE. JUST LET CATE GO.
WHAT? NO!
STRONG. POWERFUL. YOUNG. AND YOU OFFER YOURSELF? VERY WELL. THE PACT IS MADE!

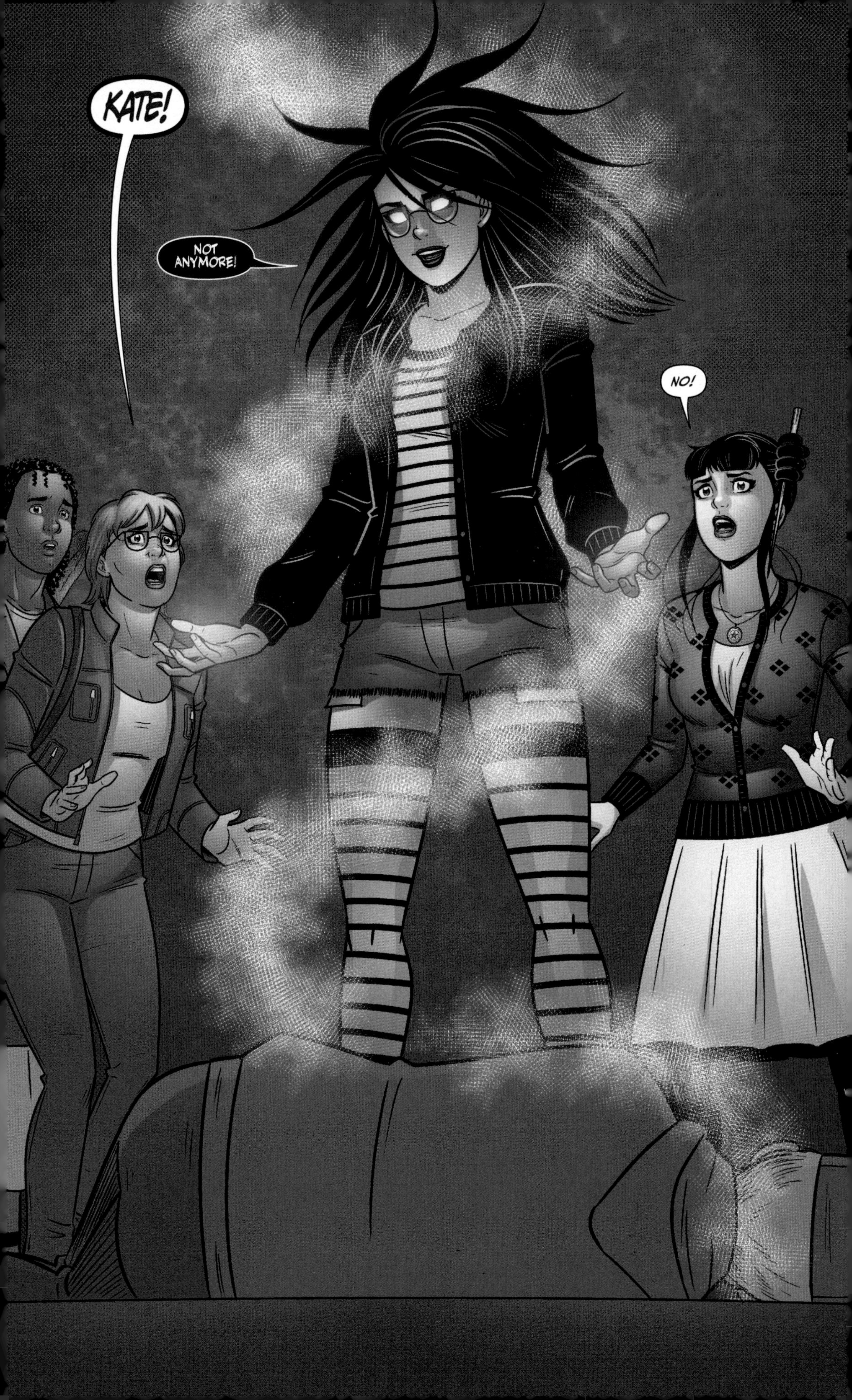
KATE!
NOT ANYMORE!
NO!

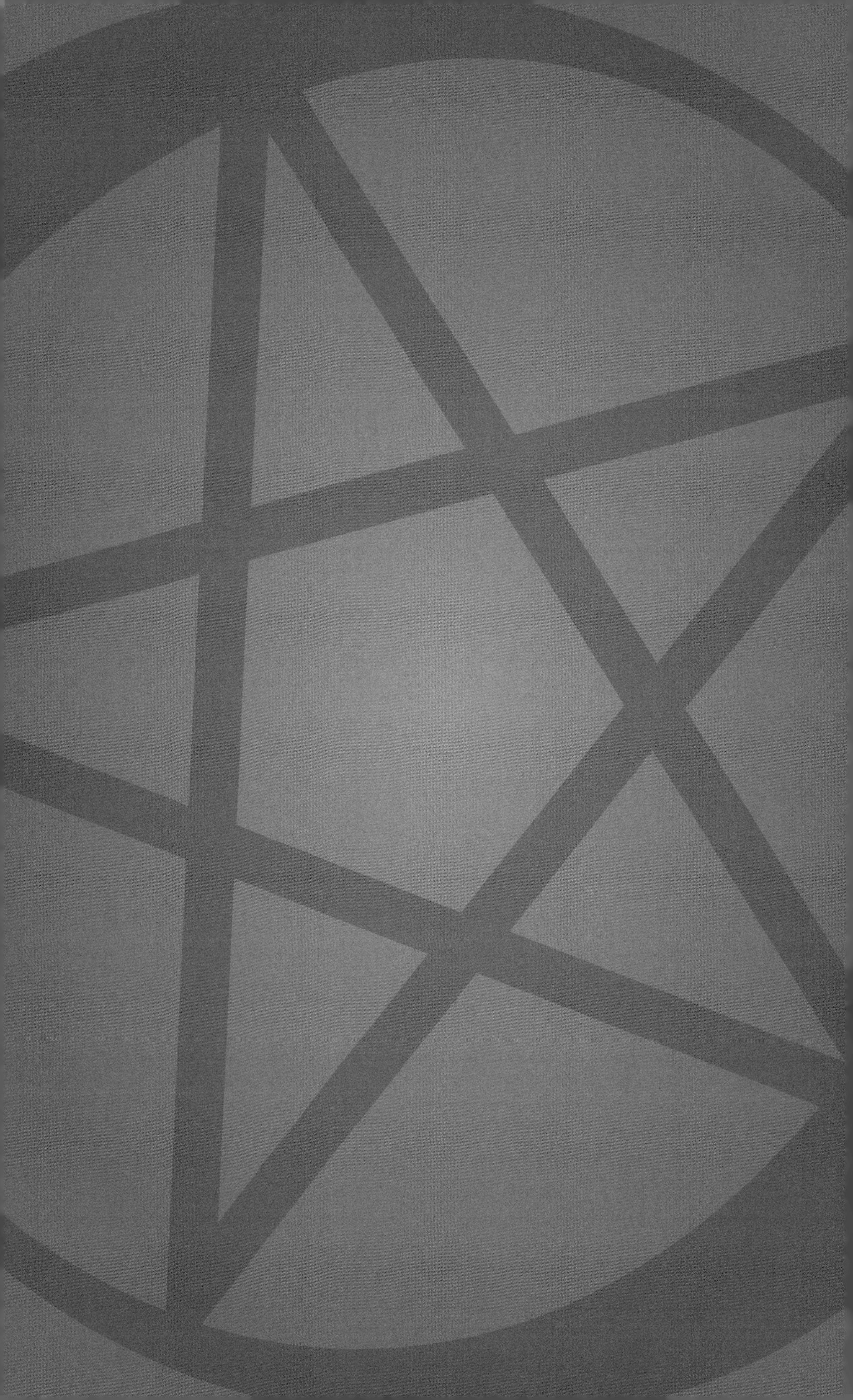

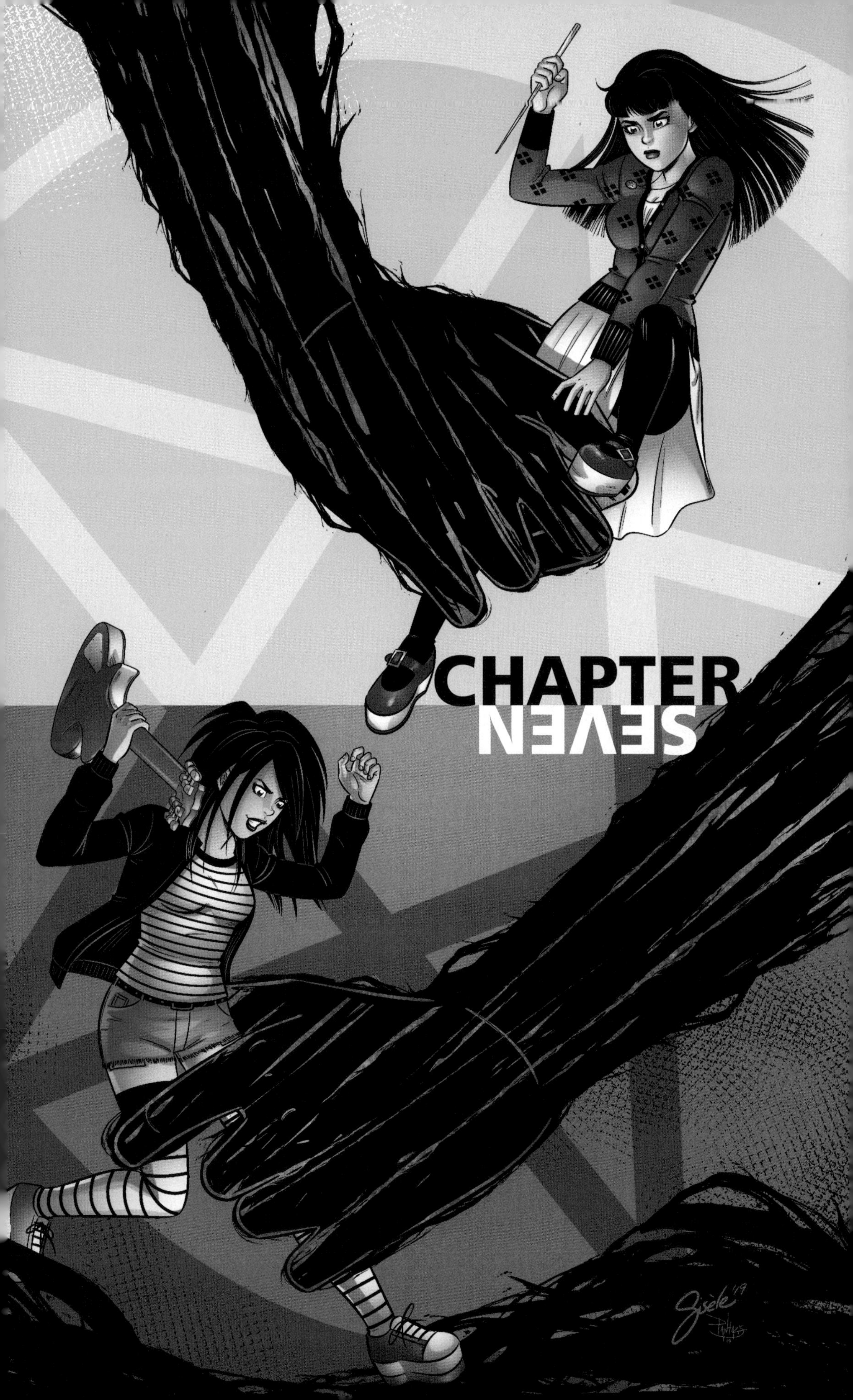
CHAPTER
SEVEN

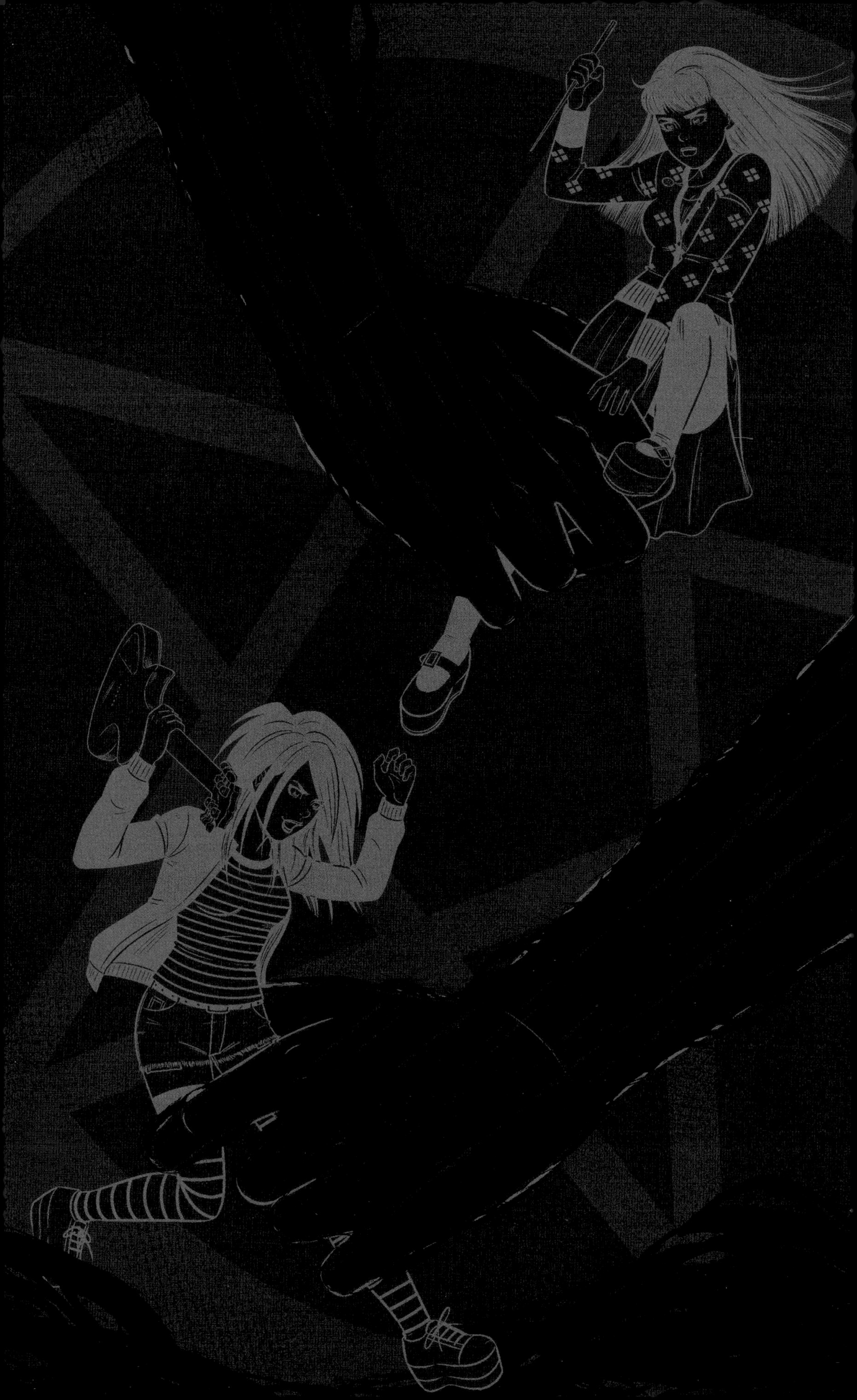

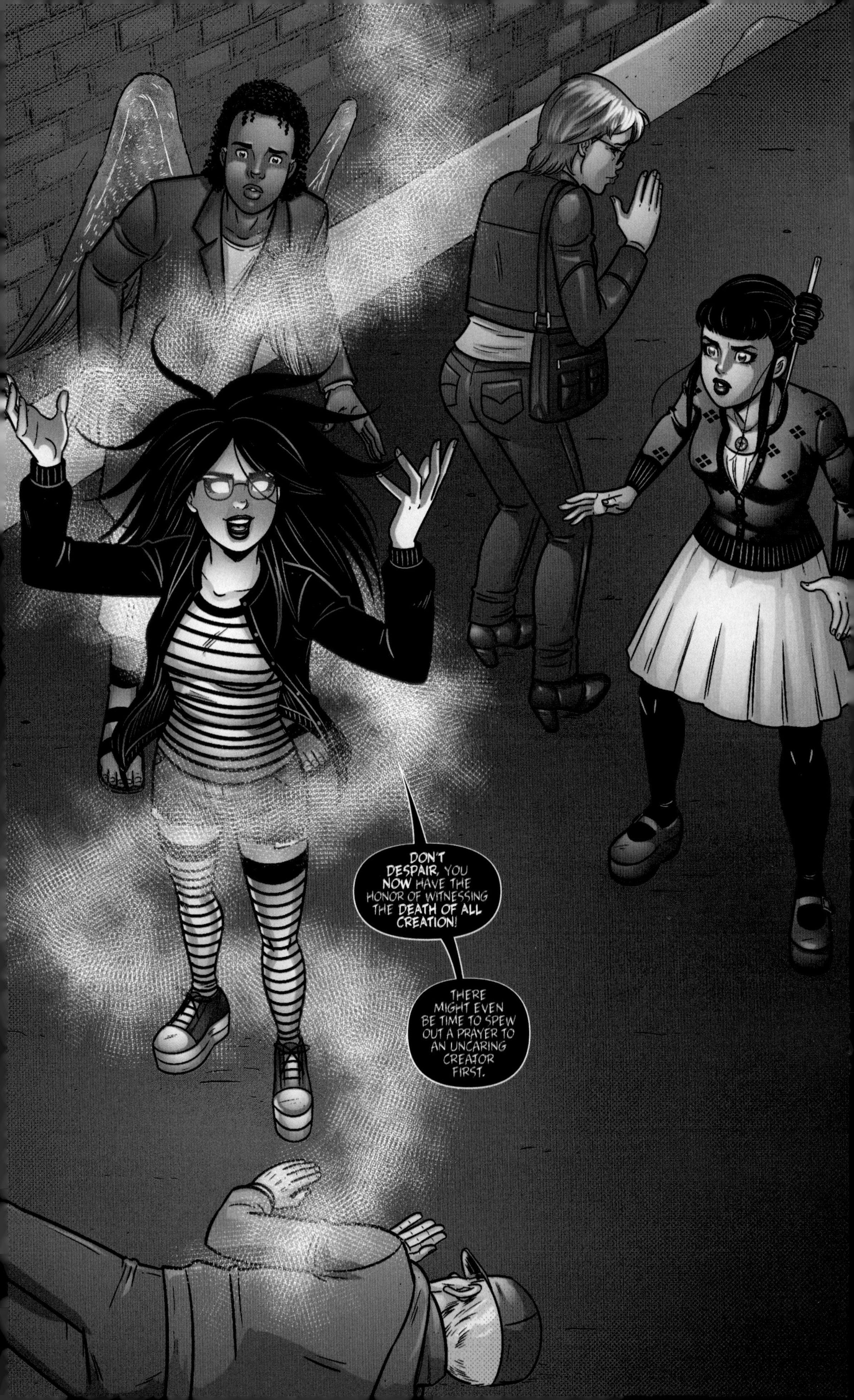
DON'T DESPAIR, YOU NOW HAVE THE HONOR OF WITNESSING THE DEATH OF ALL CREATION!
THERE MIGHT EVEN BE TIME TO SPEW OUT A PRAYER TO AN UNCARING CREATOR FIRST.

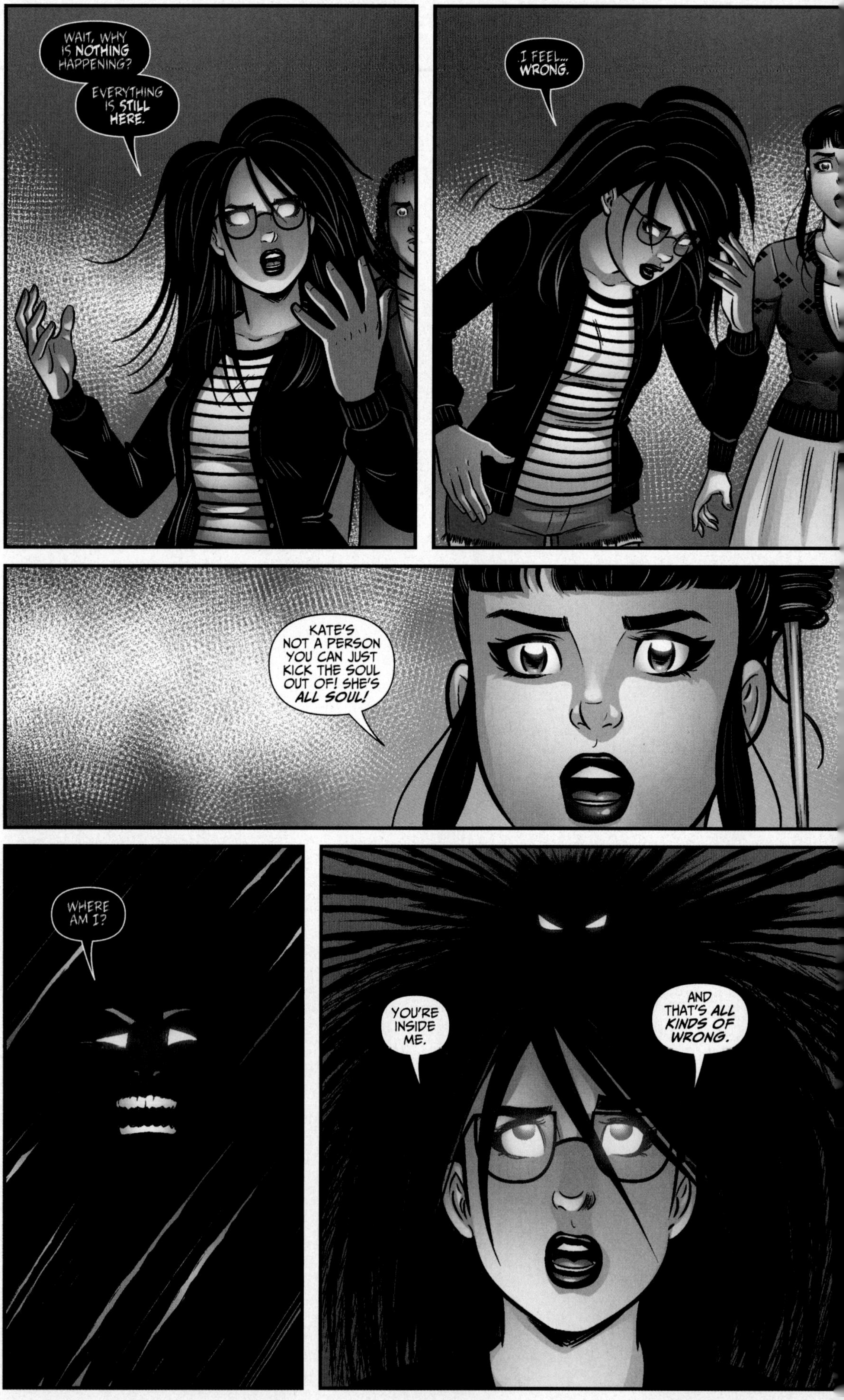
WAIT, WHY IS NOTHING HAPPENING?
EVERYTHING IS STILL HERE.
I FEEL... WRONG.
KATE'S NOT A PERSON YOU CAN JUST KICK THE SOUL OUT OF! SHE'S ALL SOUL!
WHERE AM I?
YOU'RE INSIDE ME.
AND THAT'S ALL KINDS OF WRONG.

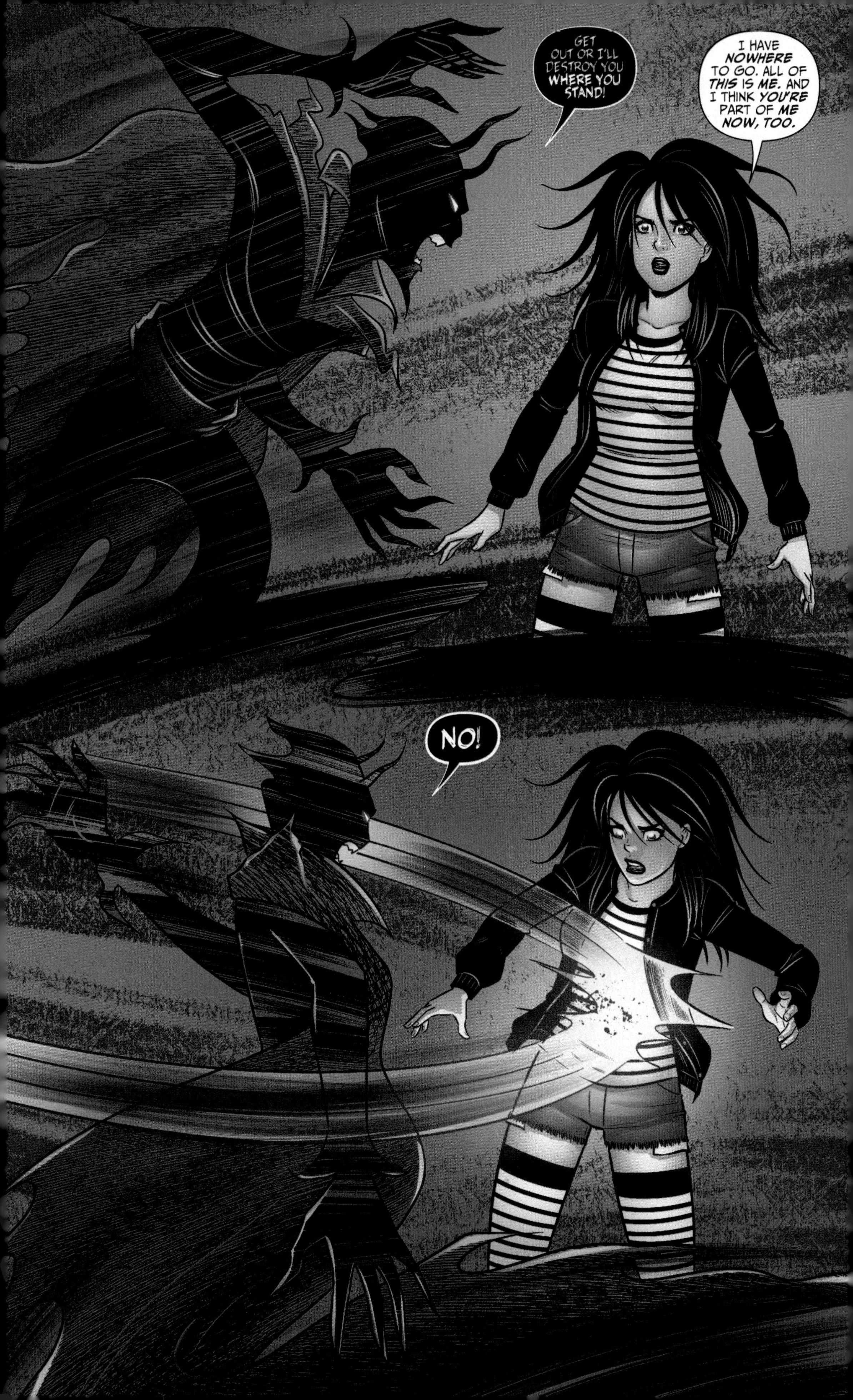
GET OUT OR I'LL DESTROY YOU WHERE YOU STAND!
I HAVE NOWHERE TO GO. ALL OF THIS IS ME. AND I THINK YOU'RE PART OF ME NOW, TOO.
NO!

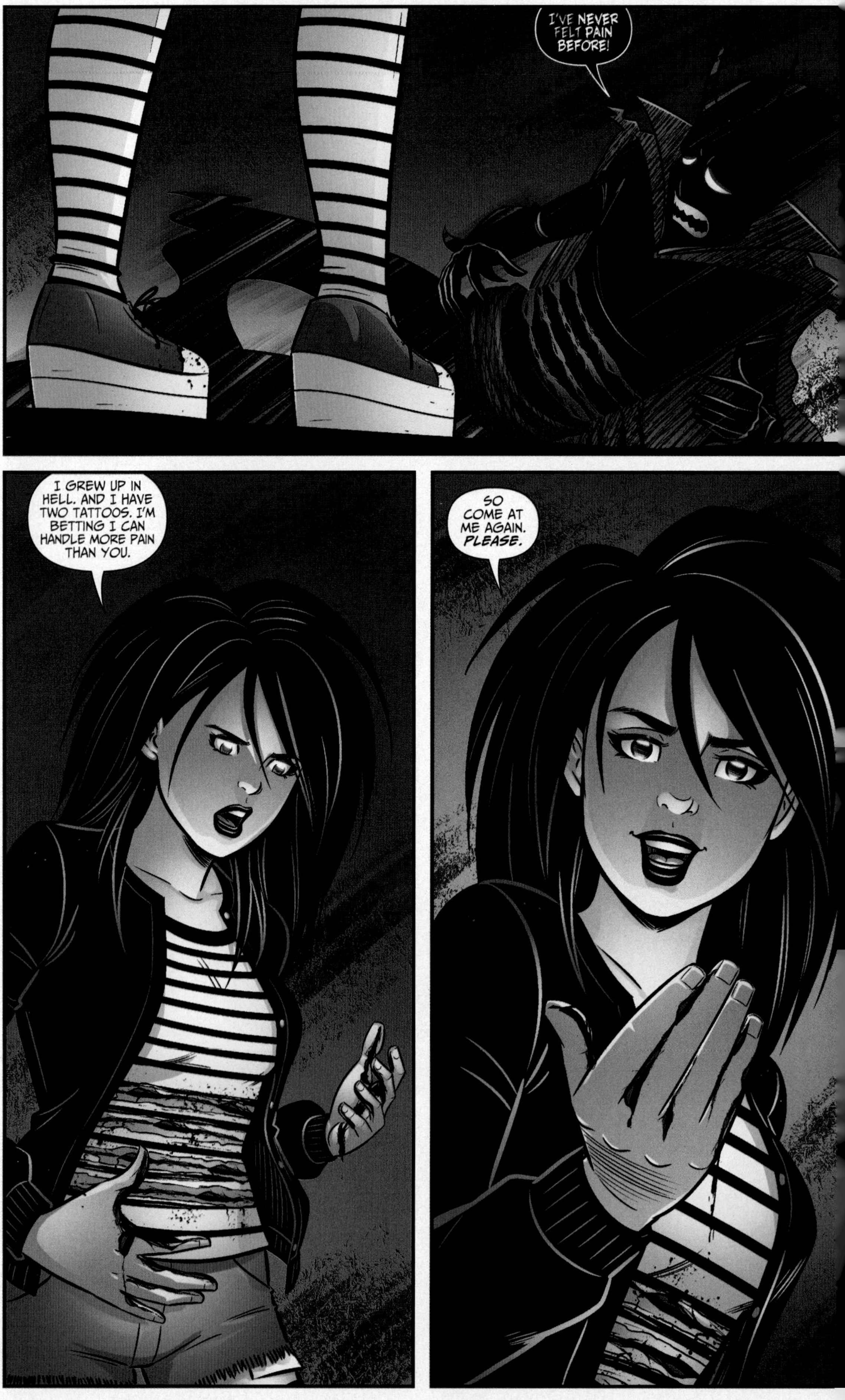
I'VE NEVER FELT PAIN BEFORE!
I GREW UP IN HELL. AND I HAVE TWO TATTOOS. I'M BETTING I CAN HANDLE MORE PAIN THAN YOU.
SO COME AT ME AGAIN. *PLEASE.*

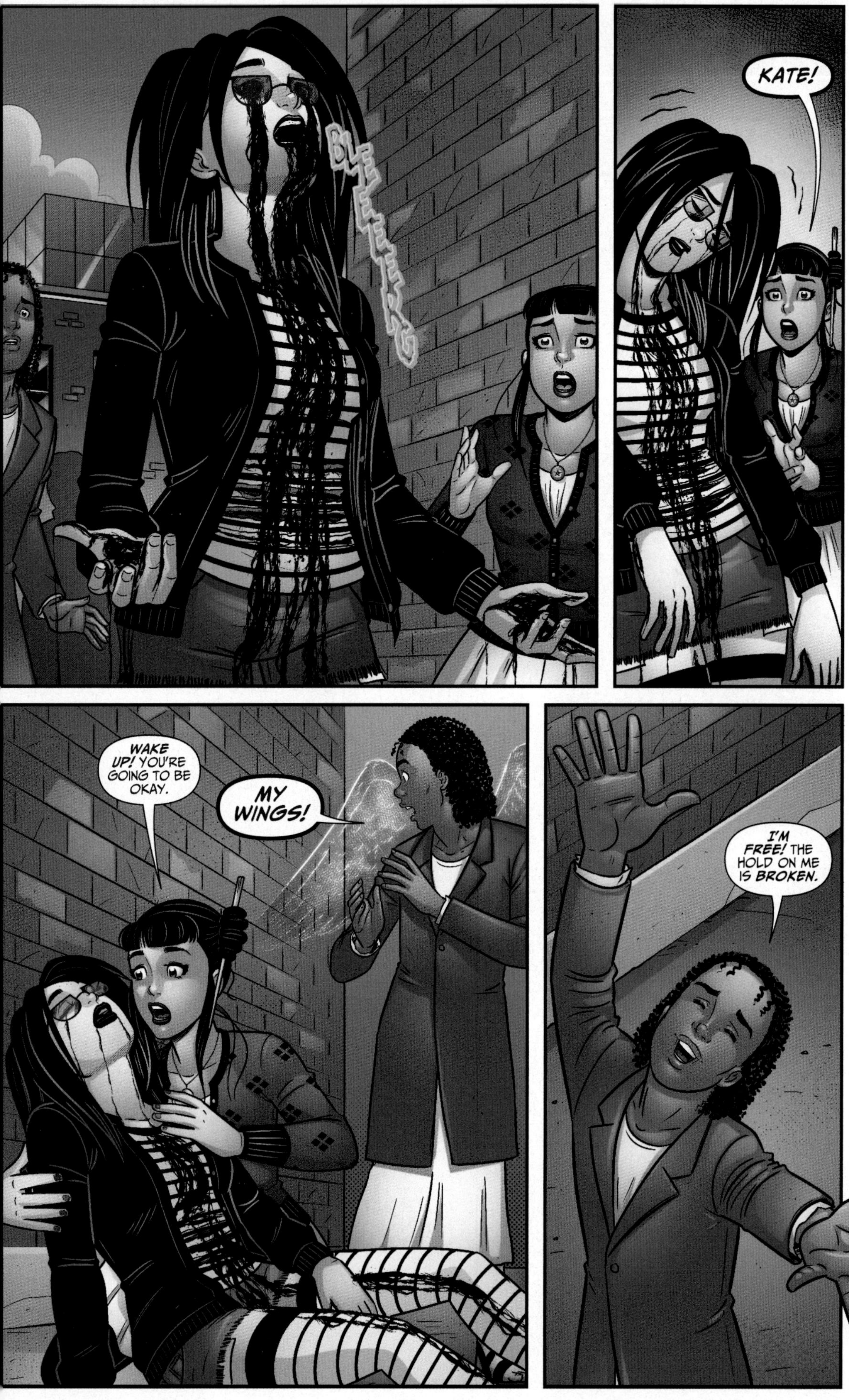
BLEEEERG
KATE!
WAKE UP! YOU'RE GOING TO BE OKAY.
MY WINGS!
I'M FREE! THE HOLD ON ME IS BROKEN.

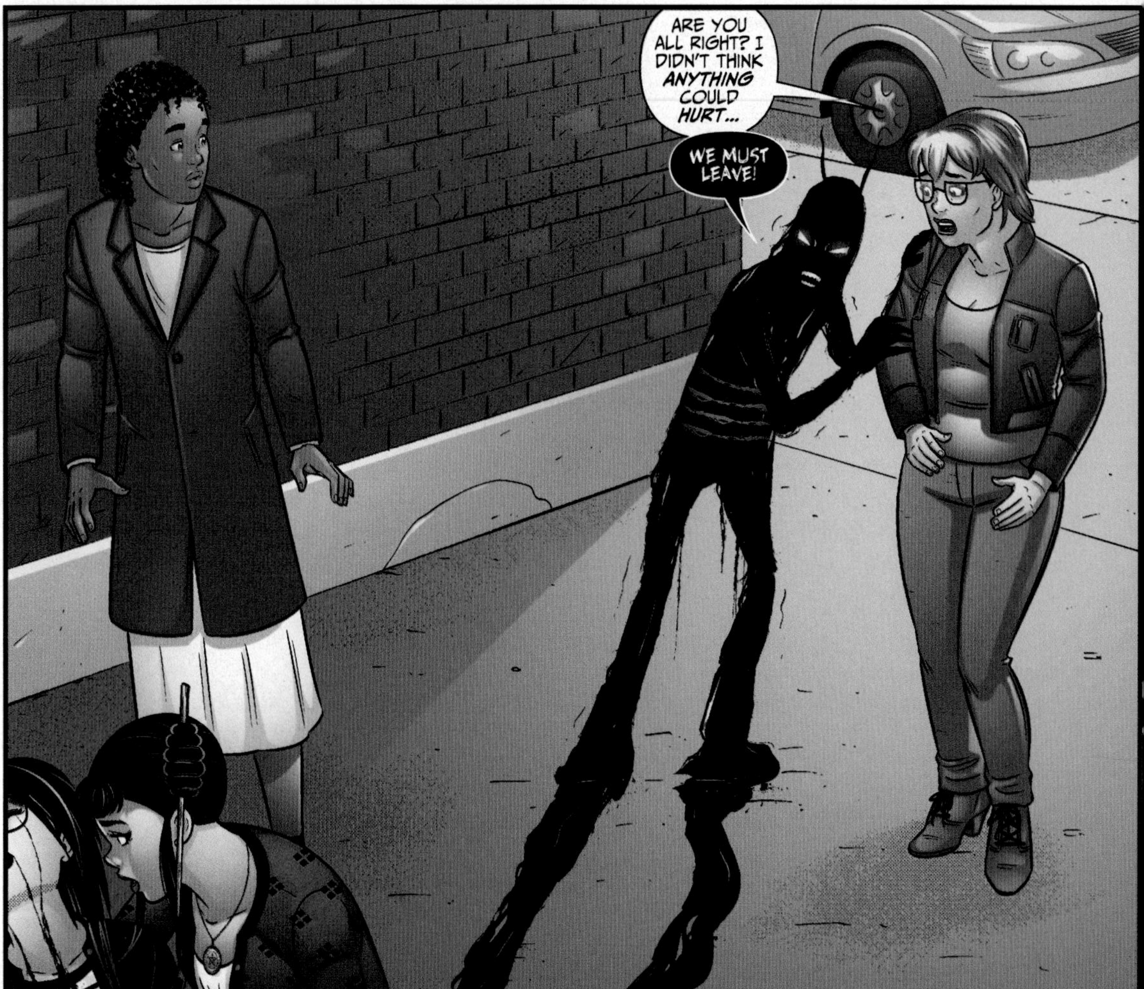
ARE YOU ALL RIGHT? I DIDN'T THINK *ANYTHING* COULD *HURT*...
WE MUST LEAVE!

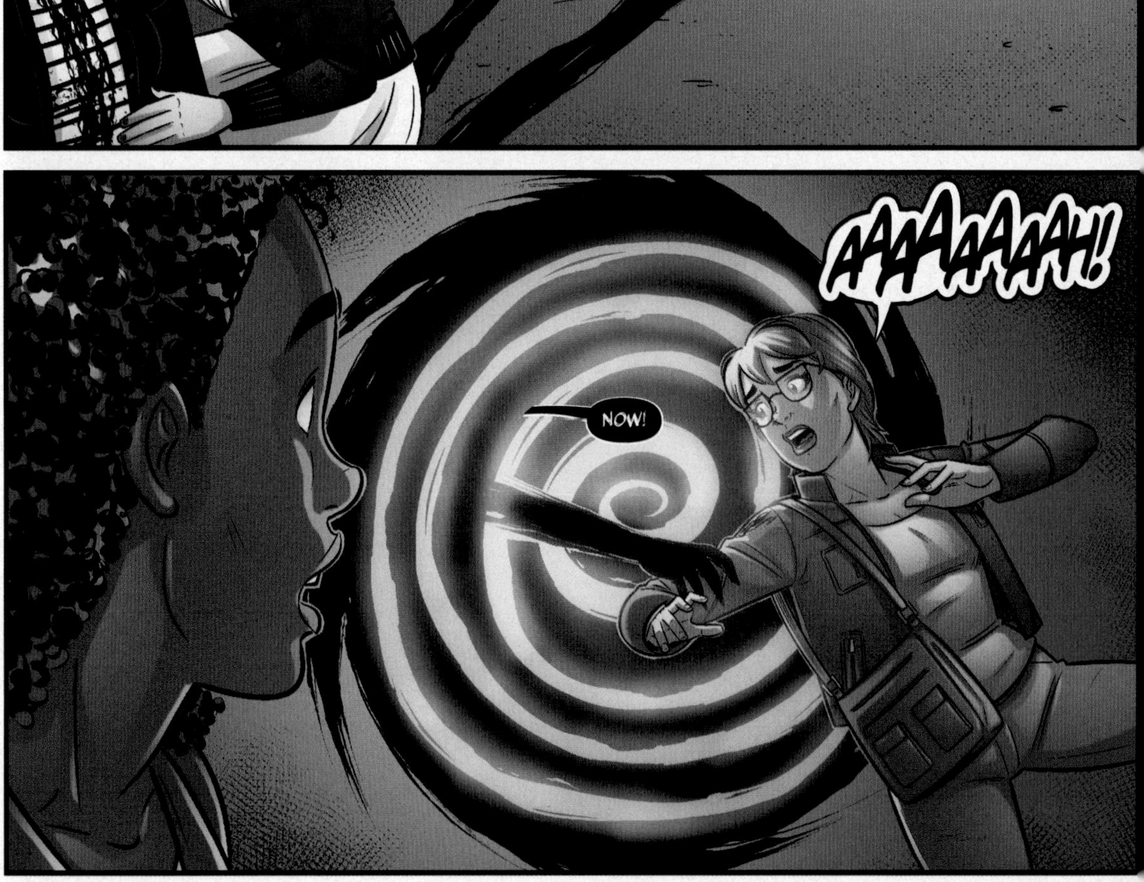
AAAAAAAAH!
NOW!

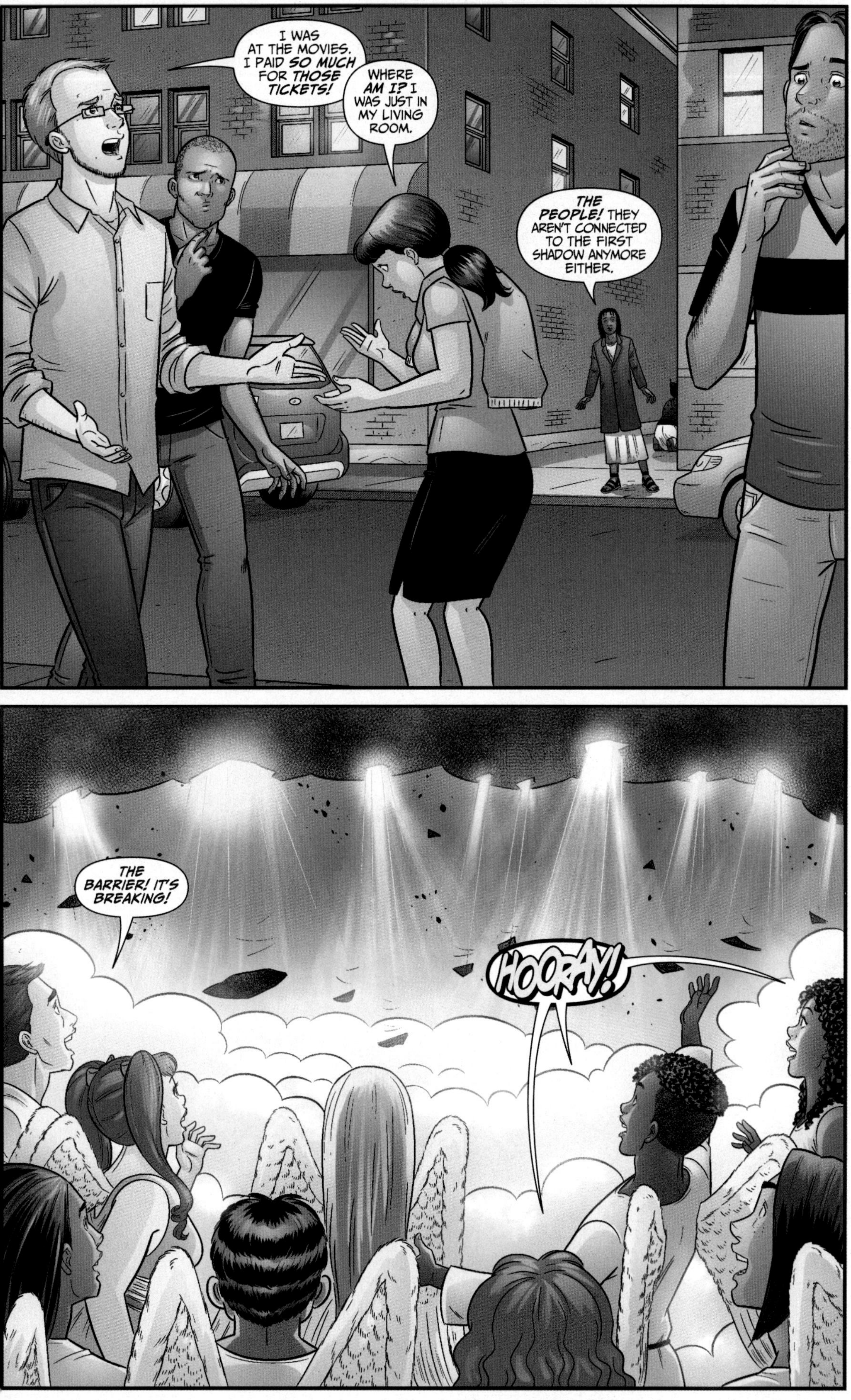
I WAS AT THE MOVIES. I PAID SO MUCH FOR THOSE TICKETS!
WHERE AM I? I WAS JUST IN MY LIVING ROOM.
THE PEOPLE! THEY AREN'T CONNECTED TO THE FIRST SHADOW ANYMORE EITHER.
THE BARRIER! IT'S BREAKING!
HOORAY!

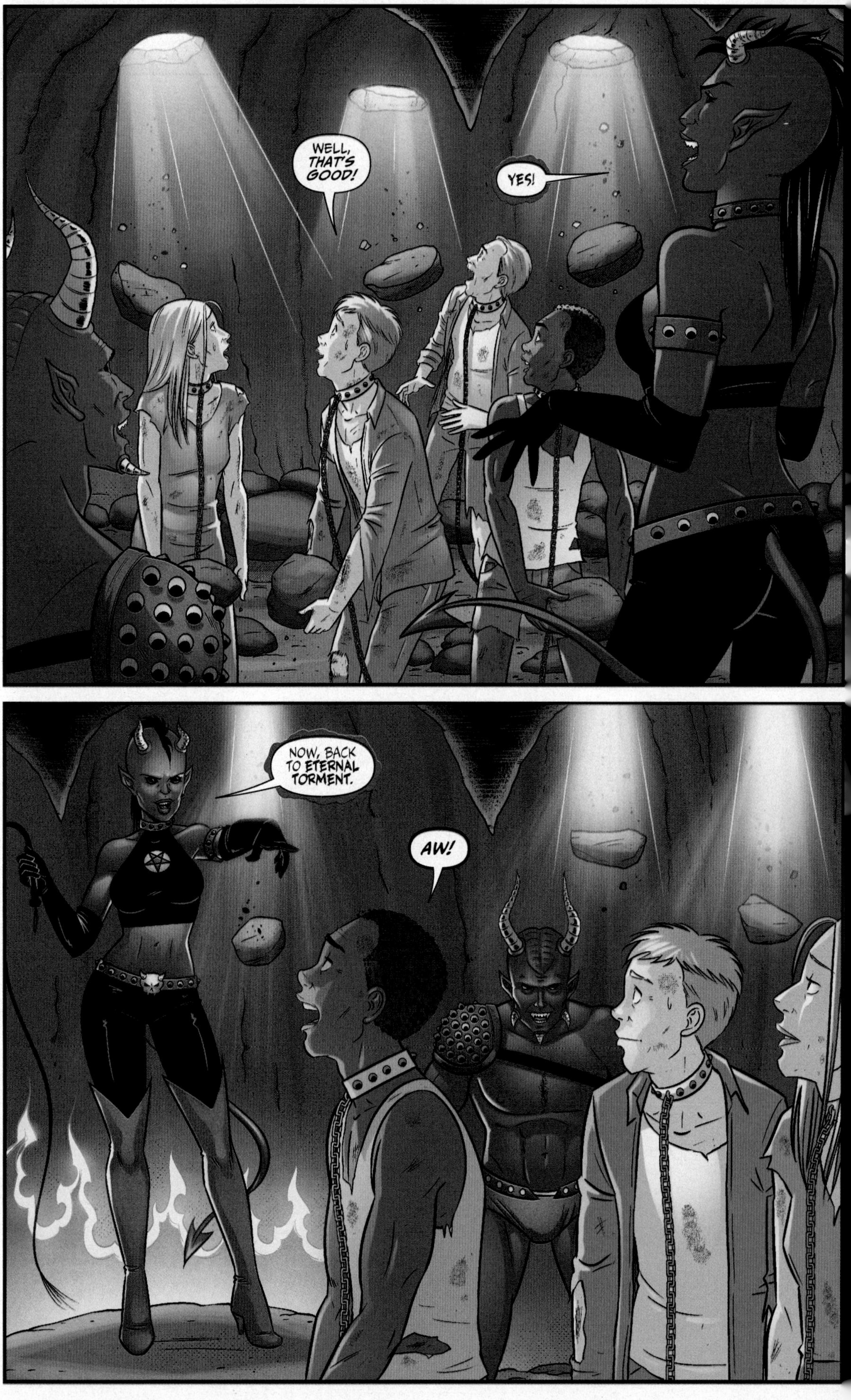
WELL, THAT'S GOOD!
YES!
NOW, BACK TO ETERNAL TORMENT.
AW!

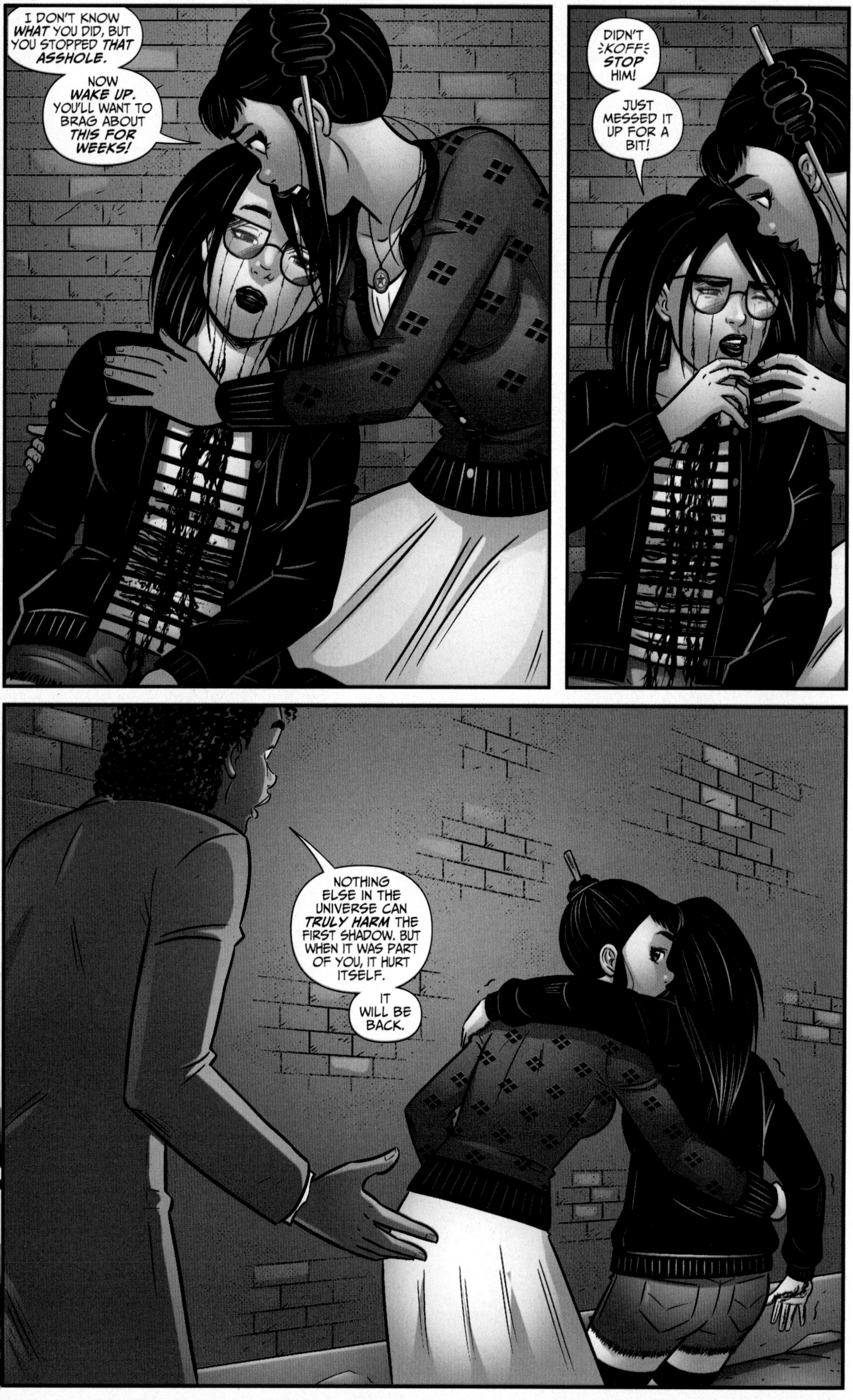
I DON'T KNOW WHAT YOU DID, BUT YOU STOPPED THAT ASSHOLE.
NOW WAKE UP. YOU'LL WANT TO BRAG ABOUT THIS FOR WEEKS!
DIDN'T KOFF STOP HIM!
JUST MESSED IT UP FOR A BIT!
NOTHING ELSE IN THE UNIVERSE CAN TRULY HARM THE FIRST SHADOW. BUT WHEN IT WAS PART OF YOU, IT HURT ITSELF.
IT WILL BE BACK.

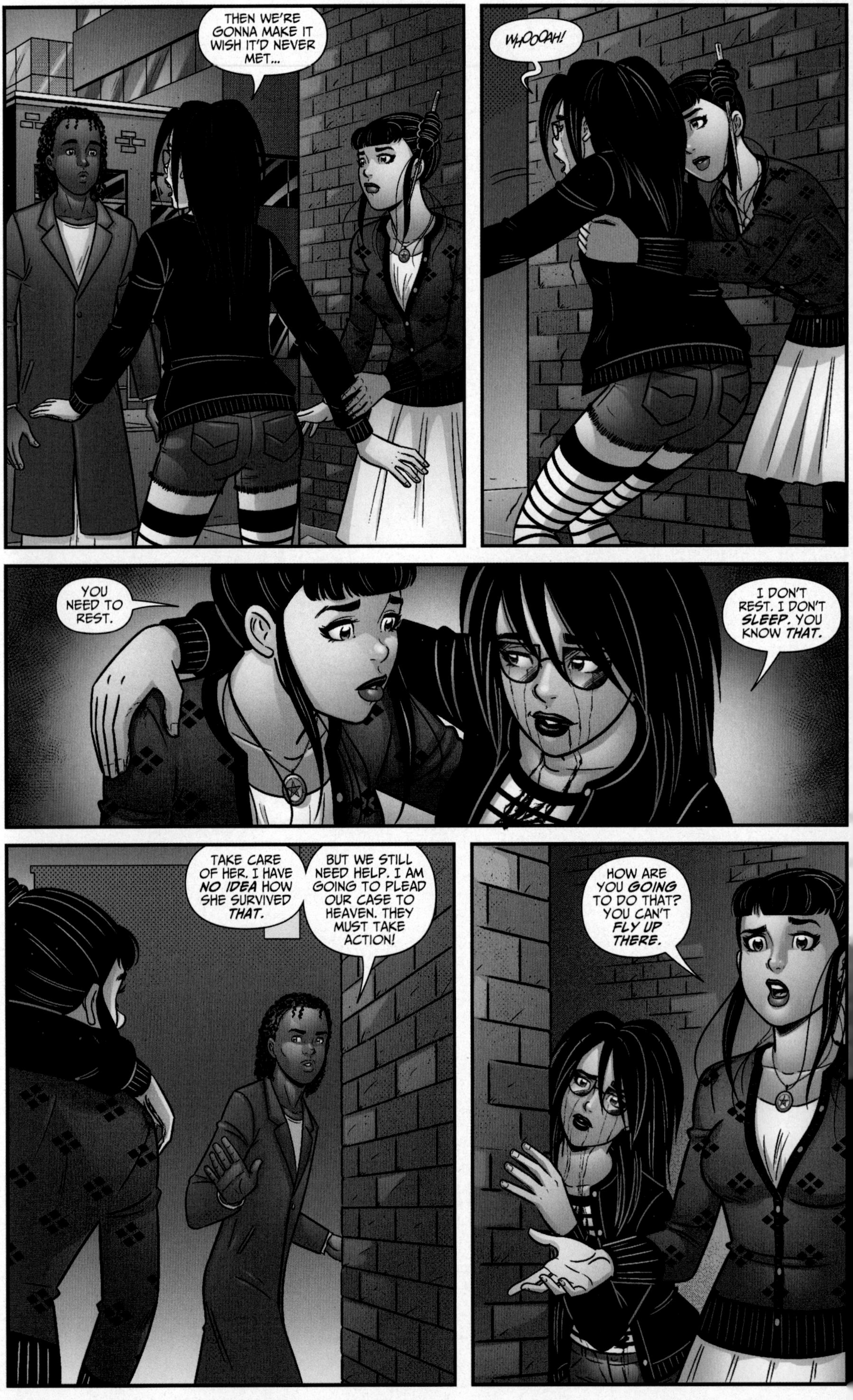
THEN WE'RE GONNA MAKE IT WISH IT'D NEVER MET...
WHOOOAH!
YOU NEED TO REST.
I DON'T REST. I DON'T *SLEEP.* YOU KNOW *THAT.*
TAKE CARE OF HER. I HAVE *NO IDEA* HOW SHE SURVIVED *THAT.*
BUT WE STILL NEED HELP. I AM GOING TO PLEAD OUR CASE TO HEAVEN. THEY MUST TAKE ACTION!
HOW ARE YOU *GOING* TO DO THAT? YOU CAN'T *FLY UP THERE.*

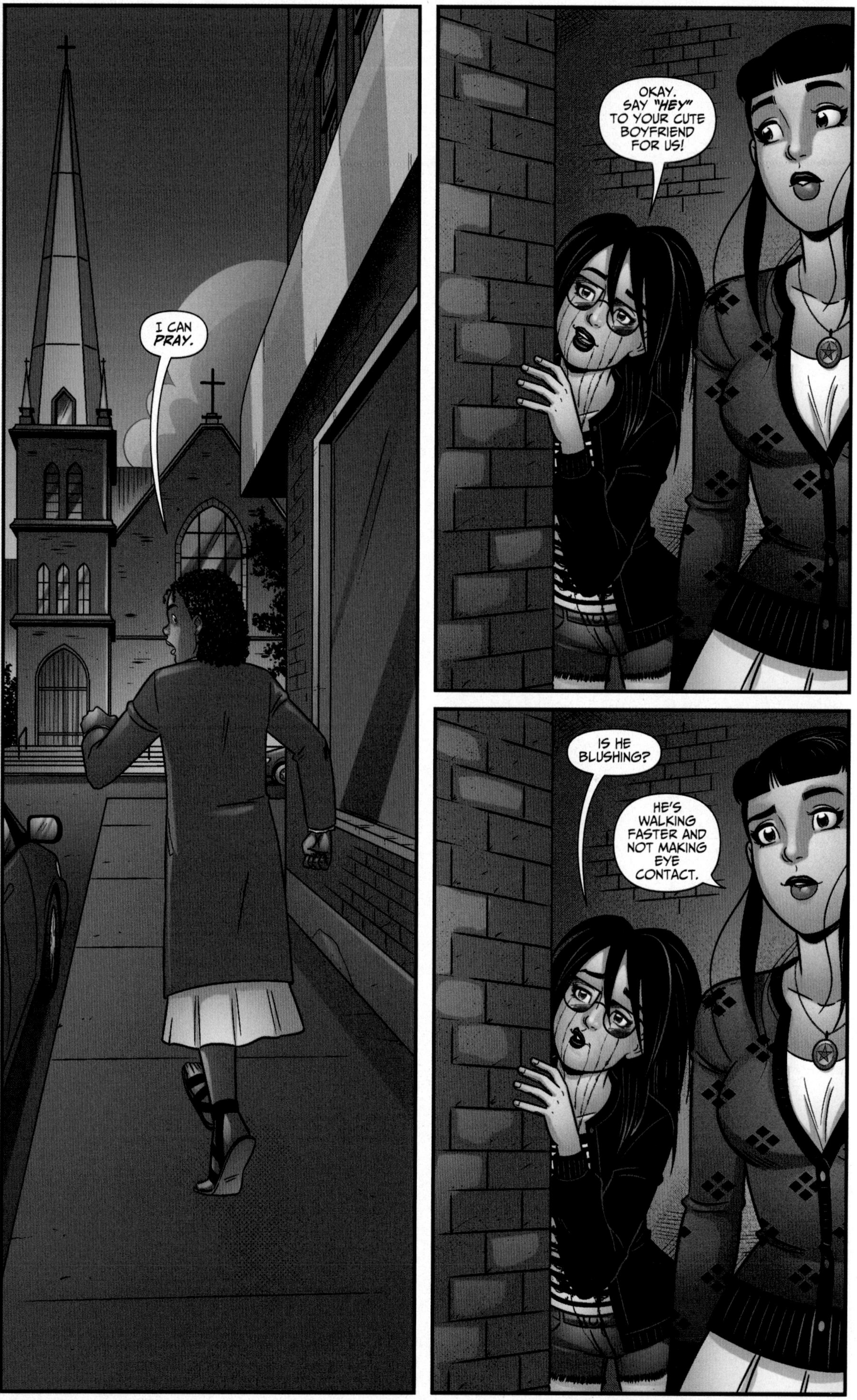
I CAN *PRAY.*
OKAY. SAY *"HEY"* TO YOUR CUTE BOYFRIEND FOR US!
IS HE BLUSHING?
HE'S WALKING FASTER AND NOT MAKING EYE CONTACT.

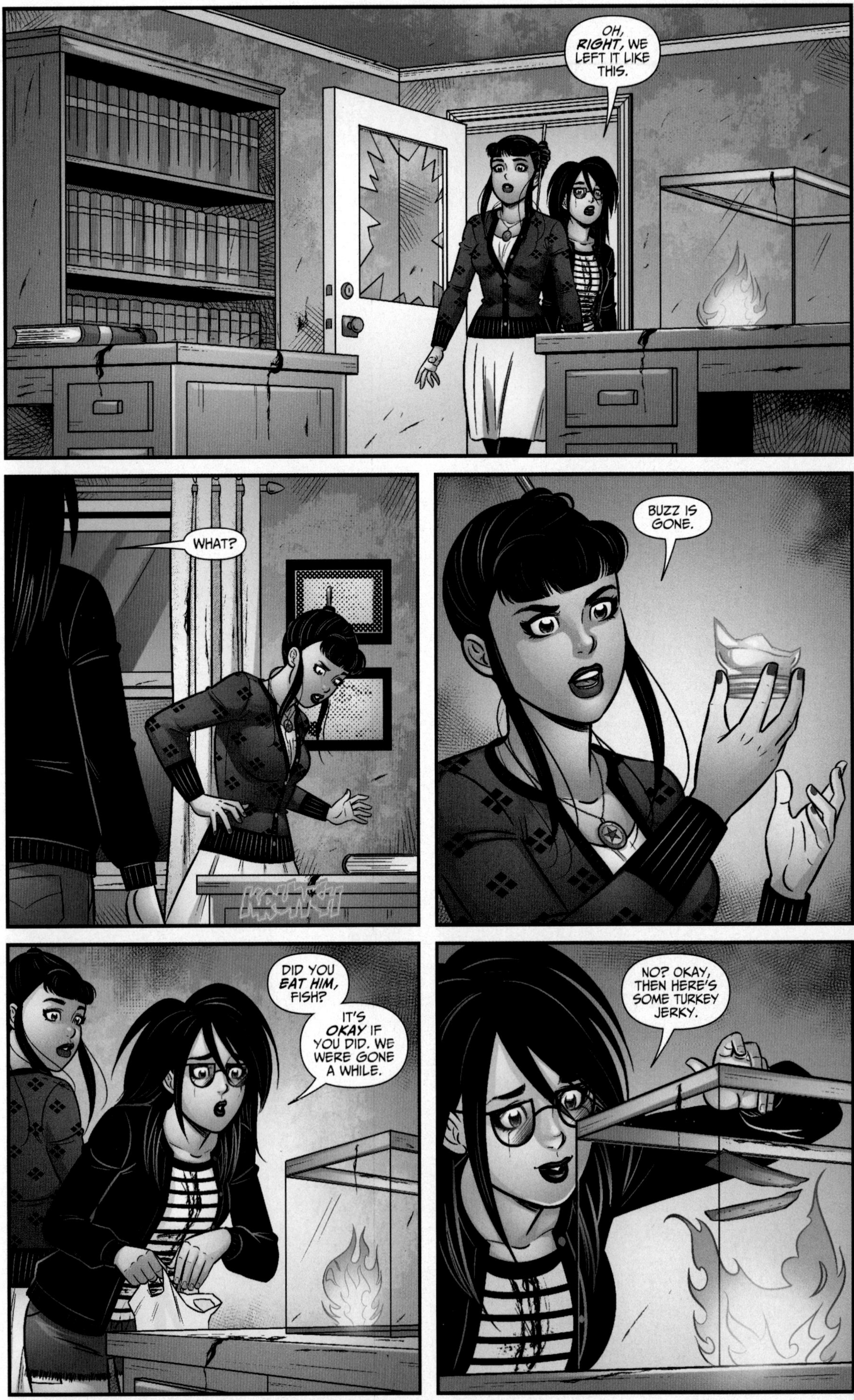
OH, RIGHT, WE LEFT IT LIKE THIS.
WHAT?
KRUNCH
BUZZ IS GONE.
DID YOU EAT HIM, FISH?
IT'S OKAY IF YOU DID. WE WERE GONE A WHILE.
NO? OKAY, THEN HERE'S SOME TURKEY JERKY.

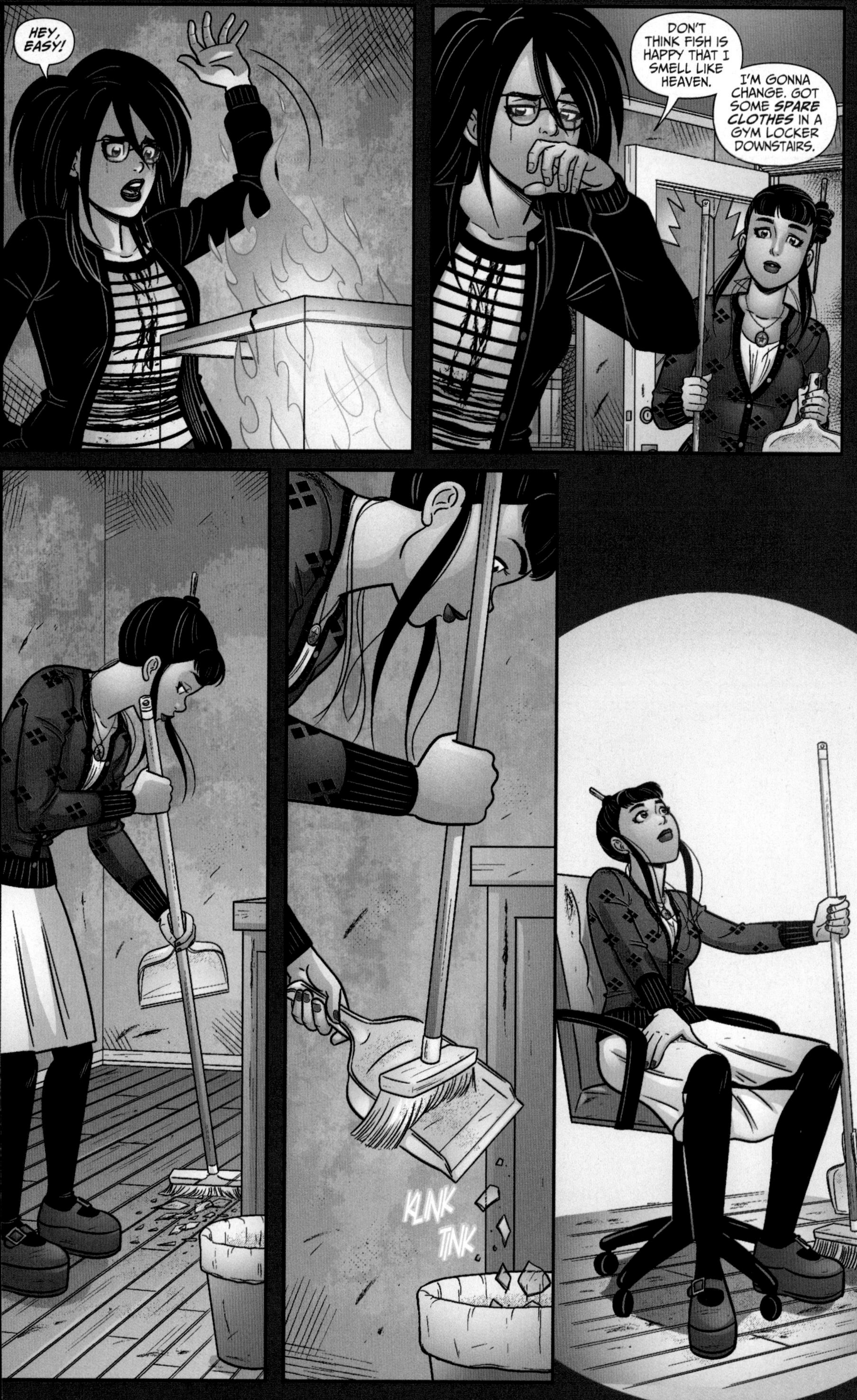
HEY, EASY!
DON'T THINK FISH IS HAPPY THAT I SMELL LIKE HEAVEN.
I'M GONNA CHANGE. GOT SOME SPARE CLOTHES IN A GYM LOCKER DOWNSTAIRS.
KLINK
TINK

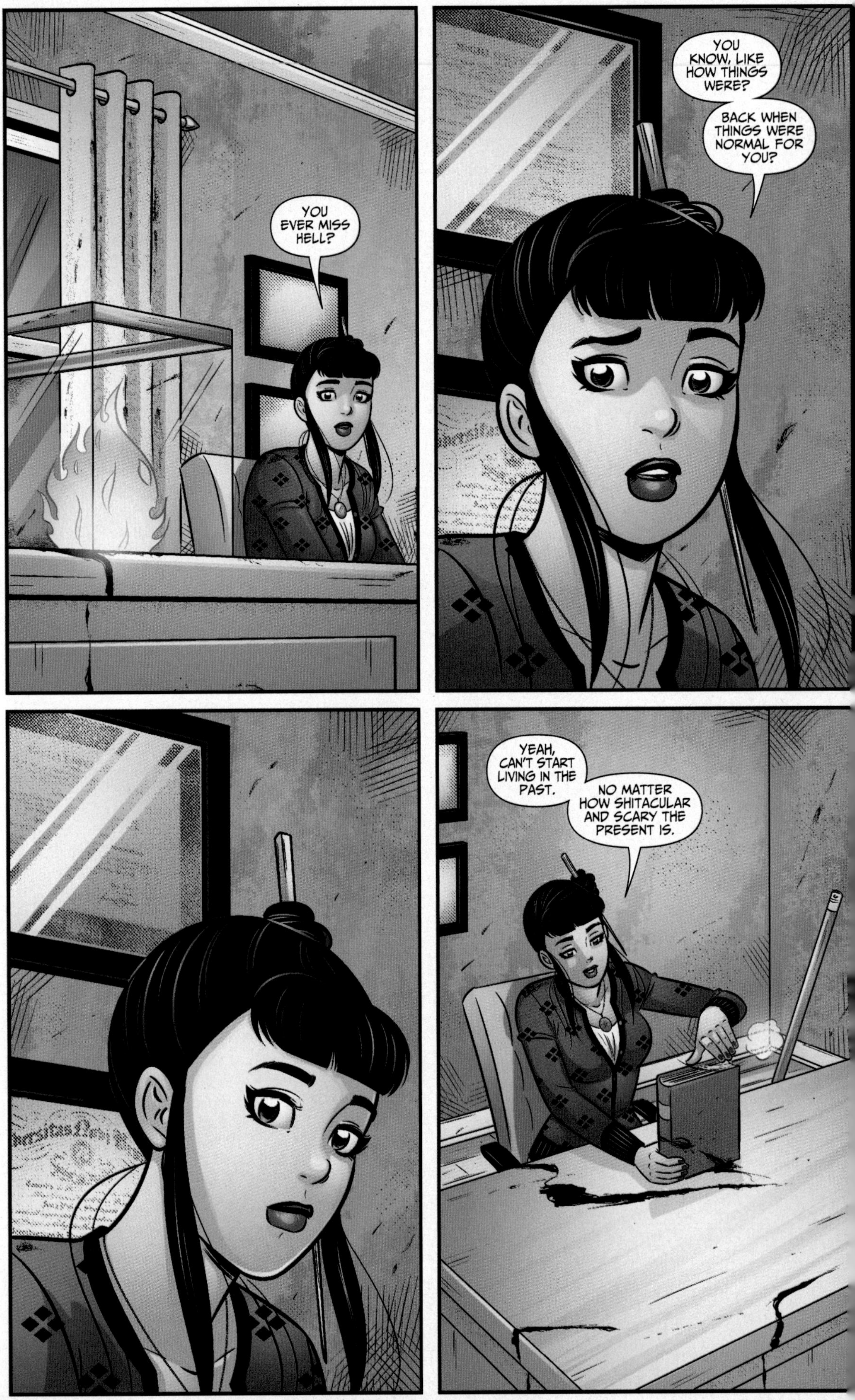
YOU EVER MISS HELL?
YOU KNOW, LIKE HOW THINGS WERE?
BACK WHEN THINGS WERE NORMAL FOR YOU?
YEAH, CAN'T START LIVING IN THE PAST.
NO MATTER HOW SHITACULAR AND SCARY THE PRESENT IS.

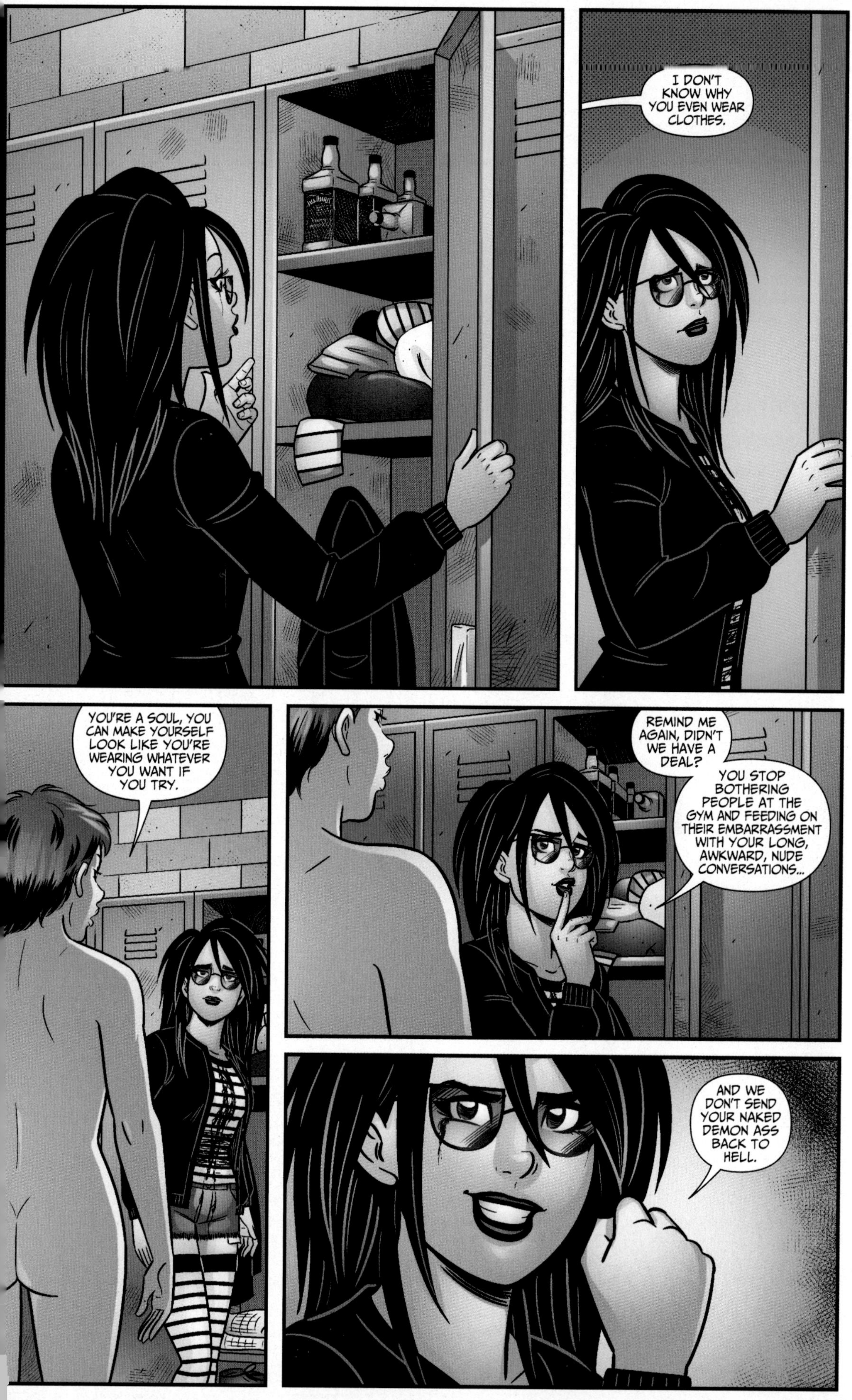
I DON'T KNOW WHY YOU EVEN WEAR CLOTHES.
YOU'RE A SOUL, YOU CAN MAKE YOURSELF LOOK LIKE YOU'RE WEARING WHATEVER YOU WANT IF YOU TRY.
REMIND ME AGAIN, DIDN'T WE HAVE A DEAL?
YOU STOP BOTHERING PEOPLE AT THE GYM AND FEEDING ON THEIR EMBARRASSMENT WITH YOUR LONG, AWKWARD, NUDE CONVERSATIONS...
AND WE DON'T SEND YOUR NAKED DEMON ASS BACK TO HELL.

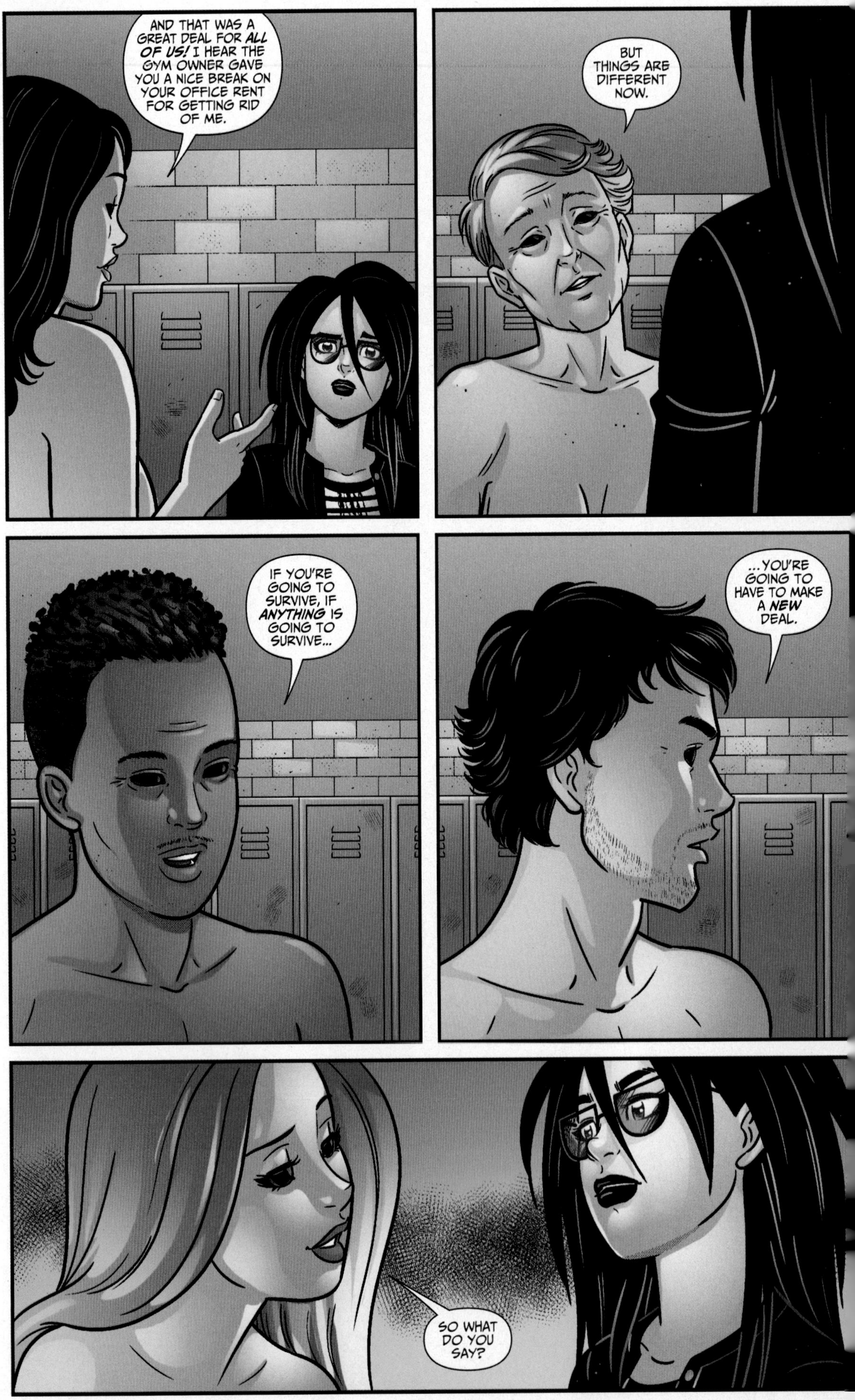
AND THAT WAS A GREAT DEAL FOR ***ALL OF US!*** I HEAR THE GYM OWNER GAVE YOU A NICE BREAK ON YOUR OFFICE RENT FOR GETTING RID OF ME.
BUT THINGS ARE DIFFERENT NOW.
IF YOU'RE GOING TO SURVIVE, IF ***ANYTHING*** IS GOING TO SURVIVE...
...YOU'RE GOING TO HAVE TO MAKE A ***NEW*** DEAL.
SO WHAT DO YOU SAY?

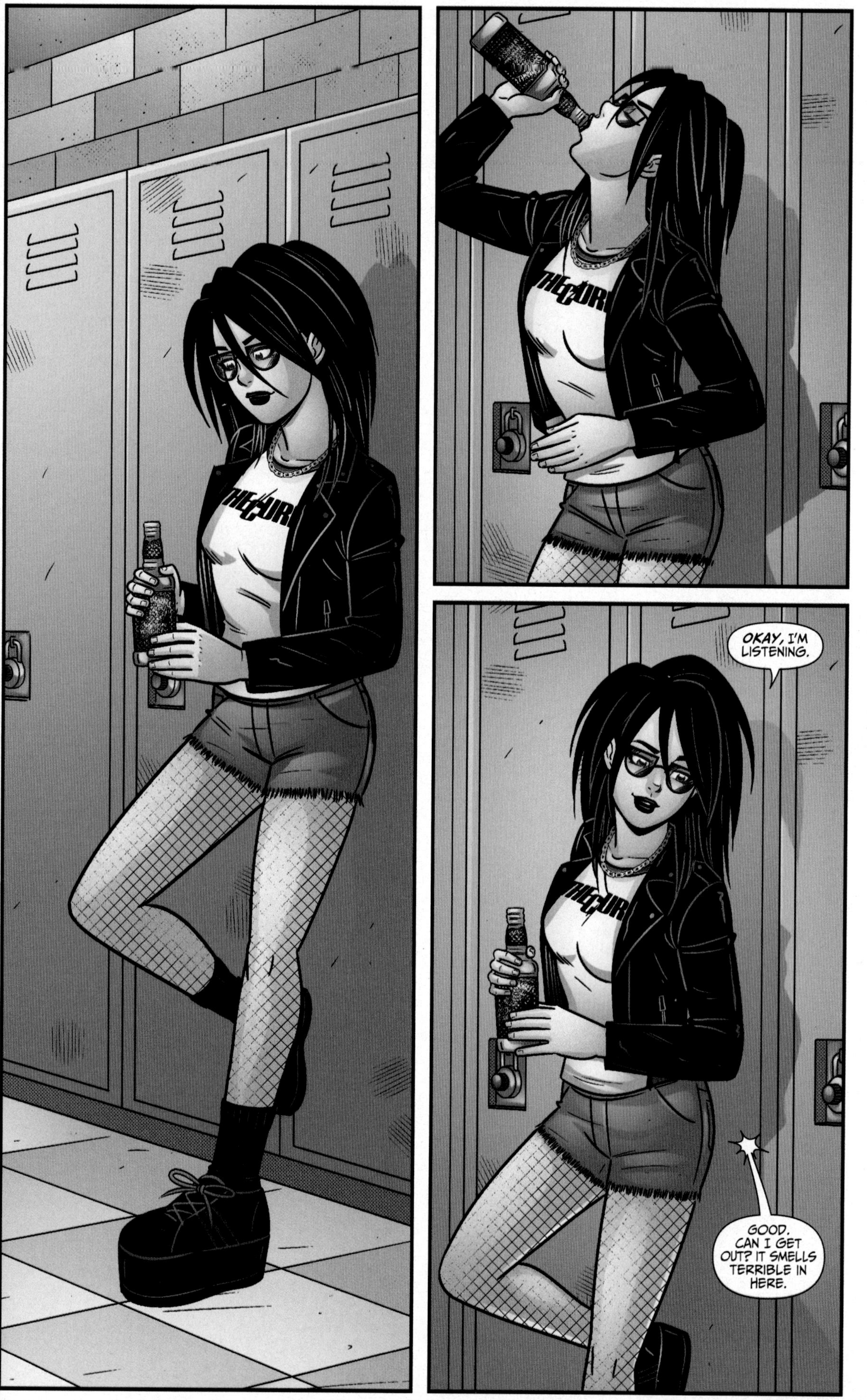
OKAY, I'M LISTENING.
GOOD. CAN I GET OUT? IT SMELLS TERRIBLE IN HERE.

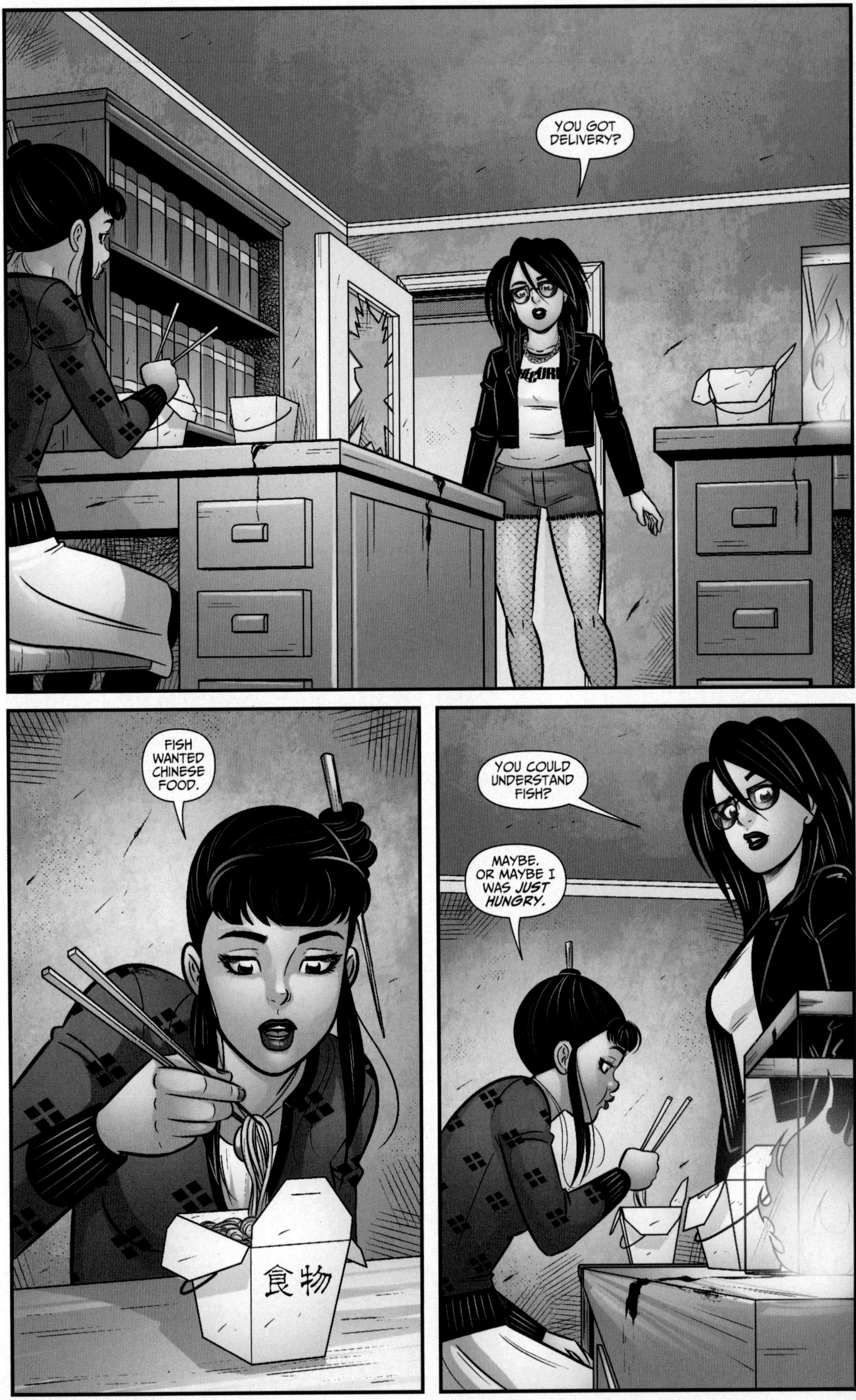

YOU GOT DELIVERY?
FISH WANTED CHINESE FOOD.
YOU COULD UNDERSTAND FISH?
MAYBE. OR MAYBE I WAS *JUST HUNGRY.*
食物

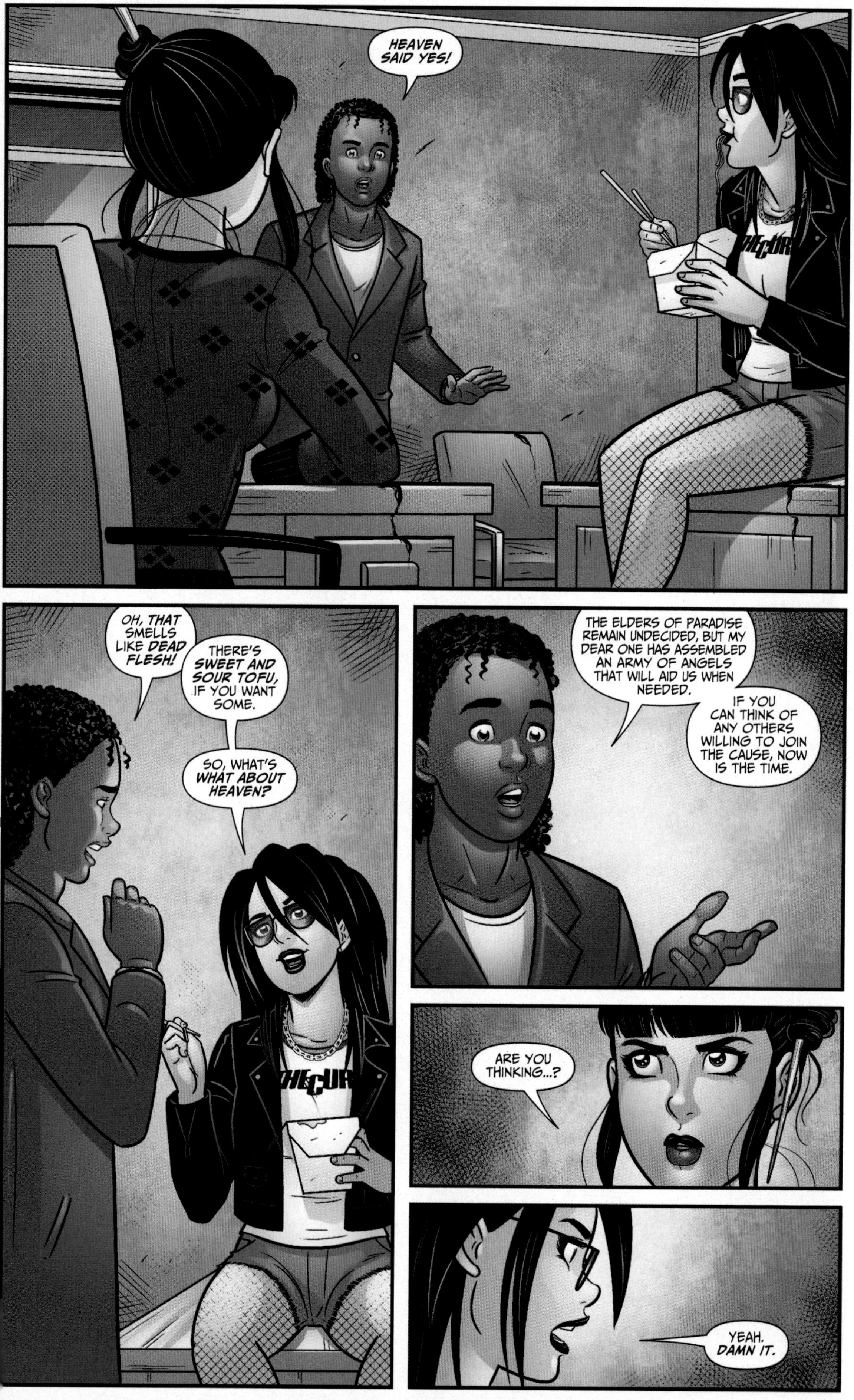
HEAVEN SAID YES!
OH, THAT SMELLS LIKE DEAD FLESH!
THERE'S SWEET AND SOUR TOFU, IF YOU WANT SOME.
SO, WHAT'S WHAT ABOUT HEAVEN?
THE ELDERS OF PARADISE REMAIN UNDECIDED, BUT MY DEAR ONE HAS ASSEMBLED AN ARMY OF ANGELS THAT WILL AID US WHEN NEEDED.
IF YOU CAN THINK OF ANY OTHERS WILLING TO JOIN THE CAUSE, NOW IS THE TIME.
ARE YOU THINKING...?
YEAH. DAMN IT.

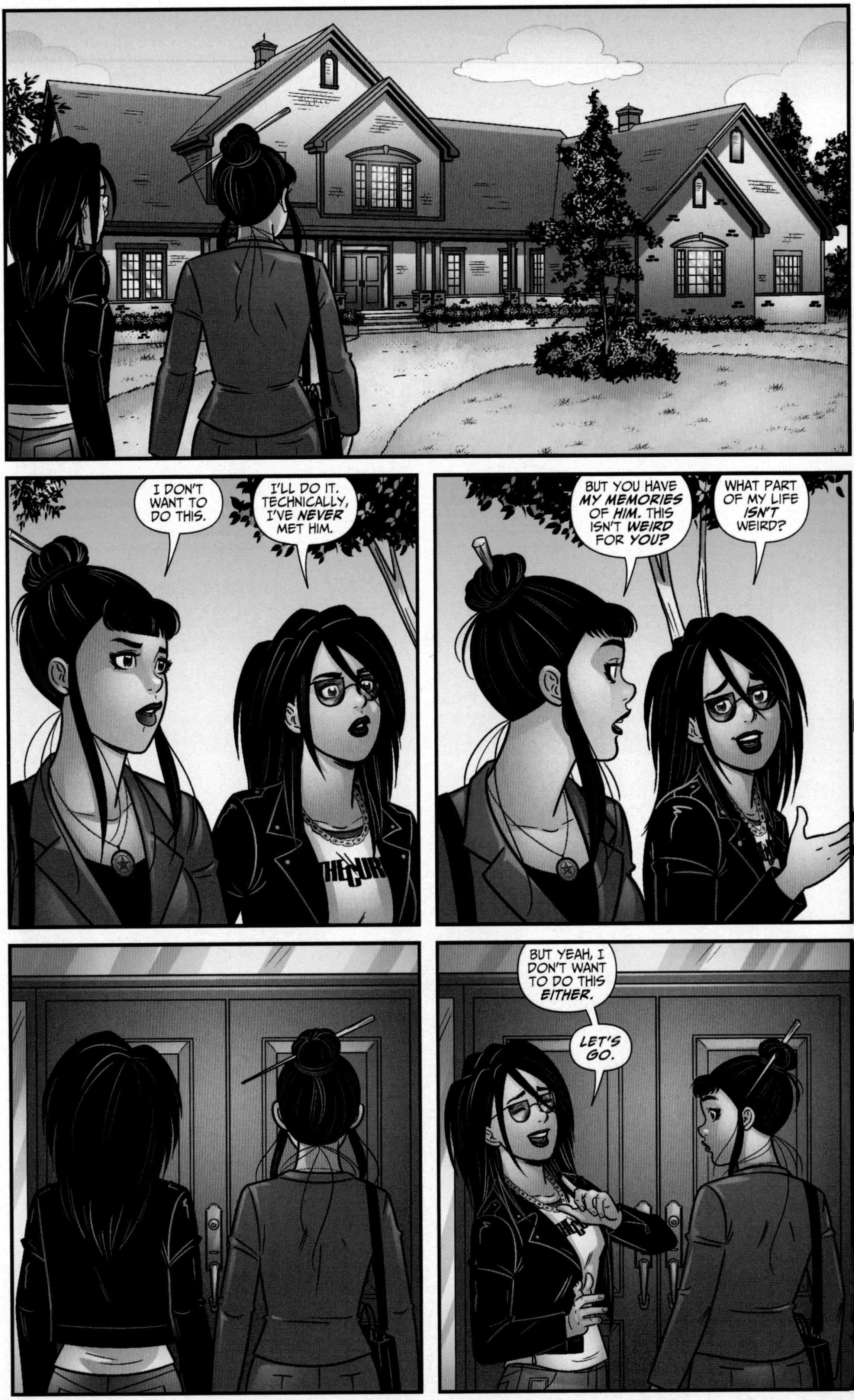
I DON'T WANT TO DO THIS.
I'LL DO IT. TECHNICALLY, I'VE NEVER MET HIM.
BUT YOU HAVE MY MEMORIES OF HIM. THIS ISN'T WEIRD FOR YOU?
WHAT PART OF MY LIFE ISN'T WEIRD?
BUT YEAH, I DON'T WANT TO DO THIS EITHER.
LET'S GO.

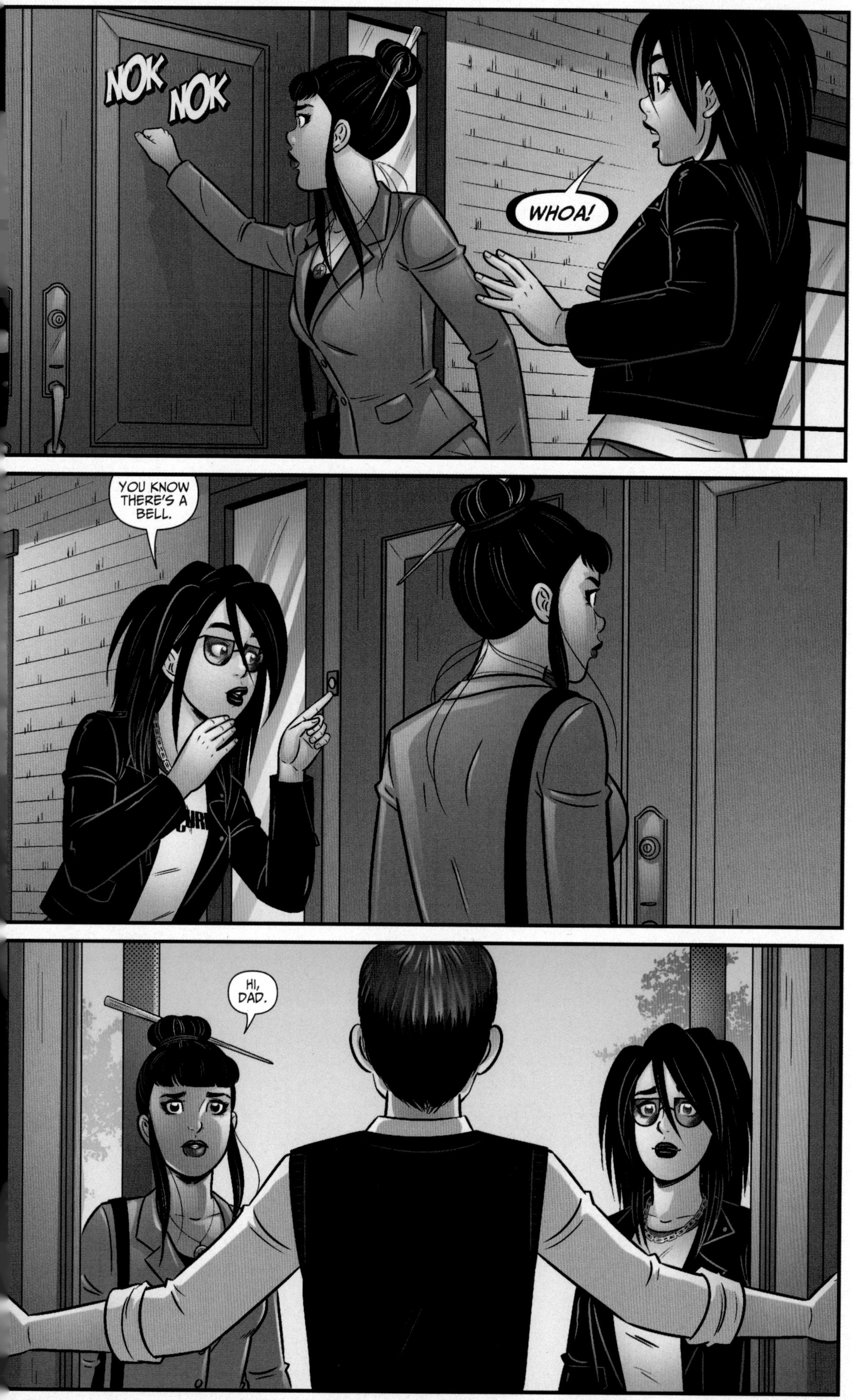
NOK NOK
WHOA!
YOU KNOW THERE'S A BELL.
HI, DAD.

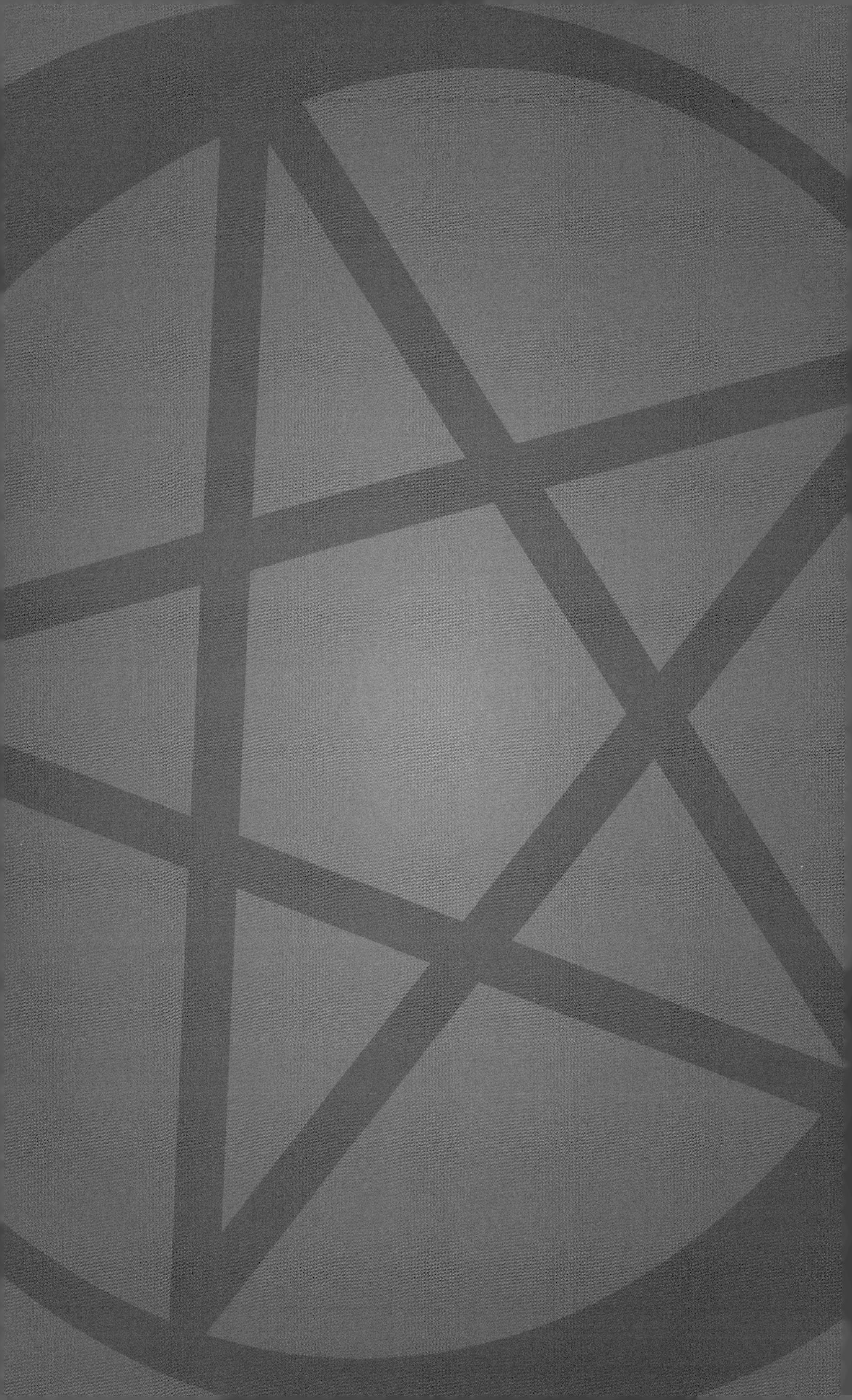

CHAPTER EIGHT

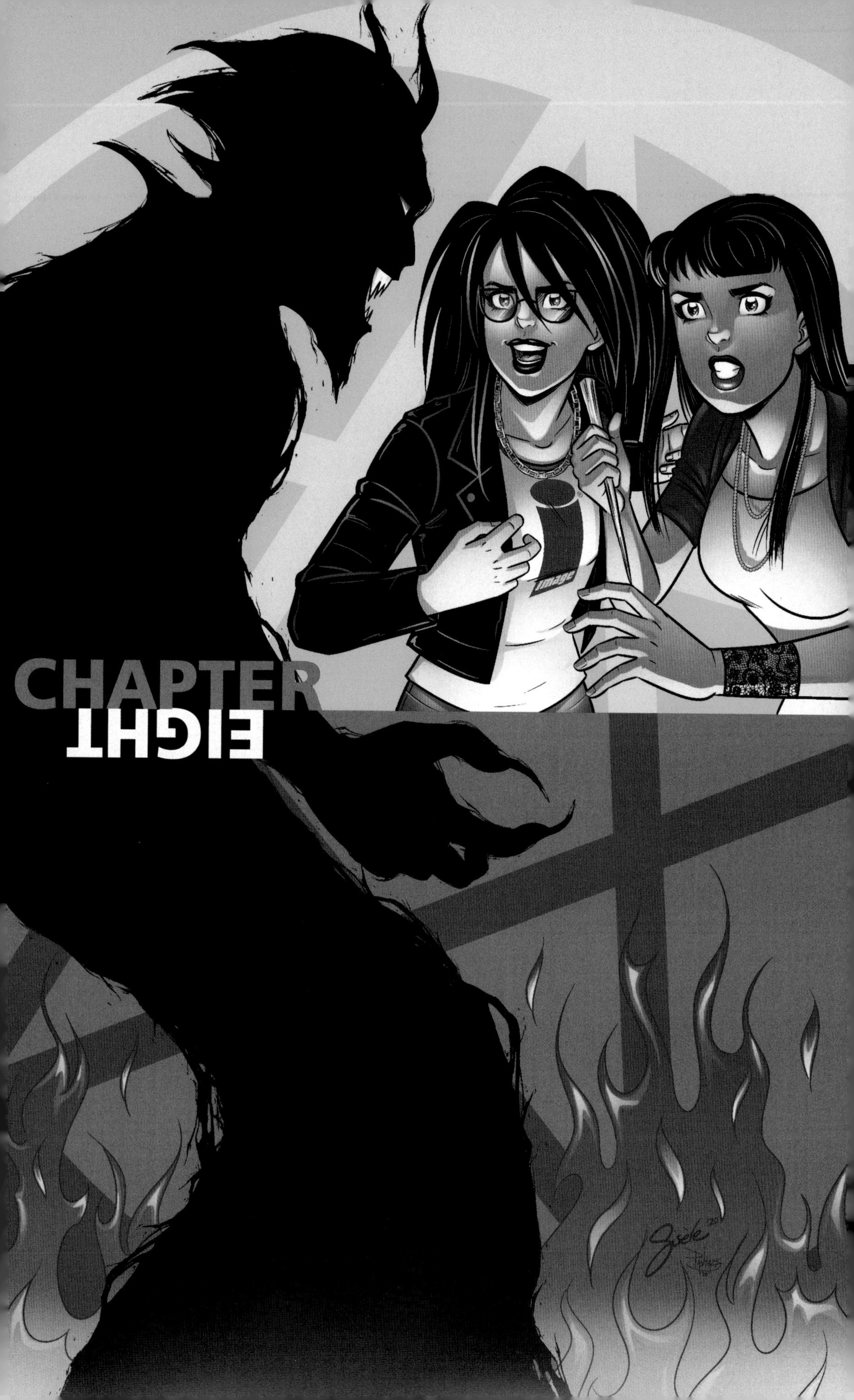

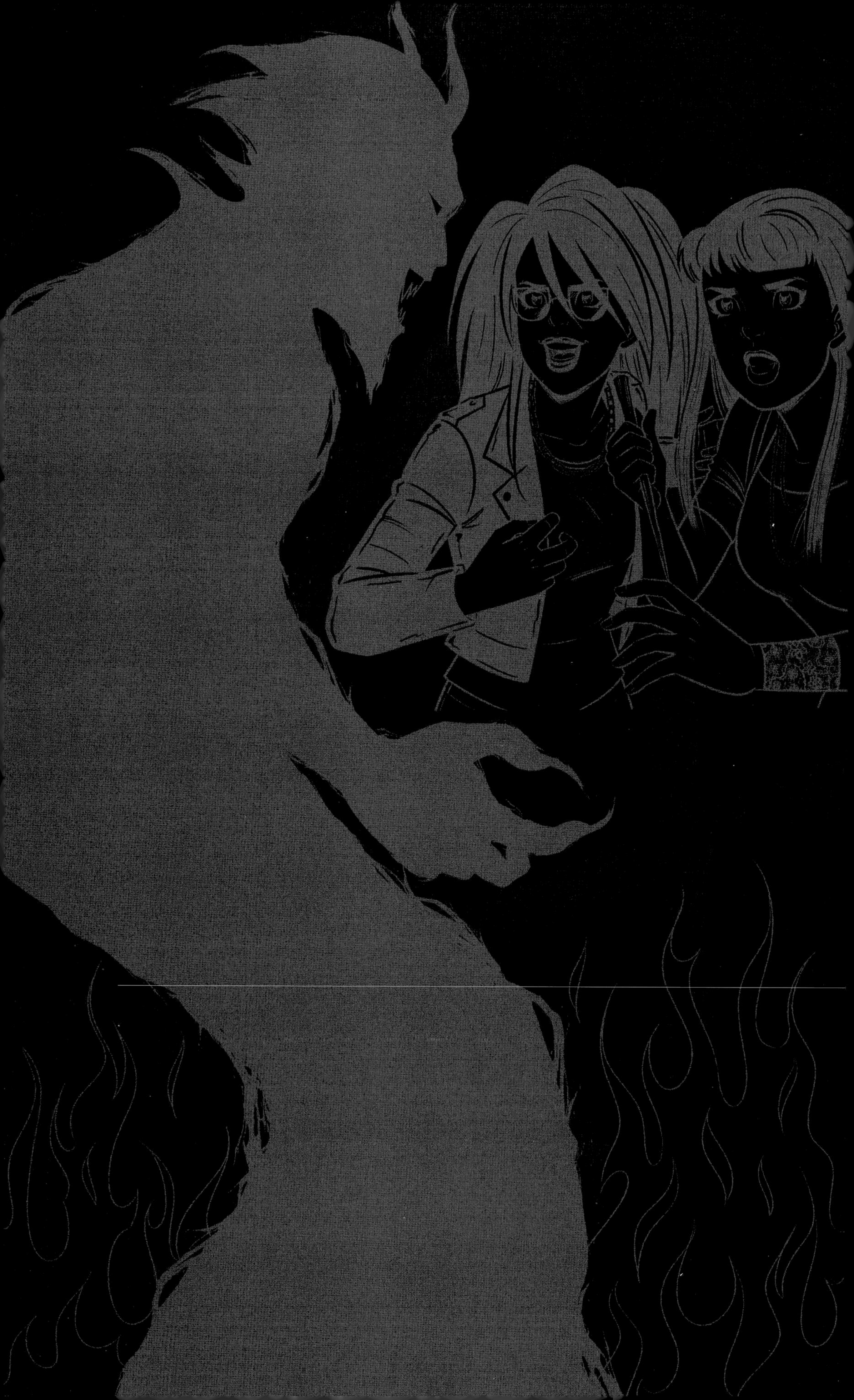

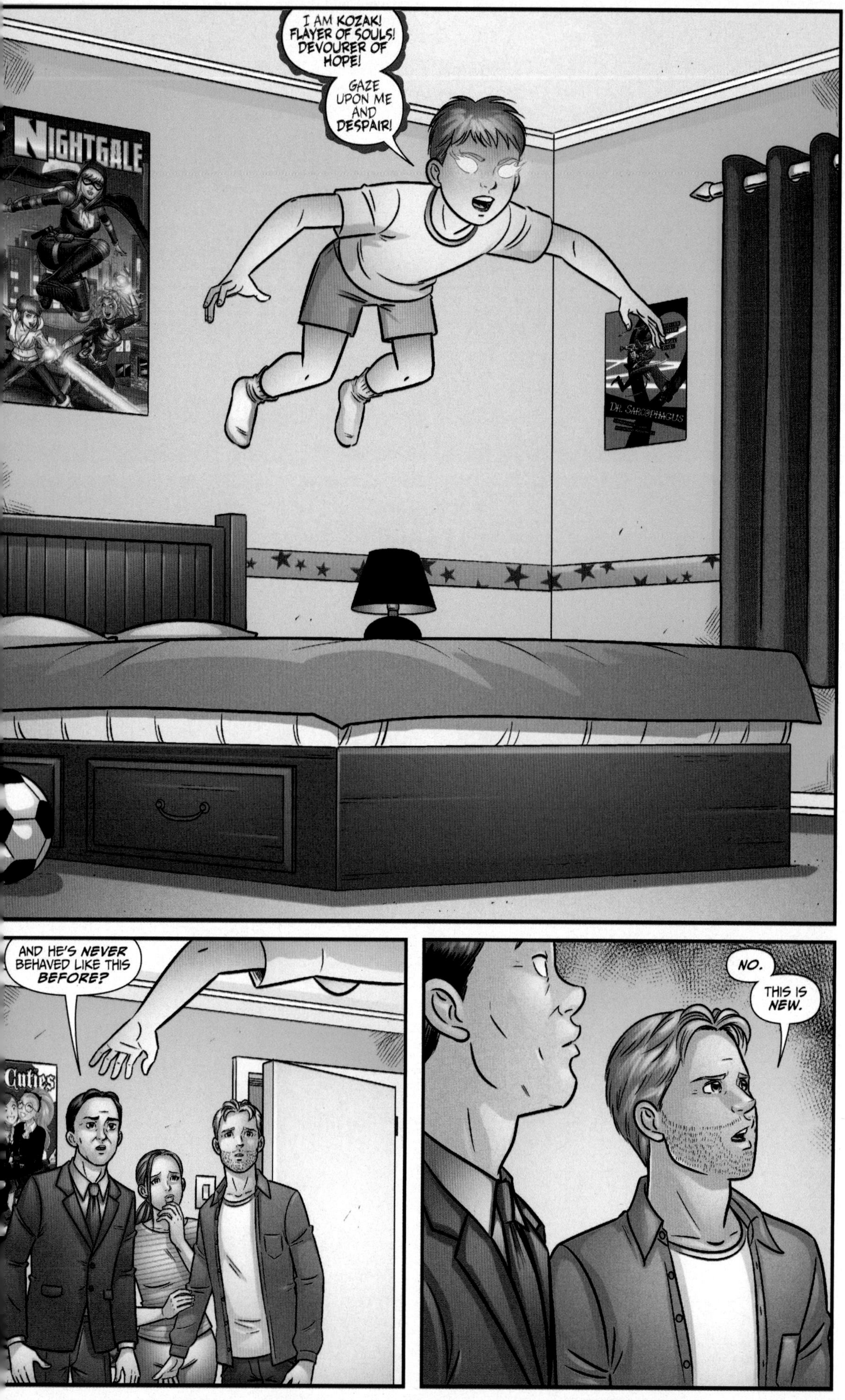
I AM KOZAK! FLAYER OF SOULS! DEVOURER OF HOPE!
GAZE UPON ME AND DESPAIR!
NIGHTGALE
DR. SARCOPHAGUS
AND HE'S NEVER BEHAVED LIKE THIS BEFORE?
Cuties
NO.
THIS IS NEW.

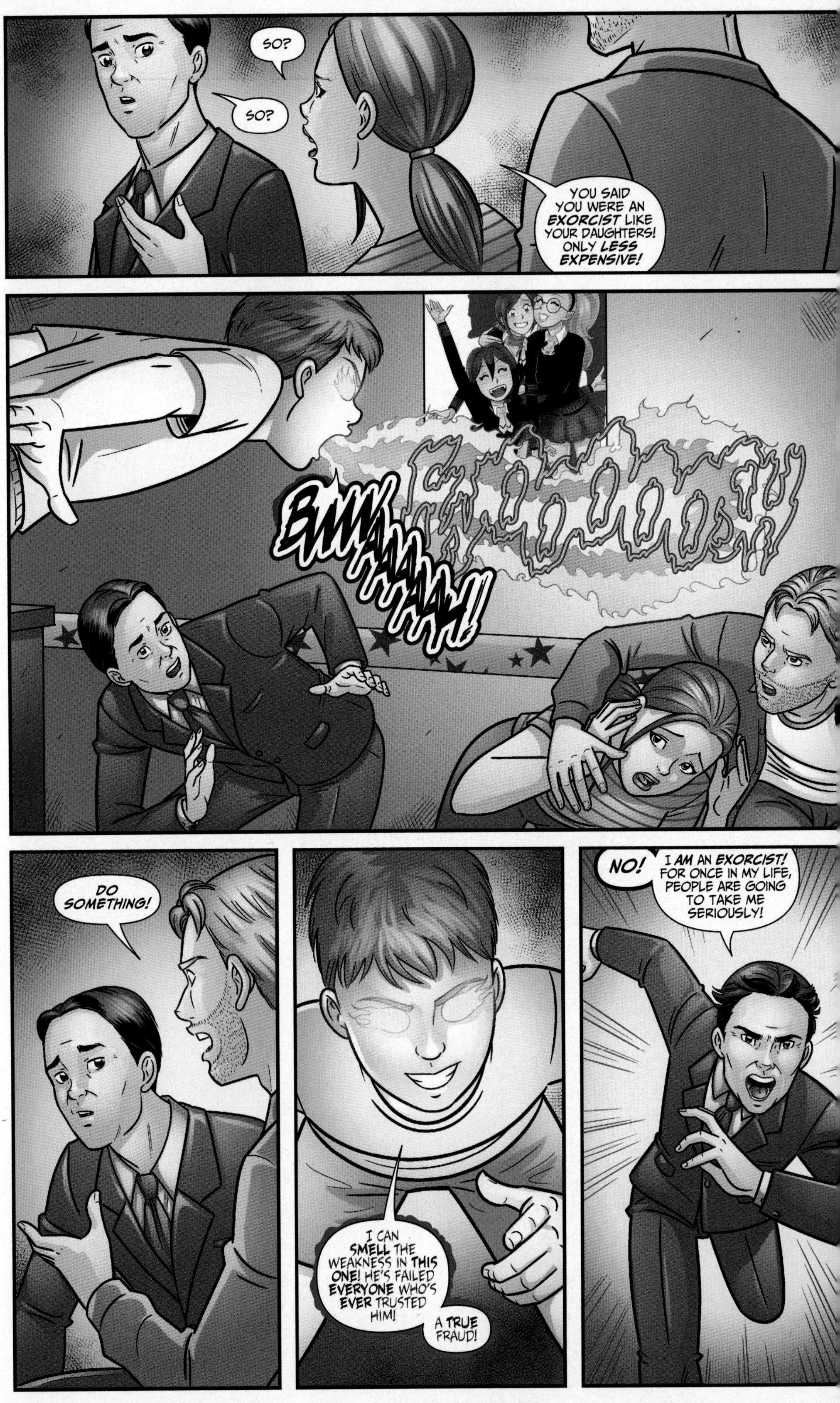
SO?
SO?
YOU SAID YOU WERE AN EXORCIST LIKE YOUR DAUGHTERS! ONLY LESS EXPENSIVE!
BWWAAAAAAH!
DO SOMETHING!
I CAN SMELL THE WEAKNESS IN THIS ONE! HE'S FAILED EVERYONE WHO'S EVER TRUSTED HIM!
A TRUE FRAUD!
NO!
I AM AN EXORCIST! FOR ONCE IN MY LIFE, PEOPLE ARE GOING TO TAKE ME SERIOUSLY!

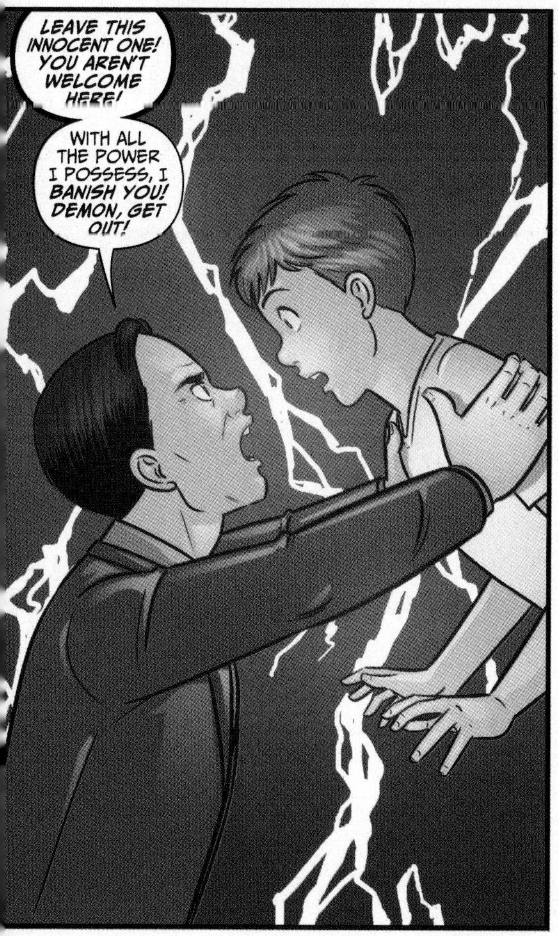
LEAVE THIS INNOCENT ONE! YOU AREN'T WELCOME HERE!
WITH ALL THE POWER I POSSESS, I BANISH YOU! DEMON, GET OUT!

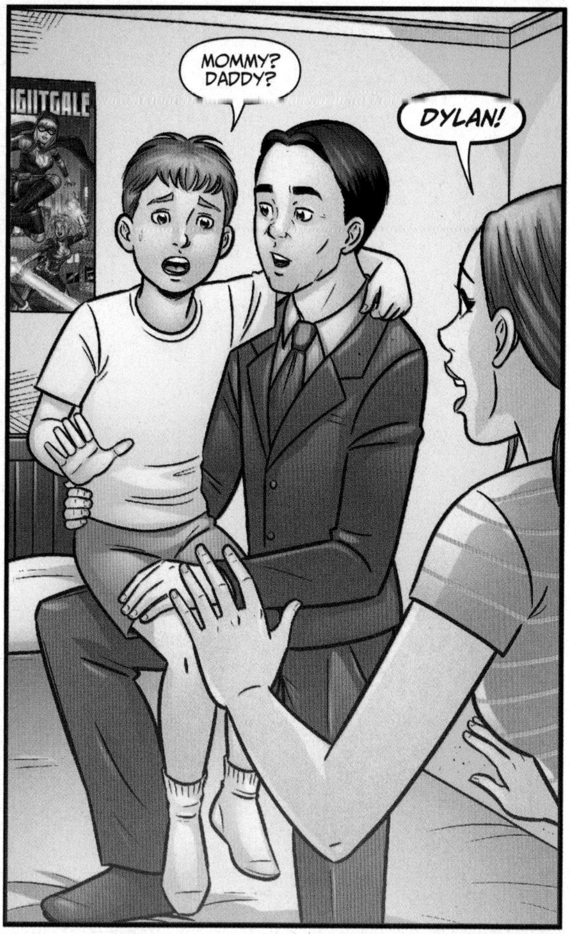
MOMMY? DADDY?
DYLAN!

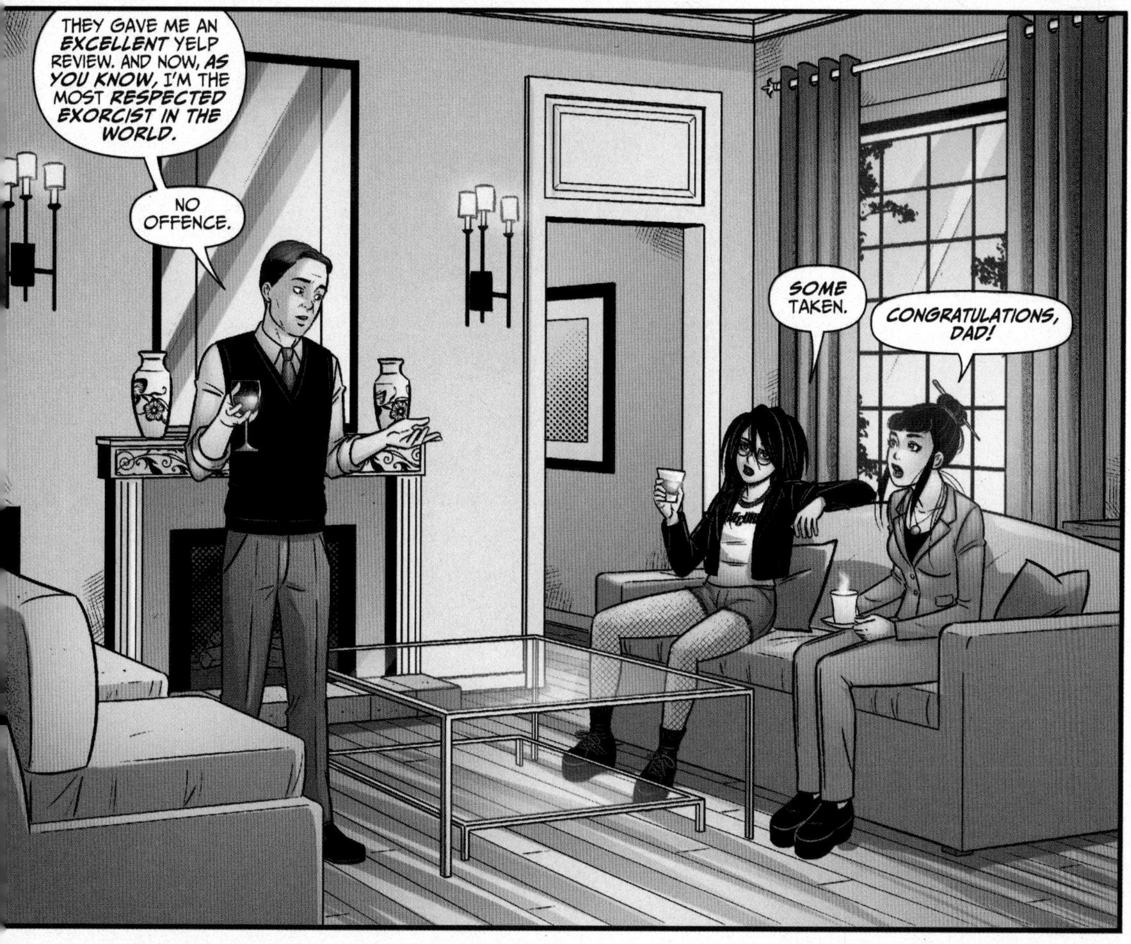
THEY GAVE ME AN EXCELLENT YELP REVIEW. AND NOW, AS YOU KNOW, I'M THE MOST RESPECTED EXORCIST IN THE WORLD.
NO OFFENCE.
SOME TAKEN.
CONGRATULATIONS, DAD!

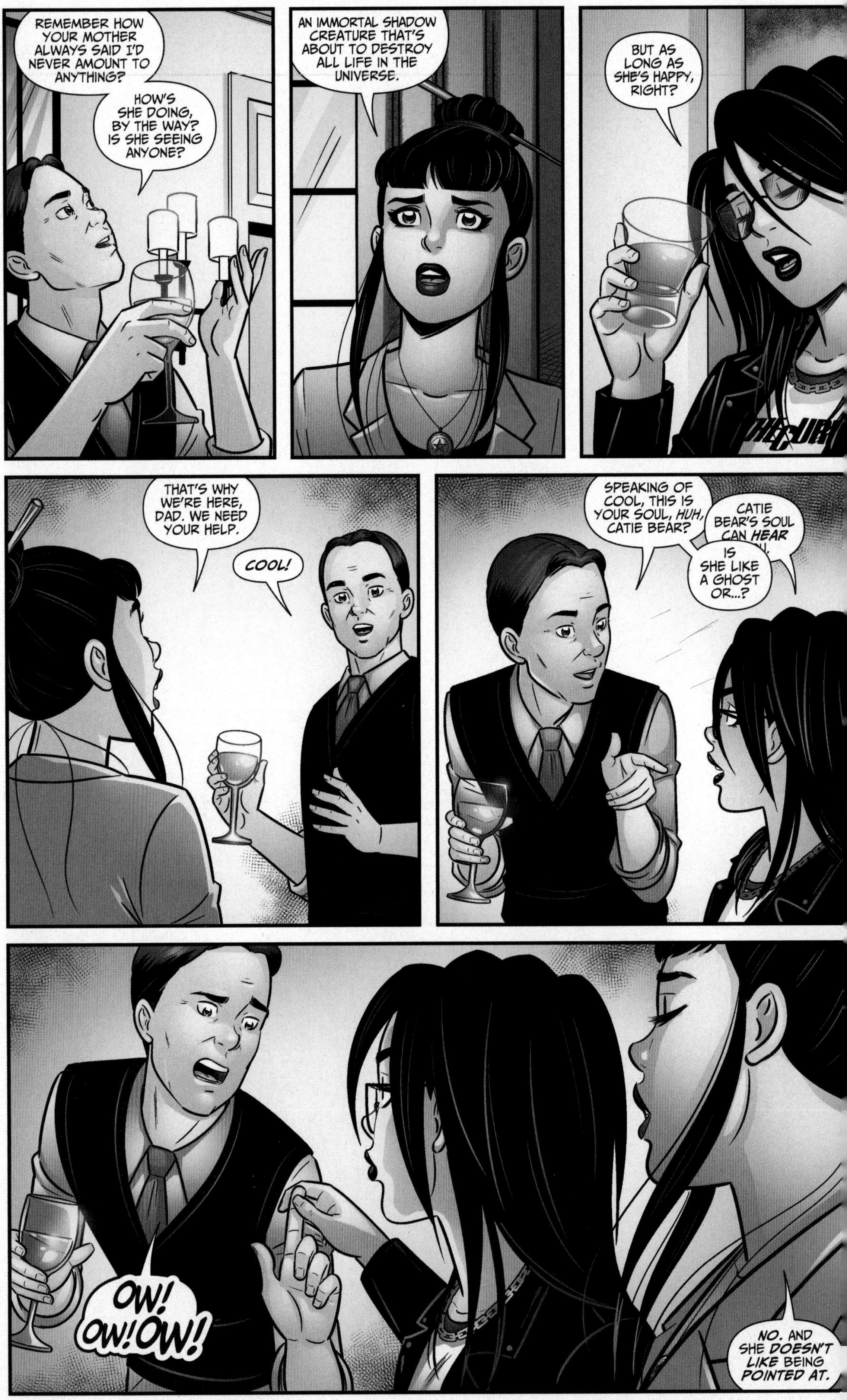
REMEMBER HOW YOUR MOTHER ALWAYS SAID I'D NEVER AMOUNT TO ANYTHING?
HOW'S SHE DOING, BY THE WAY? IS SHE SEEING ANYONE?
AN IMMORTAL SHADOW CREATURE THAT'S ABOUT TO DESTROY ALL LIFE IN THE UNIVERSE.
BUT AS LONG AS SHE'S HAPPY, RIGHT?
THAT'S WHY WE'RE HERE, DAD. WE NEED YOUR HELP.
COOL!
SPEAKING OF COOL, THIS IS YOUR SOUL, HUH, CATIE BEAR?
CATIE BEAR'S SOUL CAN HEAR
IS SHE LIKE A GHOST OR...?
OW! OW! OW!
NO. AND SHE DOESN'T LIKE BEING POINTED AT.

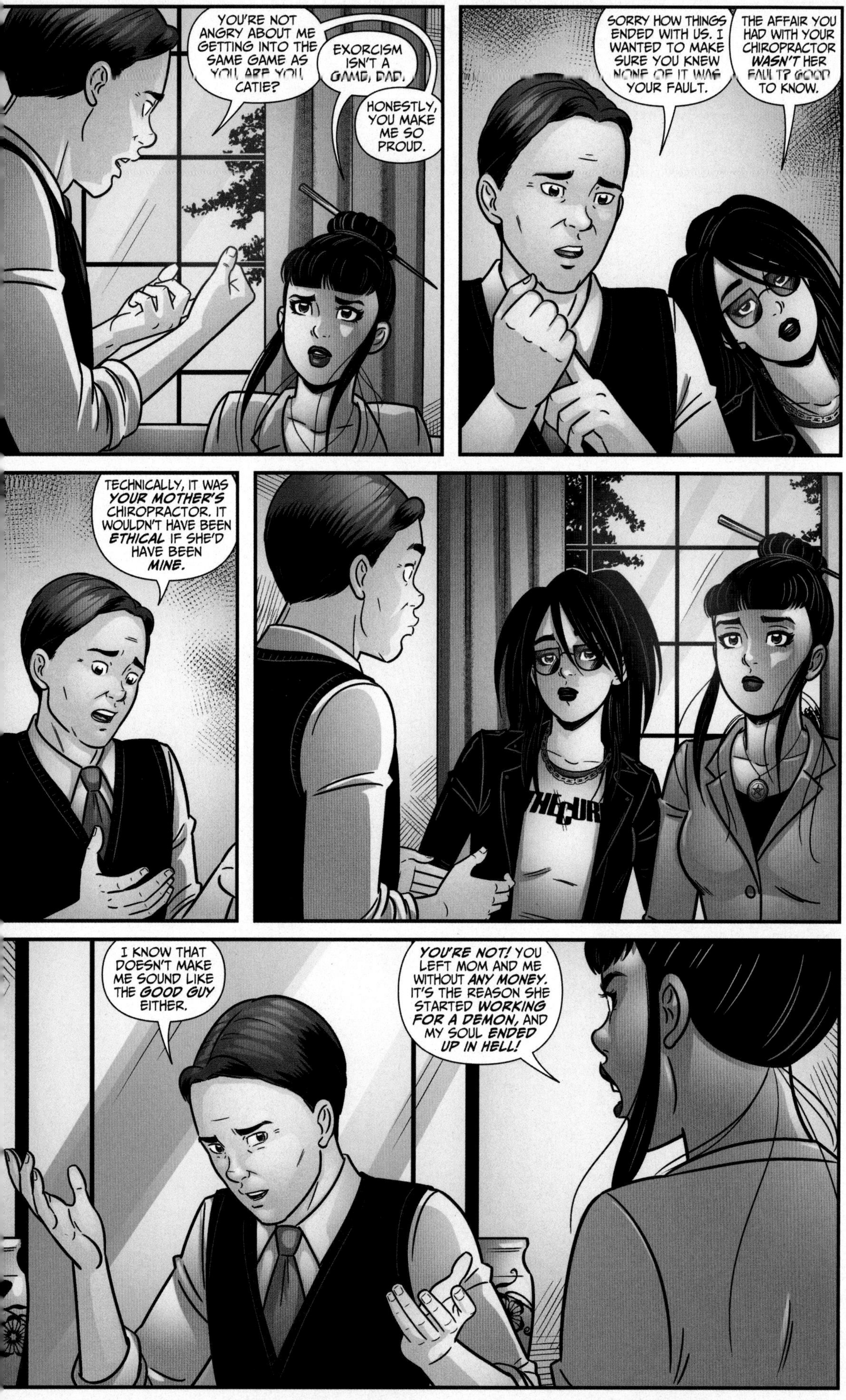

YOU'RE NOT ANGRY ABOUT ME GETTING INTO THE SAME GAME AS YOU, ARE YOU, CATIE?
EXORCISM ISN'T A GAME, DAD.
HONESTLY, YOU MAKE ME SO PROUD.
SORRY HOW THINGS ENDED WITH US. I WANTED TO MAKE SURE YOU KNEW NONE OF IT WAS YOUR FAULT.
THE AFFAIR YOU HAD WITH YOUR CHIROPRACTOR *WASN'T* HER FAULT? GOOD TO KNOW.
TECHNICALLY, IT WAS *YOUR MOTHER'S* CHIROPRACTOR. IT WOULDN'T HAVE BEEN *ETHICAL* IF SHE'D HAVE BEEN *MINE*.
THE CURE
I KNOW THAT DOESN'T MAKE ME SOUND LIKE THE *GOOD GUY* EITHER.
YOU'RE NOT! YOU LEFT MOM AND ME WITHOUT *ANY MONEY*. IT'S THE REASON SHE STARTED *WORKING FOR A DEMON*, AND MY SOUL *ENDED UP IN HELL!*

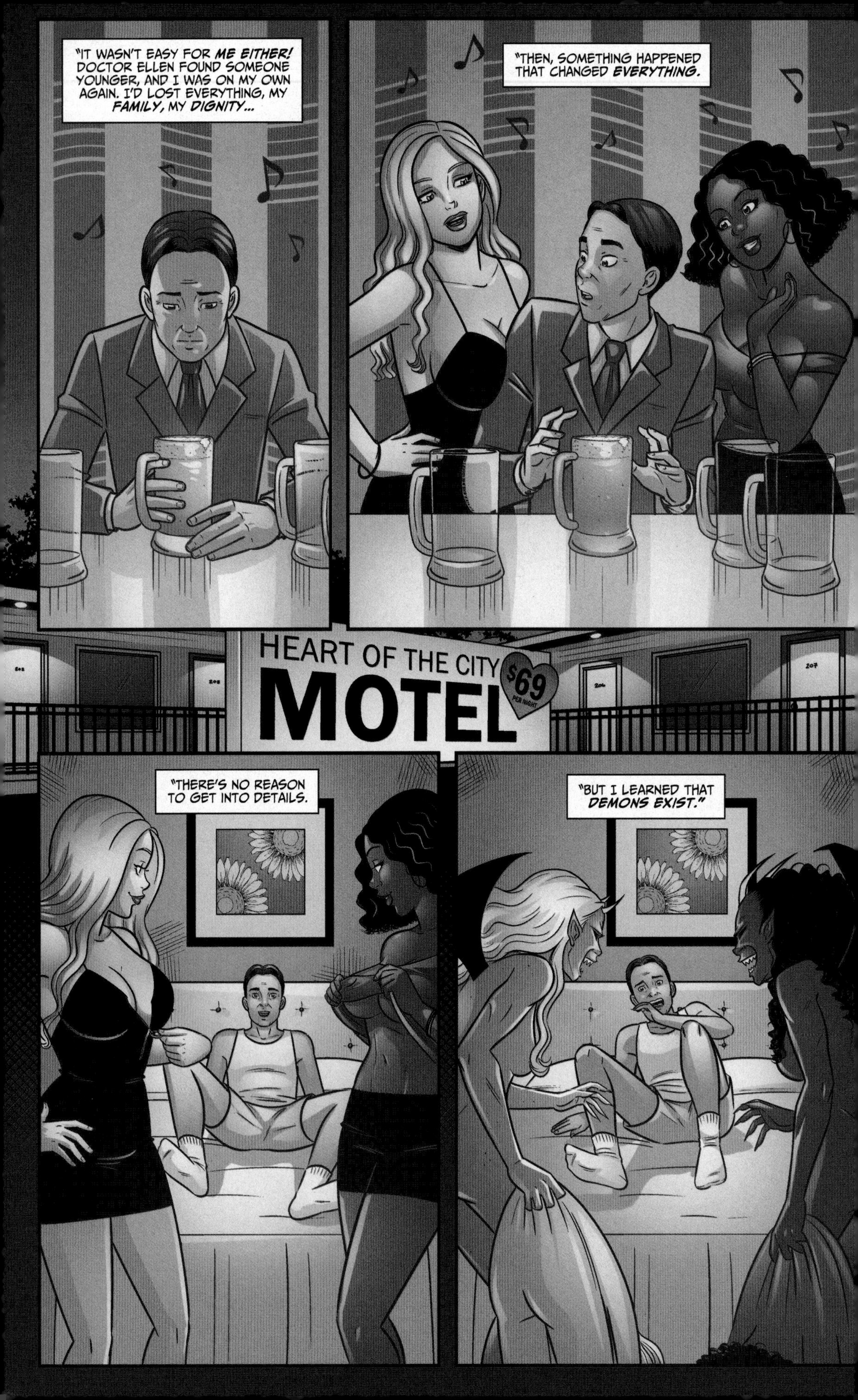
"IT WASN'T EASY FOR ME EITHER! DOCTOR ELLEN FOUND SOMEONE YOUNGER, AND I WAS ON MY OWN AGAIN. I'D LOST EVERYTHING, MY FAMILY, MY DIGNITY...
"THEN, SOMETHING HAPPENED THAT CHANGED EVERYTHING.
HEART OF THE CITY
MOTEL
$69 PER NIGHT
"THERE'S NO REASON TO GET INTO DETAILS.
"BUT I LEARNED THAT DEMONS EXIST."

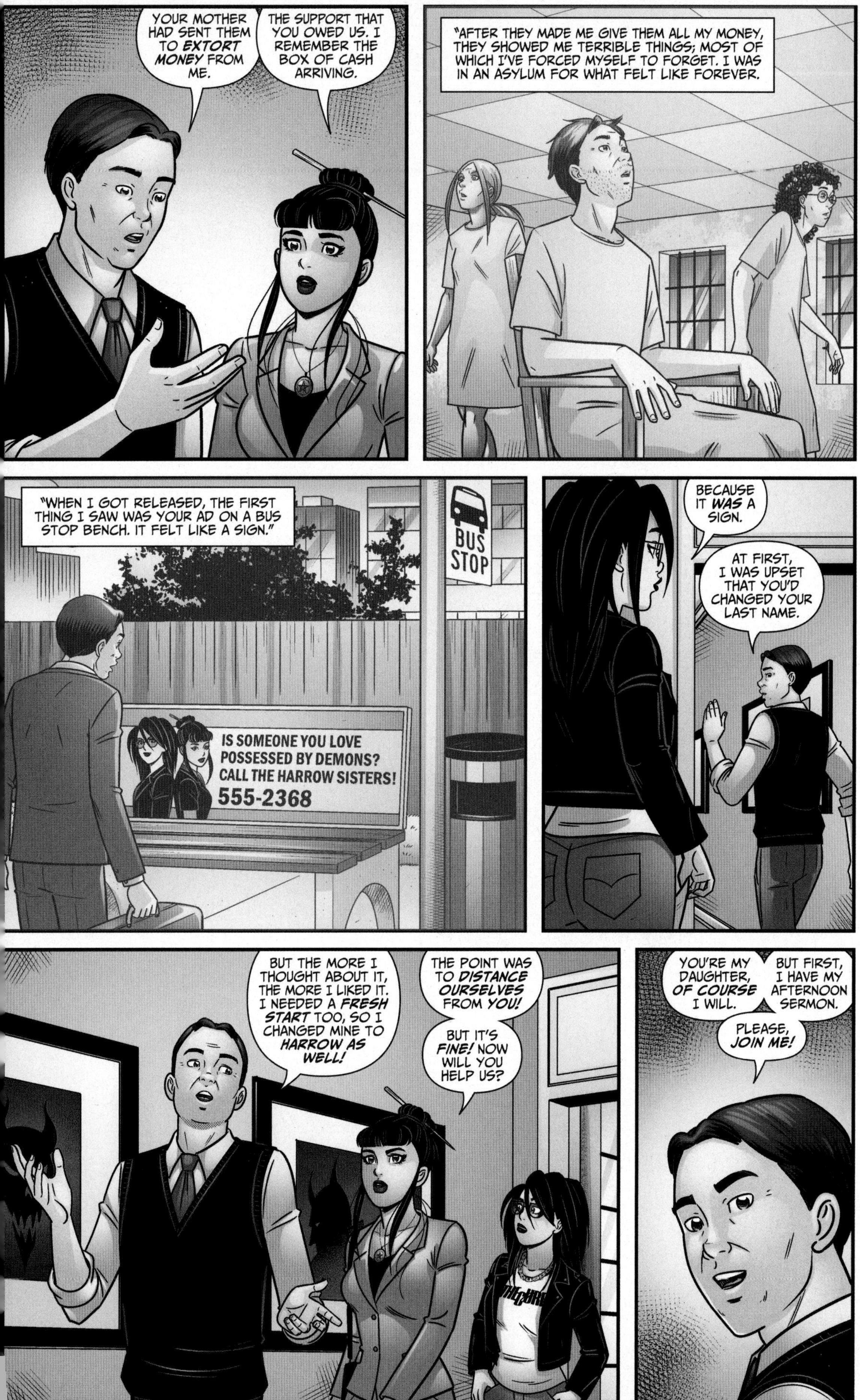
YOUR MOTHER HAD SENT THEM TO EXTORT MONEY FROM ME.
THE SUPPORT THAT YOU OWED US. I REMEMBER THE BOX OF CASH ARRIVING.
"AFTER THEY MADE ME GIVE THEM ALL MY MONEY, THEY SHOWED ME TERRIBLE THINGS; MOST OF WHICH I'VE FORCED MYSELF TO FORGET. I WAS IN AN ASYLUM FOR WHAT FELT LIKE FOREVER.
"WHEN I GOT RELEASED, THE FIRST THING I SAW WAS YOUR AD ON A BUS STOP BENCH. IT FELT LIKE A SIGN."
BUS STOP
IS SOMEONE YOU LOVE POSSESSED BY DEMONS? CALL THE HARROW SISTERS!
555-2368
BECAUSE IT WAS A SIGN.
AT FIRST, I WAS UPSET THAT YOU'D CHANGED YOUR LAST NAME.
BUT THE MORE I THOUGHT ABOUT IT, THE MORE I LIKED IT. I NEEDED A FRESH START TOO, SO I CHANGED MINE TO HARROW AS WELL!
THE POINT WAS TO DISTANCE OURSELVES FROM YOU!
BUT IT'S FINE! NOW WILL YOU HELP US?
YOU'RE MY DAUGHTER, OF COURSE I WILL.
BUT FIRST, I HAVE MY AFTERNOON SERMON.
PLEASE, JOIN ME!

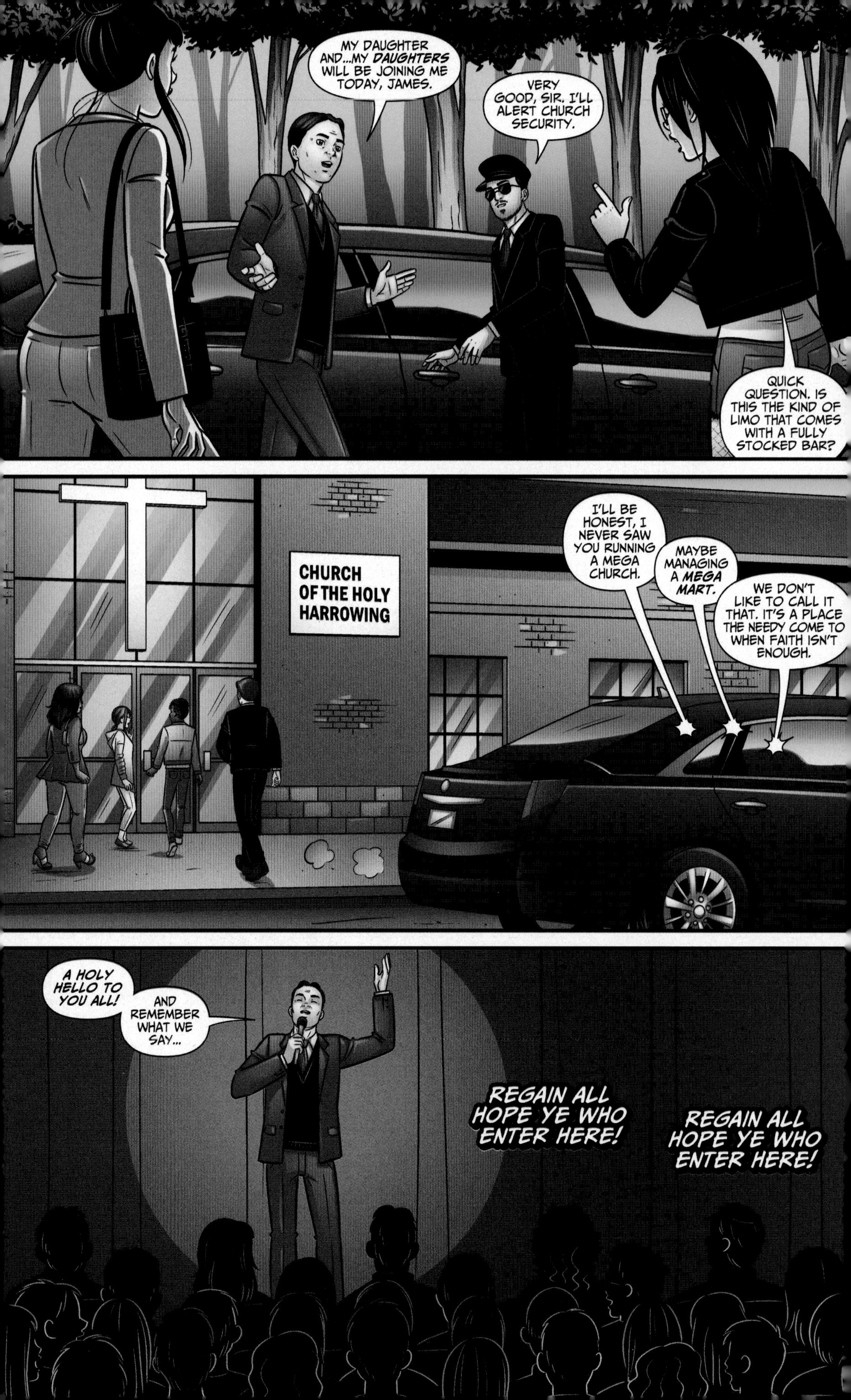
MY DAUGHTER AND...MY DAUGHTERS WILL BE JOINING ME TODAY, JAMES.
VERY GOOD, SIR. I'LL ALERT CHURCH SECURITY.
QUICK QUESTION. IS THIS THE KIND OF LIMO THAT COMES WITH A FULLY STOCKED BAR?
CHURCH OF THE HOLY HARROWING
I'LL BE HONEST, I NEVER SAW YOU RUNNING A MEGA CHURCH.
MAYBE MANAGING A MEGA MART.
WE DON'T LIKE TO CALL IT THAT. IT'S A PLACE THE NEEDY COME TO WHEN FAITH ISN'T ENOUGH.
A HOLY HELLO TO YOU ALL!
AND REMEMBER WHAT WE SAY...
REGAIN ALL HOPE YE WHO ENTER HERE!
REGAIN ALL HOPE YE WHO ENTER HERE!

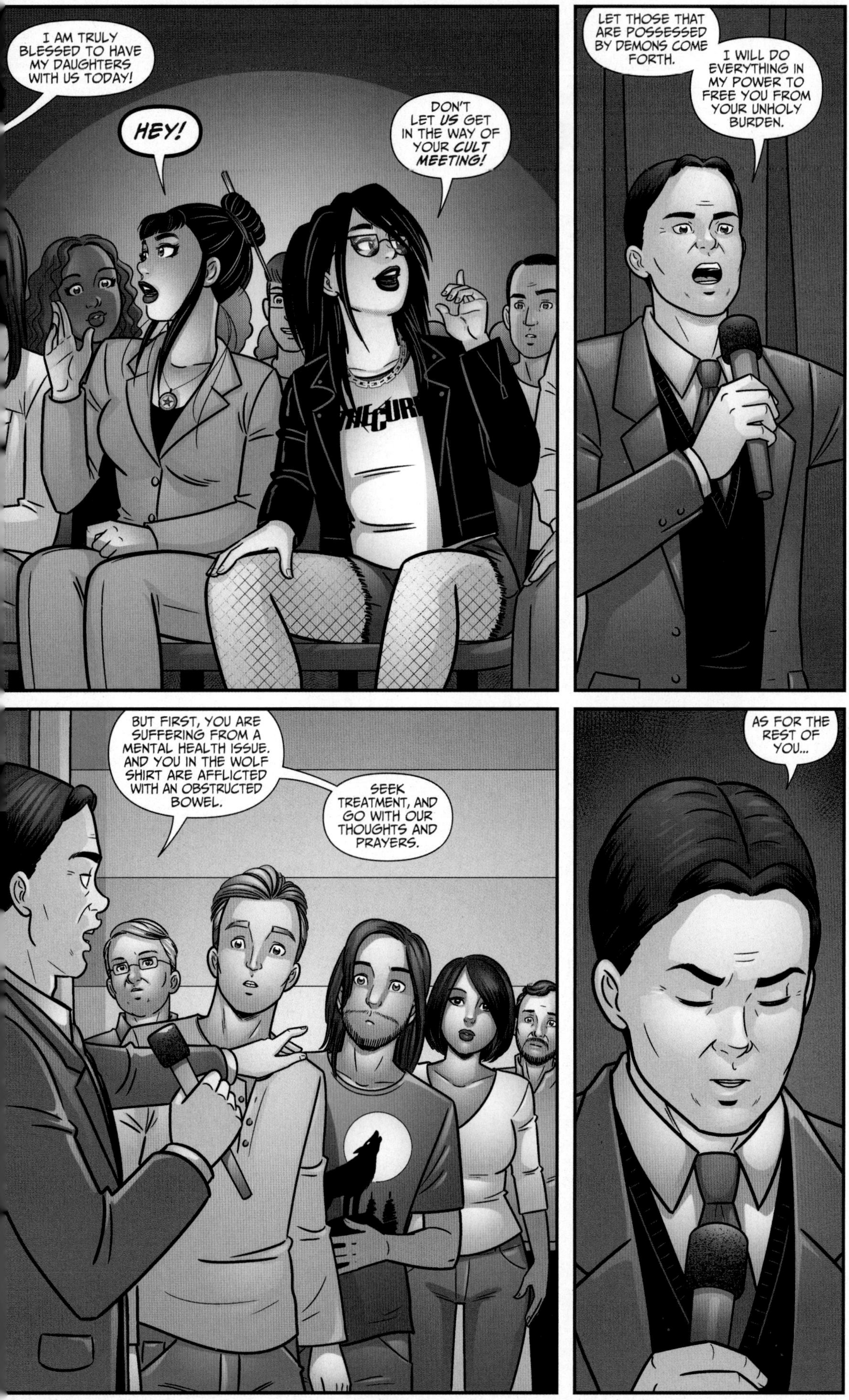

I AM TRULY BLESSED TO HAVE MY DAUGHTERS WITH US TODAY!
HEY!
DON'T LET US GET IN THE WAY OF YOUR CULT MEETING!
THE CURE
LET THOSE THAT ARE POSSESSED BY DEMONS COME FORTH.
I WILL DO EVERYTHING IN MY POWER TO FREE YOU FROM YOUR UNHOLY BURDEN.
BUT FIRST, YOU ARE SUFFERING FROM A MENTAL HEALTH ISSUE. AND YOU IN THE WOLF SHIRT ARE AFFLICTED WITH AN OBSTRUCTED BOWEL.
SEEK TREATMENT, AND GO WITH OUR THOUGHTS AND PRAYERS.
AS FOR THE REST OF YOU...

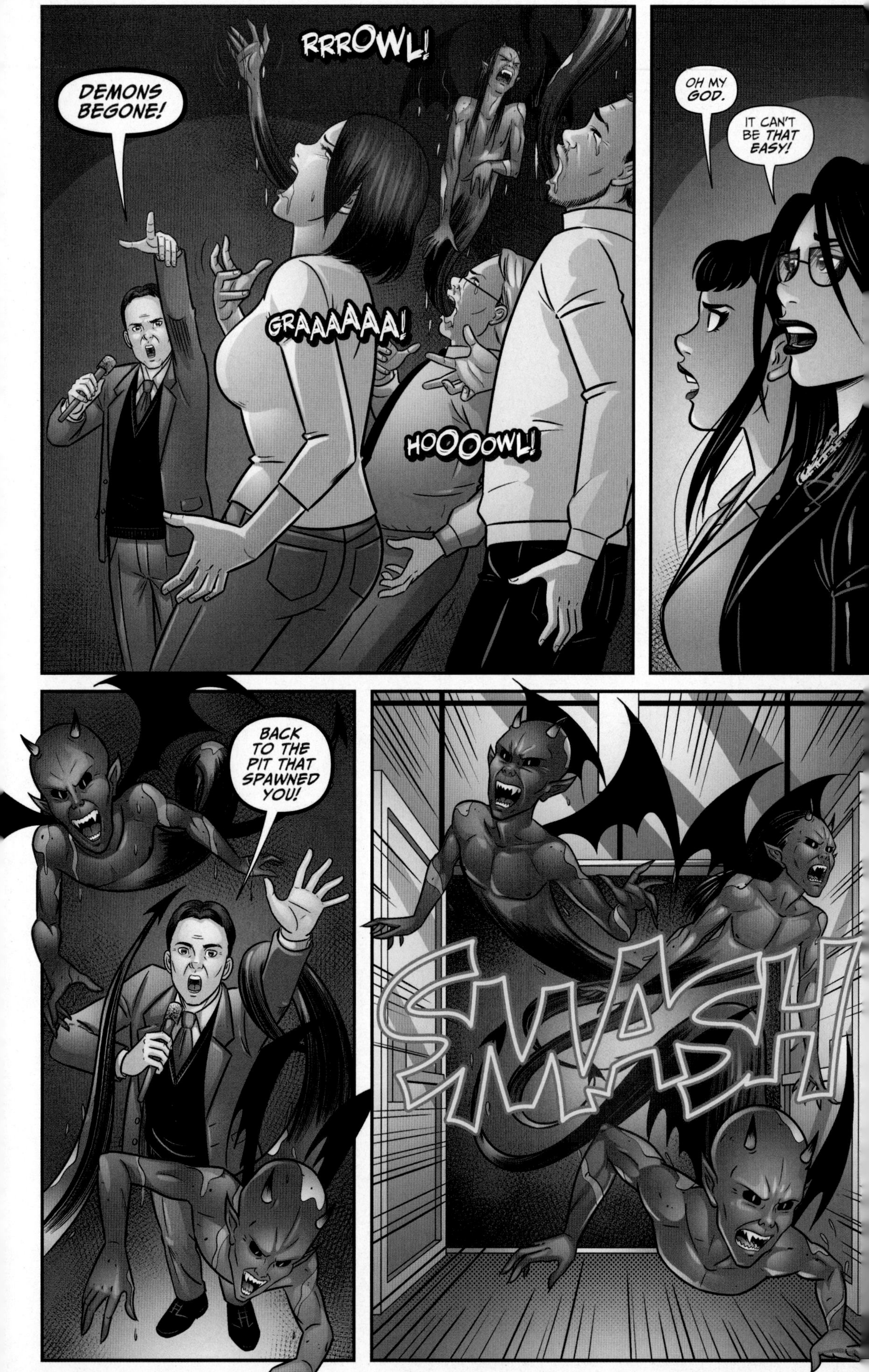
DEMONS BEGONE!
RRROWL!
GRAAAAAA!
HOOOOWL!
OH MY GOD.
IT CAN'T BE THAT EASY!
BACK TO THE PIT THAT SPAWNED YOU!
SMASH

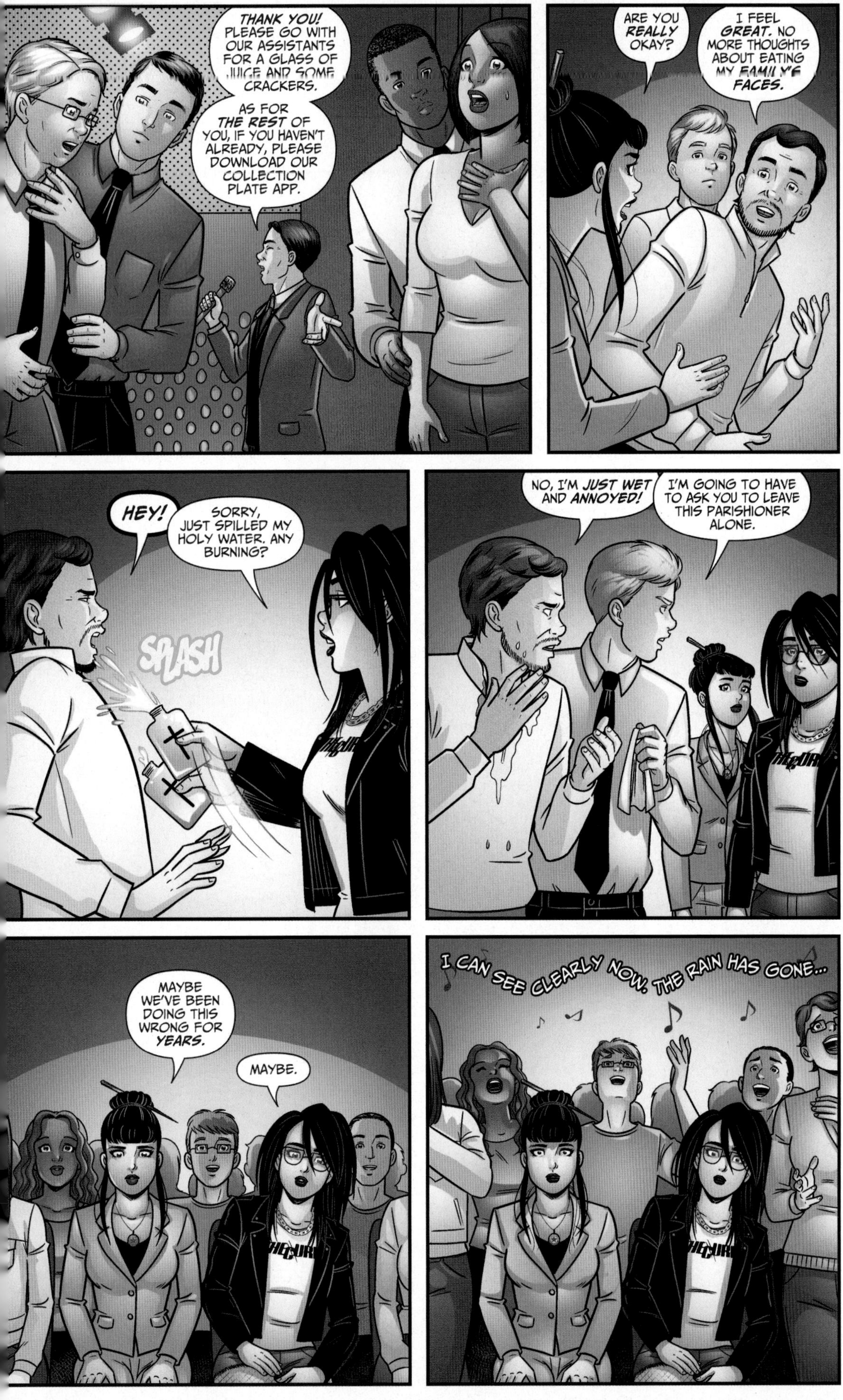
THANK YOU! PLEASE GO WITH OUR ASSISTANTS FOR A GLASS OF JUICE AND SOME CRACKERS.
AS FOR THE REST OF YOU, IF YOU HAVEN'T ALREADY, PLEASE DOWNLOAD OUR COLLECTION PLATE APP.
ARE YOU REALLY OKAY?
I FEEL GREAT. NO MORE THOUGHTS ABOUT EATING MY FAMILY'S FACES.
HEY!
SORRY, JUST SPILLED MY HOLY WATER. ANY BURNING?
SPLASH
NO, I'M JUST WET AND ANNOYED!
I'M GOING TO HAVE TO ASK YOU TO LEAVE THIS PARISHIONER ALONE.
MAYBE WE'VE BEEN DOING THIS WRONG FOR YEARS.
MAYBE.
I CAN SEE CLEARLY NOW. THE RAIN HAS GONE...

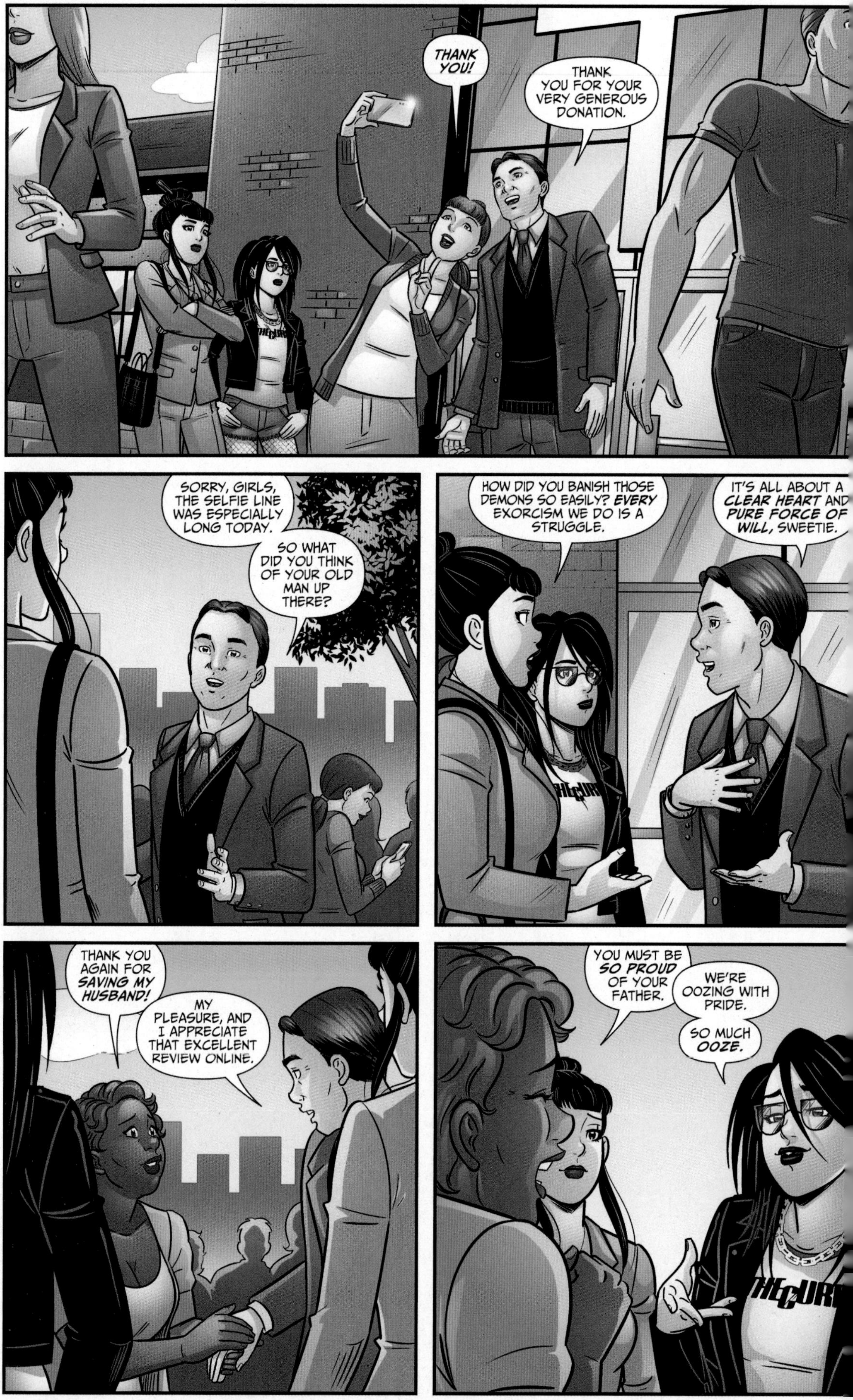
THANK YOU!
THANK YOU FOR YOUR VERY GENEROUS DONATION.
SORRY, GIRLS, THE SELFIE LINE WAS ESPECIALLY LONG TODAY.
SO WHAT DID YOU THINK OF YOUR OLD MAN UP THERE?
HOW DID YOU BANISH THOSE DEMONS SO EASILY? EVERY EXORCISM WE DO IS A STRUGGLE.
IT'S ALL ABOUT A CLEAR HEART AND PURE FORCE OF WILL, SWEETIE.
THANK YOU AGAIN FOR SAVING MY HUSBAND!
MY PLEASURE, AND I APPRECIATE THAT EXCELLENT REVIEW ONLINE.
YOU MUST BE SO PROUD OF YOUR FATHER.
WE'RE OOZING WITH PRIDE.
SO MUCH OOZE.

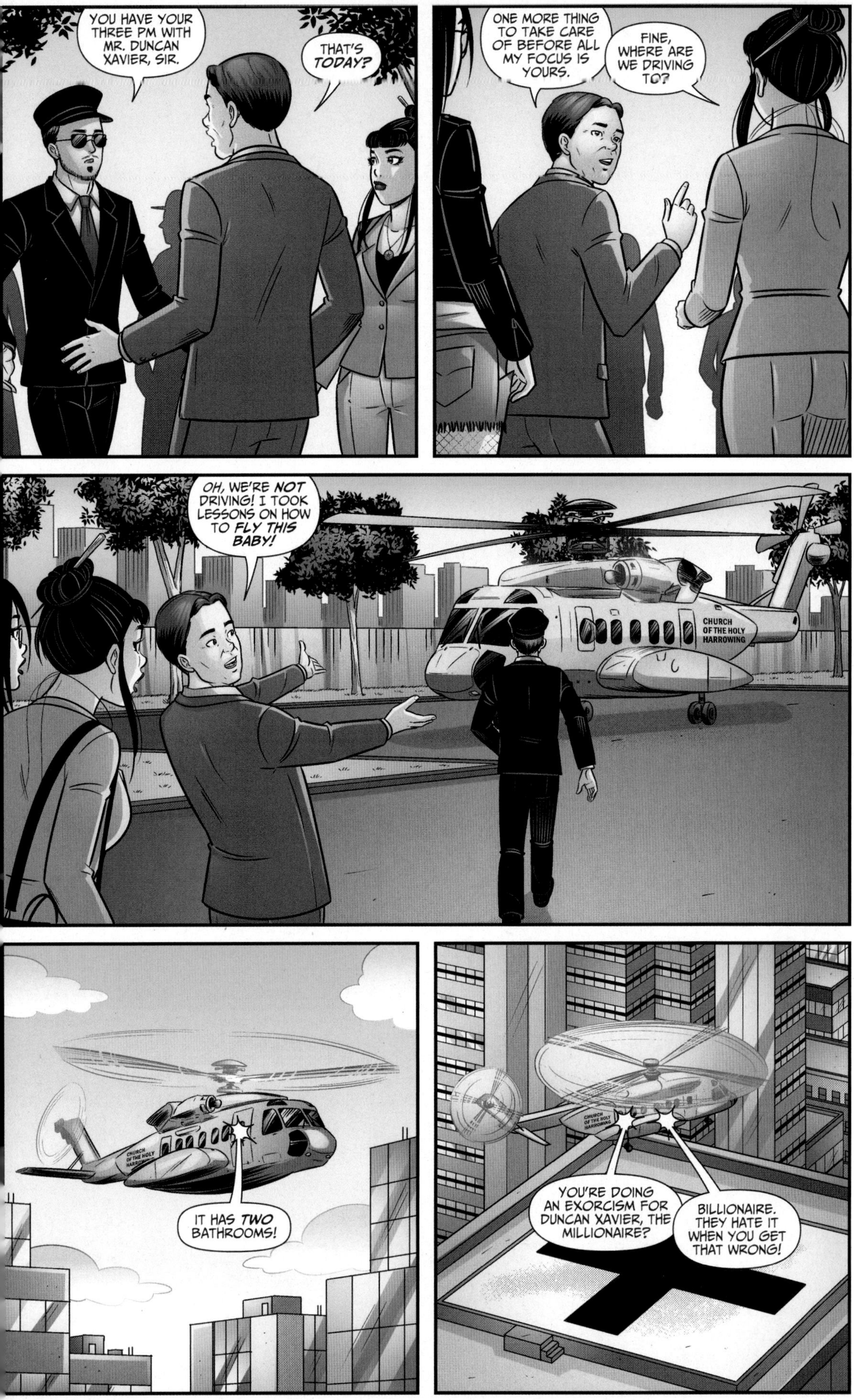
YOU HAVE YOUR THREE PM WITH MR. DUNCAN XAVIER, SIR.
THAT'S *TODAY?*
ONE MORE THING TO TAKE CARE OF BEFORE ALL MY FOCUS IS YOURS.
FINE, WHERE ARE WE DRIVING TO?
OH, WE'RE ***NOT*** DRIVING! I TOOK LESSONS ON HOW TO ***FLY THIS BABY!***
CHURCH OF THE HOLY HARROWING
IT HAS ***TWO*** BATHROOMS!
YOU'RE DOING AN EXORCISM FOR DUNCAN XAVIER, THE MILLIONAIRE?
BILLIONAIRE. THEY HATE IT WHEN YOU GET THAT WRONG!

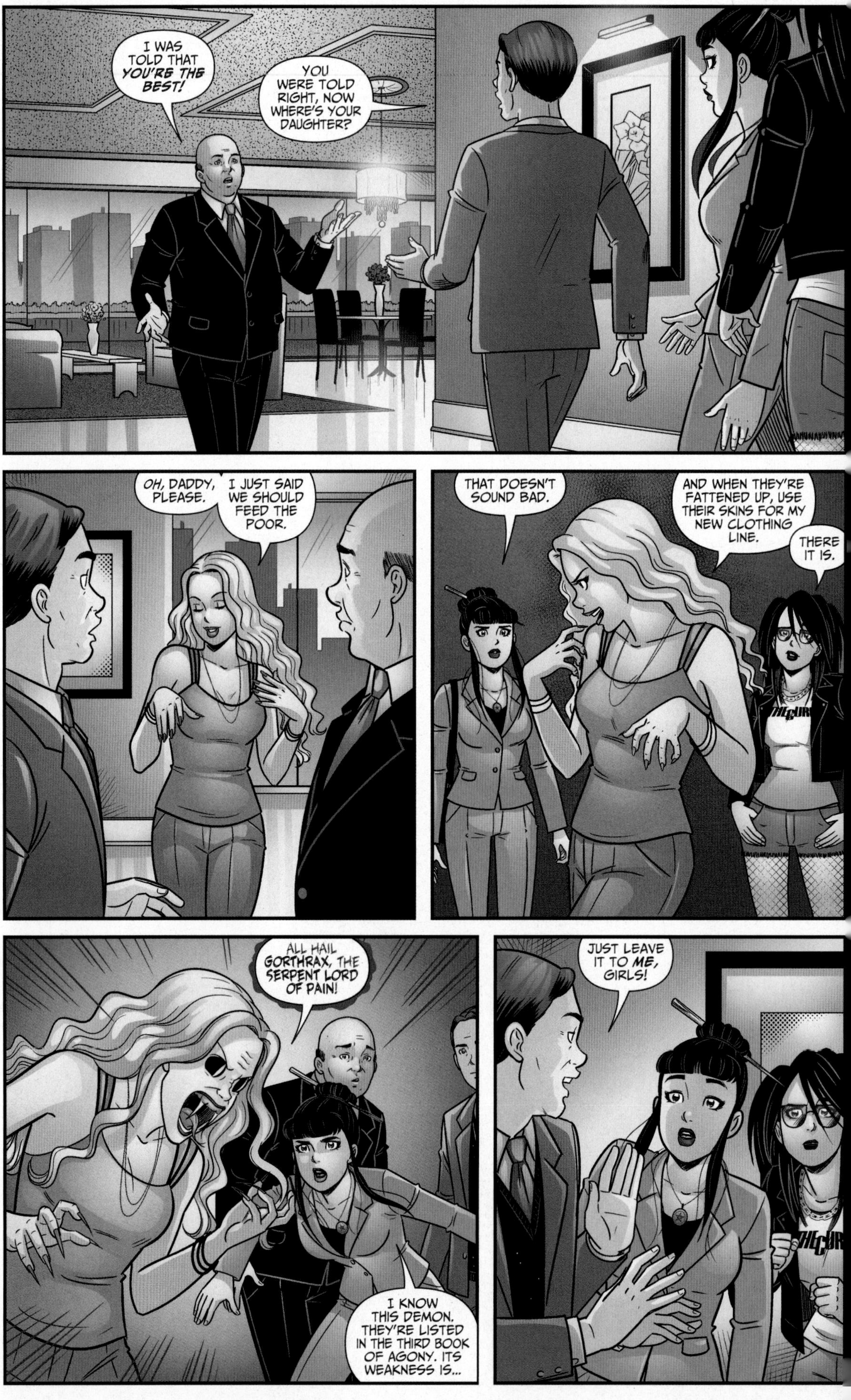
I WAS TOLD THAT *YOU'RE THE BEST!*
YOU WERE TOLD RIGHT, NOW WHERE'S YOUR DAUGHTER?
OH, DADDY, PLEASE.
I JUST SAID WE SHOULD FEED THE POOR.
THAT DOESN'T SOUND BAD.
AND WHEN THEY'RE FATTENED UP, USE THEIR SKINS FOR MY NEW CLOTHING LINE.
THERE IT IS.
ALL HAIL **GORTHRAX**, THE SERPENT LORD OF PAIN!
I KNOW THIS DEMON. THEY'RE LISTED IN THE THIRD BOOK OF AGONY. ITS WEAKNESS IS...
JUST LEAVE IT TO *ME*, GIRLS!

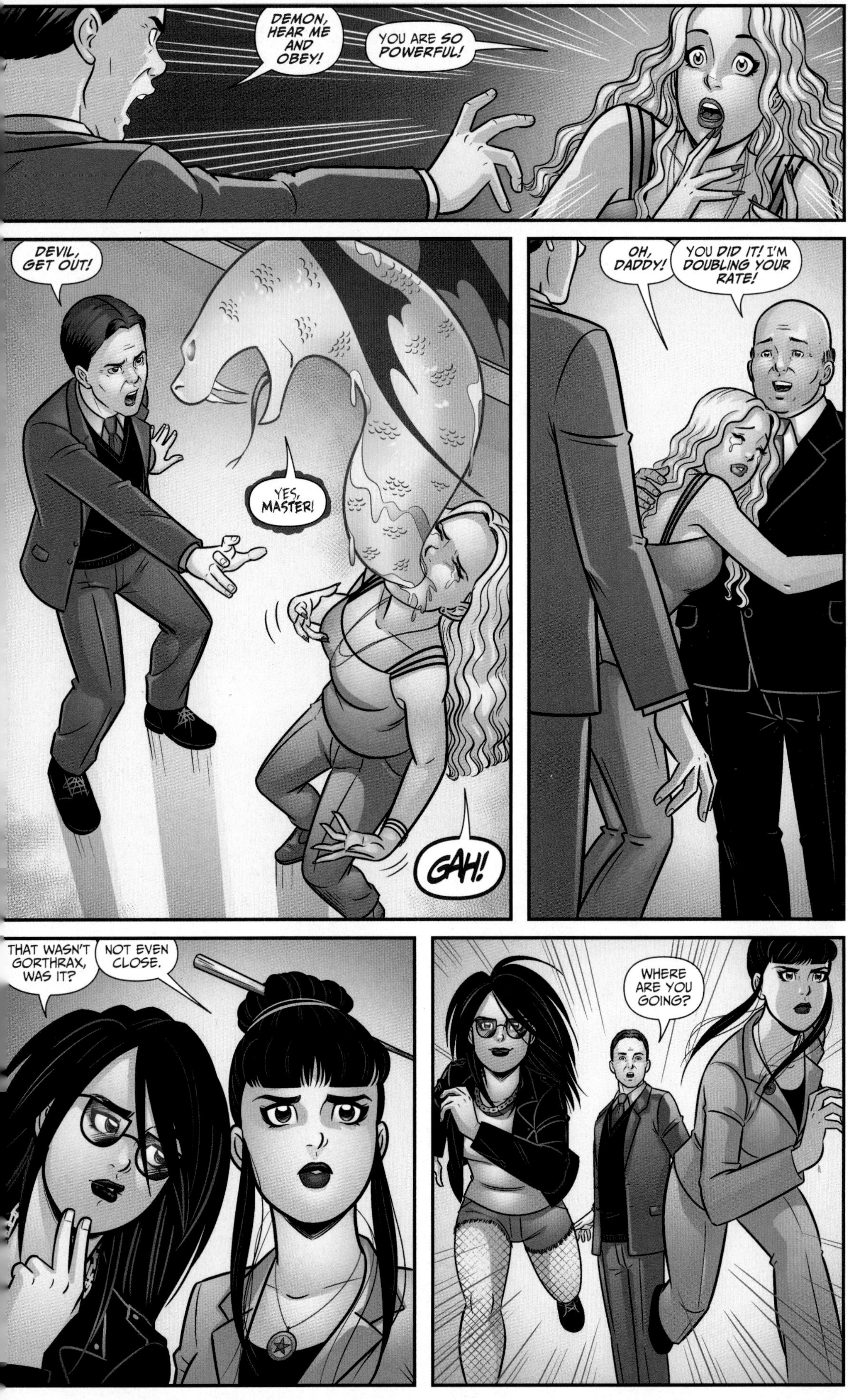
DEMON, HEAR ME AND OBEY!
YOU ARE SO POWERFUL!
DEVIL, GET OUT!
YES, MASTER!
GAH!
OH, DADDY!
YOU DID IT! I'M DOUBLING YOUR RATE!
THAT WASN'T GORTHRAX, WAS IT?
NOT EVEN CLOSE.
WHERE ARE YOU GOING?

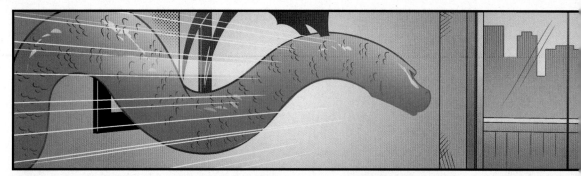

OOOF!

OW!

WHAT?

AAAAH! LET ME GO! I'M BANISHED! THAT WAS THE DEAL!

YOU'RE A LOW LEVEL IMP PRETENDING TO BE GORTHRAX.

NOW TELL ME WHAT'S GOING ON OR THIS HOLY HAIRPIN IS GOING TO END UP INSIDE YOU, AND NO SPAWN OF THE PIT SURVIVES THAT!

LET THE DEMON GO, CATIE.

IT'S CATE, AND NO, DAD! SOMETHING'S WRONG HERE!

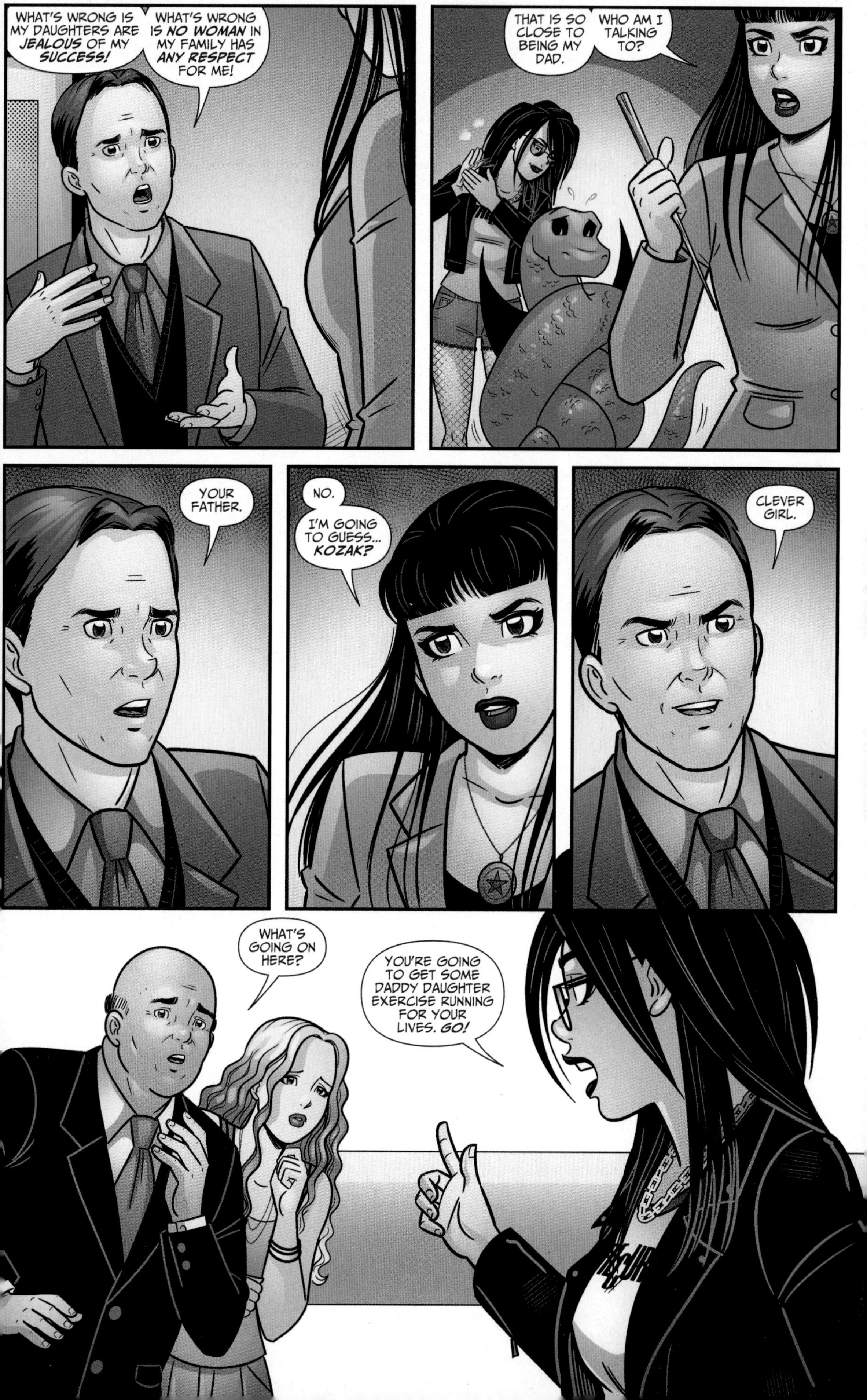
WHAT'S WRONG IS MY DAUGHTERS ARE JEALOUS OF MY SUCCESS!
WHAT'S WRONG IS NO WOMAN IN MY FAMILY HAS ANY RESPECT FOR ME!
THAT IS SO CLOSE TO BEING MY DAD.
WHO AM I TALKING TO?
YOUR FATHER.
NO.
I'M GOING TO GUESS... KOZAK?
CLEVER GIRL.
WHAT'S GOING ON HERE?
YOU'RE GOING TO GET SOME DADDY DAUGHTER EXERCISE RUNNING FOR YOUR LIVES. GO!

RRRRAAAWL!

HEY, BIG GUY!

GUESSING YOU TOOK OVER ON THAT FIRST EXORCISM!

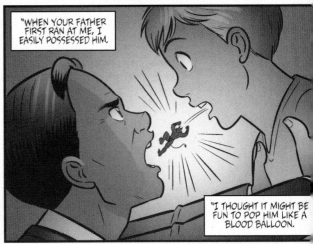

"WHEN YOUR FATHER FIRST RAN AT ME, I EASILY POSSESSED HIM.

"I THOUGHT IT MIGHT BE FUN TO POP HIM LIKE A BLOOD BALLOON.

"BUT THEN, I HAD A BETTER IDEA. I MADE DEALS WITH MY FELLOW DEMONS. I'D EXORCISE THEM, AND WE'D SPLIT THE PROFITS!"

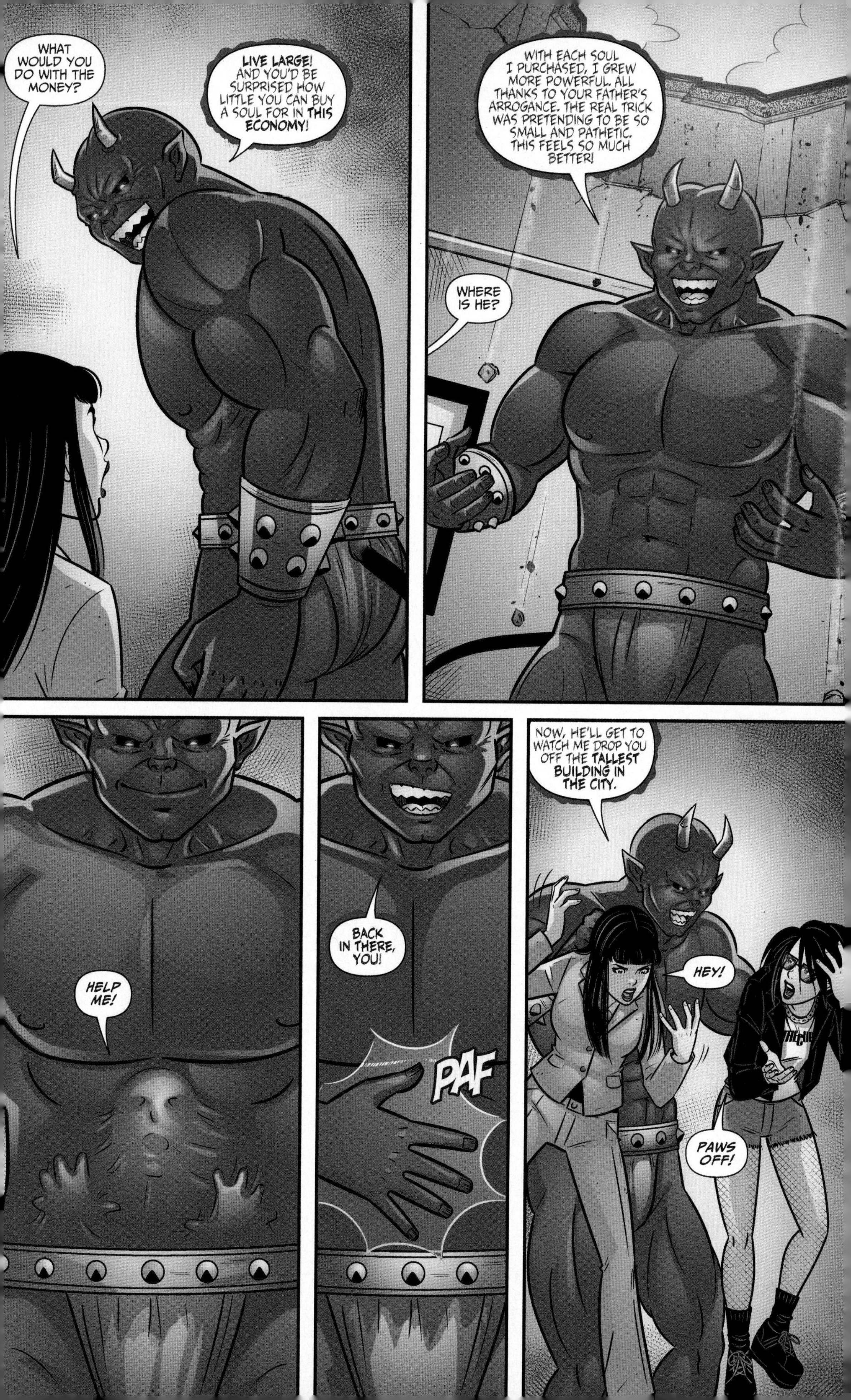
WHAT WOULD YOU DO WITH THE MONEY?
LIVE LARGE! AND YOU'D BE SURPRISED HOW LITTLE YOU CAN BUY A SOUL FOR IN THIS ECONOMY!
WITH EACH SOUL I PURCHASED, I GREW MORE POWERFUL. ALL THANKS TO YOUR FATHER'S ARROGANCE. THE REAL TRICK WAS PRETENDING TO BE SO SMALL AND PATHETIC. THIS FEELS SO MUCH BETTER!
WHERE IS HE?
HELP ME!
BACK IN THERE, YOU!
PAF
NOW, HE'LL GET TO WATCH ME DROP YOU OFF THE TALLEST BUILDING IN THE CITY.
HEY!
PAWS OFF!

A LOT OF DEMONS REALLY HATE YOU BOTH, THIS IS GOING TO HELP ME MAKE MANY MORE DEALS!

HEY, CATE! I REALLY LIKE HOW YOU LOOK WITH YOUR *HAIR DOWN!*

THANKS.

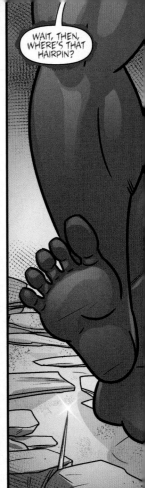

WAIT, THEN, WHERE'S THAT HAIRPIN?

GRAAAAAAH!

HE SCREAMS LIKE WHEN DAD STEPPED ON YOUR LEGO PIECES.

DAD *NEVER* EXPLODED INTO GOO, THOUGH.

HOW DO YOU *NEVER* GET COVERED?!

H-HELP!

DAD?

ARE YOU OKAY?

THERE'S TWO OF YOU. THAT'S WEIRD.

WHAT DO YOU REMEMBER?

I REMEMBER...

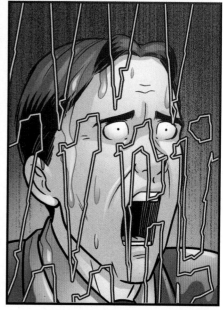

HE'S SEDATED NOW. KEEPS MUMBLING ABOUT DEMONS.

SAD. HE RAN THAT HUGE CHURCH BY THE BRIDGE. ON THE BRIGHT SIDE, HE'S GOT ENOUGH MONEY TO PAY FOR THE BEST TREATMENT.

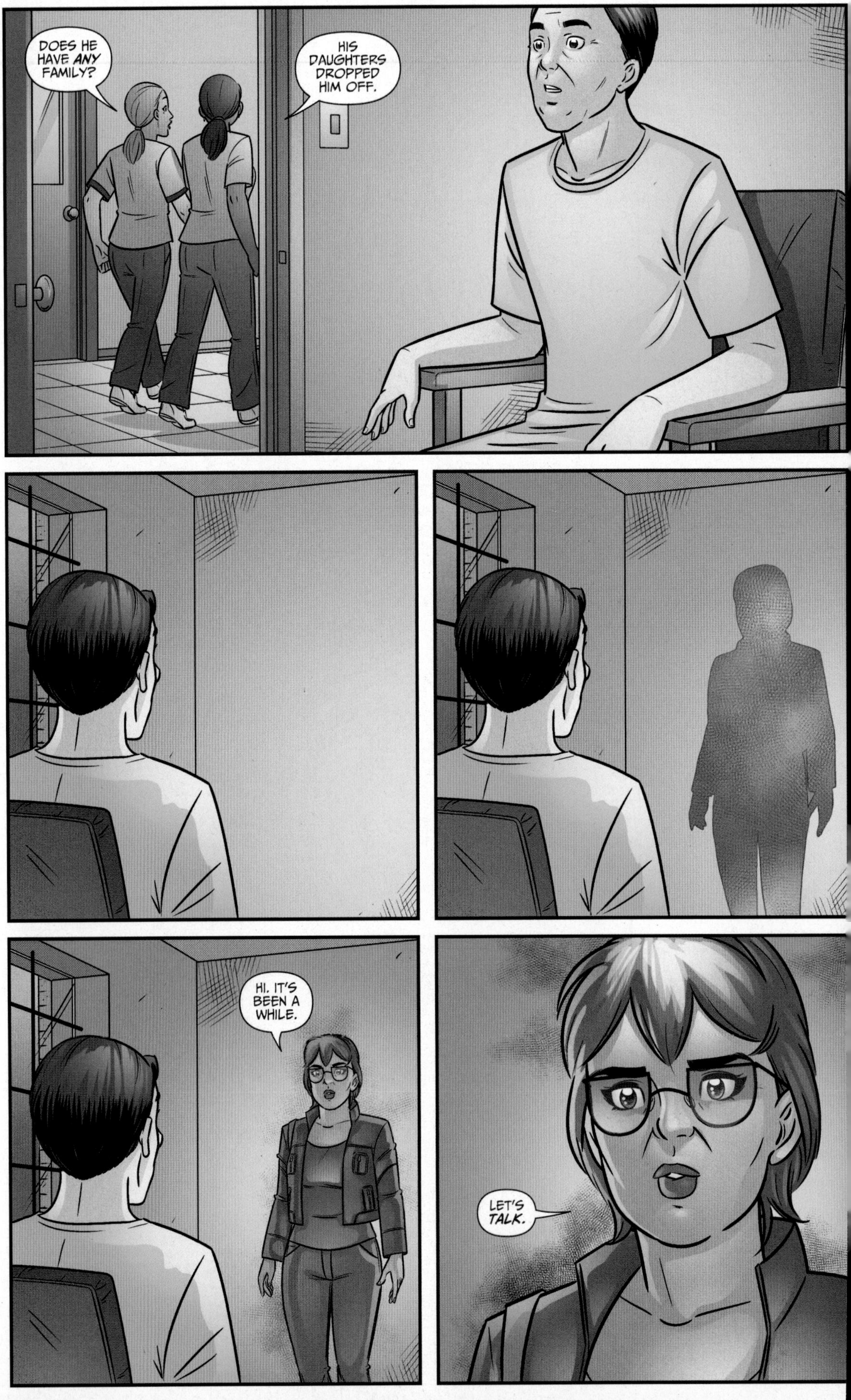
DOES HE HAVE ANY FAMILY?
HIS DAUGHTERS DROPPED HIM OFF.
HI. IT'S BEEN A WHILE.
LET'S TALK.

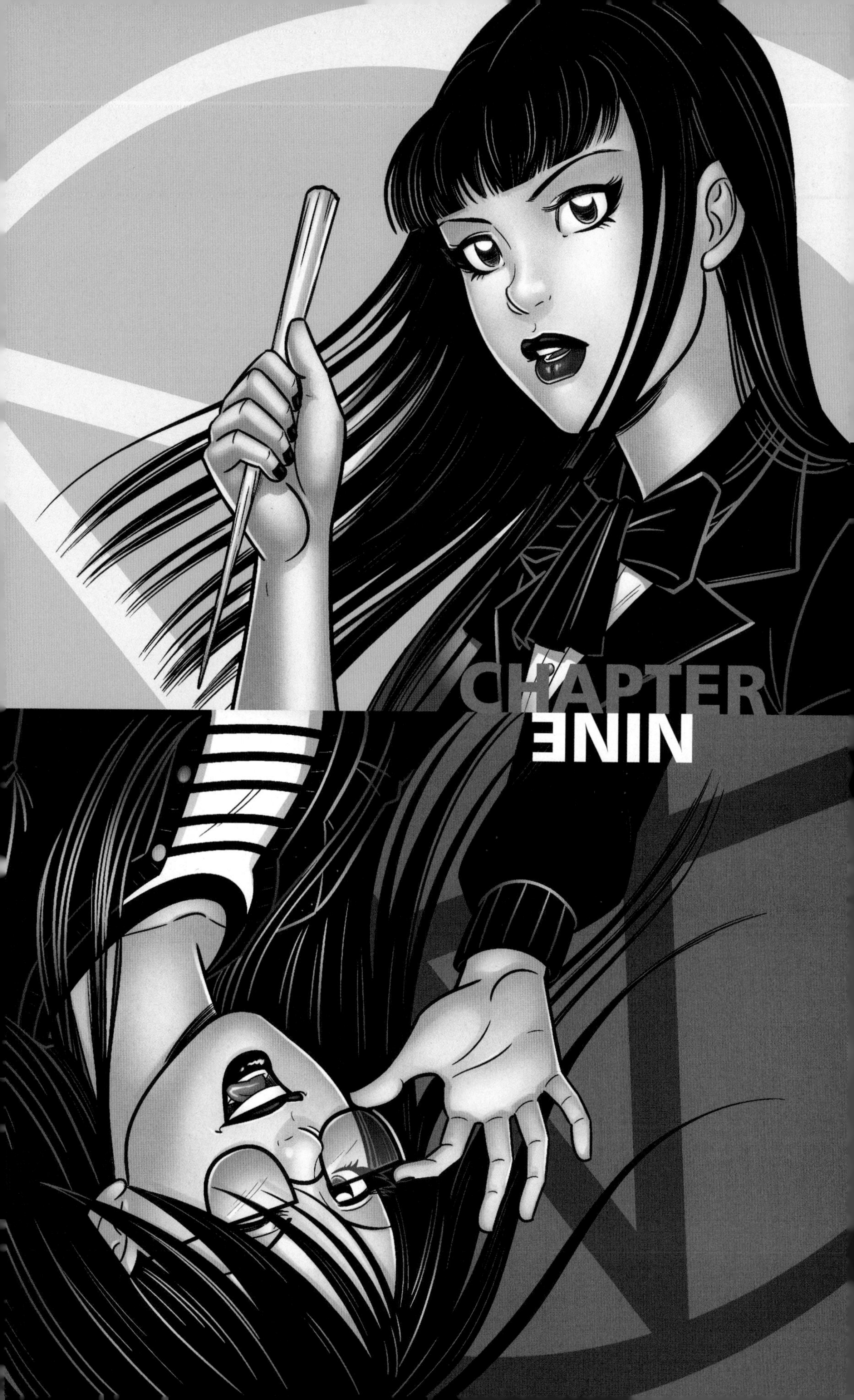
CHAPTER
NINE

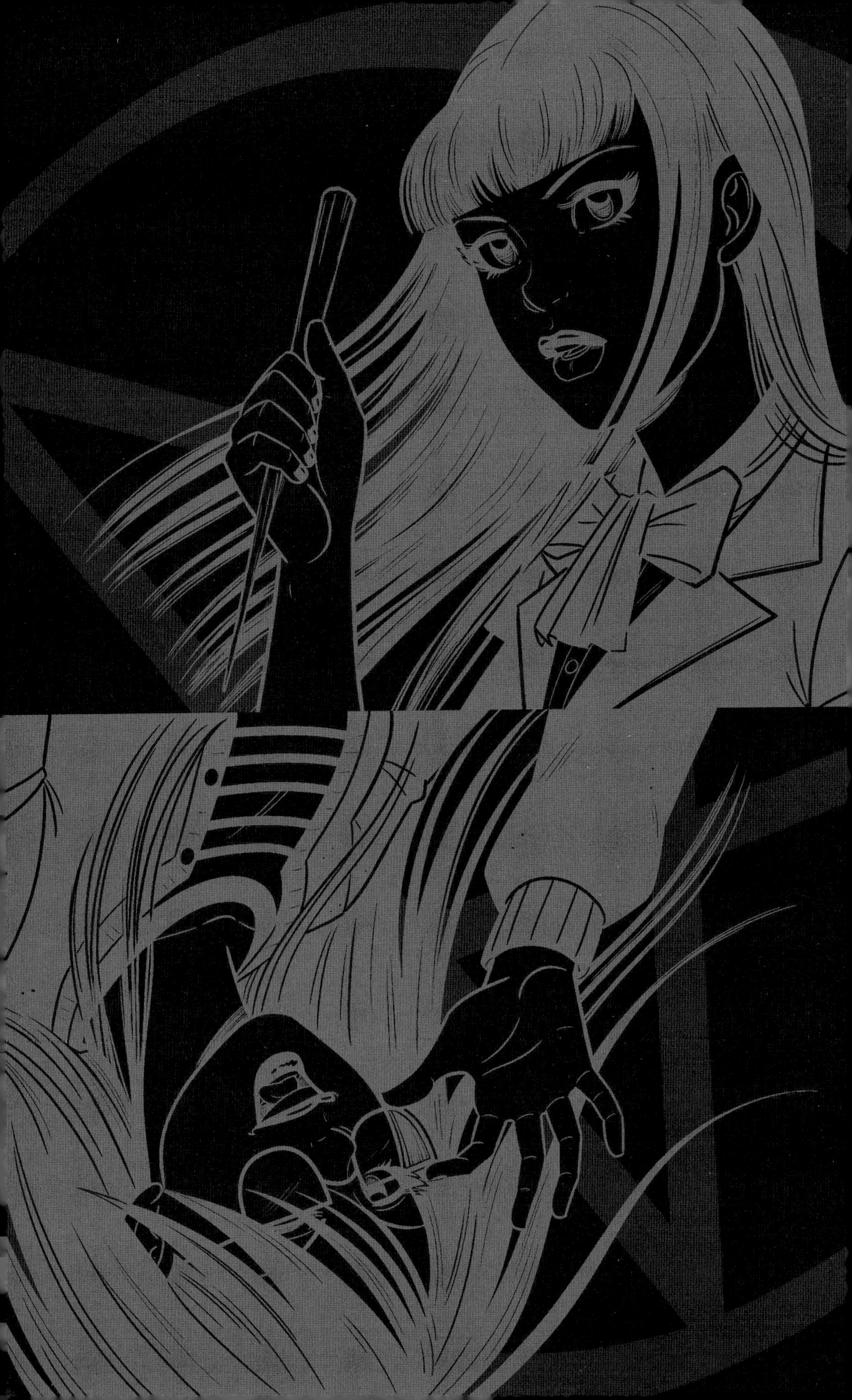

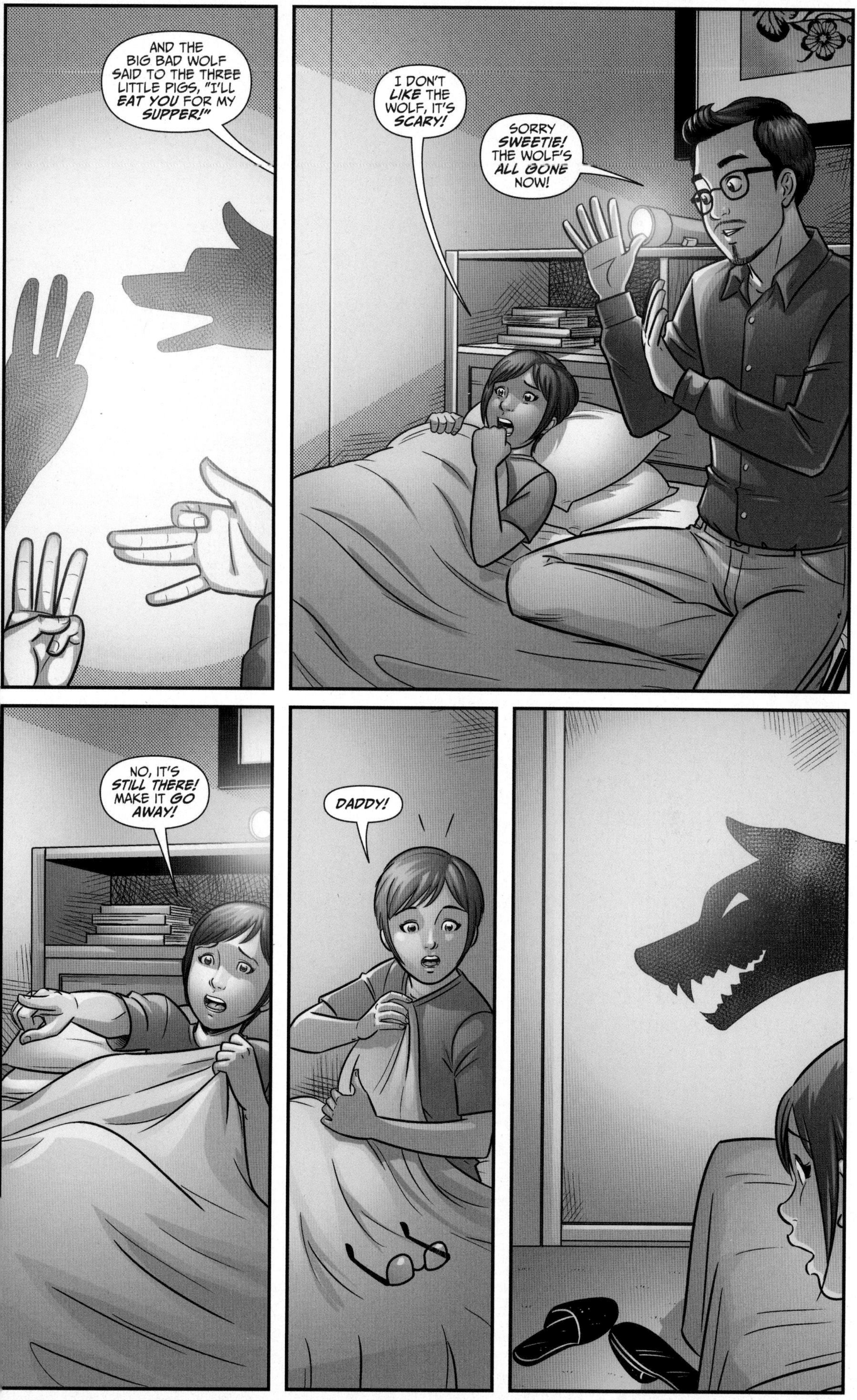
AND THE BIG BAD WOLF SAID TO THE THREE LITTLE PIGS, "I'LL *EAT YOU* FOR MY *SUPPER!*"
I DON'T *LIKE* THE WOLF, IT'S *SCARY!*
SORRY *SWEETIE!* THE WOLF'S *ALL GONE* NOW!
NO, IT'S *STILL THERE!* MAKE IT *GO AWAY!*
DADDY!

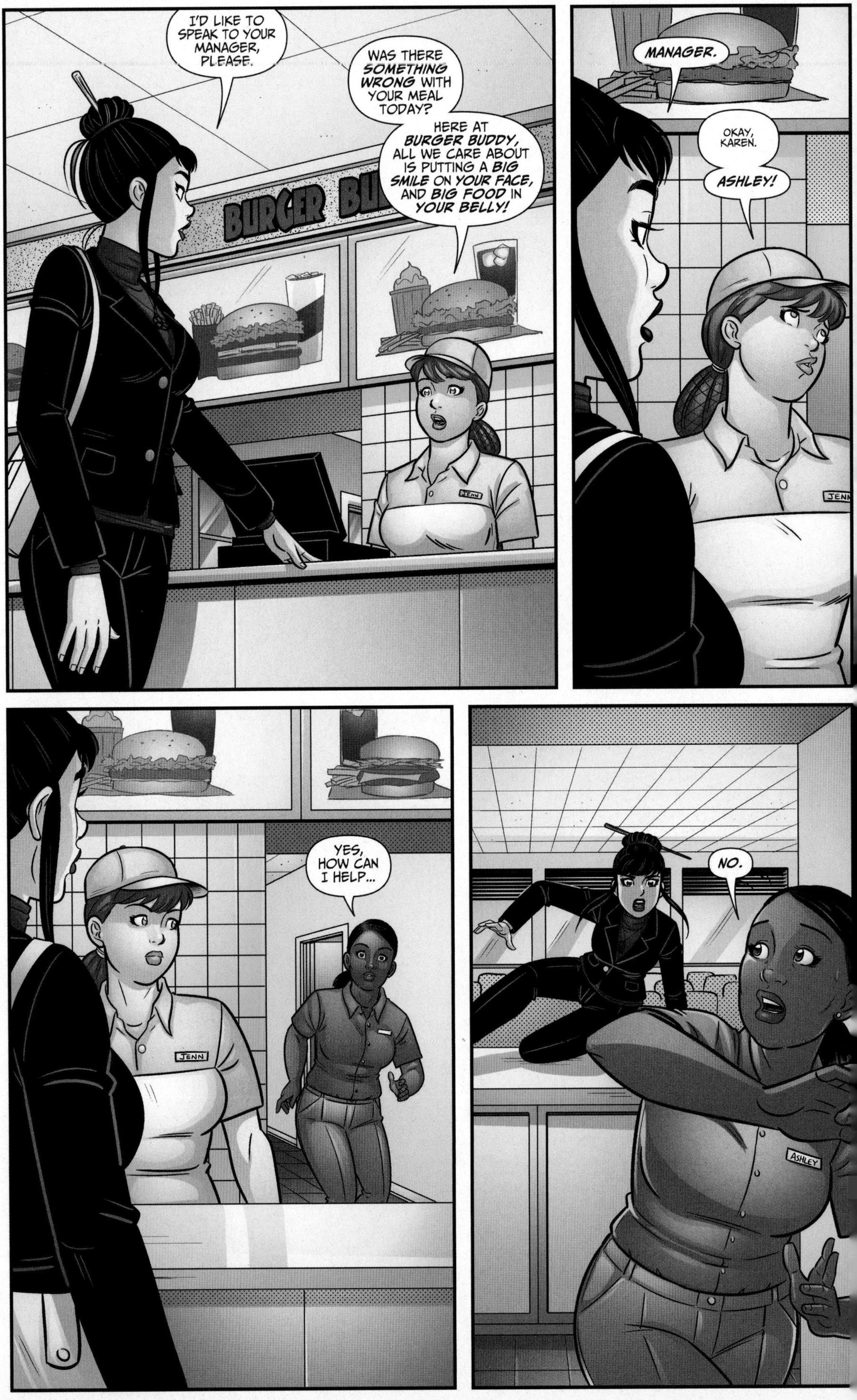
I'D LIKE TO SPEAK TO YOUR MANAGER, PLEASE.
WAS THERE SOMETHING WRONG WITH YOUR MEAL TODAY?
HERE AT BURGER BUDDY, ALL WE CARE ABOUT IS PUTTING A BIG SMILE ON YOUR FACE, AND BIG FOOD IN YOUR BELLY!
BURGER BU
JENN
MANAGER.
OKAY, KAREN.
ASHLEY!
JENN
YES, HOW CAN I HELP...
JENN
NO.
ASHLEY

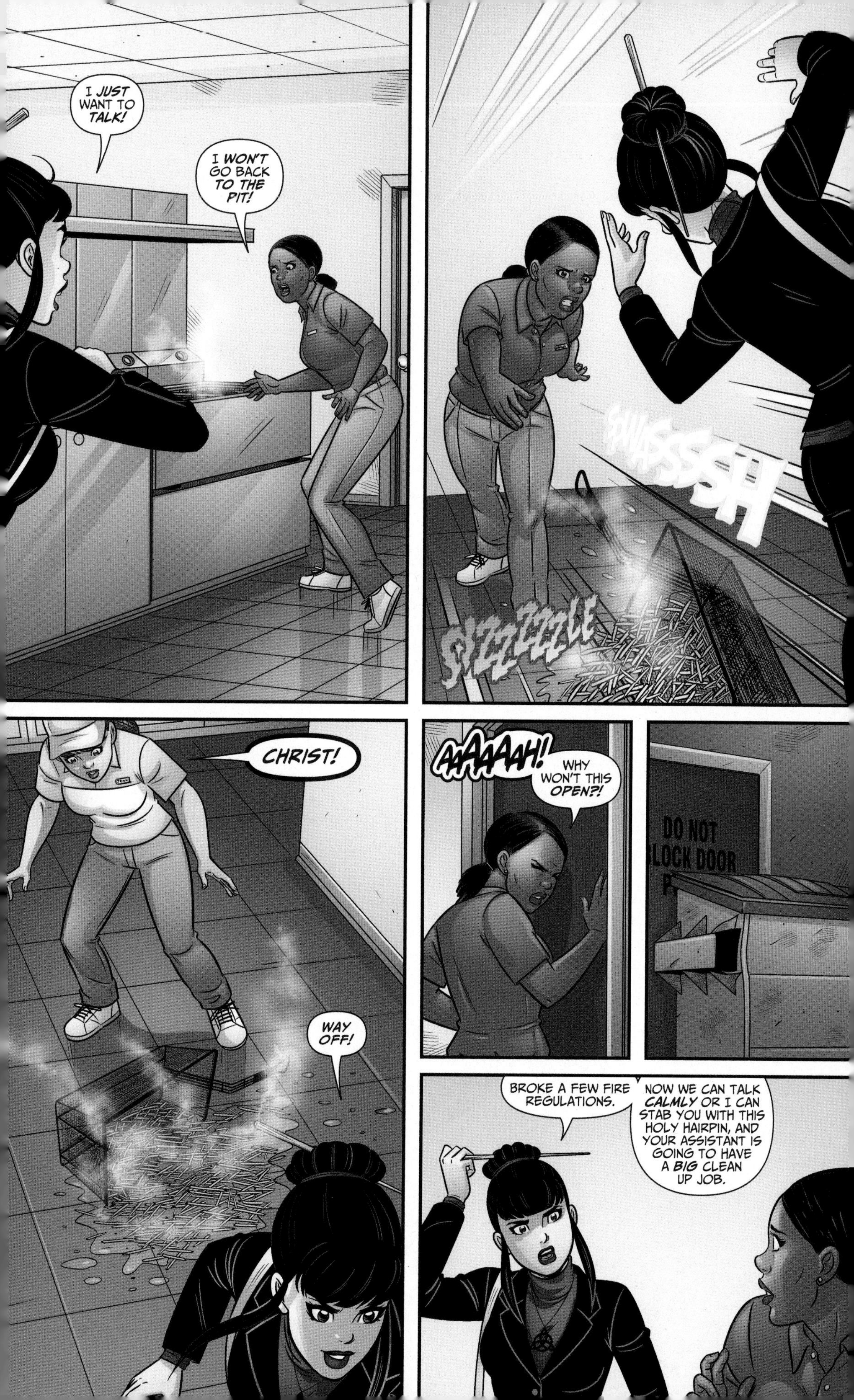
I JUST WANT TO TALK!
I WON'T GO BACK TO THE PIT!
FWASSSSSH
SIZZZZZLE
CHRIST!
WAY OFF!
AAAAAAH!
WHY WON'T THIS OPEN?!
DO NOT BLOCK DOOR
BROKE A FEW FIRE REGULATIONS.
NOW WE CAN TALK CALMLY OR I CAN STAB YOU WITH THIS HOLY HAIRPIN, AND YOUR ASSISTANT IS GOING TO HAVE A BIG CLEAN UP JOB.

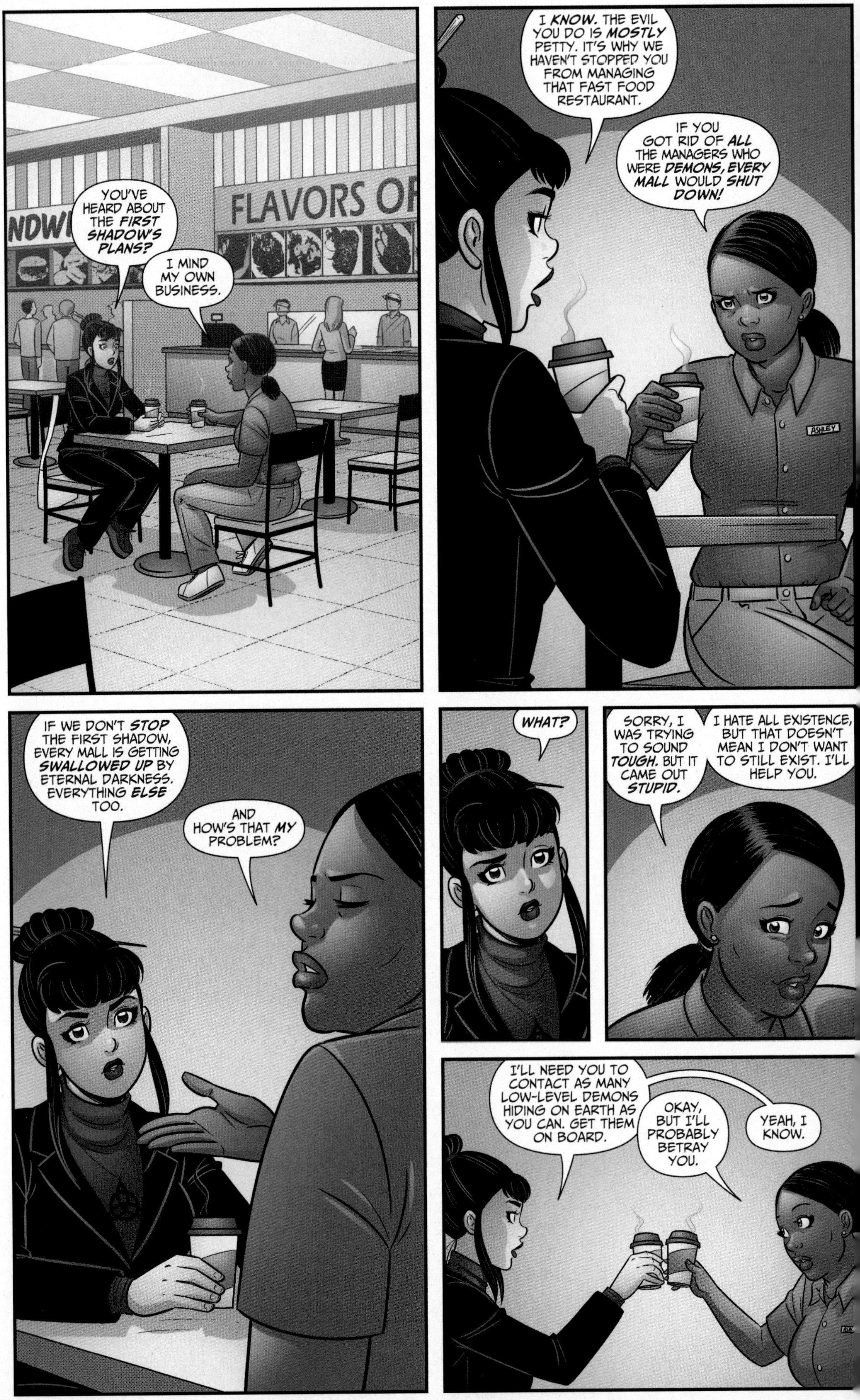

FLAVORS OF
NDWI
YOU'VE HEARD ABOUT THE FIRST SHADOW'S PLANS?
I MIND MY OWN BUSINESS.
I KNOW. THE EVIL YOU DO IS MOSTLY PETTY. IT'S WHY WE HAVEN'T STOPPED YOU FROM MANAGING THAT FAST FOOD RESTAURANT.
IF YOU GOT RID OF ALL THE MANAGERS WHO WERE DEMONS, EVERY MALL WOULD SHUT DOWN!
ASHLEY
IF WE DON'T STOP THE FIRST SHADOW, EVERY MALL IS GETTING SWALLOWED UP BY ETERNAL DARKNESS. EVERYTHING ELSE TOO.
AND HOW'S THAT MY PROBLEM?
WHAT?
SORRY, I WAS TRYING TO SOUND TOUGH. BUT IT CAME OUT STUPID.
I HATE ALL EXISTENCE, BUT THAT DOESN'T MEAN I DON'T WANT TO STILL EXIST. I'LL HELP YOU.
I'LL NEED YOU TO CONTACT AS MANY LOW-LEVEL DEMONS HIDING ON EARTH AS YOU CAN. GET THEM ON BOARD.
OKAY, BUT I'LL PROBABLY BETRAY YOU.
YEAH, I KNOW.

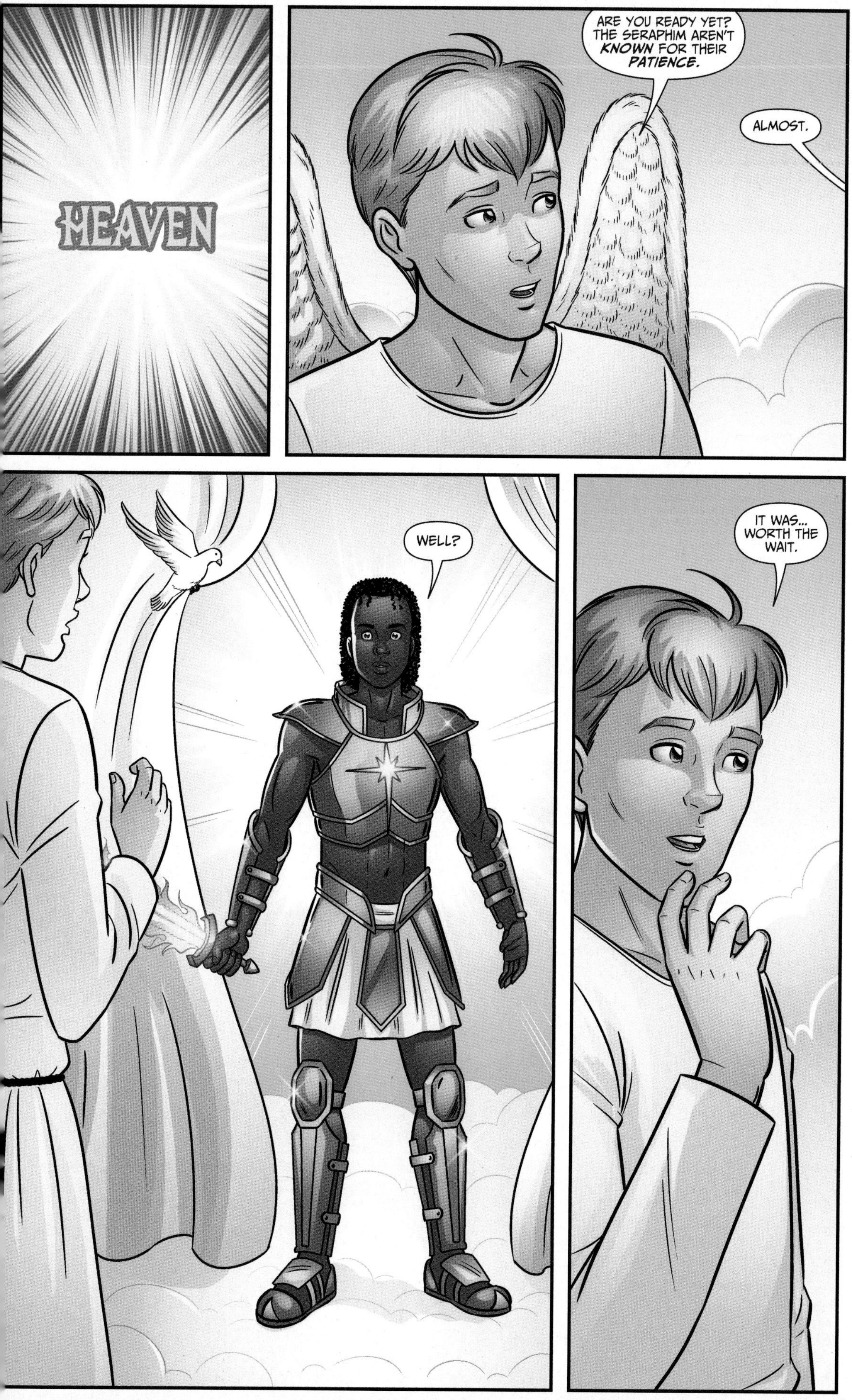
HEAVEN
ARE YOU READY YET? THE SERAPHIM AREN'T *KNOWN* FOR THEIR *PATIENCE.*
ALMOST.
WELL?
IT WAS... WORTH THE WAIT.

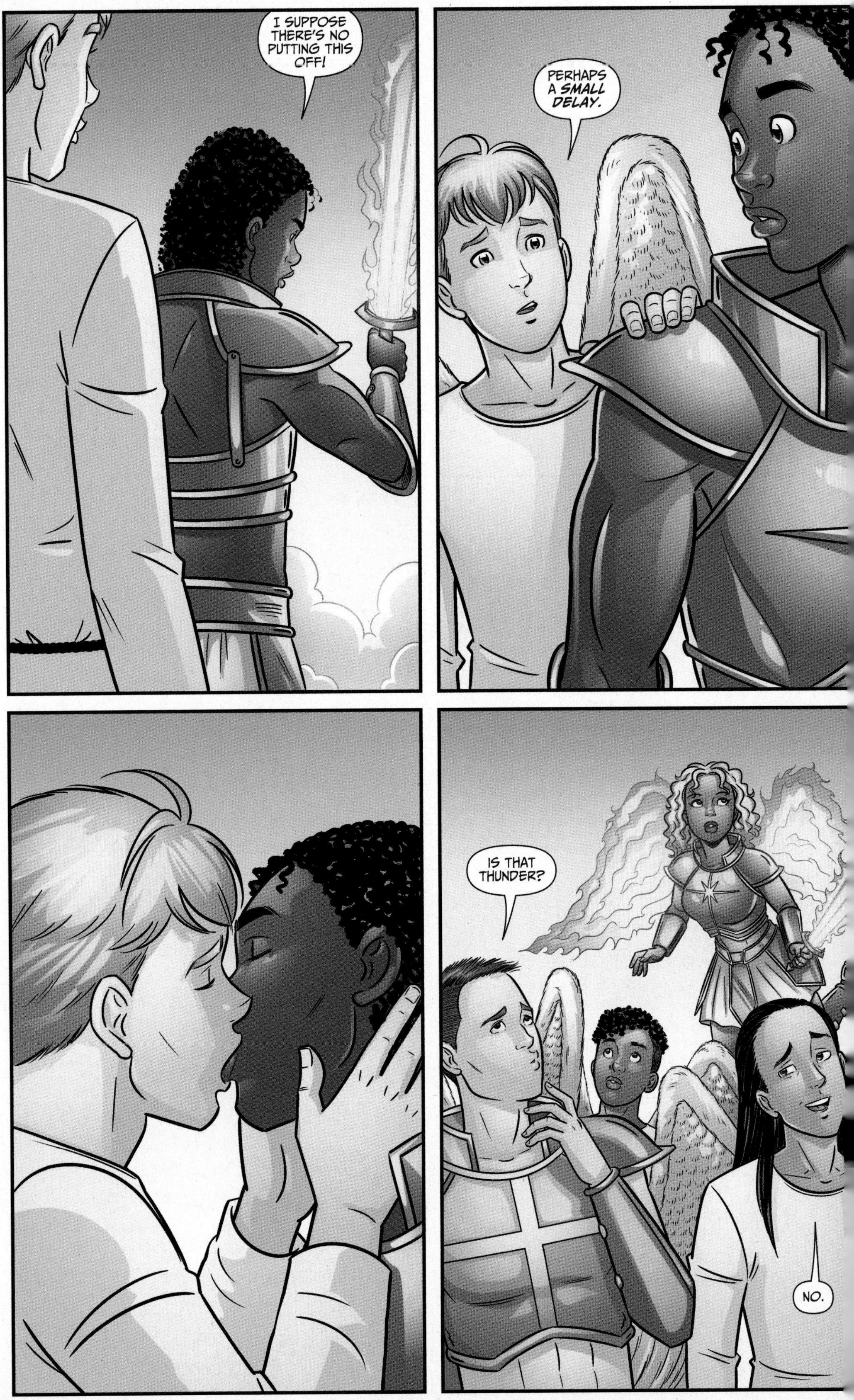
I SUPPOSE THERE'S NO PUTTING THIS OFF!
PERHAPS A SMALL DELAY.
IS THAT THUNDER?
NO.

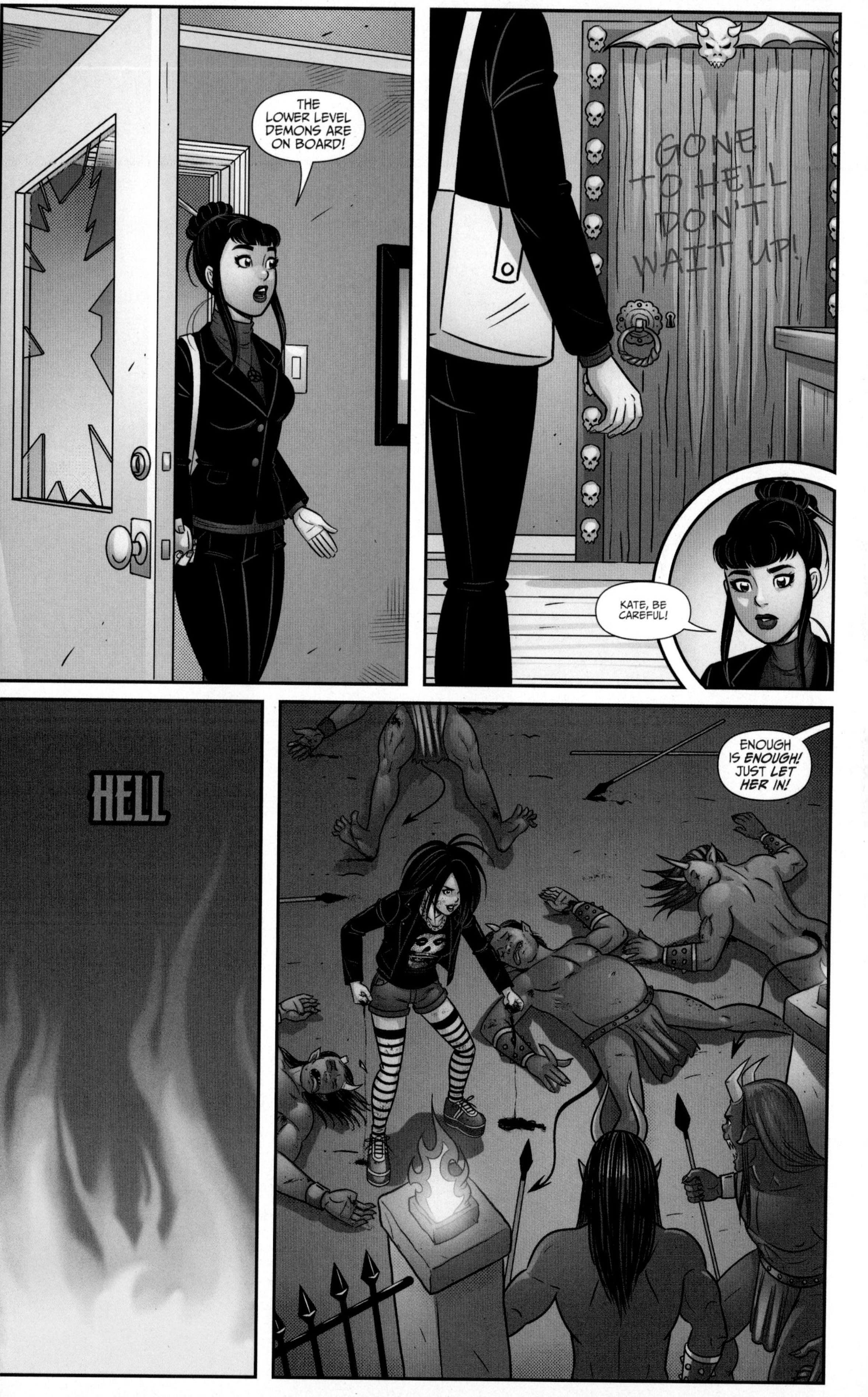
THE LOWER LEVEL DEMONS ARE ON BOARD!
GONE TO HELL DON'T WAIT UP!
KATE, BE CAREFUL!
HELL
ENOUGH IS ENOUGH! JUST LET HER IN!

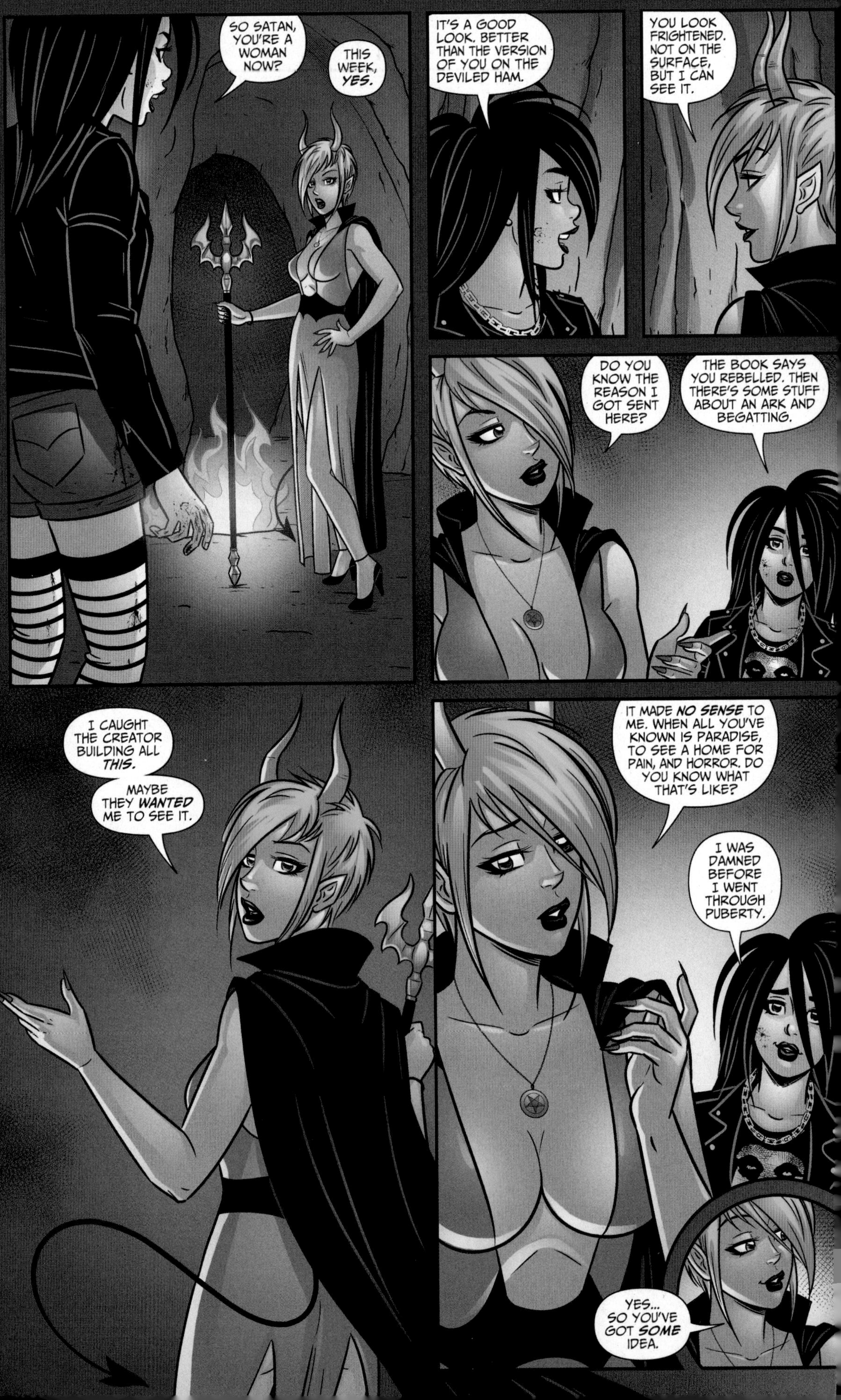
SO SATAN, YOU'RE A WOMAN NOW?
THIS WEEK, *YES.*
IT'S A GOOD LOOK. BETTER THAN THE VERSION OF YOU ON THE DEVILED HAM.
YOU LOOK FRIGHTENED. NOT ON THE SURFACE, BUT I CAN SEE IT.
DO YOU KNOW THE REASON I GOT SENT HERE?
THE BOOK SAYS YOU REBELLED. THEN THERE'S SOME STUFF ABOUT AN ARK AND BEGATTING.
I CAUGHT THE CREATOR BUILDING ALL *THIS.*
MAYBE THEY *WANTED* ME TO SEE IT.
IT MADE *NO SENSE* TO ME. WHEN ALL YOU'VE KNOWN IS PARADISE, TO SEE A HOME FOR PAIN, AND HORROR. DO YOU KNOW WHAT THAT'S LIKE?
I WAS DAMNED BEFORE I WENT THROUGH PUBERTY.
YES... SO YOU'VE GOT *SOME* IDEA.

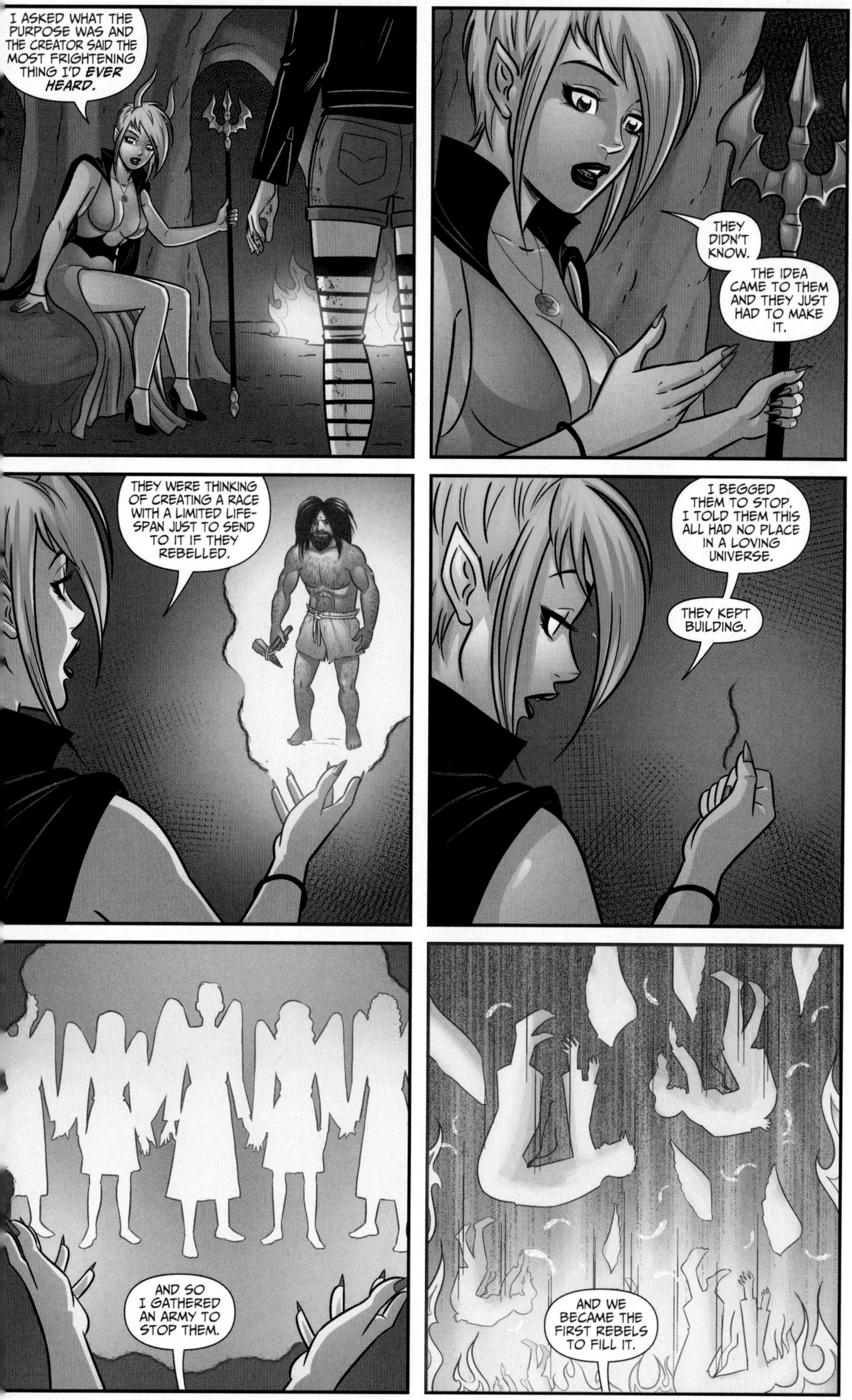
I ASKED WHAT THE PURPOSE WAS AND THE CREATOR SAID THE MOST FRIGHTENING THING I'D *EVER HEARD.*
THEY DIDN'T KNOW.
THE IDEA CAME TO THEM AND THEY JUST HAD TO MAKE IT.
THEY WERE THINKING OF CREATING A RACE WITH A LIMITED LIFE-SPAN JUST TO SEND TO IT IF THEY REBELLED.
I BEGGED THEM TO STOP. I TOLD THEM THIS ALL HAD NO PLACE IN A LOVING UNIVERSE.
THEY KEPT BUILDING.
AND SO I GATHERED AN ARMY TO STOP THEM.
AND WE BECAME THE FIRST REBELS TO FILL IT.

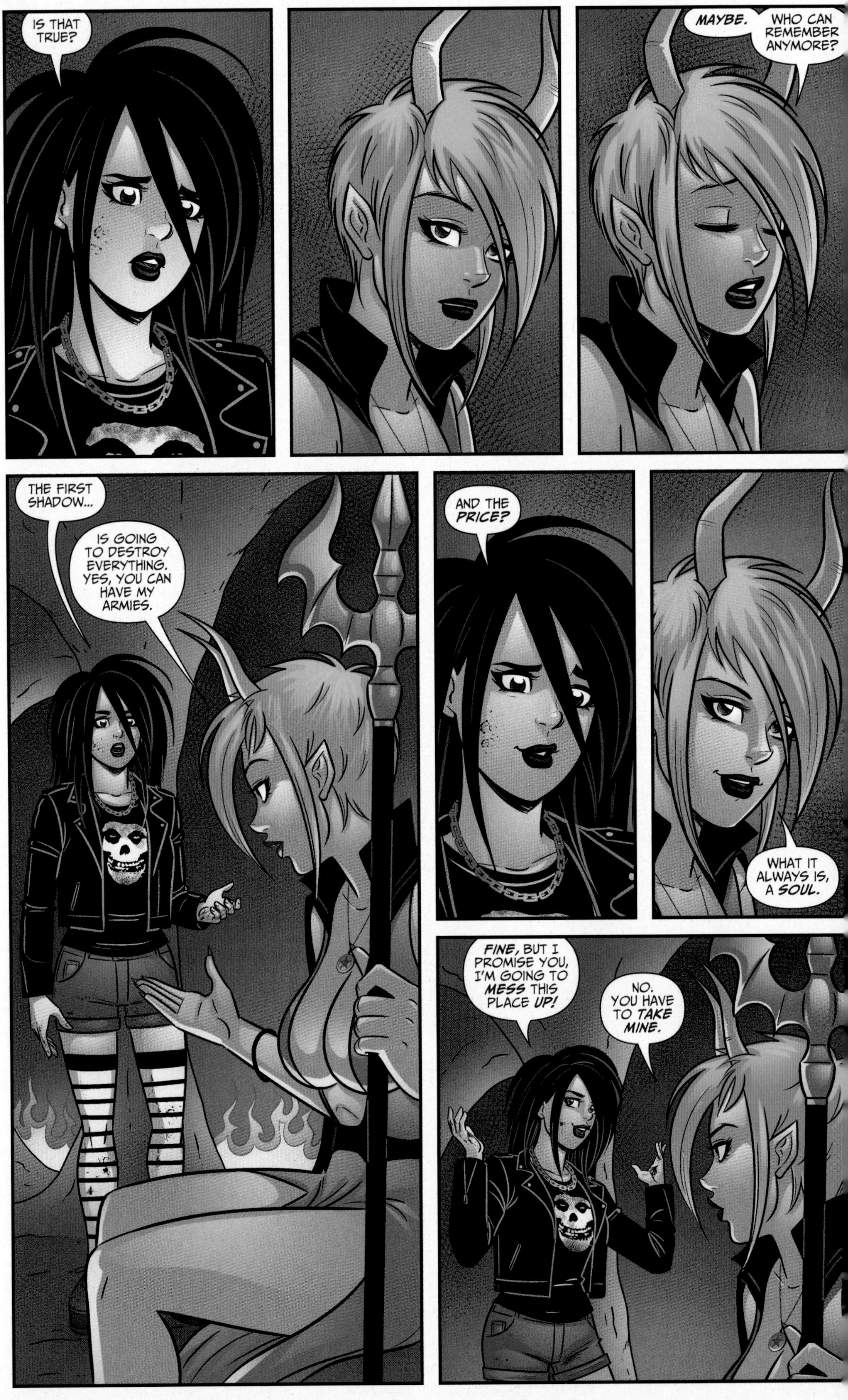
IS THAT TRUE?
MAYBE.
WHO CAN REMEMBER ANYMORE?
THE FIRST SHADOW...
IS GOING TO DESTROY EVERYTHING. YES, YOU CAN HAVE MY ARMIES.
AND THE PRICE?
WHAT IT ALWAYS IS, A SOUL.
FINE, BUT I PROMISE YOU, I'M GOING TO MESS THIS PLACE UP!
NO. YOU HAVE TO TAKE MINE.

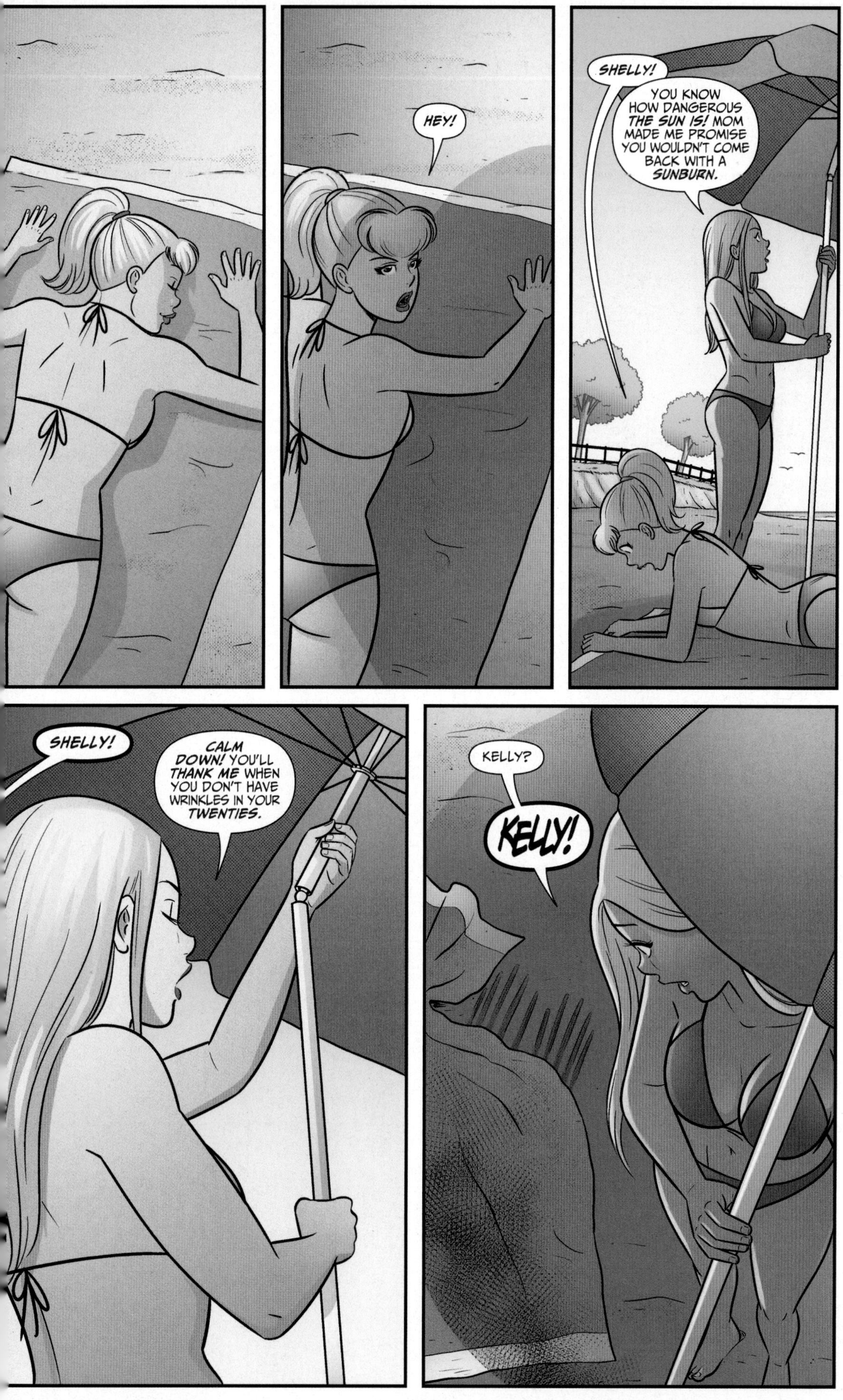
HEY!
SHELLY!
YOU KNOW HOW DANGEROUS THE SUN IS! MOM MADE ME PROMISE YOU WOULDN'T COME BACK WITH A SUNBURN.
SHELLY!
CALM DOWN! YOU'LL THANK ME WHEN YOU DON'T HAVE WRINKLES IN YOUR TWENTIES.
KELLY?
KELLY!

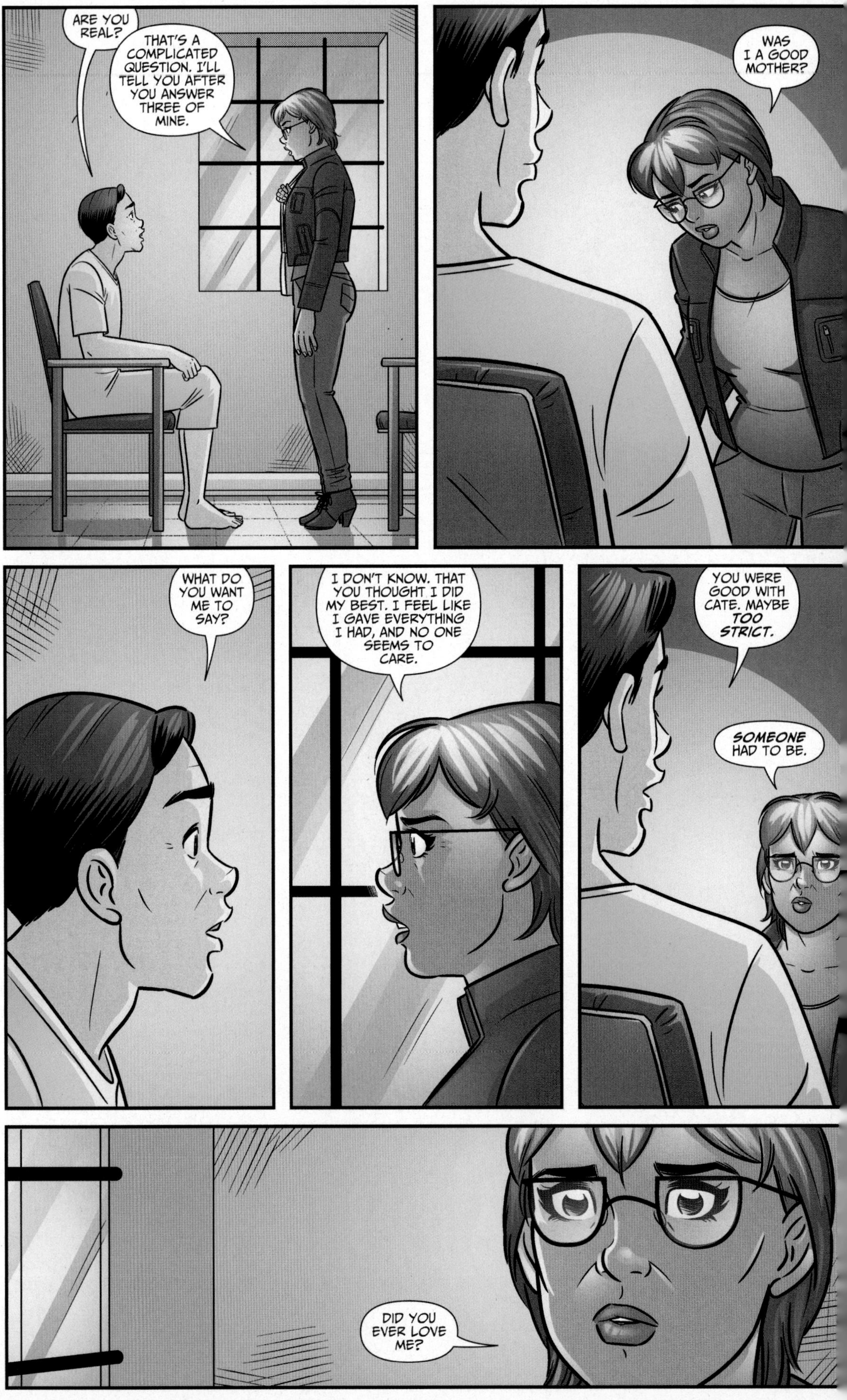
ARE YOU REAL?
THAT'S A COMPLICATED QUESTION. I'LL TELL YOU AFTER YOU ANSWER THREE OF MINE.
WAS I A GOOD MOTHER?
WHAT DO YOU WANT ME TO SAY?
I DON'T KNOW. THAT YOU THOUGHT I DID MY BEST. I FEEL LIKE I GAVE EVERYTHING I HAD, AND NO ONE SEEMS TO CARE.
YOU WERE GOOD WITH CATE. MAYBE TOO STRICT.
SOMEONE HAD TO BE.
DID YOU EVER LOVE ME?

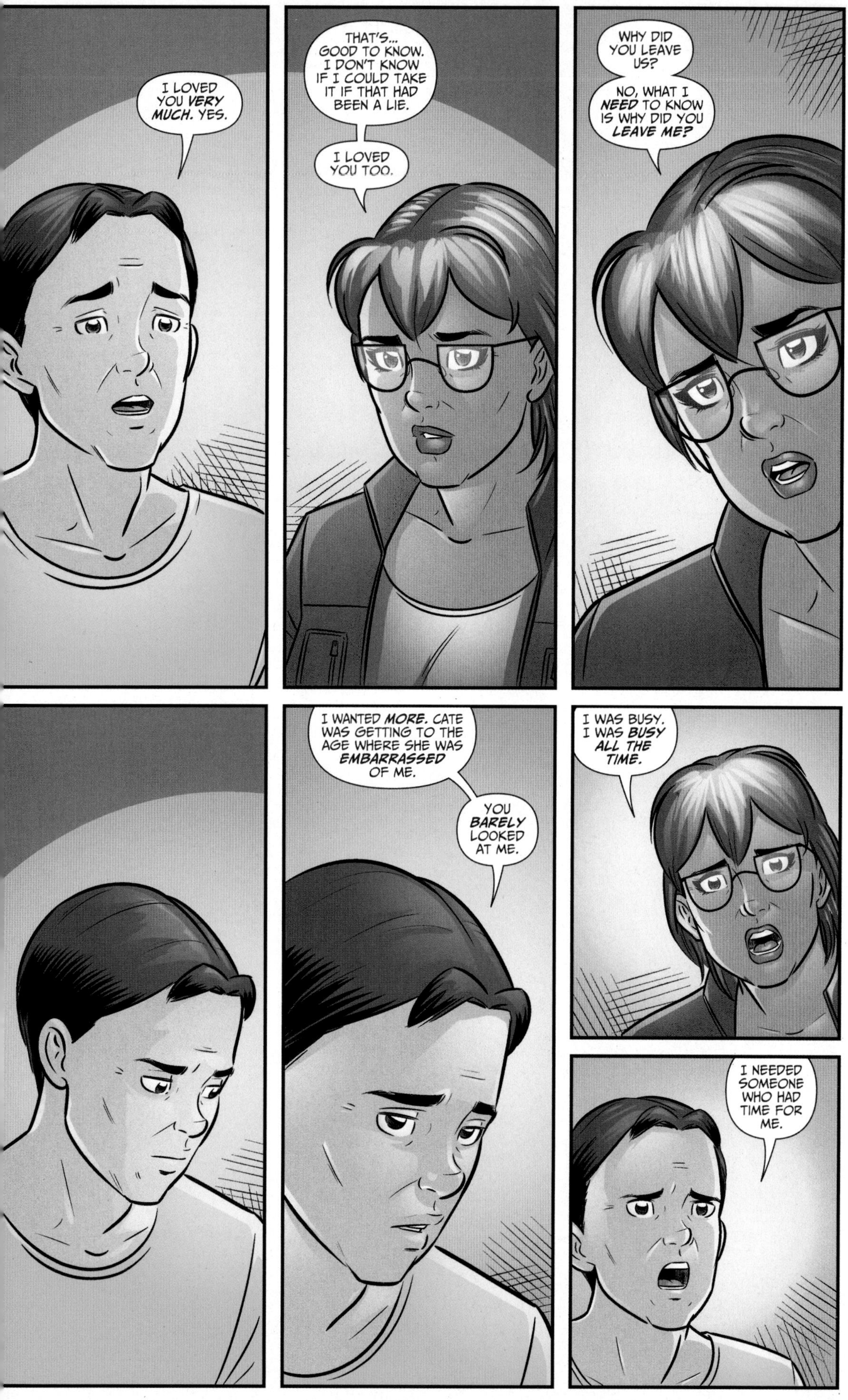
I LOVED YOU **VERY MUCH.** YES.
THAT'S... GOOD TO KNOW. I DON'T KNOW IF I COULD TAKE IT IF THAT HAD BEEN A LIE.
I LOVED YOU TOO.
WHY DID YOU LEAVE US?
NO, WHAT I **NEED** TO KNOW IS WHY DID YOU **LEAVE ME?**
I WANTED **MORE.** CATE WAS GETTING TO THE AGE WHERE SHE WAS **EMBARRASSED** OF ME.
YOU **BARELY** LOOKED AT ME.
I WAS BUSY. I WAS **BUSY ALL THE TIME.**
I NEEDED SOMEONE WHO HAD TIME FOR ME.

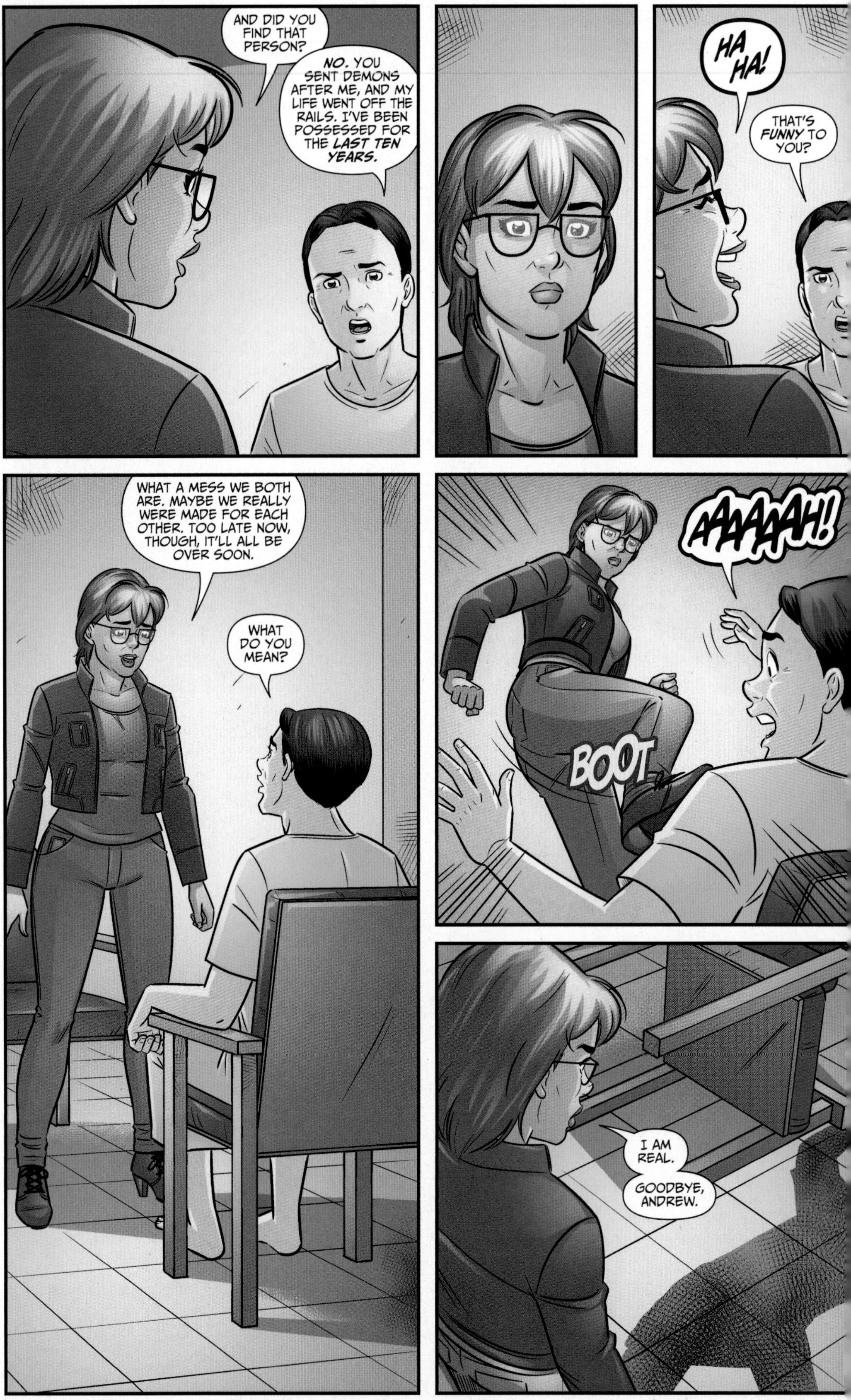
AND DID YOU FIND THAT PERSON?
NO. YOU SENT DEMONS AFTER ME, AND MY LIFE WENT OFF THE RAILS. I'VE BEEN POSSESSED FOR THE LAST TEN YEARS.
HA HA!
THAT'S FUNNY TO YOU?
WHAT A MESS WE BOTH ARE. MAYBE WE REALLY WERE MADE FOR EACH OTHER. TOO LATE NOW, THOUGH, IT'LL ALL BE OVER SOON.
WHAT DO YOU MEAN?
AAAAAAH!
BOOT
I AM REAL.
GOODBYE, ANDREW.

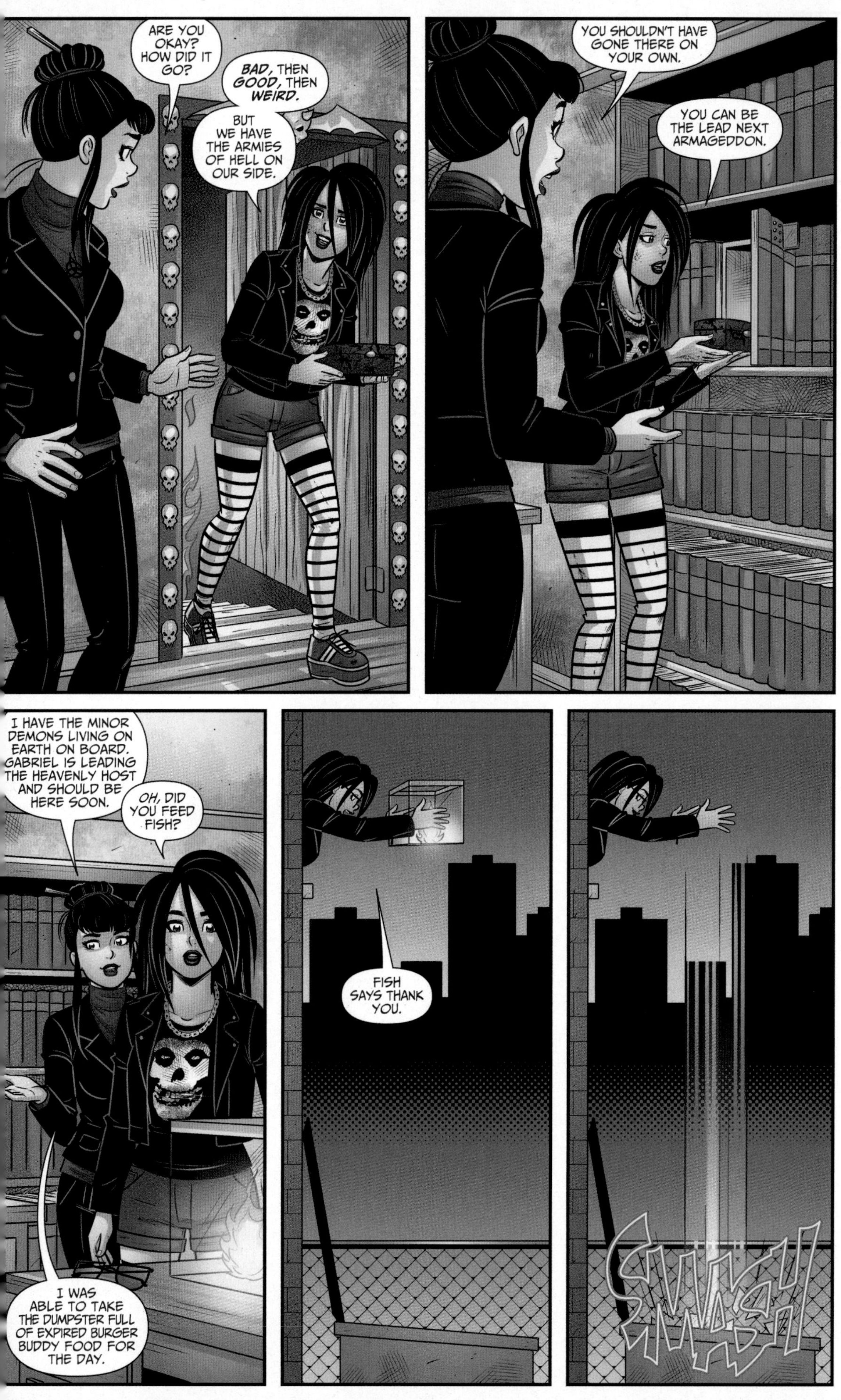
ARE YOU OKAY? HOW DID IT GO?
BAD, THEN *GOOD*, THEN *WEIRD.*
BUT WE HAVE THE ARMIES OF HELL ON OUR SIDE.
YOU SHOULDN'T HAVE GONE THERE ON YOUR OWN.
YOU CAN BE THE LEAD NEXT ARMAGEDDON.
I HAVE THE MINOR DEMONS LIVING ON EARTH ON BOARD. GABRIEL IS LEADING THE HEAVENLY HOST AND SHOULD BE HERE SOON.
OH, DID YOU FEED FISH?
I WAS ABLE TO TAKE THE DUMPSTER FULL OF EXPIRED BURGER BUDDY FOOD FOR THE DAY.
FISH SAYS THANK YOU.
SMASH

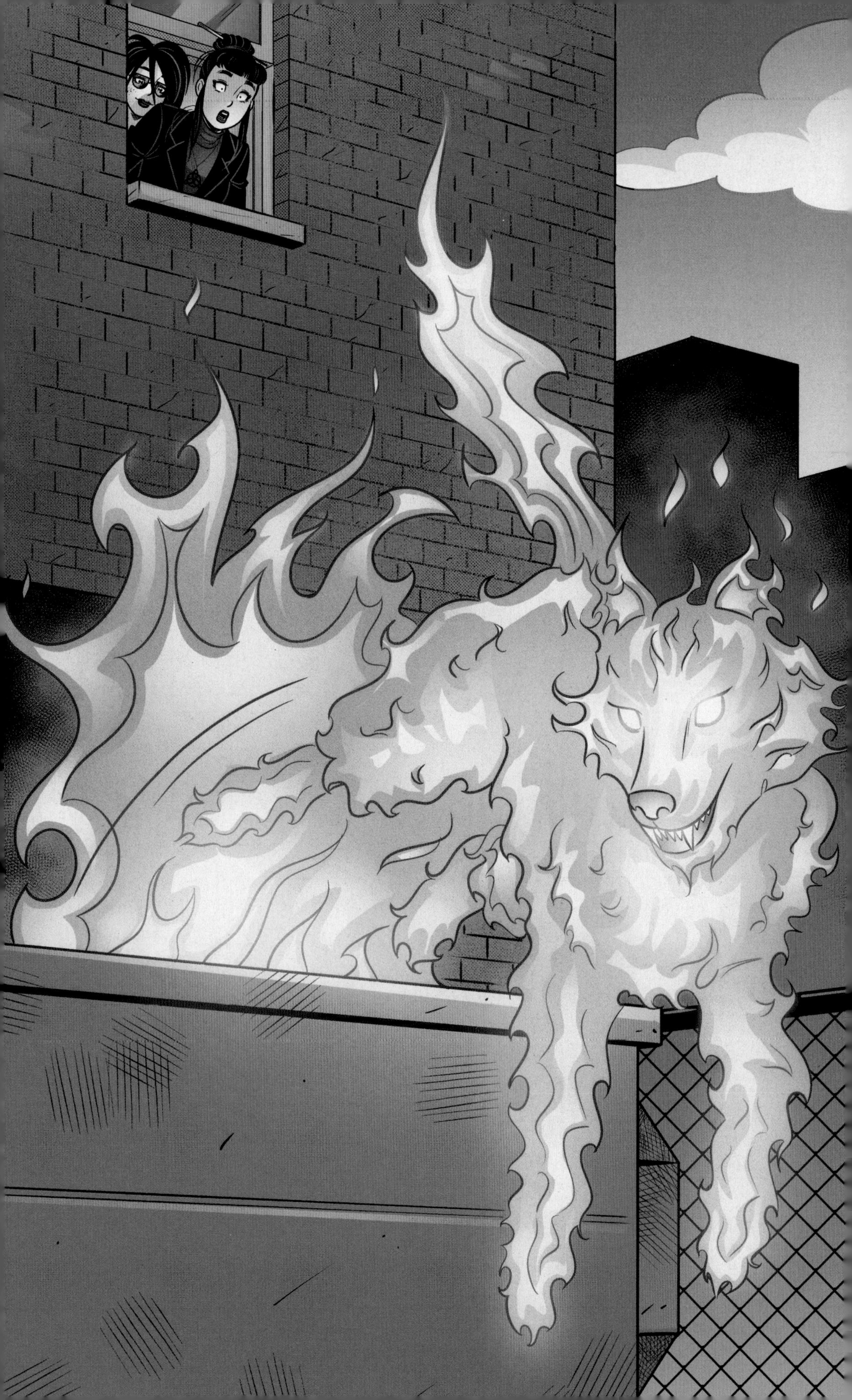

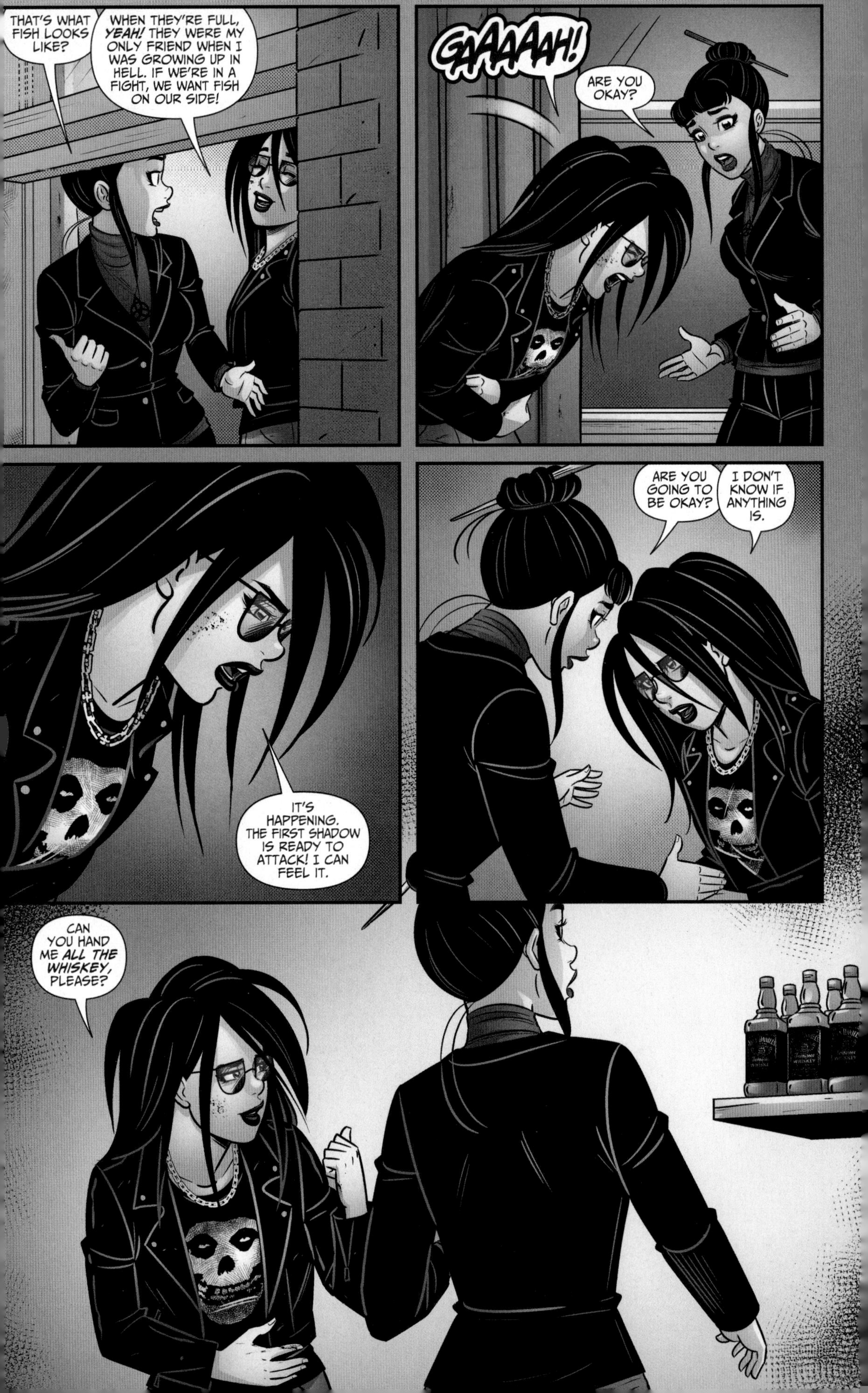
THAT'S WHAT FISH LOOKS LIKE?
WHEN THEY'RE FULL, *YEAH!* THEY WERE MY ONLY FRIEND WHEN I WAS GROWING UP IN HELL. IF WE'RE IN A FIGHT, WE WANT FISH ON OUR SIDE!
GAAAAAH!
ARE YOU OKAY?
IT'S HAPPENING. THE FIRST SHADOW IS READY TO ATTACK! I CAN FEEL IT.
ARE YOU GOING TO BE OKAY?
I DON'T KNOW IF ANYTHING IS.
CAN YOU HAND ME *ALL THE WHISKEY*, PLEASE?

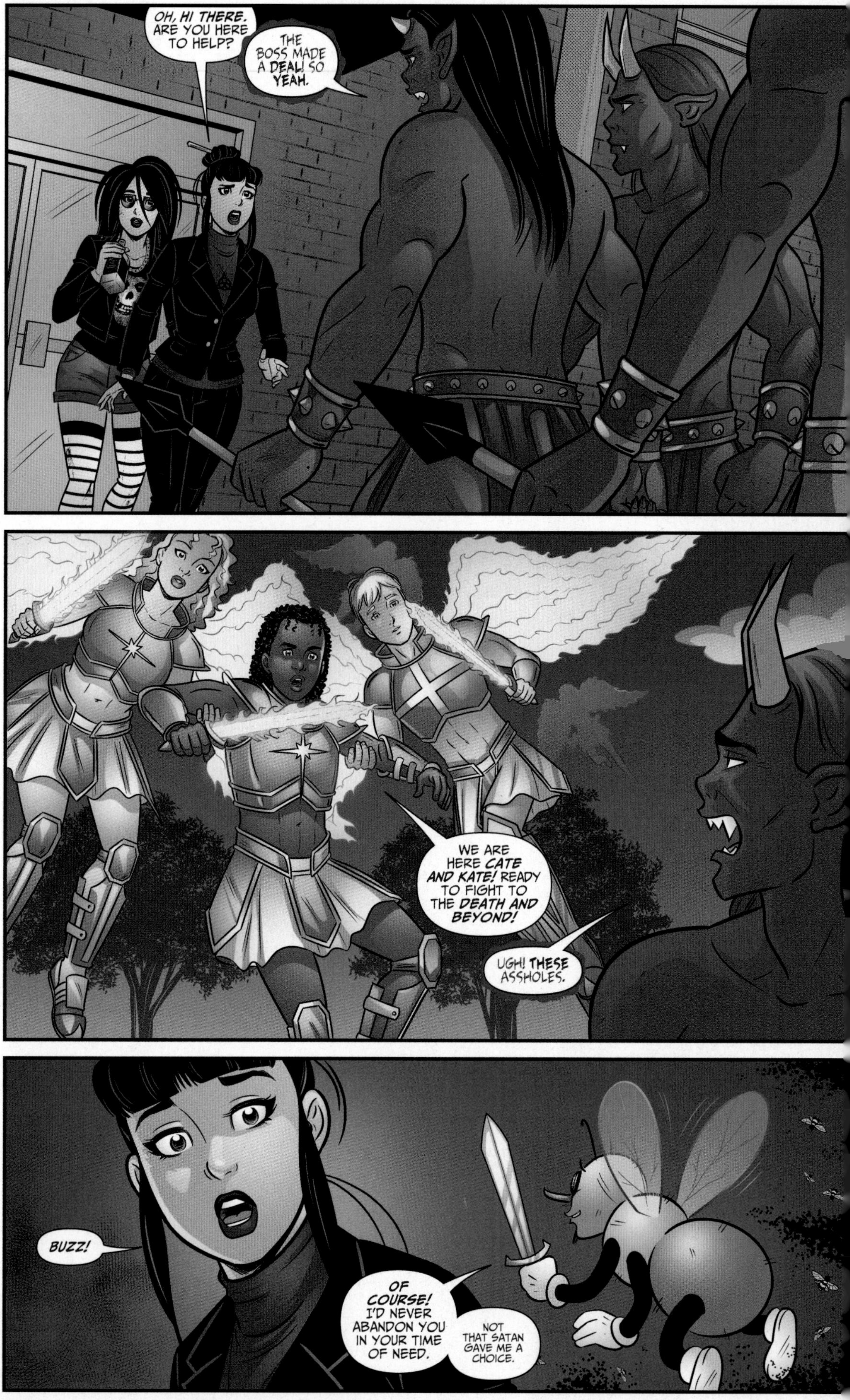
OH, HI THERE. ARE YOU HERE TO HELP?
THE BOSS MADE A DEAL! SO YEAH.
WE ARE HERE CATE AND KATE! READY TO FIGHT TO THE DEATH AND BEYOND!
UGH! THESE ASSHOLES.
BUZZ!
OF COURSE! I'D NEVER ABANDON YOU IN YOUR TIME OF NEED.
NOT THAT SATAN GAVE ME A CHOICE.

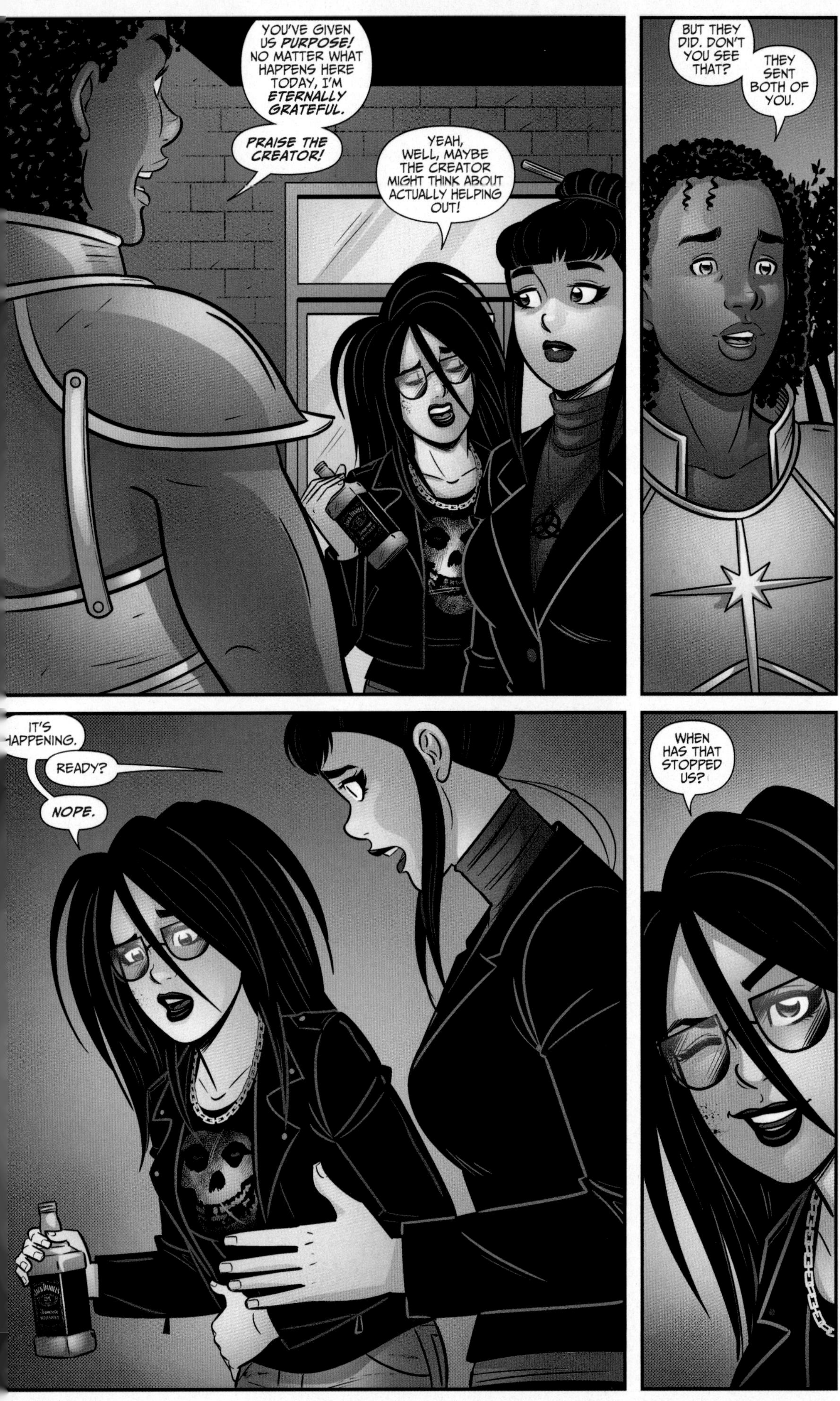
YOU'VE GIVEN US PURPOSE! NO MATTER WHAT HAPPENS HERE TODAY, I'M ETERNALLY GRATEFUL.
PRAISE THE CREATOR!
YEAH, WELL, MAYBE THE CREATOR MIGHT THINK ABOUT ACTUALLY HELPING OUT!
BUT THEY DID. DON'T YOU SEE THAT?
THEY SENT BOTH OF YOU.
IT'S HAPPENING.
READY?
NOPE.
WHEN HAS THAT STOPPED US?

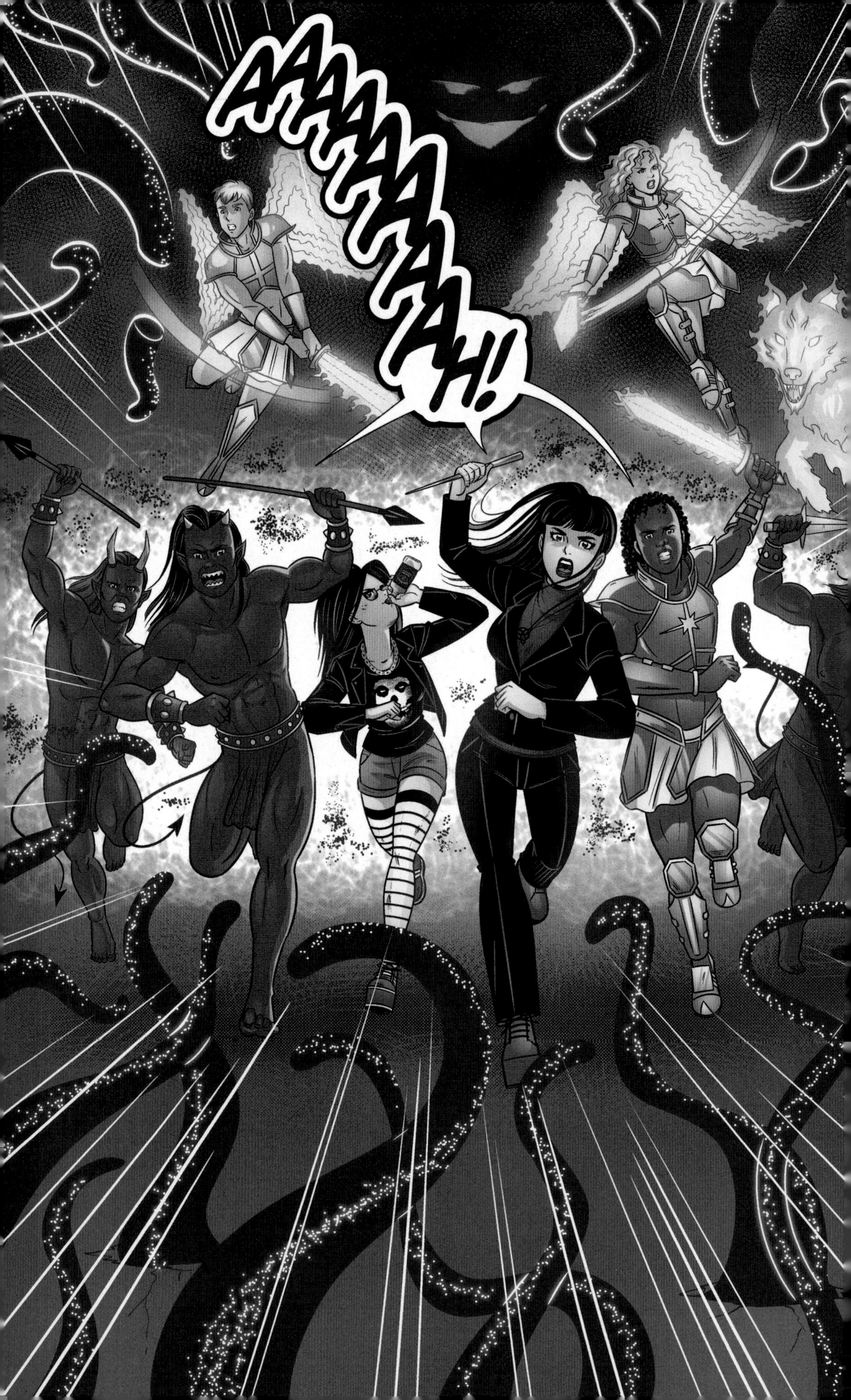
AAAAAAAAH!

CHAPTER TEN

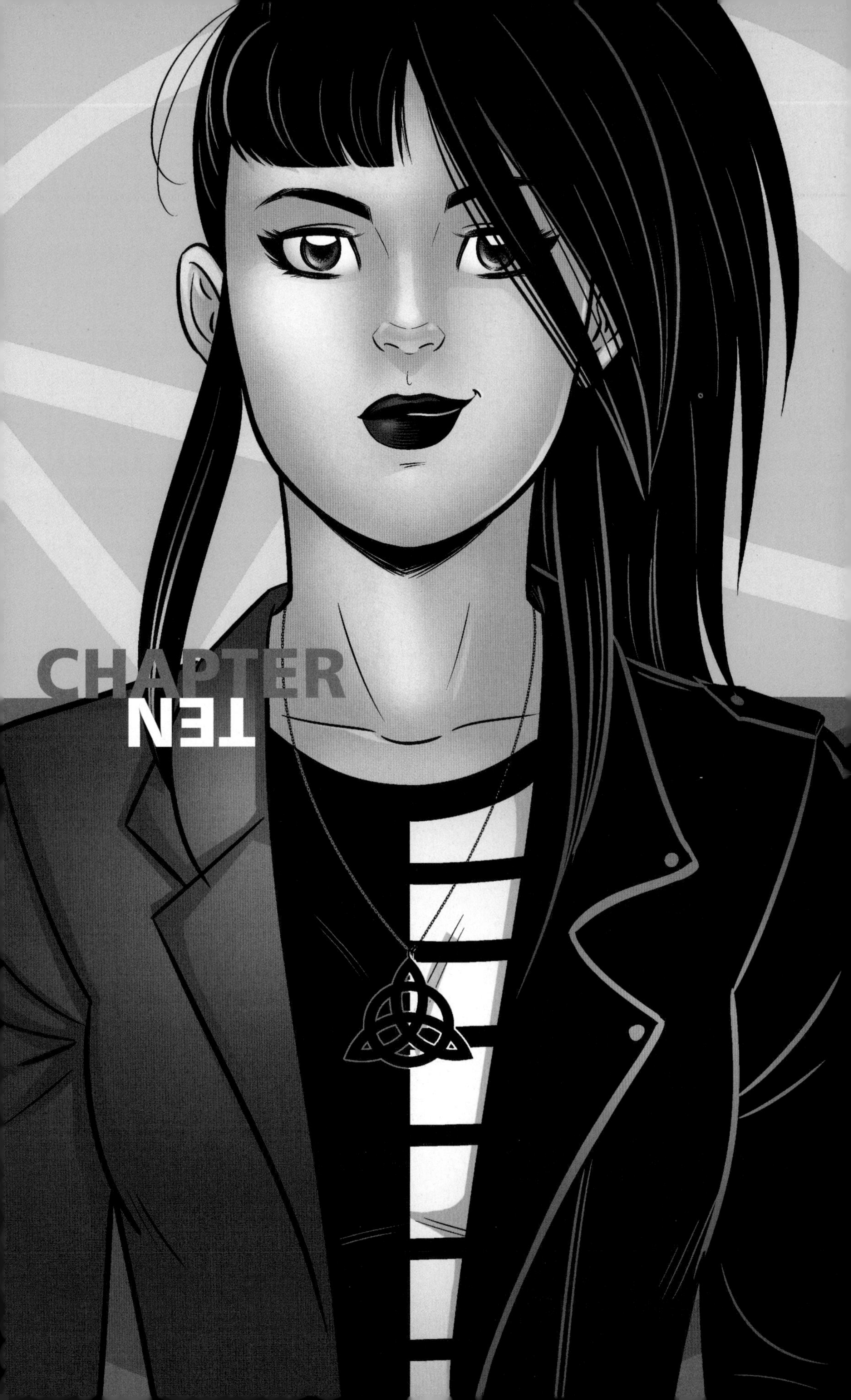

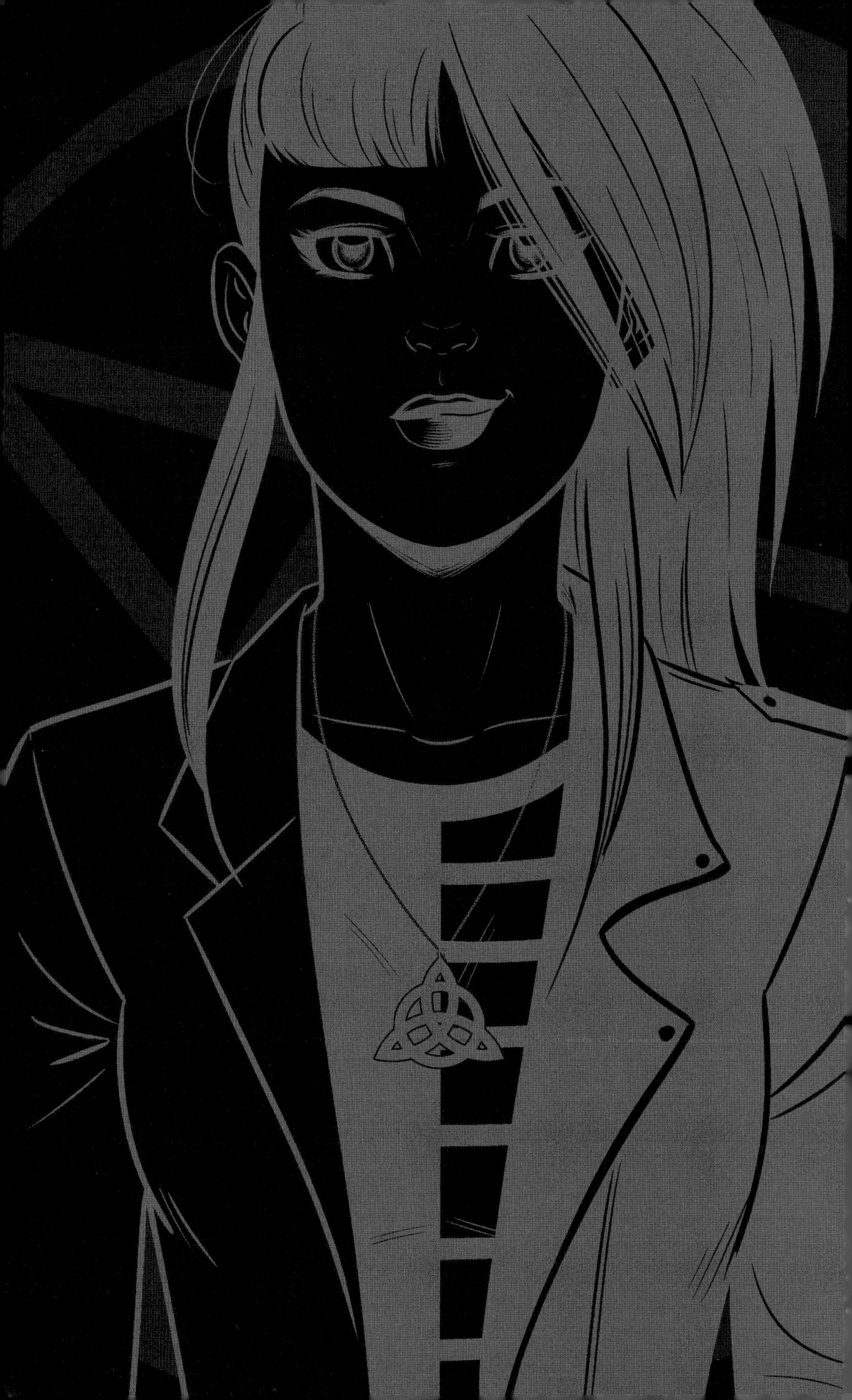

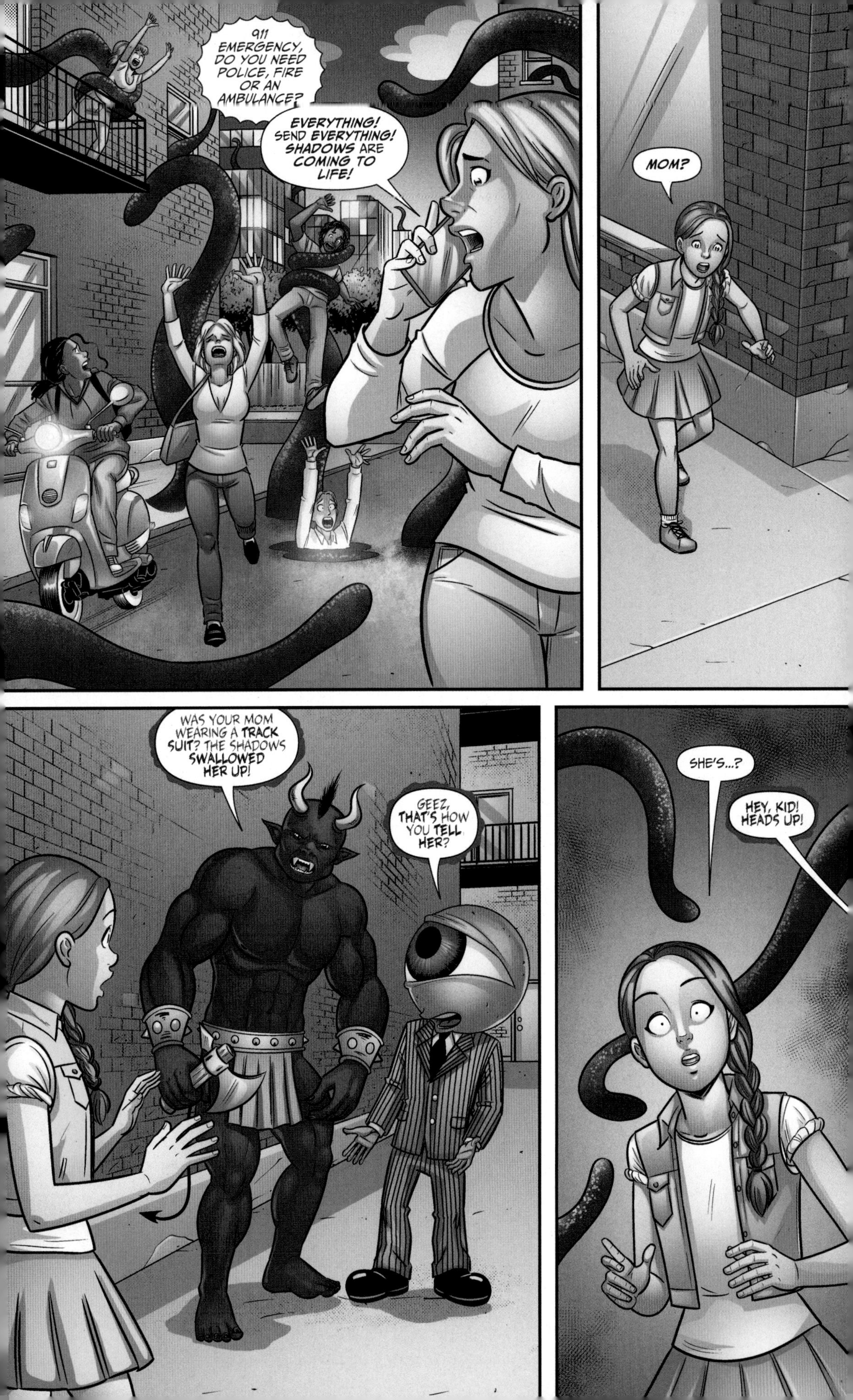
911 EMERGENCY, DO YOU NEED POLICE, FIRE OR AN AMBULANCE?
EVERYTHING! SEND EVERYTHING! SHADOWS ARE COMING TO LIFE!
MOM?
WAS YOUR MOM WEARING A TRACK SUIT? THE SHADOWS SWALLOWED HER UP!
GEEZ, THAT'S HOW YOU TELL HER?
SHE'S...?
HEY, KID! HEADS UP!

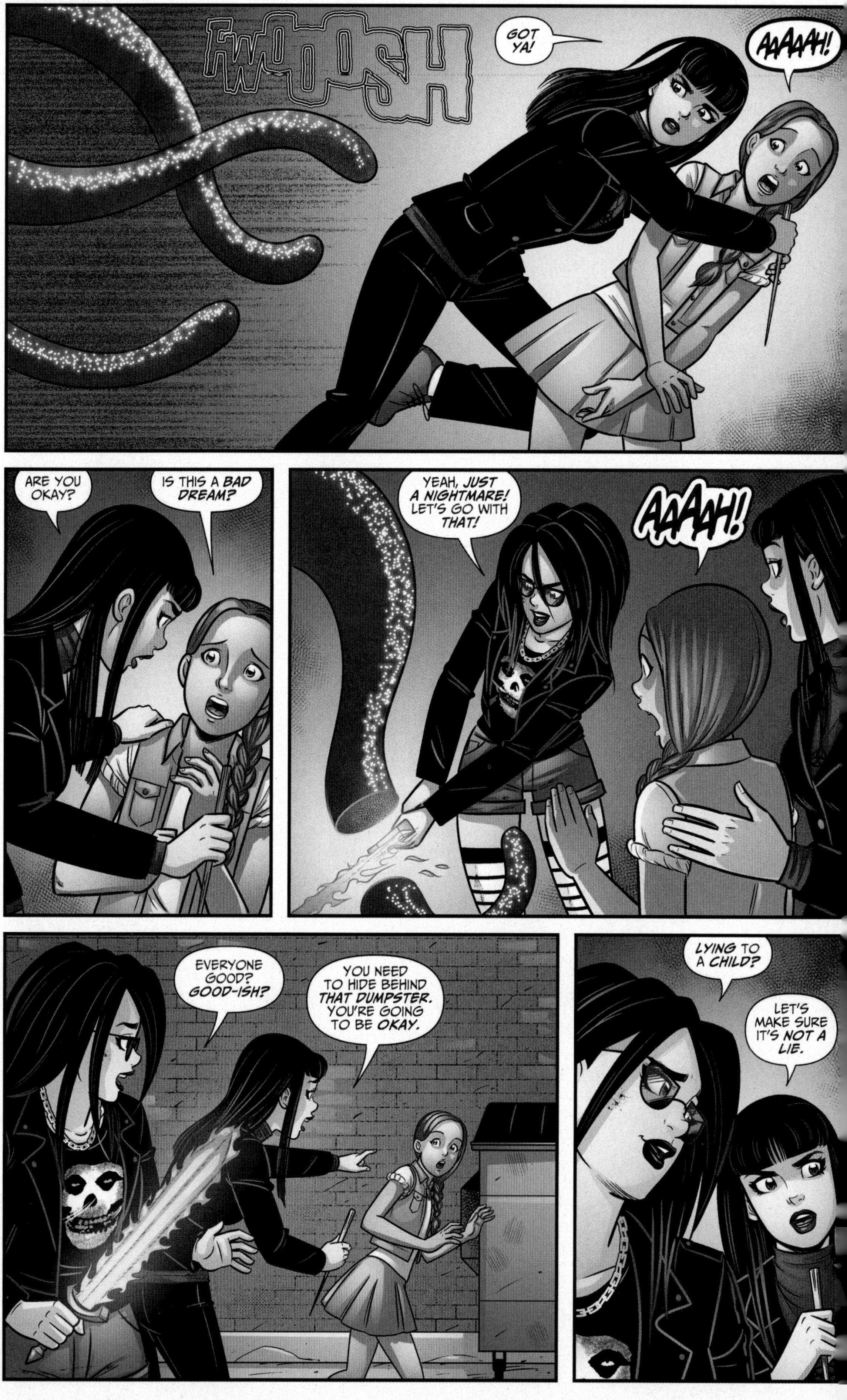

FWOOSH
GOT YA!
AAAAAH!
ARE YOU OKAY?
IS THIS A BAD DREAM?
YEAH, JUST A NIGHTMARE! LET'S GO WITH THAT!
AAAAH!
EVERYONE GOOD? GOOD-ISH?
YOU NEED TO HIDE BEHIND THAT DUMPSTER. YOU'RE GOING TO BE OKAY.
LYING TO A CHILD?
LET'S MAKE SURE IT'S NOT A LIE.

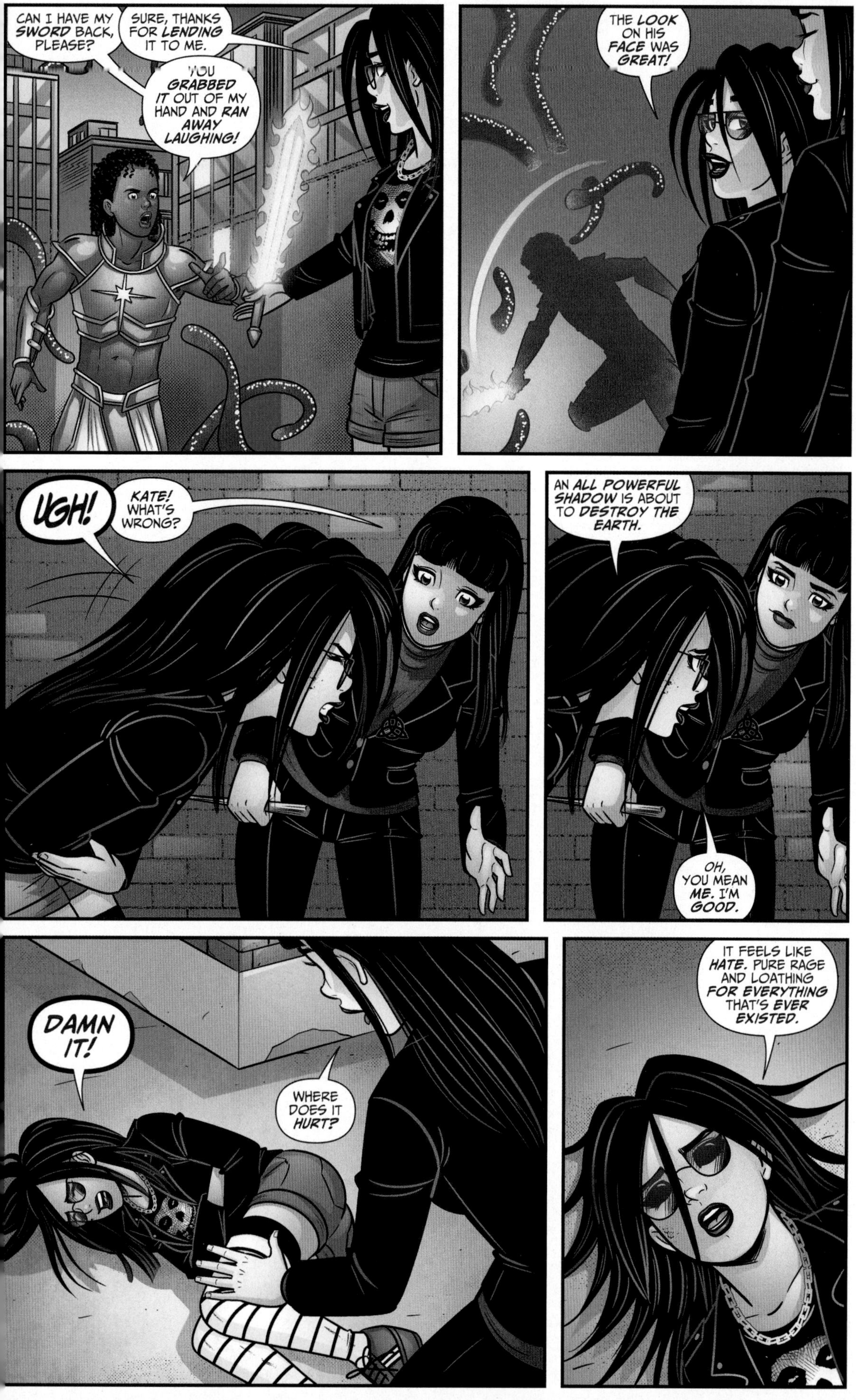
CAN I HAVE MY SWORD BACK, PLEASE?
SURE, THANKS FOR LENDING IT TO ME.
YOU GRABBED IT OUT OF MY HAND AND RAN AWAY LAUGHING!
THE LOOK ON HIS FACE WAS GREAT!
UGH!
KATE! WHAT'S WRONG?
AN ALL POWERFUL SHADOW IS ABOUT TO DESTROY THE EARTH.
OH, YOU MEAN ME. I'M GOOD.
DAMN IT!
WHERE DOES IT HURT?
IT FEELS LIKE HATE. PURE RAGE AND LOATHING FOR EVERYTHING THAT'S EVER EXISTED.

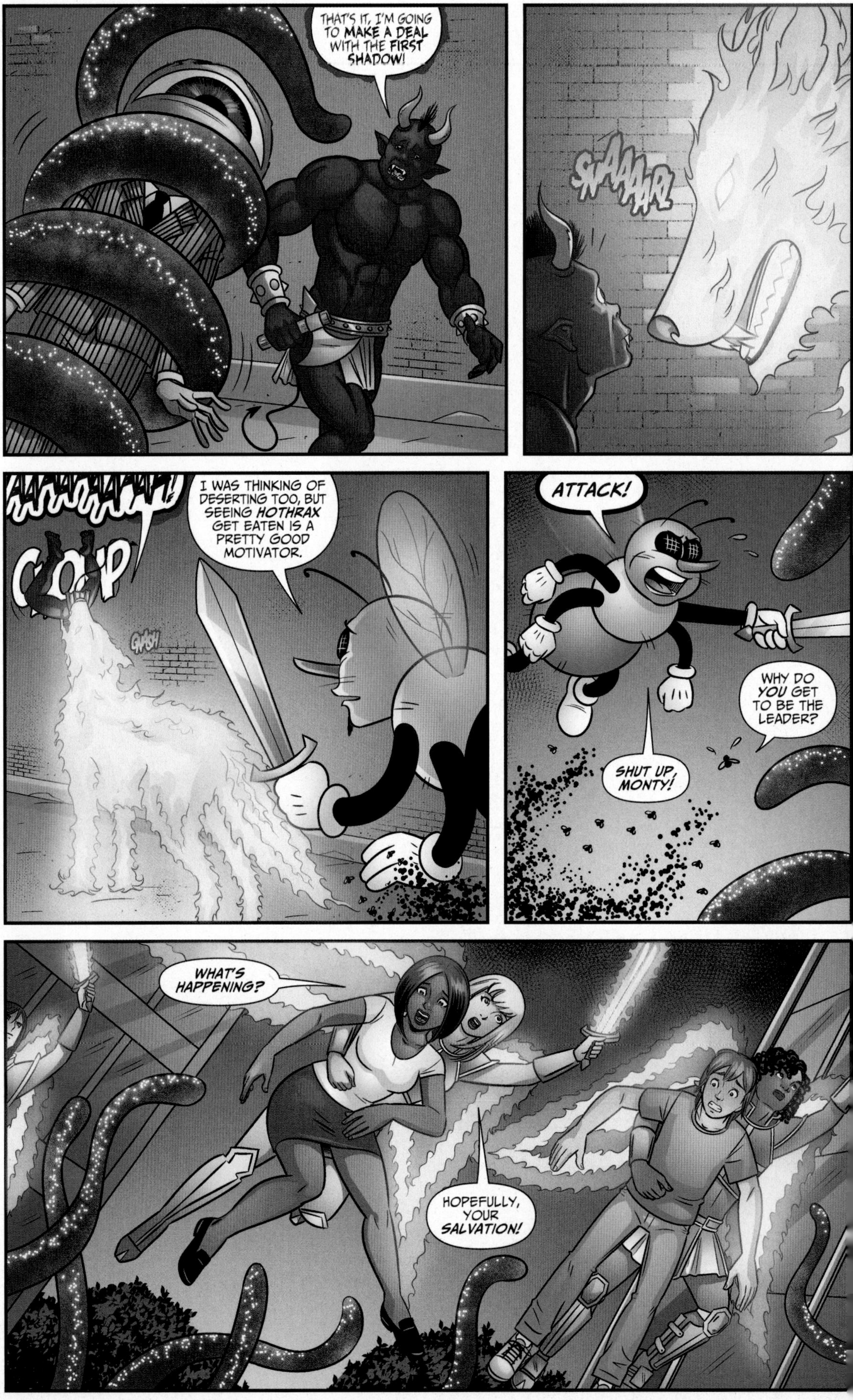
THAT'S IT, I'M GOING TO MAKE A DEAL WITH THE FIRST SHADOW!
SNAAAARL
AAAAAAAAH!
CHOMP
GNASH
I WAS THINKING OF DESERTING TOO, BUT SEEING HOTHRAX GET EATEN IS A PRETTY GOOD MOTIVATOR.
ATTACK!
WHY DO YOU GET TO BE THE LEADER?
SHUT UP, MONTY!
WHAT'S HAPPENING?
HOPEFULLY, YOUR SALVATION!

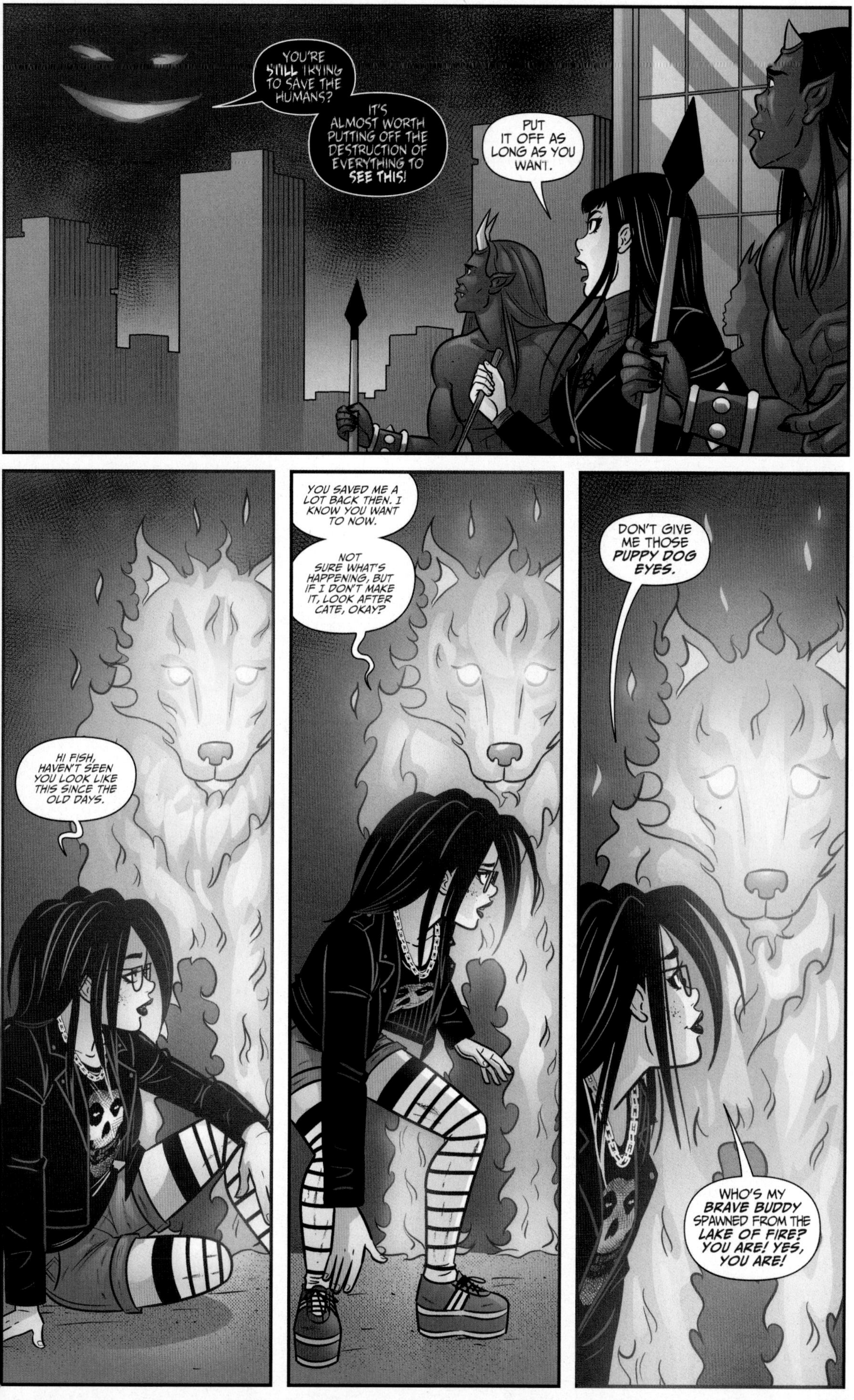
YOU'RE STILL TRYING TO SAVE THE HUMANS?
IT'S ALMOST WORTH PUTTING OFF THE DESTRUCTION OF EVERYTHING TO SEE THIS!
PUT IT OFF AS LONG AS YOU WANT.
HI FISH, HAVEN'T SEEN YOU LOOK LIKE THIS SINCE THE OLD DAYS.
YOU SAVED ME A LOT BACK THEN. I KNOW YOU WANT TO NOW.
NOT SURE WHAT'S HAPPENING, BUT IF I DON'T MAKE IT, LOOK AFTER CATE, OKAY?
DON'T GIVE ME THOSE PUPPY DOG EYES.
WHO'S MY BRAVE BUDDY SPAWNED FROM THE LAKE OF FIRE? YOU ARE! YES, YOU ARE!

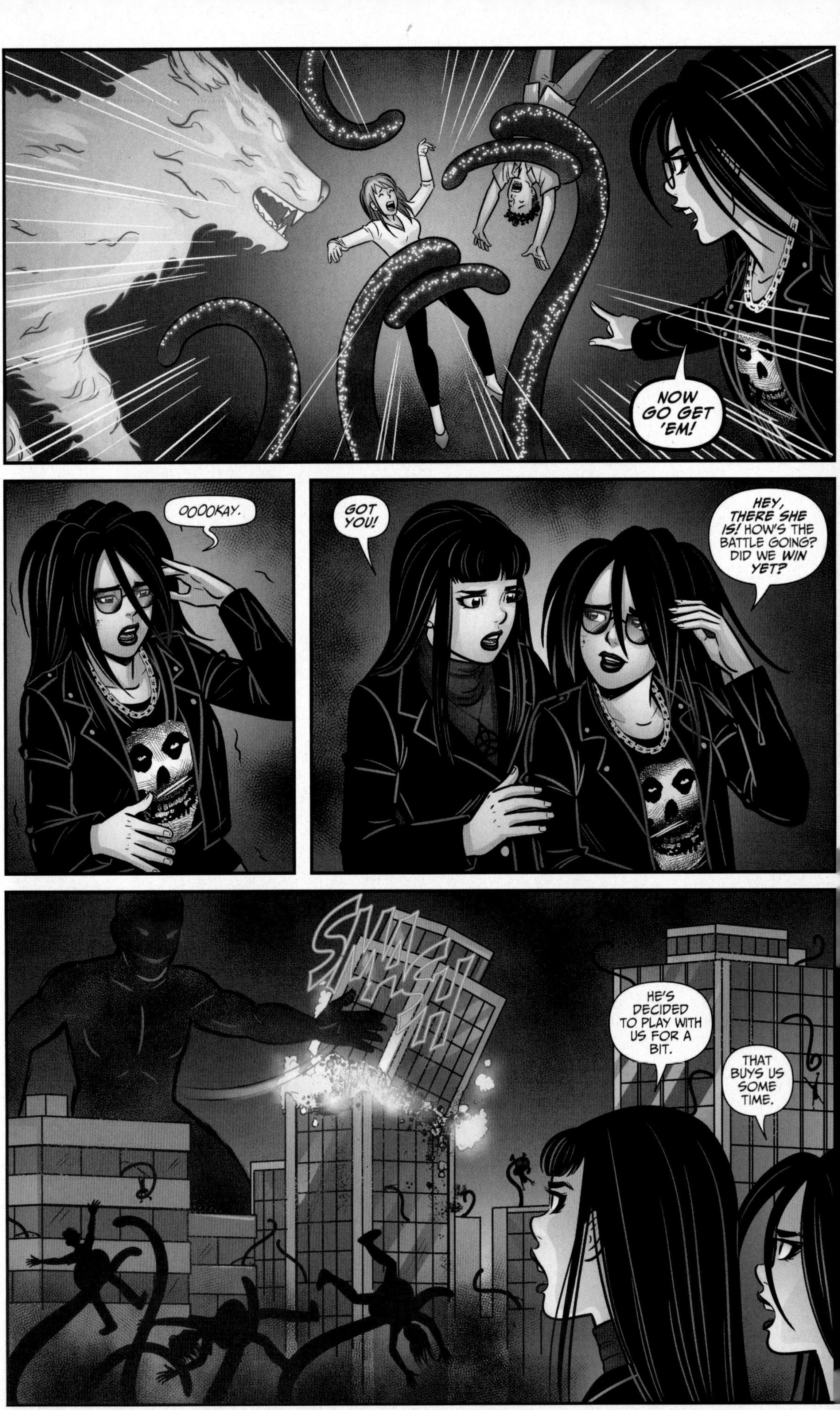
NOW GO GET 'EM!
OOOOKAY.
GOT YOU!
HEY, THERE SHE IS! HOW'S THE BATTLE GOING? DID WE WIN YET?
SMASH
HE'S DECIDED TO PLAY WITH US FOR A BIT.
THAT BUYS US SOME TIME.

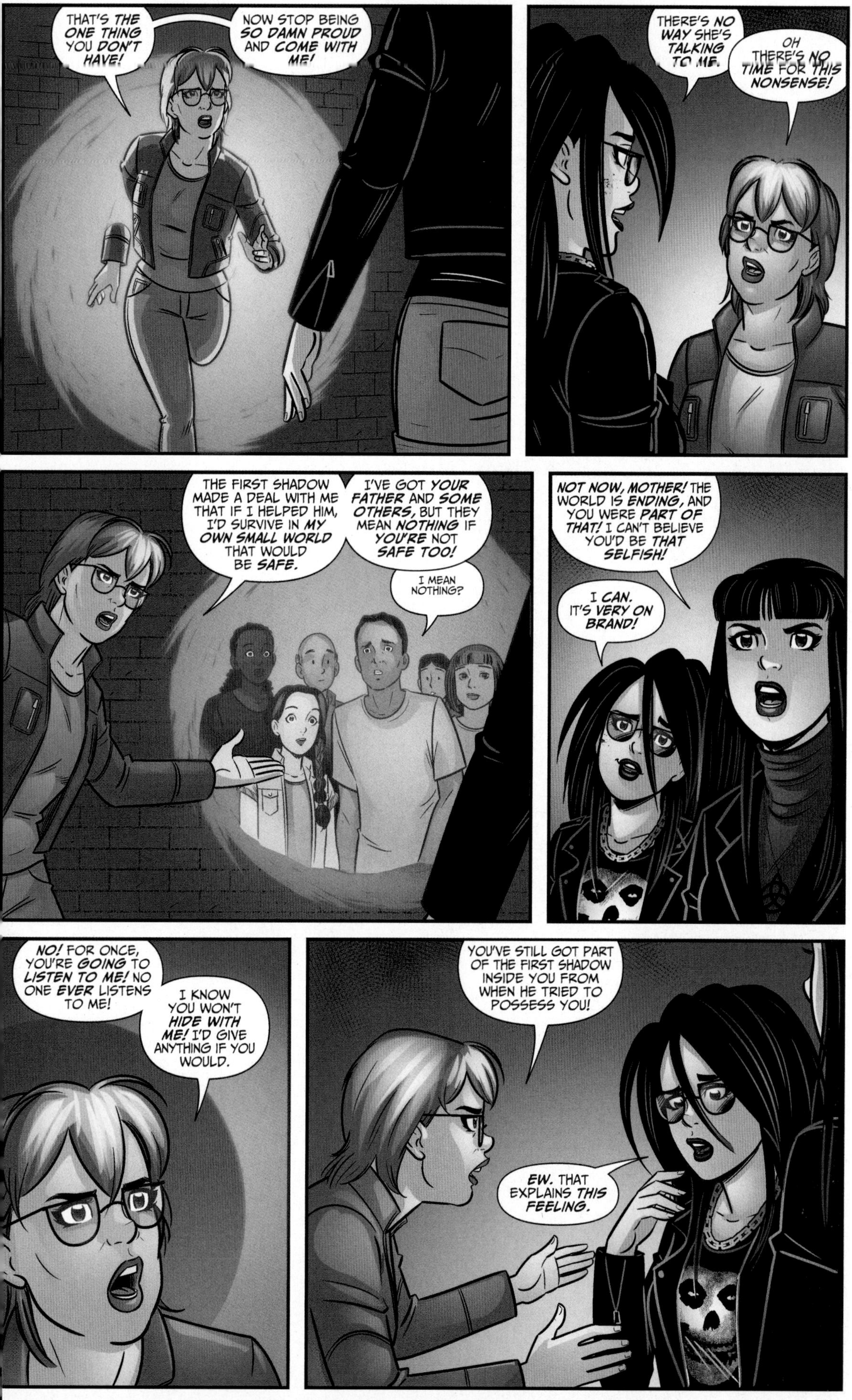
THAT'S THE ONE THING YOU DON'T HAVE!
NOW STOP BEING SO DAMN PROUD AND COME WITH ME!
THERE'S NO WAY SHE'S TALKING TO ME.
OH THERE'S NO TIME FOR THIS NONSENSE!
THE FIRST SHADOW MADE A DEAL WITH ME THAT IF I HELPED HIM, I'D SURVIVE IN MY OWN SMALL WORLD THAT WOULD BE SAFE.
I'VE GOT YOUR FATHER AND SOME OTHERS, BUT THEY MEAN NOTHING IF YOU'RE NOT SAFE TOO!
I MEAN NOTHING?
NOT NOW, MOTHER! THE WORLD IS ENDING, AND YOU WERE PART OF THAT! I CAN'T BELIEVE YOU'D BE THAT SELFISH!
I CAN. IT'S VERY ON BRAND!
NO! FOR ONCE, YOU'RE GOING TO LISTEN TO ME! NO ONE EVER LISTENS TO ME!
I KNOW YOU WON'T HIDE WITH ME! I'D GIVE ANYTHING IF YOU WOULD.
YOU'VE STILL GOT PART OF THE FIRST SHADOW INSIDE YOU FROM WHEN HE TRIED TO POSSESS YOU!
EW. THAT EXPLAINS THIS FEELING.

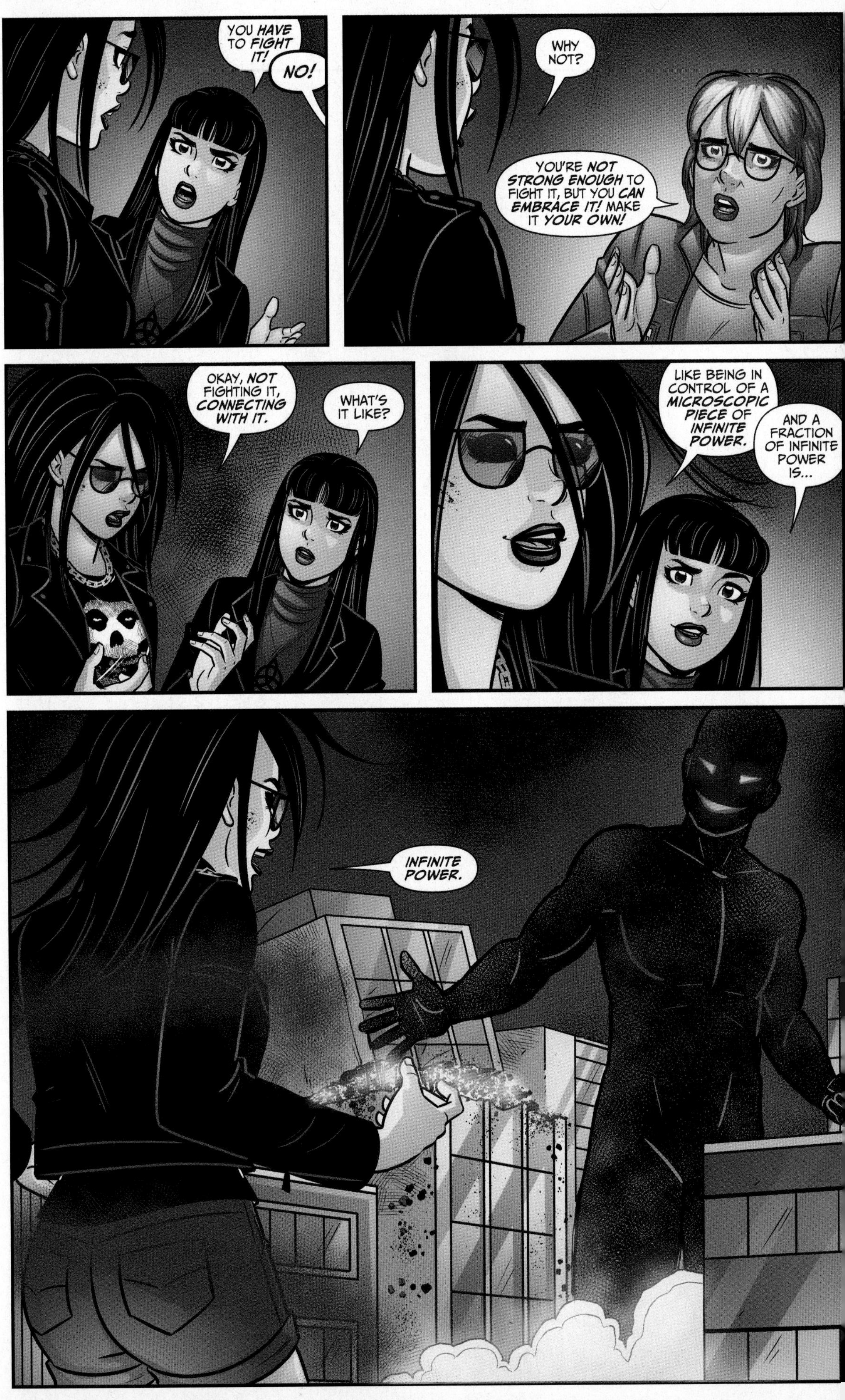
YOU HAVE TO FIGHT IT!
NO!
WHY NOT?
YOU'RE NOT STRONG ENOUGH TO FIGHT IT, BUT YOU CAN EMBRACE IT! MAKE IT YOUR OWN!
OKAY, NOT FIGHTING IT, CONNECTING WITH IT.
WHAT'S IT LIKE?
LIKE BEING IN CONTROL OF A MICROSCOPIC PIECE OF INFINITE POWER.
AND A FRACTION OF INFINITE POWER IS...
INFINITE POWER.

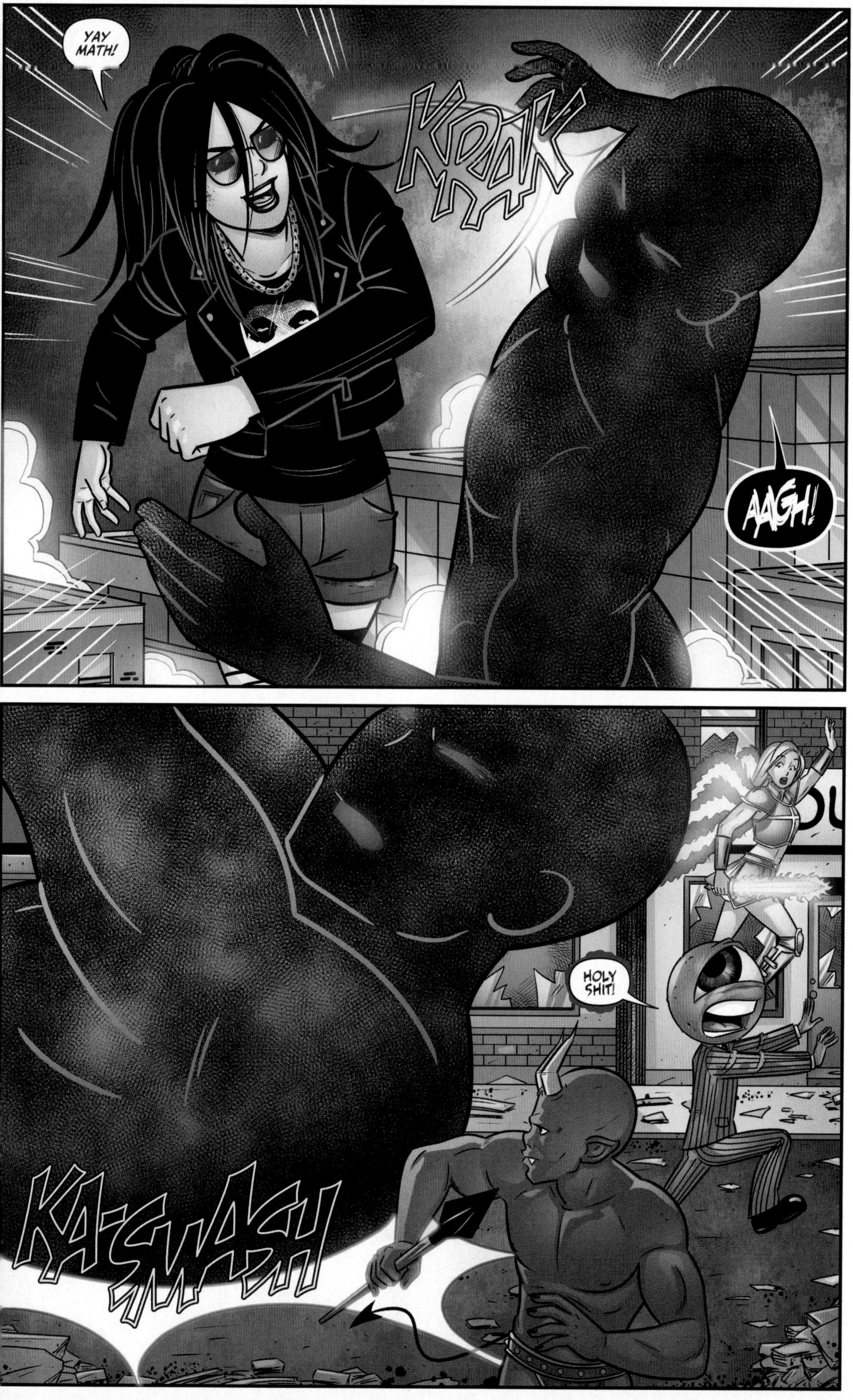
YAY MATH!
KRAK
AAGH!
HOLY SHIT!
KA-SMASH

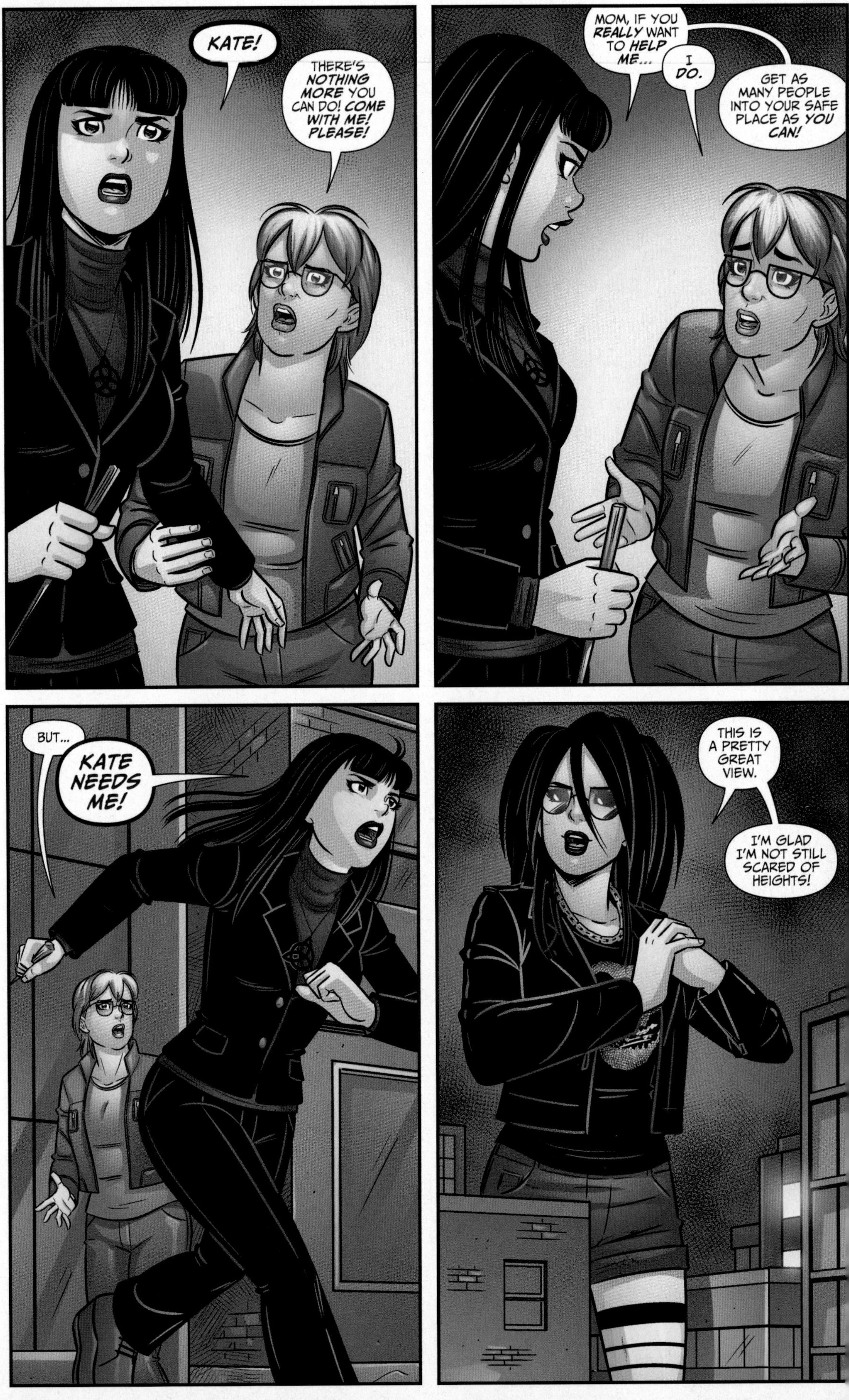
KATE!
THERE'S NOTHING MORE YOU CAN DO! COME WITH ME! PLEASE!
MOM, IF YOU REALLY WANT TO HELP ME...
I DO.
GET AS MANY PEOPLE INTO YOUR SAFE PLACE AS YOU CAN!
BUT...
KATE NEEDS ME!
THIS IS A PRETTY GREAT VIEW.
I'M GLAD I'M NOT STILL SCARED OF HEIGHTS!

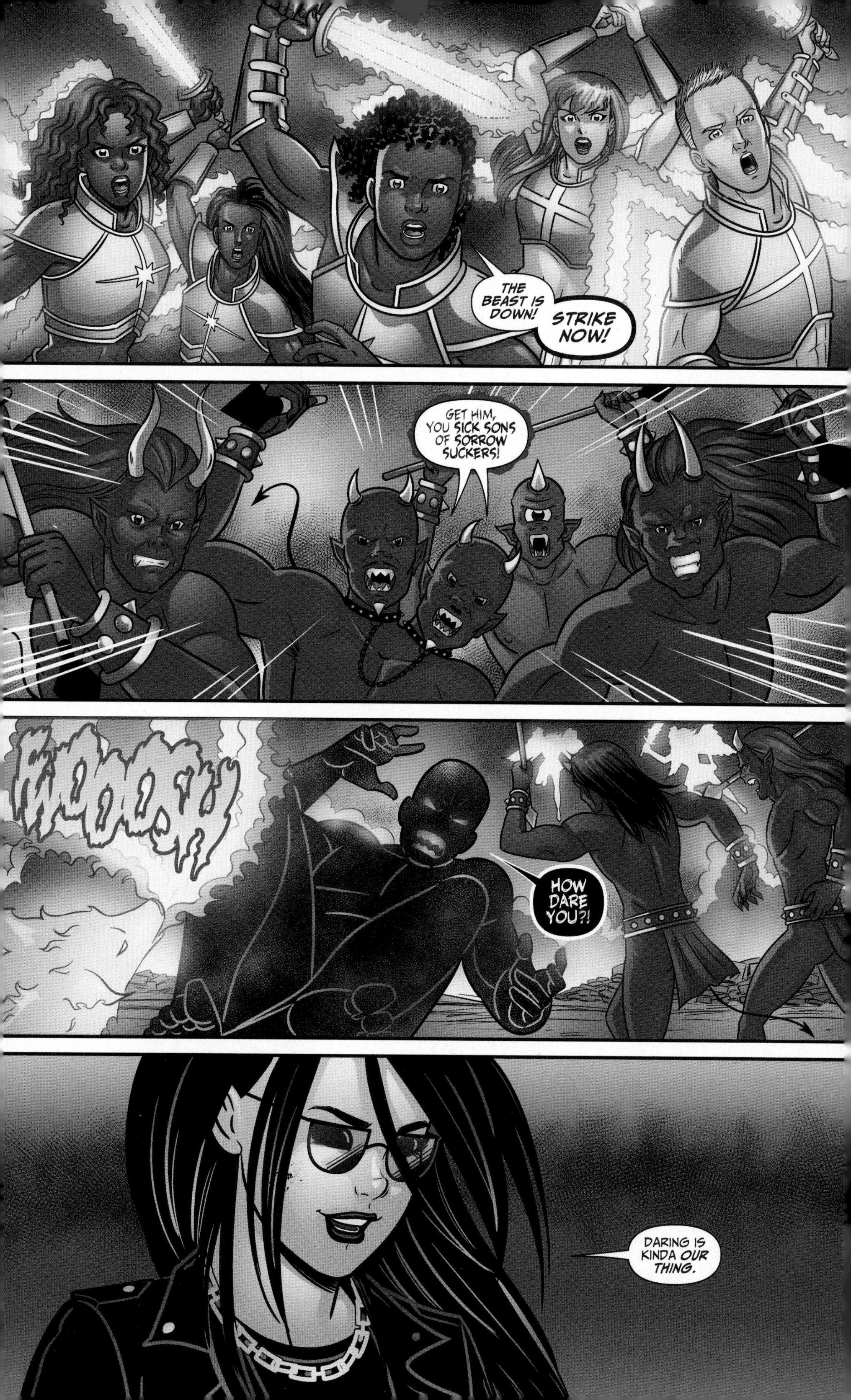
THE BEAST IS DOWN!
STRIKE NOW!
GET HIM, YOU SICK SONS OF SORROW SUCKERS!
HOW DARE YOU?!
DARING IS KINDA OUR THING.

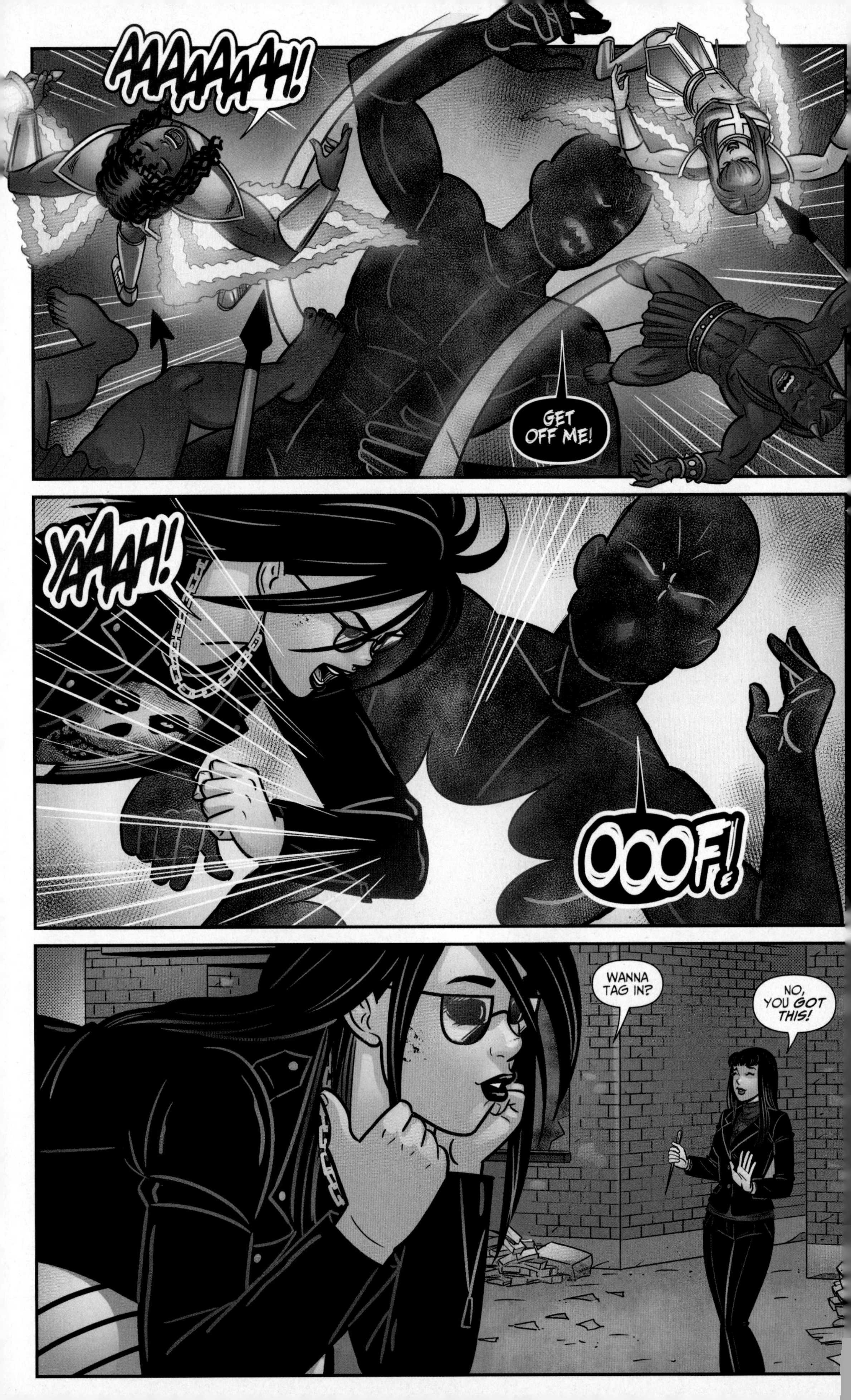
AAAAAAAH!
GET OFF ME!
YAAAH!
OOOF!
WANNA TAG IN?
NO, YOU GOT THIS!

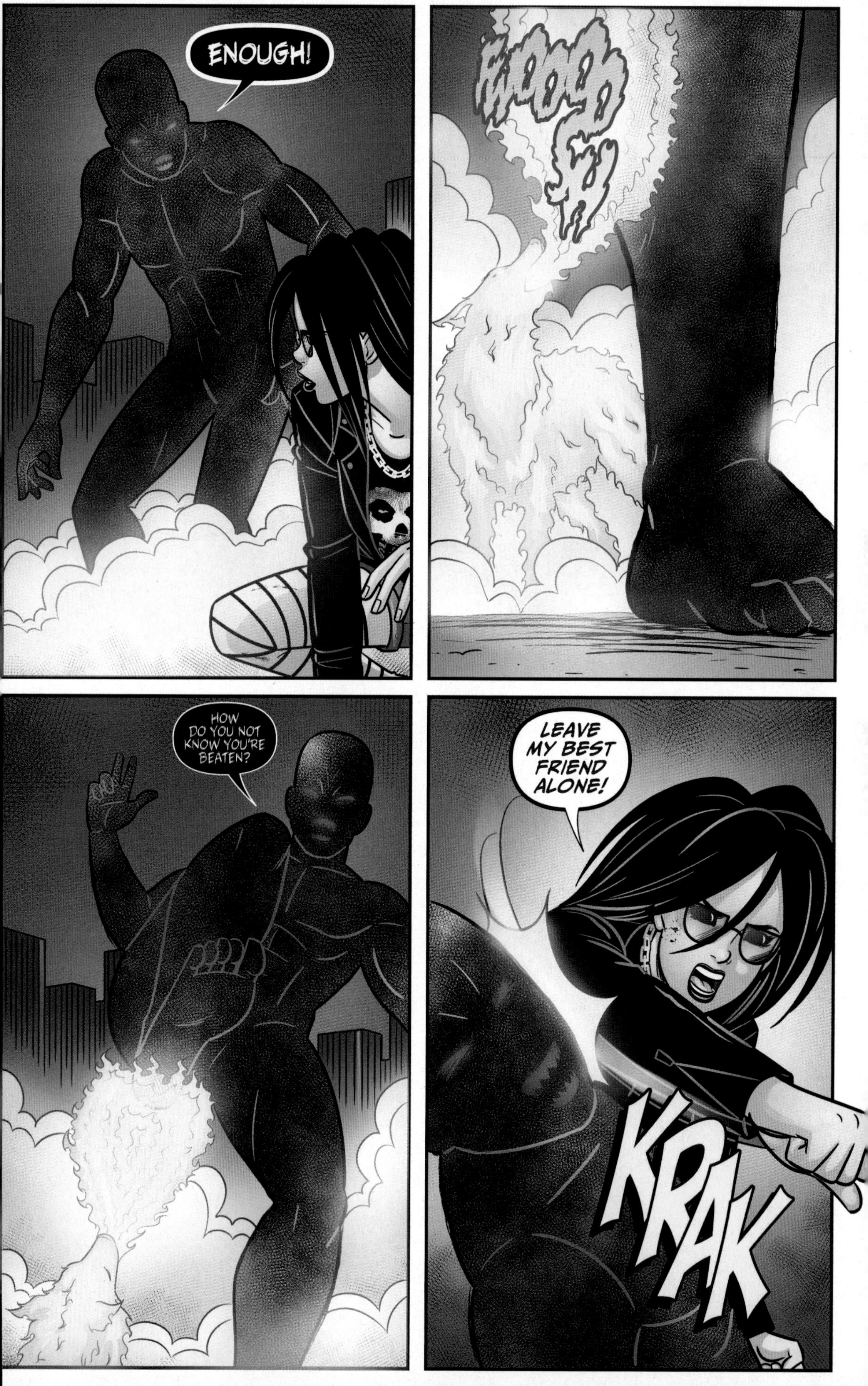
ENOUGH!
HOW DO YOU NOT KNOW YOU'RE BEATEN?
LEAVE MY BEST FRIEND ALONE!
KRAK

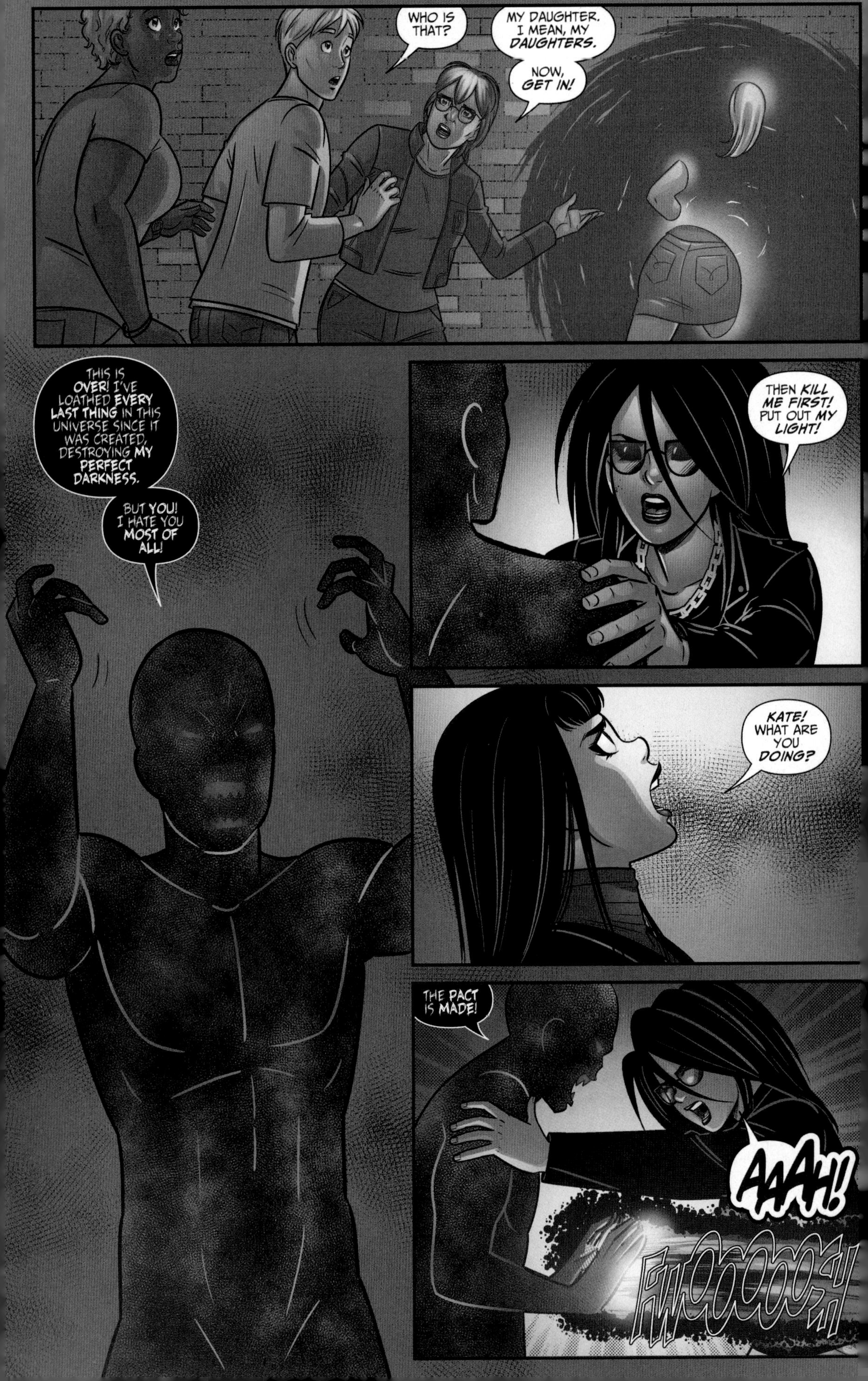
WHO IS THAT?
MY DAUGHTER. I MEAN, MY DAUGHTERS.
NOW, GET IN!
THIS IS OVER! I'VE LOATHED EVERY LAST THING IN THIS UNIVERSE SINCE IT WAS CREATED, DESTROYING MY PERFECT DARKNESS.
BUT YOU! I HATE YOU MOST OF ALL!
THEN KILL ME FIRST! PUT OUT MY LIGHT!
KATE! WHAT ARE YOU DOING?
THE PACT IS MADE!
AAAH!
FWOOOOOOSH

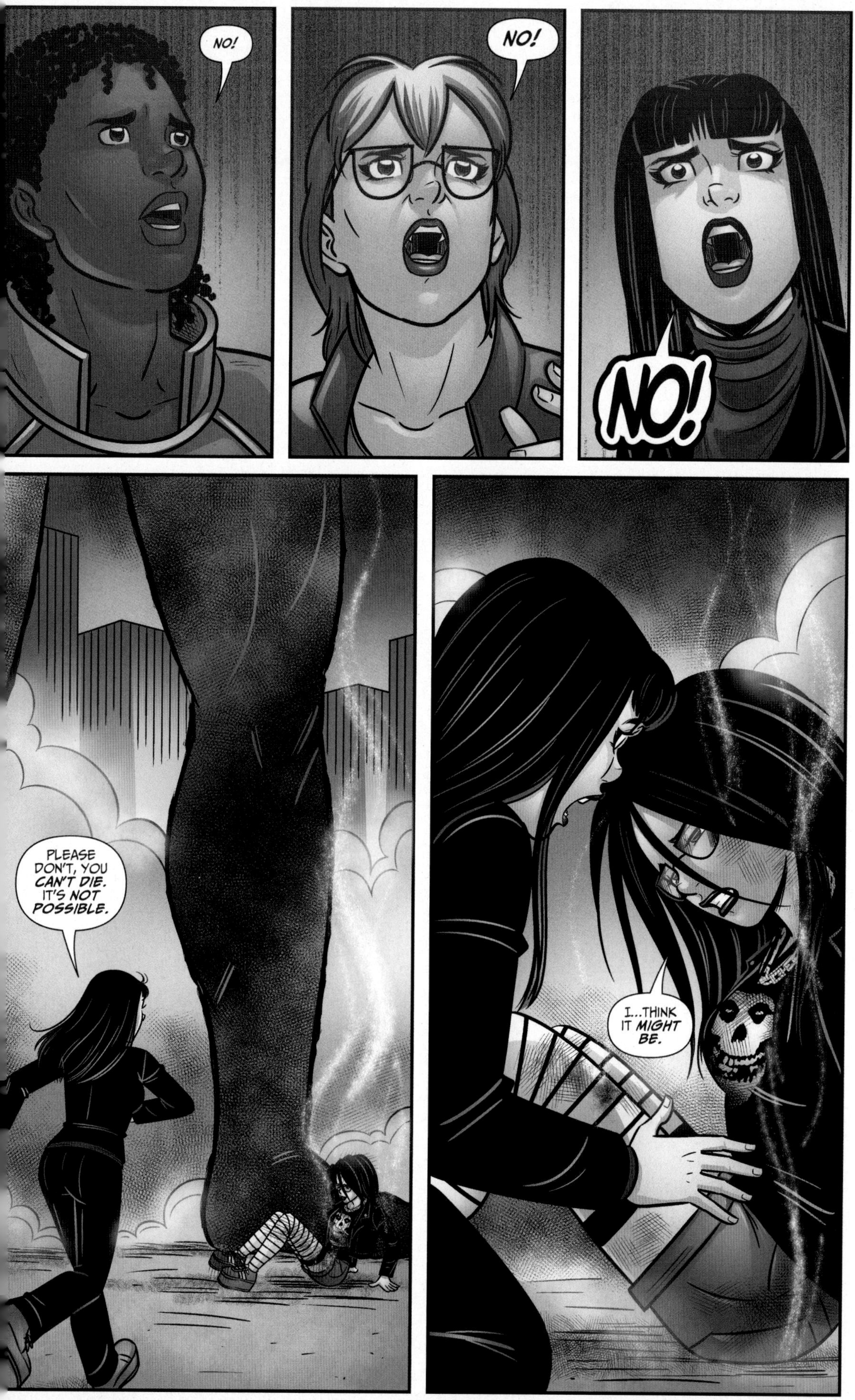
NO!
NO!
NO!
PLEASE DON'T, YOU *CAN'T DIE.* IT'S *NOT POSSIBLE.*
I...THINK IT *MIGHT* BE.

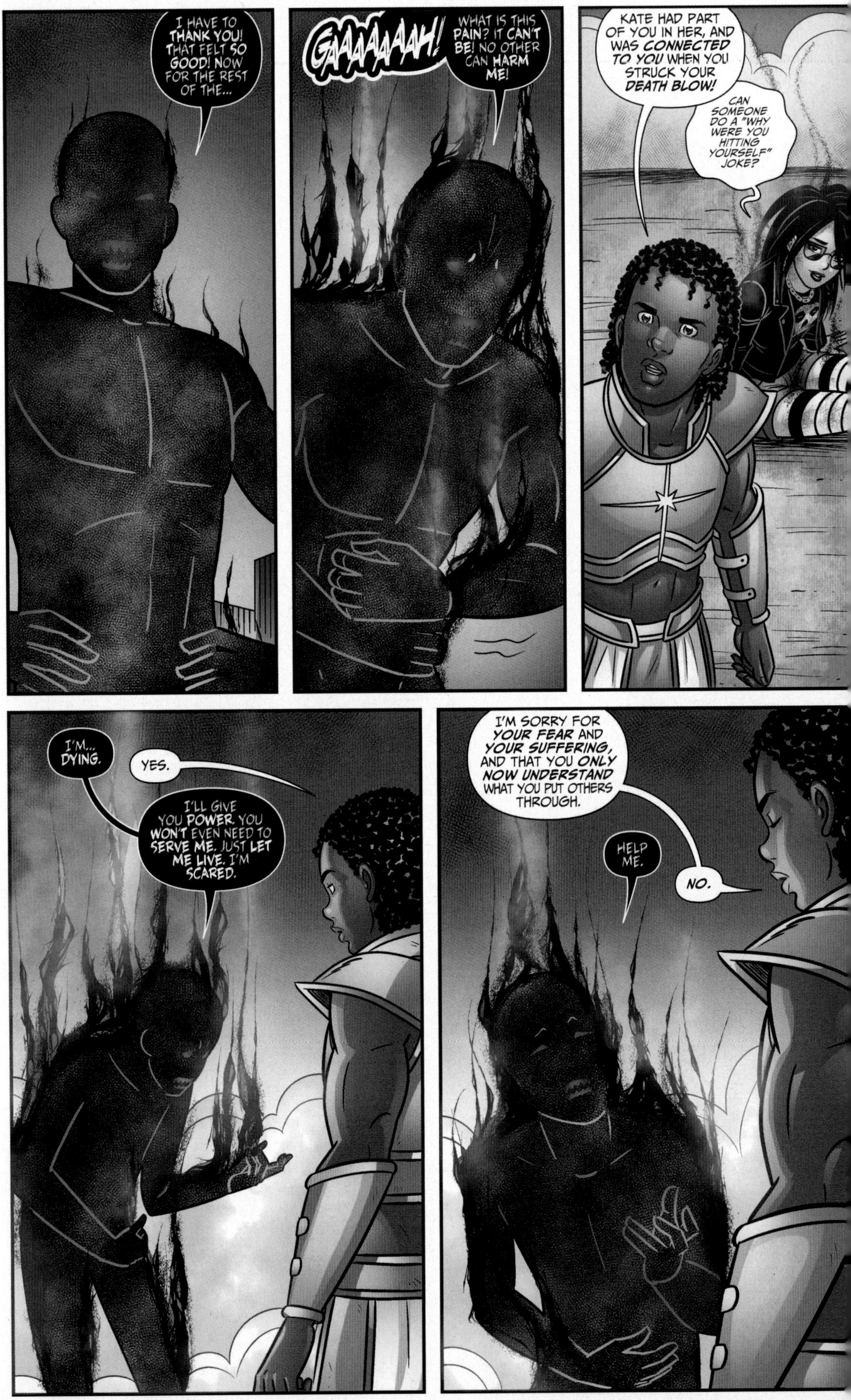
I HAVE TO THANK YOU! THAT FELT SO GOOD! NOW FOR THE REST OF THE...
GAAAAAAAH!
WHAT IS THIS PAIN? IT CAN'T BE! NO OTHER CAN HARM ME!
KATE HAD PART OF YOU IN HER, AND WAS CONNECTED TO YOU WHEN YOU STRUCK YOUR DEATH BLOW!
CAN SOMEONE DO A "WHY WERE YOU HITTING YOURSELF" JOKE?
I'M... DYING.
YES.
I'LL GIVE YOU POWER. YOU WON'T EVEN NEED TO SERVE ME. JUST LET ME LIVE. I'M SCARED.
I'M SORRY FOR YOUR FEAR AND YOUR SUFFERING, AND THAT YOU ONLY NOW UNDERSTAND WHAT YOU PUT OTHERS THROUGH.
HELP ME.
NO.

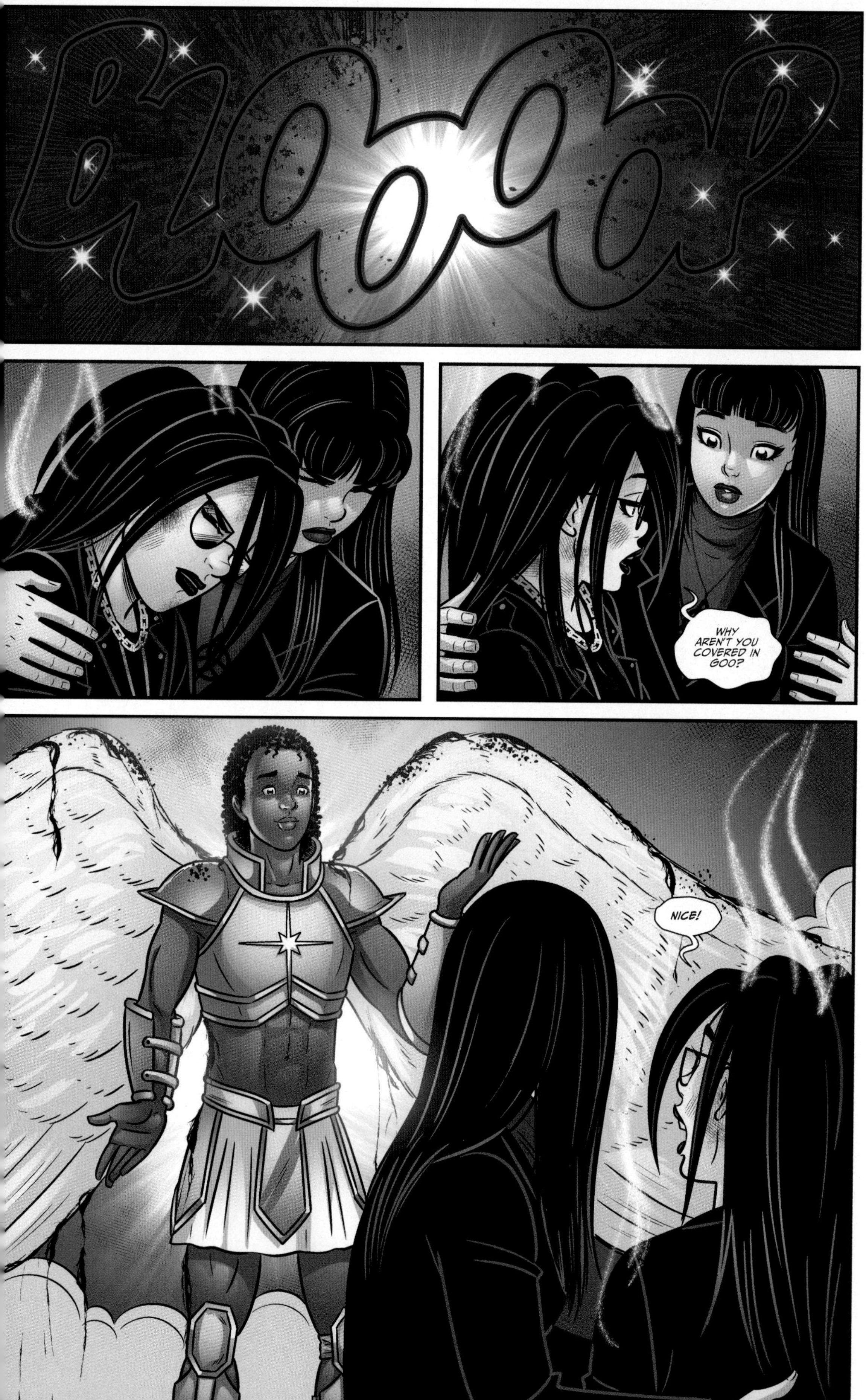
BLOOOOP
WHY AREN'T YOU COVERED IN GOO?
NICE!

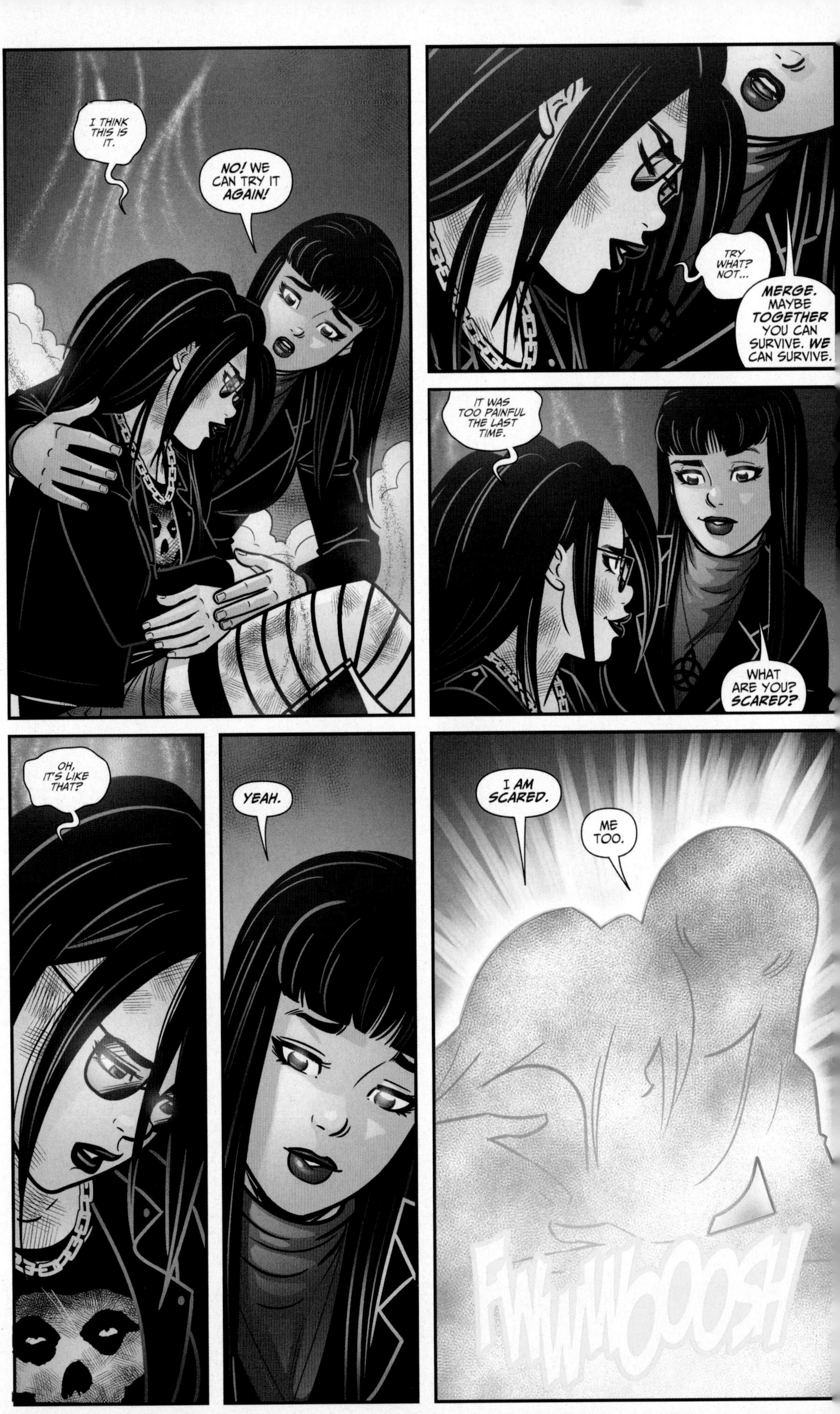

I THINK THIS IS IT.
NO! WE CAN TRY IT AGAIN!
TRY WHAT? NOT...
MERGE. MAYBE TOGETHER YOU CAN SURVIVE. WE CAN SURVIVE.
IT WAS TOO PAINFUL THE LAST TIME.
WHAT ARE YOU? SCARED?
OH, IT'S LIKE THAT?
YEAH.
I AM SCARED.
ME TOO.
FWWWOOOSH

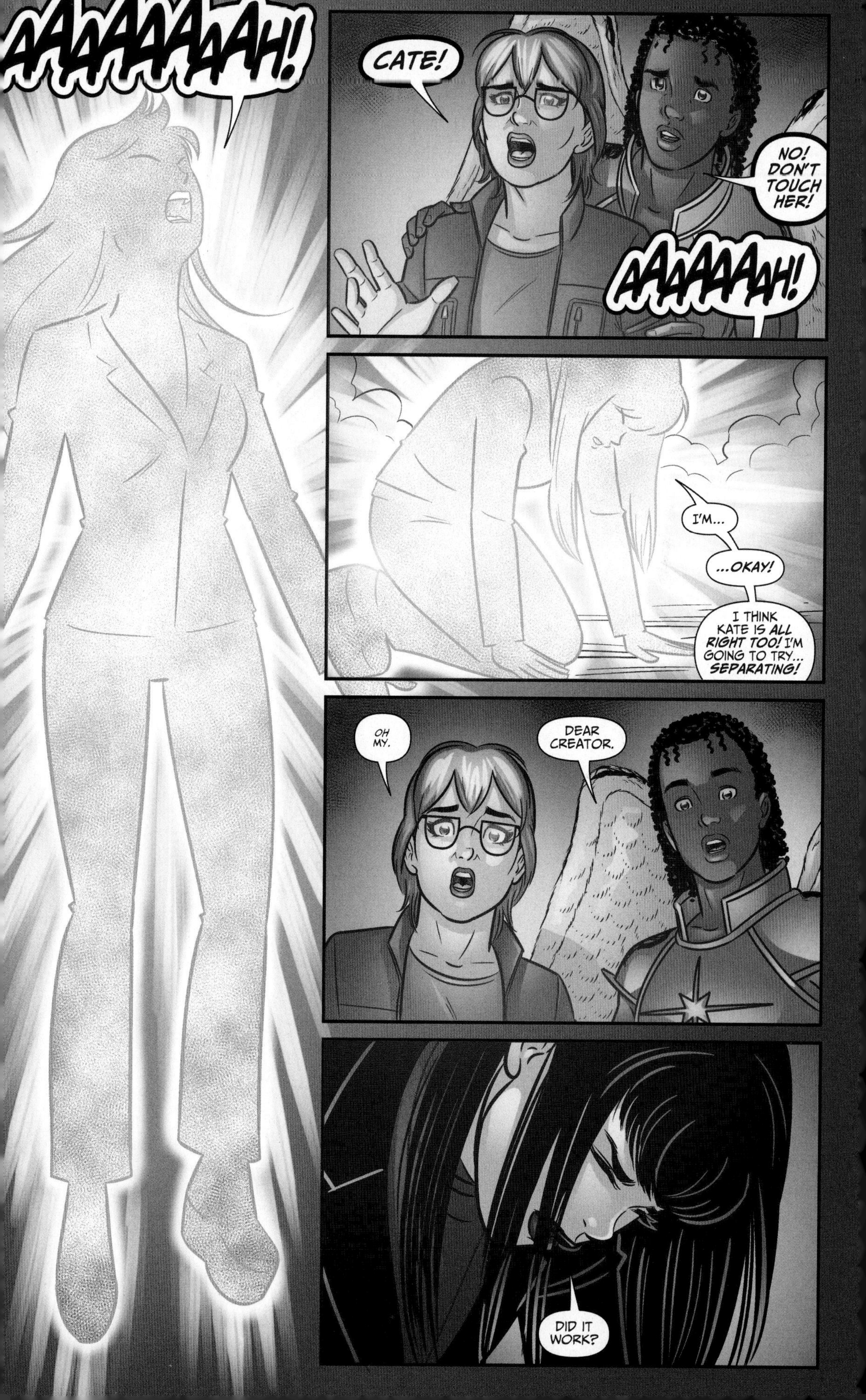
AAAAAAAAAH!
CATE!
NO! DON'T TOUCH HER!
AAAAAAAH!
I'M...
...OKAY!
I THINK KATE IS ALL RIGHT TOO! I'M GOING TO TRY... SEPARATING!
OH MY.
DEAR CREATOR.
DID IT WORK?

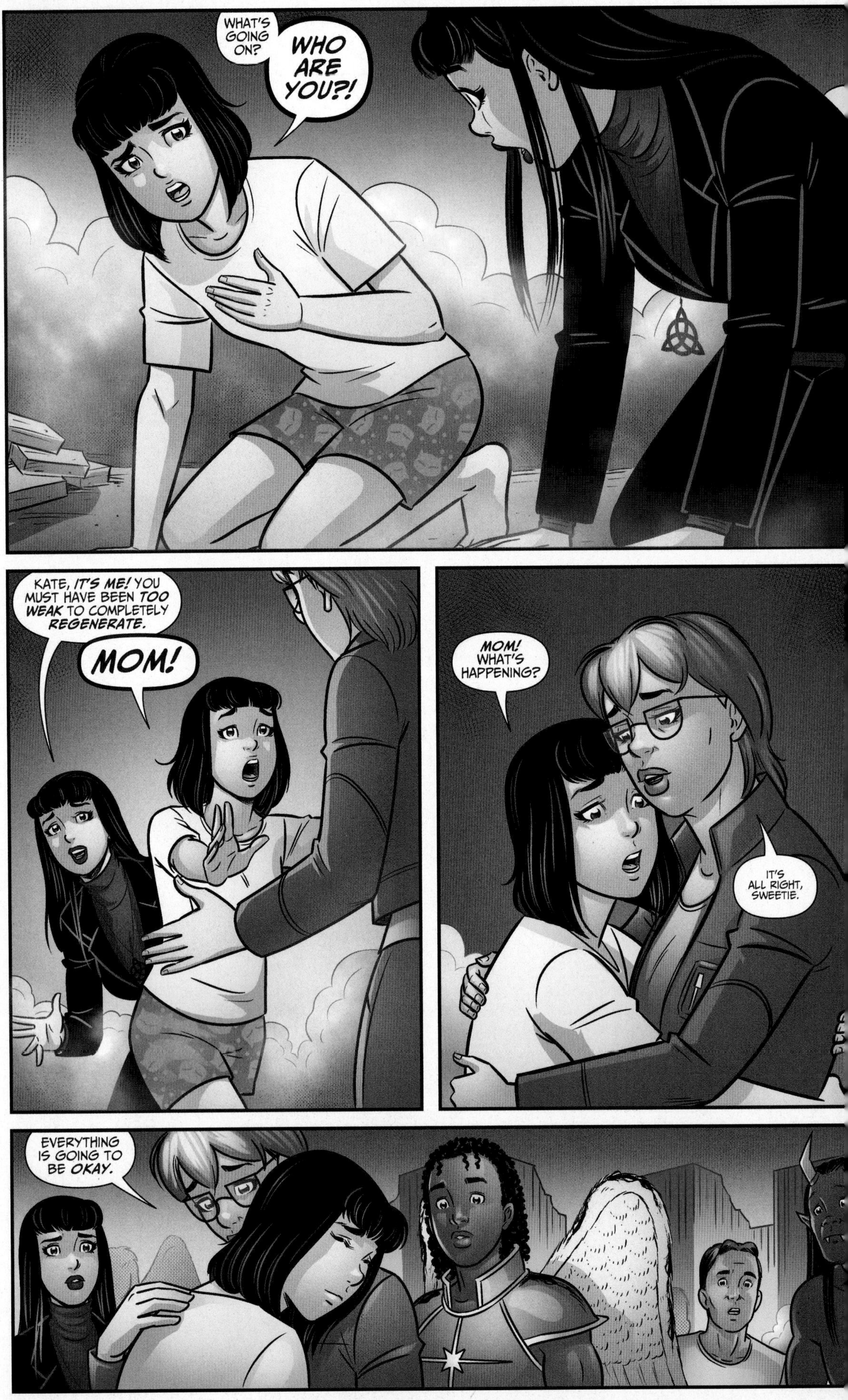
WHAT'S GOING ON?
WHO ARE YOU?!
KATE, IT'S ME! YOU MUST HAVE BEEN TOO WEAK TO COMPLETELY REGENERATE.
MOM!
MOM! WHAT'S HAPPENING?
IT'S ALL RIGHT, SWEETIE.
EVERYTHING IS GOING TO BE OKAY.

PIN-UP
GALLERY

ART BY

Brenda Hickey

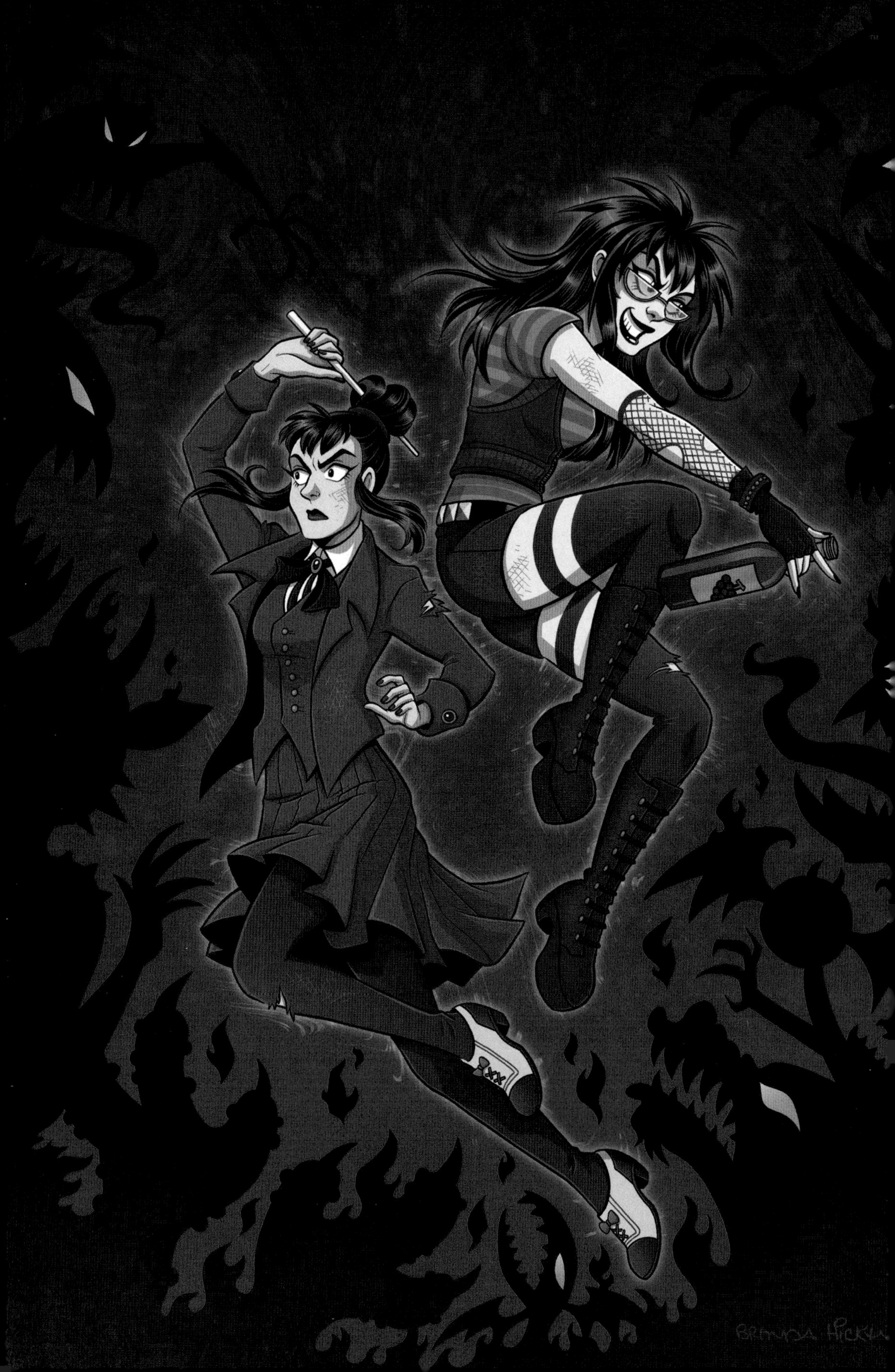

ART BY
Jenn St-Onge

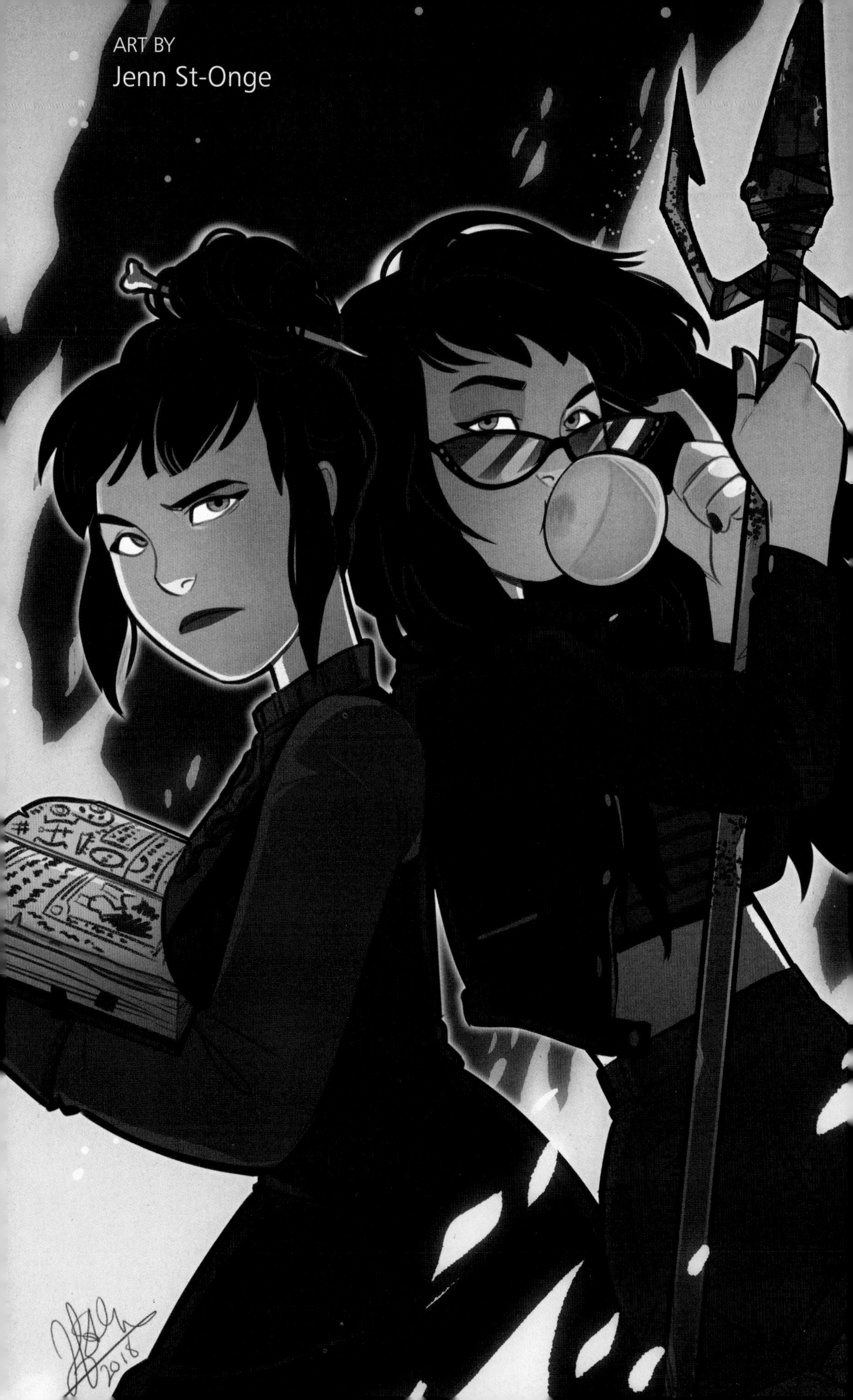
2018

ART BY
Michael Shelfer &
Anwar Hanano

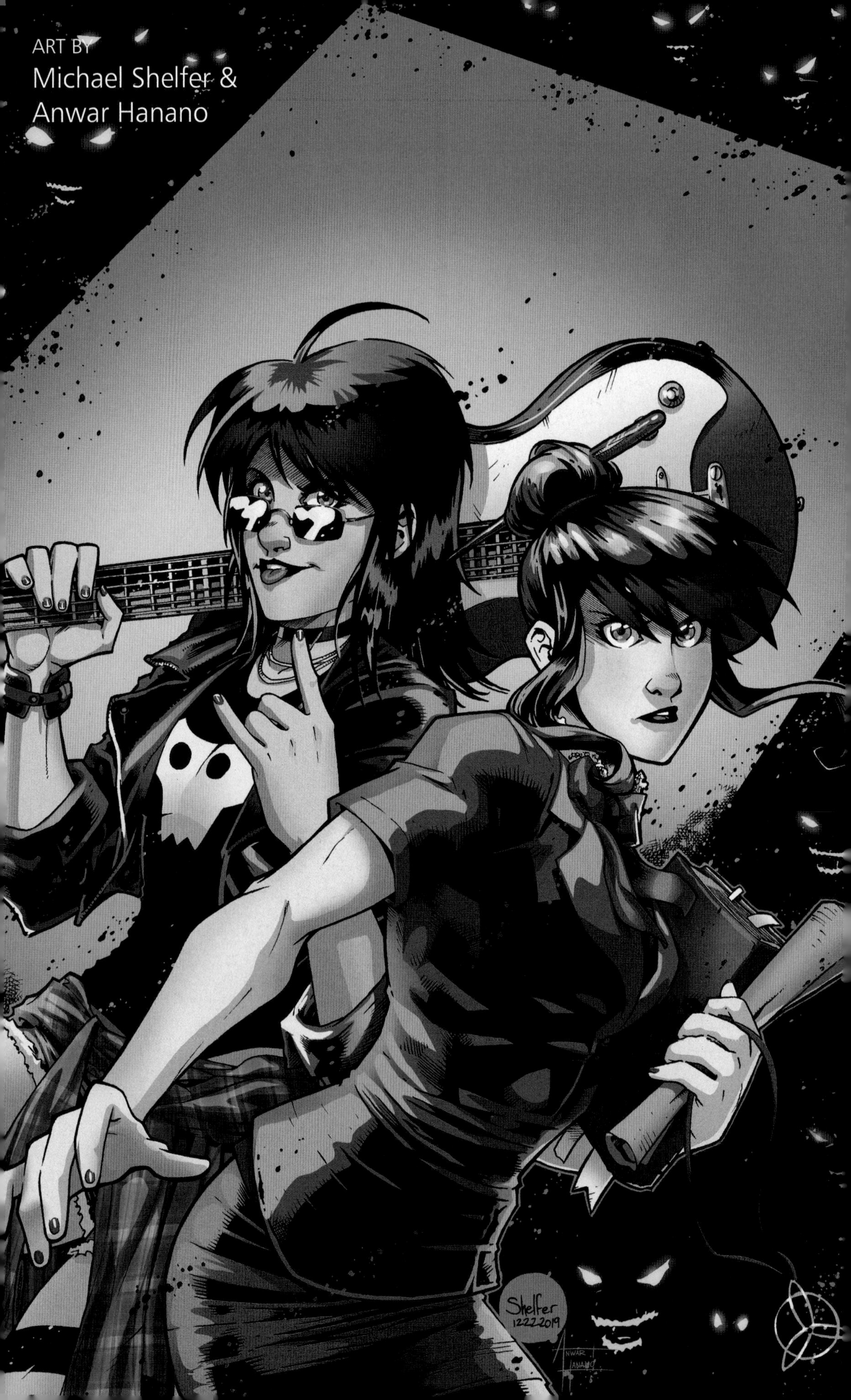
Shelfer

ART BY
Rossi Gifford

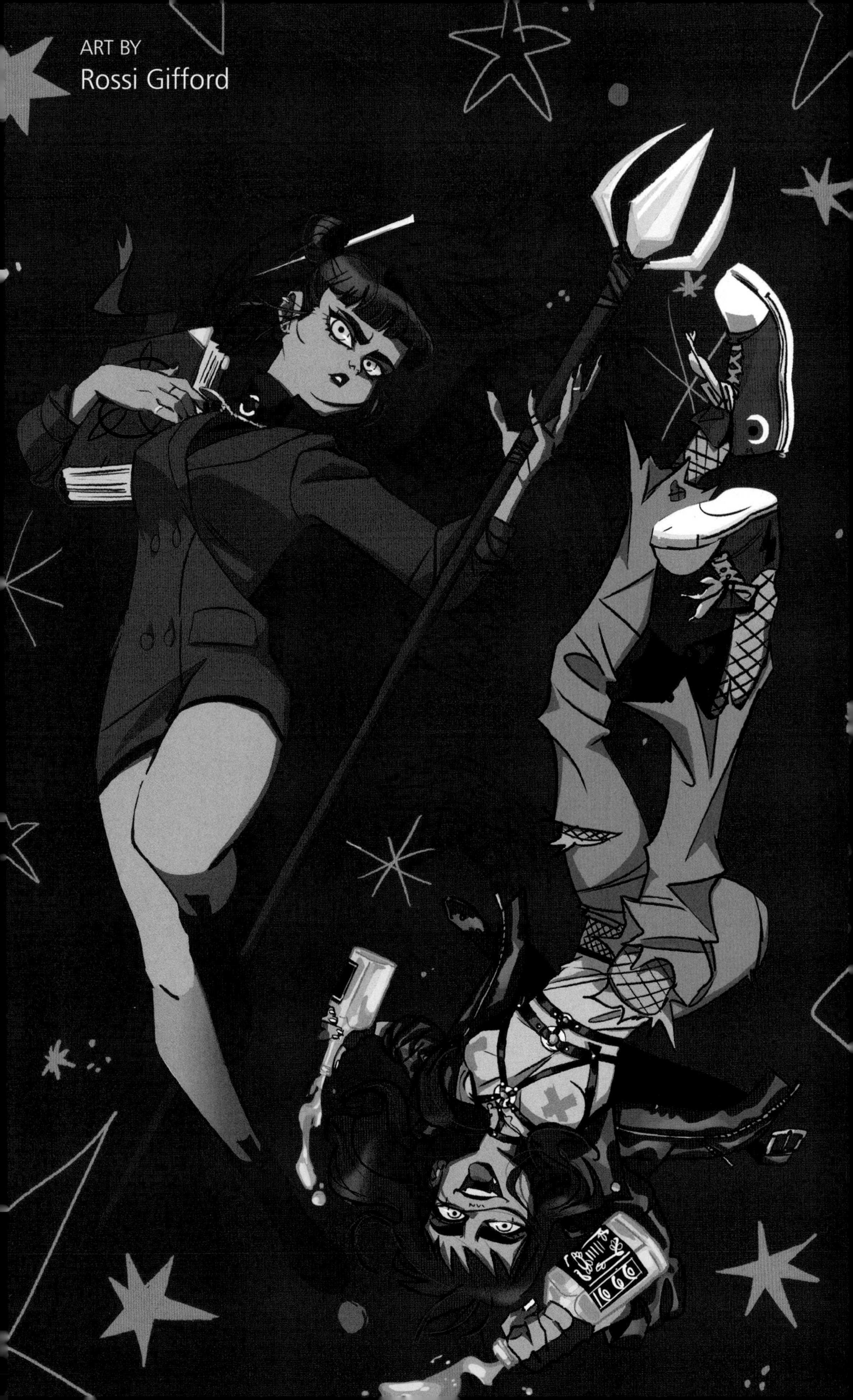